BOUND IN SILVER

Marie Grace

Book One in the Clock Keeper Chronicles

BOUND IN SILVER

By Marie Grace

Bound in Silver by Marie Grace

https://m.facebook.com/m.gracebooks

@mariegracebooks

Second edition 2019

Library of Congress Card Number Pending
ISBN: 9781794459021

Independently published

Cover Art Courtesy of Spark Adobe

Cover by Marie Grace

To my mom, this book would have fallen face first
into the dirt if you hadn't had helped it to crawl.
Also, to the rest of my family, who saw it walk
and said it could run.
Love you, sillies ;)

Contents

Prologue: Crumbling to Pieces and Pebbles.

A man stood alone amongst the rubble. Bits of broken cement littered the ground, crumbling to pieces and pebbles underfoot. His gaze swept across the small village. It was utterly destroyed. Just like the rest of the world, it was now little more than ashes. Everything that he dreaded had come to pass, and there was no way to stop the terror that rained from the sky.

"Humans," he scoffed, "they never learn, do they?" the man questioned himself with a heavy sigh. Sorrow danced around the edge of his mind as he tried to block the horrific scenes that wanted to race through it- each one more horrifying than the last. Memories of war and destruction, children crying while... he shook his head and tried to erase the images once more.

The man nudged a piece of debris out of the way with the steel tip of his boot. They were military standard and they reminded him once more of why he was headed to his destination. He trudged forward toward a hill. This place was supposed to be safe, he had made sure of it. A small village in the middle of Switzerland, Appenzell, was supposed to be safe. The hill's silhouette nothing more than a dot on the horizon, he crossed the road that bordered the village and led the way home.

On top of the gentle rise stood a house, it was mighty and foreboding in nature. It was the centerpiece of ghost stories and legends that swept through this little valley on stormy nights. In a way, it was fitting for it to be represented in this manner, because he knew something the locals didn't know- nor now would ever know- it was the center of all supernatural power. It was a beacon of sorts; its energy spread to the farthest corners of the Earth and everywhere in between. And it was his home.

When he reached the heavy oak door, he realized that he himself and one other creature were the only living things left standing. *That's the thing about humans,* he mused, they never think about anything except the fight to be on top. They ignore everything else, especially what truly matters in life.

He walked along the empty corridors. Now not even radios could fill the silence. He finally reached the grand library and pushed open the doors. The man immediately went to the farthest bookshelf and climbed the ladder, looking for...**that**. The book was large and leather bound with an ancient air surrounding it. Its tang of musty parchment filled his nose. He choked on the dust that assaulted him as he retrieved the heavy tome from its slumber.

The archaic text firmly in his hands, he climbed back down the ladder. He proceeded to walk across the room to one of the many wooden tables that covered the space. Pushing aside most of his journals, he paused for a second. He had an idea. Pulling the most recent journal forward, he began scrawling a new entry.

September 2, 1945,

In all the years that I have been alive - which has been a great many- never have I seen so much destruction. The human race has gone too far this time. They have annihilated all of Earth's inhabitants. All life is gone- flora, fauna, creatures of the supernatural, and humans as well. That is how far they have gone in their quest for power. But then again, all beings strive for the same. Humans more than most. And when they attain it, they lose all that _makes_ them human. They struggle for control and only achieve chaos. This time, however, they destroyed everything. Gone. Everything is gone. They created the apocalypse and have left only death in their wake. I am nearly all that is left.

That is why what I am about to do has to be done. I am going to fix this. No matter the cost. That is also why this is going to be my last entry. All I ask of my successors, is to not let the good in the this world die a second death, to follow the instructions I have created here. Think of this as my Last Will and Testament- to spare humanity destruction from their own atomic weapons.

I am writing this letter to whom it may concern. Humanity's future generations shall be protected by two factions; the Book Keepers and the Clock Keepers- separate, but equally important.

They are hereby created on this day and will be sustained through the ages by my timeless power as The Mage.

I leave my house to the Book Keepers. They shall keep my journals and study the spells within. My one request is that they protect the power of knowledge and the power of free will, so that they may always maintain peace and ensure that history never repeats itself. To them do I not only leave my journals, my house, and all of my Earthly possessions, but also half of my power. The powers of a Book Keeper shall be passed down from grandparent to grandchild in the order of honor and strength. They will defend the precious wisdom and magic within these walls, as well as the Clock Keepers themselves.

I leave to the Clock Keepers- The Haunt. Named so, because just like a ghost, it can disappear and reappear. It can only be used by those who hold its key. It shall be utilized as a gathering place and safe haven for the Clock Keepers. I also leave to the Clock Keepers the joy and sorrow of all Humankind, to watch and keep them always. I bestow upon them the Clocks, so that time may keep moving. I leave them the tools to protect the ones they love. The Clock Keepers shall be the Mothers of Time- the sacred responsibility will be passed down through the generations from grandmother to granddaughter; they will nurture and protect time as is their divine feminine birthright.

These groups shall work together secretly in perfect harmony, as the yin and yang, to maintain balance in the world and be called upon in times of peril. With these final words, I wish the future generations good luck, and farewell.

He finished his entry and closed the journal, only to open the heavy text next to it. This book of enchantment had been with him since the beginning of time, it had seen wars, destruction, and hope. He opened it to the correct page, almost without thinking, and gave another sigh. It would be worth it- he knew it would. He started to chant. His voice was deep and booming and full of passion for what he believed in. Singing the words like a familiar tune, he became one with the spell. It swirled and danced around the room with colors and music and power.

His gaze wandered toward one of the expansive windows that lined the walls of the library, their large glass bodies spanning from floor to ceiling. In awe, he watched his work unfold. He watched the sky reverse from a dull grey to a wonderful and alluring blue. He watched as the village rose from the rubble and remade itself like new. He watched as the world around him brightened and came back to life.

Then, even as he felt his power lessen and his

shoulders droop, he smiled, content in the knowledge that he had left humanity's fate in the capable hands of those he had foreseen would come after him to keep this world safe. Their children's children would carry on with this most important of duties, as was their birthright, well into the bright and beautiful future. A small smile was still playing on his features when he dropped to the floor.

Chapter 1: Everyday and Simply Mundane.

Arabella Grace's day started like any other Tuesday. It began something like this: she woke up. Pretty simple, right? She focused through sleepy eyes at her alarm. The bright red, digital lights read...7:30 a.m.! *I'm late!* She thought in alarm (pun intended). Arabella jolted out of bed.

Suddenly, something flashed to mind.

With a light sigh of relief, Arabella realized that she wasn't late after all. It wasn't Tuesday, it was Saturday.

Laaaa, choirs of angels, accompanied by trumpets and all, sang in her head. *Every Saturday,* she mused. She had been certain today was a school day. She kept doing this, sleeping in on weekdays, yet finding herself wide awake on Saturday morning. So with a flop, Arabella Grace flourished back to bed and closed her heavy lids. And... the dogs started barking.

You have got to be kidding, she huffed with a mixture of annoyance and amusement. Her family's two adorably annoying Pomeranians never gave it a rest. *Looks like I'm up now,* she realized. Lazily rolling sideways, she fell with purpose out of bed. Her legs felt like dead weight as she sleepily sauntered out the door, already planning on trying to stay in her pj's all day, if her mom would let her. A proudly self-proclaimed nerd, the type of person who counted money in how many books she could buy and the passage of time in songs, she was hoping to catch up on the

latest episode of *Arrow*. Arabella made her way down the
hall, its walls covered in pictures of her family. Each
individual photo was fastened by a clothes pin to a twine
line, as if they were laundry hanging out to dry, or at least
she was pretty sure that's what her mother was going for. It
was sort of shabby-chic, she and her mom had agreed.
There were several photos of her and her siblings, parents,
cousins, aunts, uncles and grandparents. The photographs
hung all the way up the short corridor from the bedrooms
and office to where it opened up into the vaulted ceilings of
the kitchen, living room, and dining room. It was bright,
full of natural light, and open and airy. It felt like home.

    The whole house was made up in a color scheme of
cheery blues, reds and yellows- all the primary colors- with
a lot of pops of varying shades of turquoise, her mom's
favorite color. She beelined for the kitchen, her slumped
shoulders slightly straightening at the thought of breakfast.
The kitchen- her favorite spot in the house- had an island in
the middle, stainless steel appliances, granite counter tops
and dark wood cupboards of which there were more than
she could count. Most of them sat empty; Arabella's family
ate out more than they cooked at home. Arabella Grace
opened the first set of cupboards and snatched her *Star
Wars* bowl. She trudged over to the fridge and grabbed the
milk out, slogged over to the pantry and poured herself a
generous portion of her cereal of choice, Captain Crunch.
Life was good. She considered calling Cadence or Diana,

or both, to ask them to come over, but decided to wait until after she had a few lazy hours of reading and lounging under her belt. No need to rush a good thing.

She put everything away, then found her way to the couch and turned on the TV while the dogs jumped up next to her and stared at her with pleading eyes. *Yes! Harry Potter* was on. She had recently re-read all the books. It had instantly become one of her favorite series as a young girl and had stayed dear to her heart. She watched the movie for a while, but soon her mind wandered toward deeper things than whether or not Harry was going to be able to continue on his quidditch team.

She closed her eyes as her daydream quickly took her away to a place where her life was more than the everyday and simply mundane. It carried her to a place where soulmates existed, along with strange creatures with powers beyond her imagination. She yearned for it deep in her bones; its burn spread through her limbs. She felt the familiar ache of wishing so badly that it could be real, yet knowing that it could not. It seemed like a faded dream or forgotten memory playing through her mind. Flickering images, like an old movie, of flying high over towers and skyscrapers, with silver wings billowing behind her, were suddenly shattered by the sound of small feet padding toward her. Her little sister, Kathryn, followed by her parents, crashed the peace of her Saturday morning sanctuary as they bustled into the room grabbing breakfast, chatting, and generally making way too much noise that early on her weekend. Their eyes searched for a book at hand; they seemed pleasantly surprised by the fact that she had decided to join the living this morning. Her mom clanged hurriedly about, making Arabella and her sister some of her not-so-famous healthy smoothies.

The only one who was missing was her older brother, Thomas. He was a little more than two years her senior and had recently moved out of the house. That fact wasn't shocking in itself, but where he went was. Thomas had always been more of the scholarly type, like her grandfather. She and Thomas had both been born with an athletic build and were also both very tall. But unlike her, Thomas never really acted that interested in utilizing his athleticism. While Arabella dabbled in many sports in her youth, and enjoyed them, none had really stuck. So that's why it came as such a shock when Thom didn't go immediately to a College or University, like Harvard or Princeton or something equally as studious, but instead enlisted in the Army.

One day, she and Kathryn were sharing a room, the next, he was gone, and she got her own space to decorate with as many books and bookish things as she pleased; there was already a fair amount of fan art on the walls from the previous occupant that she happily left up. She and Thomas had always shared a bond over reading. He just didn't appreciate the male characters as much.

Arabella snapped back to reality (that seemed to happen a lot) with her 8 year old sister in front of her. Kat's family trait cornsilk hair was pulled back in a braid, and she had a yellow sundress dotted with little purple tulips on. She was obviously waiting for something, as was made evident by her foot tapping to an impatient beat. She cleared her throat and raised one eyebrow, which was normally one of Arabella's favorite expressions, especially when Kat was wearing it (well besides the laughing/crying emoji and Andrew Garfield's face in general). But this time, it was directed at her in a less than sisterly bonding kind of way.

"Well?" she inquired, her inflection clearly conveying her exasperation.

"Yes?" Arabella replied, mimicking her tone.

"Did you forget?" she questioned, now both eyebrows raised and her hands thrown in the air dramatically.

"Forget what?" Arabella's face was a frown of confusion as she probed Kat's green eyes for an answer to the mysterious crisis. That was the only feature she didn't have in common with her siblings- they both had bright, grass green eyes, while hers were a glacier blue.

"I have dance practice!" Kat fumed. "You promised you would run me this week."

"Crap!" Arabella yelled, and together they bolted

out the door to the car, Arabella forgetting that she was still in her *Spider-Man* pj's and had left her bowl on the coffee table for the eighth time that week. She had totally spaced that she was supposed to take Kat today. Unlike Arabella and their older brother, Kat was still using her natural athleticism. They rushed to the studio, Arabella's hair acquiring strange looks from the people in the cars next to them.

Great. It probably resembles a lion's mane, she realized. *Yay.* Yes, that was sarcasm.

Kat jumped out of the car without so much as a goodbye.

Really? Arabella thought with a sigh.

She pulled out of the parking lot and began to gently weave through the light traffic of Boise, Idaho. She loved living in her one story, gingerbread colored house with white trim that was nestled in the suburbs between the foothills and the Boise River. She pulled into the familiar driveway, hopped out of the car, and made the walk of sleep deprived shame through the yard that displayed a colorful array of yard art, hoping that none of the neighbors were looking out their windows. She attempted to open the white door the wrong way. *Duh, push. Every. Time.* She tried again successfully, crossed the threshold and threw her shoes off in the foyer. She somehow made it back to the couch without any bodily harm (she sustained three stubbed toes last time), and was almost successful in resuming her lazy day, only to be interrupted. Again. What did she ever do to the Universe to make it hate her so? Caution filled her as she threw an impish glance at her mother, who was standing in front of her with a very pointed look on her face.

Her mother, Sarah Grace, was an extremely beautiful woman. She had a mess of white blonde hair, a tall, 5'9", willowy form, bluish/green eyes, and striking, yet refined features. Plus, she had a gorgeous singing voice with a rustic, classic country feel to it that all the greats had. She was a throwback to a bygone era.

Her hobbies included: making Arabella work out, working out herself, making Arabella clean, cleaning herself, anything to do with warm weather- hiking, kayaking, swimming, and of course singing around the house; sometimes real songs, but most of the time, made up ditties or play on words. She was the most amazing person Arabella knew. She loved her children fiercely. She was also super laid-back and kind, always putting others before herself. She got that quality from her mom- Arabella's grandmother. But don't let that sweetness fool you, she had a very fiery soul, just like Arabella's southern aunt, who had a temperament to match her wild red hair.

Arabella was beginning to think that she was about to get the full blast of that fiery soul. Sarah had her hands on her hips. But what troubled Arabella, was that in one of Sarah's hands, she held Arabella's *Star Wars* cup. Also,

Arabella's Dad, Mitch Grace, was nowhere to be found, which was usually a pretty good sign that something was about to go down.

"Arabella, I found this on the coffee table," her mom stated, holding the cup higher. "Care to explain?"

Crap. This was the eighth time she was going to have this conversation with her mom this week. "I, uh... well, you see, I took Kat to dance rehearsal, and well... I forgot..." Arabella trailed off, giving her an apologetic expression and a sheepish shrug.

Sarah sighed. "You just need to be more responsible, that's all," then softened and added, "but thank you for driving your sister, I know it means a lot to her to spend time with you." Again with the responsibility. Arabella was about as responsible as any almost-sixteen-year-old could be, probably more so than most.

The phone started ringing, saving her from any further scolding.

Arabella had always hated the smell of hospitals. It was cliché, she knew, but it was the truth. The smell of bleach perfectly complimented the stark walls, but even the bleach couldn't cover up the smell of decay and disease that drifted through the emergency room. Everything was the same pristine white, even the modern looking plastic chairs. It was the type of white that hurt to look at and left you feeling cold and exposed. There was a sterile-ness to it that felt unwelcome and alien. Plus, Arabella was kind of a hot mess, and white didn't last five seconds in her presence. Seeing so much of it in one place wasn't natural. In the back of her mind, she morbidly wondered if it was easier to clean the blood off the white surface.

Trying to clear the buzzing from her ears and the strange thoughts that barely drifted through her murky mind, she focused on the nurse's bright red nails- the only color in the place- as she typed away on her white computer.

Tap. Tap. Tap.

Her mom and dad were speaking anxiously with the nurse. Arabella's little sister stood fearfully behind them as they tried to figure out what was going on. Arabella was dully aware of the nurse telling them to take a seat as she pointed to said horrid plastic chairs.

Arabella followed behind the rest of her family, taking Kat's small hand in hers in an attempt to give her comfort, but not knowing how. She wanted to protect her from all of this. She only heard muffled bits of dialogue and the sound of crying and coughing. They all sat, her father running his hand through his brown hair, his usual teasing attitude replaced with worry lines and stress. Tears pooled in his uniquely colored eyes- one green, one blue.

His display of raw emotion caused tears to trail down Arabella's own cheeks, carving silent paths.

After a few moments of waiting, she numbly realized that the nurse with the red nails was back, probably speaking, but she wasn't sure, because the buzzing noise was too loud. *Maybe I'm having a panic attack. Wouldn't be a bad place to have one.* Again, the thoughts were watered down and distant, as if she weren't the one thinking them.

The nurse led them through a pair of swinging doors. After a short -too short- walk up a corridor, with cracked, white linoleum floors, they reached their destination. The nurse pushed open the door in a quick, down-to-business manner, acting oblivious to the fact that they were dreading what lay behind the door. Acting as if there weren't tears streaking down their reluctant faces. Yet, soon the door was open all the way, and the nurse stood aside to follow them through. Arabella trailed her parents, still clutching Kat's hand.

Her eyes searched the room, but avoided the bed in the middle of it, the woman in the bed, and the man beside it. Her ears started begging to have that buzzing sound again, because now everything was crystal clear. The nurse's shoes scuffing on the floor, the rustling of blankets, and the fluffing of pillows. Worst of all, what stood out the most were the sobs of the man. He cried harder than she thought someone could cry, with such... heartbreak, that it broke her own heart in two, even more so than it already was. Out of the corner of her eye, she saw his fragile frame shake like a leaf in the wind. Her own heavy tears made it difficult to see the man, but she didn't dare turn and see him more clearly and face reality. Two new laments of frightful sobbing resounded, and soon a third, as the rest of her family moved to join him by the bed, leaving her to stare at the wall.

The doors closed and the nurse left them to their privacy. That's when she lost it. With a sob that nearly cracked her ribs, she finally faced the bed, her heart now in thirds. There in the white bed, surrounded by white walls, was an elderly woman whose face didn't have its usual glow and whose hair didn't have its usual luster. Her breathing was shallow, and her color was pallid. A thick layer of bandages covered her face and almost every place her skin was visible.

"How bad... how bad is it?" Arabella forced out, her voice cracking as tears choked her throat; it burned.

Arabella's grandfather's British accent was usually not noticeable, but was now thick with grief. He took a moment to collect himself and replied in a shaky breath, "it's bad," he croaked. "They... they don't know if she'll wake up, and..." He closed his eyes tightly, forcefully shielding himself from the sight in front of him. "Your grandmother was finishing her weekly womens' hike and was headed to her car, but never made it. It was pretty early, and no one really saw it happen, but they did see a black SUV peeling away. They found your grandma laying on the sidewalk unconscious. It was so early, and she was so cold when they found her... She hasn't regained consciousness, but they say she's stable, and hopefully..." He shook his head. "But they don't know if she'll wake up. They said..." he trailed off, deep in thought, "that her vitals and brain activity have been promising. It must have been an accident, and some scared idiot didn't want to take responsibility and decided it was better to hit and run than face the cops." He usually did that when he was upset. He used logic to outweigh grief.

Arabella placed her grandmother's hand in her own. She studied the hand as a way to distract herself. It was small, but strong, with years of work evident in her callouses. She noticed her grandma's fingers twitch and her cheek spasm. One steel blue eye suddenly fluttered open, while one remained swollen shut. Arabella's grandpa all but pushed her out of the way.

"Love," he whispered and gave her a lingering kiss on the forehead. "You scared me there for a second."

A weak chuckle escaped her lips. "You should know better by now Harris, you can't get rid of me that easily."

He sighed deeply in relief, but it sounded mainly amused. "Axelia."

Arabella was profoundly relieved to see them back

to their normal banter and hoped it meant that everything was going to be okay. Maybe her grandma couldn't come home right now, but she would eventually. Everything would be fine. She felt her body unclench.

She glanced at her grandma's face to see her watching Arabella with deep concern. "I want to talk to Arabella for a moment. Alone."

Her grandpa nodded gravely and led the rest of her confused family out of the room after a few brief, misty embraces, and hushed, sweet well-wishes from her other granddaughter, son-in-law and devoted daughter.

"Why do you need to talk to *me*?" Arabella questioned once it was just the two of them. Her grandma got a far off look in her one good eye and cleared her throat. "They knew- you must understand- they knew where I was going to be, they waited in the shadows. They caught me when I was alone... I shouldn't have been so foolish. It had been years, though, and you are so close. I thought I was safe and that I was strong enough. I thought that I could be alone." She sounded delirious, and Arabella was curious how strong her pain medication was.

Guilt settled over Arabella like shrink wrap; would this have happened if she had gone with her grandma that morning? She tried to attend the womens' walks with her, but had totally spaced that morning. She had offered the night before, but had ended up being busier, and more forgetful, on her Saturday morning than she had anticipated.

Her grandma read her face and hastily waved it off. "No, no. Don't feel bad. Something like this would have happened eventually. I'm not as strong as I used to be. You need to be careful, after what happened to Ember... I knew they were coming here, I knew they were going to come after me and you. You need to watch yourself, Arabella. You need to stay out of the shadows. Watch yourself, they will kill you if they get the chance." Seeing her confused look, her grandmother closed her eyes tightly as if to prepare herself. "I had hoped to tell you this on your birthday. I didn't want to tell you before it was absolutely necessary, but-" Suddenly her words were cut off with a dry, violent cough. With every word, her voice got weaker. Arabella couldn't begin to understand what any of this meant and chalked it up to medication and lack of REM sleep. She was just about to suggest that her grandmother get some rest and that she come back tomorrow when they were interrupted.

The doors opened, revealing red nails and the nurse they belonged to. "I'm sorry, but visiting hours are over. You can come back tomorrow," she said with a forced smile and overly cheerful voice. *She must be near the end of her shift and struggling through exhaustion to remain polite to stragglers like me.*

Arabella got up, already planning on coming back

as soon as visiting hours allowed, so that she could figure out what her grandmother's cryptic words meant. Before she was halfway out of her seat, her grandma grabbed her hand. "Goodbye, darling," she almost whispered. "I love you so much, and I will always be proud of you." Her face grew grave. "No matter what happens, follow your heart. And oh," she quirked her mouth almost into a smile. "Your present is in my room in a cherrywood box, engraved with mother of pearl." Then she pulled Arabella in close so that the nurse couldn't hear and gripped her hand painfully tight. "Watch yourself, they will kill you if they get the chance."

"What?" She shook her head. Her grandma had just gone through a lot- she deserved a little crazy. And her words were truly crazy. "I'm coming back tomorrow, and even if you miss my birthday, grandpa can give it to me," Arabella reassured her. "And I'll visit everyday, anyway. I love you."

"I love you." Her grandma gave a soft smile. *It must be painful with a split lip.*

Arabella walked out as her grandpa walked back in. He gave her a hug that conveyed so many unspoken words.

"I love you so much. Tell your brother that I'm so proud of him, just like I'm proud of you. Never forget that."

She gave him a confused look. "I love you too."

She was going to question him about the strangely ominous
words he had shared, but he was already leaving. How
come they seemed to know something she didn't?

Arabella joined her family in the waiting room, and
they all headed home. They got the call as soon as they got
there.

Her grandparents were both gone.

It rained the day of their funeral.

Something about that didn't sit right with Arabella.
Both of her grandparents were larger than life, with
personalities that shined more brilliantly than the sun itself.
They brightened the lives of all whose paths they crossed.
She had always assumed that even when they left, she
would still feel that warmth, but it seemed that their
absence had left her cold and devoid of light; all that was
left were ashes from a long dead fire. She felt utterly and
completely alone. The rain that beat into her dark dress was
nothing but a minor annoyance in the grand scheme of
things. She couldn't help but realize, however, that any
other day, she would have been worried about how the rain
had ruined the princess curls she had spent an hour on, or
how her carefully constructed makeup- especially her
mascara- had melted off her face, like wax that got too
close to a flame. Arabella Grace feared, especially after her

grandmother's warning, that she would get too close, and the flame would consume her. She came to the realization that none of that mattered. What was the point of any of it when the people she loved, looked up to, and cared so deeply for were...

Gone.

The rain went on all through the memorial service, and she found that either way her mascara would have run. Fat tears streamed down her face and her frame shook as though a tornado whipped around her. Her parents stood behind her crying, and her younger sister, Kat, was sobbing into her mother's long skirt. Even Thomas was there, in his military garb, his hair tucked into a hat. He was as close to their grandpa as Arabella was to their grandma. Finally, when the time came, they each laid a rose onto both of the coffins- one coffin was the final resting place of someone dear to her who had been in the wrong place at the wrong time, and the other housed someone, also dear to her, who had died of a broken heart when he had found out about his wife's passing. His body just couldn't handle the stress and heartbreak, and he had suffered a heart attack on the spot, shortly after Arabella's family had departed the hospital.

The service ended in a blur, and right before they left the cemetery, Arabella thought her eyes deceived her when she glimpsed a woman through the cemetery mist, watching her with pale green eyes. She wore a look of sad determination.

After that day, Arabella Grace's life consisted primarily of sitting in her room- and she didn't plan on moving anytime soon. Even when the calendar marked October 25, her birthday. She wished it wasn't. Meant to be a benchmark occasion, it was the day she turned 16, but all she could think about was that they weren't there to share it. Tears gathered in her eyes and leaked out of the corners as she thought about their parting words.

She had tried to figure out the cryptic message behind them, but she couldn't find any. All she knew was that they weren't there; she sobbed again. Lately, it was the only sound in the mourning house.

It hit the whole family really hard, but everyone else wasn't left with the confusion, worry, and irrational fear that caused Arabella to look over her shoulder every few minutes as her grandmother's words played through her head on a loop. *You need to watch yourself, Arabella. You need to stay out of the shadows. Watch yourself, they will kill you if they get the chance.* Worry filled her again... Why? *Why would someone be after me, why would someone want to kill me?* Her grandma's death had been an accident, hadn't it? That night, nightmares of demons plagued her.

Chapter 2: Her Mind Whirled, and Her Heart Raced.

It had been two weeks since Arabella Grace's birthday, and three since their deaths. Three weeks of constantly looking over her shoulder, three weeks of hiding the paranoia and forcing uneasy smiles. On top of that, the house had become unbearably tense. Everything was so quiet. Everyone spoke in a whisper. To make matters worse, well meaning friends and neighbors wouldn't stop bringing casseroles over. It was as if the whole neighborhood had decided that's what you give someone when they're mourning. If she ate one more casserole this week, she was going to scream.

Not that she wasn't doing plenty of that lately. Sometimes it just all got to be too much. She would clench her teeth so tight, they would groan and creak in protest. She would squeeze her hands into fists with the same fierceness, so tightly that it caused her fingernails to break the skin and create bloody crescents on her palms. Yet those things didn't stop the suffocating feeling that rose inside her, drowning her from the inside out until she had no choice but to... let it out.

That was how it had been for the past two weeks. So it came as a relief when her mom gently woke her up and told her that the school had called requesting information on Arabella and whether or not she would be feeling well enough to return. She had decided today was as good a day as any, although she was beginning to regret it when math class rolled around. Math wasn't exactly her favorite subject. In fact, it was her least. The fact that she had missed three weeks of it- and all of her other classes- wasn't a comforting thought, either.

She found herself remembering the time when she was in third grade and her mom and grandma were helping her learn multiplication by teaching her silly little riddles and tricks with her fingers. She could almost feel the warm sunlight filtering into the kitchen and could almost smell chicken noodle soup simmering on the stove. Her fingers tightly wrapped around her pencil as she chewed on the eraser, her mom would rub comforting circles on her back and point out the answers she missed in a soft voice while her grandma laughed and kissed her on the cheek when she got one right. Then her grandpa would walk in and kiss her grandma's cheek, and they would smile at each other in the way they always did. With so much.. *love.*

Arabella closed her eyes tightly, shielding herself from the memory. A tear escaped, and she willed it away quickly and sniffed. Then she shot a quick glance around the room. She wouldn't cry in front of these people. And she was NOT going to cry in math class. But she saw that most of them weren't even paying attention to the teacher, let alone her. She bit at the end of her pencil, then continued working on quadratics. It didn't help that every time she shifted slightly in her seat, her freshly inked tattoo would get irritated. Yes, tattoo.

When her grandmother was young, she had gotten a tattoo similar to her own grandma's. When the family had been reading her grandparents' Will, she had been shocked to discover that her grandmother had wanted Arabella to keep the tradition by getting one of her own. She had left a sketch of the tattoo, and arranged a place where she could get the artwork done. She had even paid for it ahead of time. Arabella was surprised by how much she wanted to get the tattoo to honor her grandmother. Her parents didn't say no. They didn't exactly seem pleased, and were slightly hesitant, but they quickly came to the agreement that if Arabella wanted to follow through with it, they would respect her strange request as well. How could they refuse her grandmother's last wishes? Going in and getting the actual tattoo had been surreal. The shock that she was actually doing it, and why she was doing it, were fresh in her mind. She remembered snippets of a British accent, the intense and extremely prolonged pain, and the eventual numbness that graciously envelopes one when getting your whole back tattooed. She had to go back three times for it to be completely finished, and each time, she felt more out of it than the last. But when it was finished... it took her breath away. She had magnificent, flowing wings. They looked so life-like that they could almost have been real.

They had been done completely in silver, grey, and white ink, reminding her of shimmering angel wings.

Back to Math. *Yay.* Oh, the joyful subject, how she had missed it. Just to prove her love for arithmetic, she wrote a little poem on the outside of her binder: *Math sucks and makes me want to die, when I do it I cry, I'm not a poet, so why do I try? Well...because it's better than doing mathematic equations that make me sigh.*

Arabella's platonic soulmate, Cadence, leaned over from the desk behind her and read her poem and snorted. "Nice." He chuckled under his breath, "I really hope you've been paying more attention than I have, because if I have any chance of passing the test next week, this weekend I'll need you and Diana to come over and help me study." His voice was light and teasing. But when she looked back, his eyes were filled with worry. He was clearly trying to distract her. "Why is it," he started in the same light tone, "that in any teenage movie or TV show, they always have, like, a ton of time in between classes? They can plan how to take down the villain, rob a bank, and travel the world- all between classes. We only have four minutes. Either we're getting hosed, or they have great time management skills."

Now it was her turn to snort. "You're weird." She couldn't tell if her laughter was real or fake, and she couldn't tell if that was good or bad. But if anyone could cheer her up, it would be Cadence. She had wanted to tell him about her grandmother's cryptic words and how scared she was, but couldn't find the strength. Who was going to believe what even she had brushed off as the ramblings of an old woman on pain medication? Who would believe that she was starting to suspect that it was an actual warning- that it was forming into a hard stone of worry that was becoming a constant resident in her gut?

Gabriel finished bringing the last box into his room and sagged back onto his frameless bed. He pulled a sketchbook from his backpack. He started to lightly sketch a musician he had seen playing on a street corner in downtown Boise to distract his wandering mind from his scattered life, most of which was stuffed in the boxes littering his floor.

But he had his backpack, which meant it couldn't be all bad. The print was a patchwork of various Marvel comics, and the inside contained his most precious Earthly possessions. It had safeguarded his belongs since his mom bought it for him, when he was 10, at a comic book store somewhere in Somerville, Massachusetts. It was filled with an assortment of items from the last 6 years: multiple sketchbooks, pencils, sharpies, his camera, pictures of his family, his favorite books, comics, a Walkman, his favorite tapes, a Rubik's cube, and a random Nick Fury action figure. The books, comics, music and toys had been his (only) constant companions for a long time. Now there wasn't as much need for them. Well, he hoped there wouldn't be- he assumed starting school meant making friends. Still, it was bittersweet. Wanting a distraction, he focused once more on the picture. But before his pencil could touch the page, his world went black.

After about an hour and a half, Arabella Grace was about to go crazy and was regretting her hasty decision to return to school. Finally the bell rang, its annoying and shrill buzz blaring through the corridors. As abrasive as it was, it still signaled freedom. So with a withering glance thrown around at the cracked white walls, white boards, smart board and inspiring posters, Arabella fled the classroom. Cadence was already gone, having sprinted to get his lunch. *Boys.*

The minute she got to the lunchroom, she took out her phone and headphones. She adored music. Music sometimes felt like her only solace in life. Her favorite band, Infinity At Its Best, screamed through her earbuds-their loud punk rock and indie beat keeping time with her own heartbeat; it momentarily drowned out the worries that swam in her head. The lead singer wailed out a melody that carried her far from her troubles with a voice as smooth as water- perfect glass. It didn't hurt that said frontman was pretty cute.

Arabella made her way to the back of the cafeteria where she usually sat with her friends. It made her sad to have it flash to mind why she hadn't been there lately. Her friends were the best. There was Diana- the classic, quiet, good girl... with a crazy side. Claire, who didn't try to hide her crazy, but was as sweet as they come. Cadence, Arabella's awesome best friend and soon to be pilot, because he was that smart and hard working. Zuriel, Claire's boyfriend, who was basically the older brother she didn't want. Zuriel's twin brother, Luke, was a big clown and video game nerd- even at that moment, he was tapping away at his phone...and, she was pretty sure he was wearing his shirt inside out. That was her group, and Arabella thought they were probably the best group of friends she could have.

Arabella stole an apple from Cadence, having forgotten to pack a lunch and refusing to eat the presumably poisoned cafeteria food. She pulled one earbud out so that she could explain this to him, but all thoughts of explaining herself instantly flew out the single paned window.

She suddenly saw the most beautiful bird perched upon the big oak tree outside; the sunlight filtering through the leaves reflected off its white, glittering wings. The bird looked to be some sort of bird of prey- maybe a falcon or a hawk-except it was pure white, from feather to talon to beak. It had a deadly look about it, with its razor like claws and viciously sharp beak. Its eyes were wide with what appeared to be curiosity. It made eye contact with Arabella before flying away.

Arabella's glacier blue eyes were huge with shock to discover that Cadence's hand was waving in front of her, his booming voice calling her name.

"W-what?" she questioned, tearing her gaze from the window and focusing on Cadence. She rubbed at her wrist automatically, feeling like she was missing something there- it was the same feeling she got when she would lose a bracelet. But then she remembered that she hadn't worn a bracelet today.

He gave her a challenging look, shook his head, and peered at her once more, relief at last relaxing his features. "Um," he responded, sounding confused, then more confidently added, "you zoned out for, like, several minutes. Are you okay?" he inquired, his voice still filled with concern.

Arabella turned toward the rest of the group and was surprised to find that all gossiping and chatter had died down, and they were instead staring at her with similar looks of concern on their faces.

"Didn't you see the bird...?" Arabella inquired, then drifted off when she saw their confusion deepen.

"There wasn't a bird there, Bella," Diana replied,

looking at her with a worrisome expression.

Cadence touched her shoulder gently, causing her to look his way. He murmured, "you sure you're okay?"

She may have nodded on the outside, but inside she wasn't sure.

Then Luke broke the tension. "So what are you on, and where can I buy some?"

Everyone laughed, and just like that, it was forgotten about. But she couldn't forget. She was scared. And she missed her grandmother.

Gabriel realized with a start that he was outside of his house. He wasn't entirely sure how he had gotten there. The last thing he remembered was starting to draw in his bedroom, and then... nothing. *Not again,* he thought, realizing he had blacked out. He gave a deep sigh and stared down at his own hands. For some reason, he was expecting them to look unfamiliar, but they were the same graphite and paint-stained hands he had been looking at his whole life.

She returned home that night tired and confused.

After watching a movie with her family and finishing her homework, she went to bed. Or she tried to, but for hours she tossed and turned. She read and watched Netflix, trying to get her mind off of her grandmother and to get the pit out of her stomach. When she finally slept, all she dreamt of were shadows. Arabella Grace was no stranger to nightmares and had recently had more than her fair share. Ever since she was a child, her dreams had ran deep and vivid. Sometimes she was a hero and had a prince, while other times, demons hunted her through the night. Despite this, she always woke up the next day fully rested, content and reassured that the demons couldn't follow her into the real world. This dream was different.

Shadows that were more than mere darkness slunk toward her, changing from formless blobs of inky black into shapes with warped humanoid features, with hunched shoulders, long, twisted arms, and claw-like hands. They slithered and withered as if they were made of thick, oozing oil. One creature reached for Arabella, and a scream emerged in her throat. As the demon clawed and scratched at her arm with its gnarled, trowel-like fingers, she felt ice sink into her bones. Wherever it scoured, the warmth was immediately extracted, almost as if it had never been there at all. She glanced down, gasping, and saw three long bleeding marks right above her elbow. She accelerated her backpedal, wheezing and choking for her breath. Each rasp she took hurt, and her throat felt as if the creature had reached down and scraped the flesh from her esophagus. Continuing to retreat, she stared in horrified amazement as the creature wriggled faster toward her, its unnaturally elongated arms clutching for her. The shimmering blackness of its face looked right at her with nothing, but somehow she knew it was staring at her.

Suddenly, power gusted through her and filled her lungs. Her choked breath hitched. The bird, the silver bird from outside her lunchroom, swept in front of her, talons out-stretched. The talons shimmered in the low lighting of the room she was in, as if silver coated them. It swept through the demon, The Shadow, dissolving it as easily as you would scatter dust through the air. The rest of the monster melted into the floor. And when the silver bird flew away, it didn't have tar on its wings like she expected. As quickly as that demon was dispersed, though, another took its place, and she continued her panicked escape.

The feeling of being a caged animal returned to claw at her insides, and claustrophobia clung around her neck like a noose. Every step The Shadows took tightened it more and more until she felt as if she was being hung. Her ragged breath grew more frantic, and the need for air pushed through her and made her desperate for survival. She was enclosed- no escape. She couldn't help thinking of others in her life and prayed the demons would never get to them. *No, no, no, no, no, no, no.* The word raced through her head on an endless loop. "No!" The sound tore free from her shell-shocked lips. "This can't be happening, this can't, this can't, it can't. Not real, not real, not real," she repeated, shaking her head. She raised her hands to her head, her long fingers gripped tightly in her fine hair, pulling hard enough to make a burning pain spread throughout her delicate scalp wherever she pulled. She was terrified and just wanted it to stop. All the color drained from her face- her skin turned from pale to pasty. Her feet resumed their backpedaling, her boots padding softly against the concrete; their frantic march matched her heartbeat. Suddenly, her back hit something solid.

Turning in desperate horror, she was praying what she hit was a wall. When she turned around, she instead saw a hooded figure; relief swept through her. It was a person- she wasn't alone. Then she noticed that under the hood, he had a sickly sweet smile. He gave her a feeling like she had eaten too much candy. It made the hairs on the back of her neck stand up, and not even the thought of demons behind her could keep her from backing up. Then the rest of his features became clear in her frantic vision. His pure black eyes stared down at her. The thing lunged out and captured her within its arms, bony fingers digging painfully into the flesh of her upper arm. Its right hand dug into the scratches left by the demon and blood trickled from them. If Arabella had ever considered herself pale, it was nothing compared to the albino hue of this creature's skin.

With a voice like rusted nails screeching across a

tin roof, it hoarsely whispered,"ahh, Arabella, we meet at last."

She shot awake, a cold sweat breaking out on her forehead and terror clinging to her like a second skin. She had felt sure that she was never going to escape that dream and the man-creature in it. Thinking of the void in his eyes, her heart rate sped up, and a gut-wrenching scream ripped through her vocal chords and shattered her own eardrums, followed by a silence that seemed to weigh on the night air. "Please!" she wailed and called into the dark, begging for her nightmares to stay in her dreams. She drew her knees from under her soft covers and up to her chest, cradling them to her as a sob broke free. She mourned the death of her grandparents and she mourned some nameless thing she felt she was about to lose.

The door of her room cracked open and her mom stood there, maternal worry etched on her face. Yellow light flooded her room- it was too bright for her already sore eyes, and she burrowed her face even farther into the fleece of her *Spider-Man* pj pants. She heard the steps of her mother's soft tread as she neared her bed and suddenly drew Arabella into the warmth of her motherly love. It was the tender, but fierce, type of embrace that moms wrap their children in to reassure them that they are safe and that everything will turn out alright. Sarah Grace didn't say any of this out loud, nor did she have to. Arabella knew exactly what her mother's hugs meant by now, and right now, she needed one. Yet, as she rested her head on her mom's shoulder and cried her heavy heart out, she noticed pain radiating from her right arm where her mom hugged her- right where The Shadow-demon-monster had scratched her. When she glanced down through her tears, she saw three raised lines that looked like recently healed scars.

The next two days weren't any better. Weird things kept occurring. First, it was the silver falcon bird-thing. For someone to understand what made the next event so abnormal, they would have to know a little bit about Arabella Grace. While being tall and halfway athletic, Arabella was extremely... what was a good way to put this? She was... a day-dreamer. She got easily caught up in her own head- big things, like: how she would make a difference in the world and leave her indelible mark on it. This, ironically, led her to be pretty unaware of her current world and surroundings. She was outside on an unnaturally warm, Idaho November day; in fact, everyone seemed to be outside that day. A group of Freshman and Junior boys (typical show-offs) were playing baseball nearby while a group of girls sat on the grass eating their lunch. She was soaking up the warm rays of the sun as they heated her leather jacket and was re-reading *City of Glass*. She was in a state of total enthrallment, when suddenly, her hand shot up, and before her mind could catch up with her subconscious, she realized that she had caught the stray baseball the boys had been playing with- without looking- right before it was about to tag her square in the face. Not exactly one to live in the present, the miraculous snag shocked her and everyone around her.

As for the third incident, well... some jerk that had always given Cadence a hard time was once again lamely teasing him about the fact that he was adopted- she **hated** that- and she stepped in like she often did. But this time, she didn't just cut off the conversation and do the usual girl thing by putting her hands on their chests and pushing them apart like she would have normally done. No. She stepped in front of the bully so fast that he didn't even realize she moved. Not only did she move lightning quick, but she was able to block the punch he had thrown wildly in Cadence's direction, and then she slugged said jerk with a solid Rocky-style left hook. So, yeah. That happened... *What was going on?* she questioned herself afterwards as she played with her braid- undoing and redoing it- a nervous habit of hers. She kind of hoped that this meant she had super speed, and that S.H.I.E.L.D. was going to come pick her up. Instead, she was in confinement of a different kind.

The incident had led her to her latest dilemma: she was in detention. She had never been in detention! Not once! *And why?* All because she broke some dude's nose who got his kicks from making other people miserable.

Worst of all, she couldn't even listen to music, which was the only thing she currently felt that she would miss if the world ended. The English teacher and detention Nazi, Mrs. Tallas, hated her! She always had, ever since her Freshman year, two short years ago. She was ready to be done with this conformist prison that they called High School. She didn't ever want to hear the words, 'future' or 'college' again.

But back to her current sad state. The clock ticked at such a slow pace, you'd think Kronos, the Titan of Time, was purposely slowing it to a maddening standstill just to slowly drive her insane. Maybe he was, and she was about to be whisked away on a terrifyingly awesome adventure. But as the clock continued to tick, and a certain black haired boy didn't burst through the door, she felt her hope dwindle. Time kept moving agonizingly slow. She attempted to master the art of self control by not tapping her pencil too loudly. Every time she did, the witch- by witch she meant teacher- would look up from the papers she was grading and glare at her over her wire-rimmed glasses.

Gabriel was outside trying to calm down. He loved his dad, but sometimes he could be oblivious to Gabriel's feelings. When he said stuff like, 'we're better off without her,' it made him so mad, because no matter how hard he tried not to, there was a part of him that blamed his dad for the divorce- that blamed him for her leaving. Back then, he had actually wanted to leave, when the fighting never stopped and words were said that couldn't be taken back. He breathed in deeply and tried to sketch a picture of Bogus Basin. Suddenly, something painful tugged in his stomach, pulling his legs out from under him as his world once again went black.

A flash of light distracted Arabella Grace from further exploring the subject of what would happen if she became a superhero. Her unfocused gaze swept toward the open window. It looked to be the same bird from a few days before. It had the same silver wings and sharp gaze. A sudden urge to go outside struck her swiftly in the gut and tugged at her intestines. Fortunately, the alarm on her teacher's desk sounded, signaling the end of her imprisonment. She rocketed out of her seat the moment the alarm rang, its irritating buzz loud enough to shatter ear drums. Her feet raced across the tiles, her shoes slipping and sliding upon its freshly waxed surface. *Oh, the janitor is going to hate me.* The fleeting thought was swept away as she threw open the doors.

There it was. Waiting. For her. Somehow....she just

knew. They made eye contact as it launched itself upward in a graceful, fluid motion. She couldn't fight the invisible thread that was hooked to her mind and gut, pulling her along- it seemed as if a cord was tethered to the bird's wings, and she was compelled to let it lead her. She was so enthralled by following the bird, she didn't even stop to think what it could possibly mean. It was like something out of her fantasies. Maybe it was a 'were', or they ran out of owls at Hogwarts, or maybe it was something more sinister- like a poltergeist. She hoped she still had salt in her lunch bag. Or maybe it was a figment of her imagination. Either way, when it flew away, she followed it, unable to do anything else. She watched as it soared just out of reach, its wings spread majestically. *How amazing it must feel to be able to do that.*

The bird led her all the way across town, following the Boise River Greenbelt, crossing one major highway, and venturing deep into the suburbs. With her binder close to her chest, she raced through traffic, trying to stay on the trail of the bird, who, as soon as she would catch up with it, would zoom just out of sight again. She was also trying to avoid getting hit by a car or bike. When it finally did stop, Arabella gasped involuntarily for two reasons: one, they were at her grandma's house; two, the bird had instantly and inexplicably blinked out of existence before her eyes. One second it was there, the next, it had vanished. *It's official, I've gone crazy,* Arabella Grace couldn't help but think. Suddenly, the force that had been causing her to follow the bird switched to an equally painful tug, propelling her toward the empty home. She stopped. No matter how uncomfortable it was to have the cramp-like pain in her stomach, it couldn't be worse than going into the house.

She gazed up at the towering Victorian mansion. Blinking in shock and surprise, she slowly moved, unable to ignore the excruciating, invisible thread pulling her toward it. She stumbled in her boot-clad feet through the newly fallen leaves and lifted one hand to shield her eyes from the sunlight that filtered through what was left of their lingering gold and red companions in the trees. The closer she got to the front door, the more frequently she had to rub her clammy palms on the front of her artfully-destroyed, black skinny jeans to dry the sweat. At the same time, her throat became almost unbearably dry. *Yet, I can't turn back,* she thought ruefully. It was as if gravity was pushing her sideways instead of keeping her on the ground. It seemed to be forcing her toward the once comforting, but now imposing home, with its thin flower print curtains in all six front windows, and its bright yellow door- a stark contrast against the dark grey paint that covered the rest of the house. It felt as if a golfball was working its way through her throat as she swallowed. In her head, she imagined it traveling down the parched surface of her esophagus, causing it to bleed as it scraped its way down at an agonizing pace.

Desperation ripped at her insides like a terrible fanged beast, with sharp claws that could tear through steel like butter. But alas, she just kept moving forward. She tried, again, to take a deep breath and stop, but no matter how hard she screamed at her body to halt, it wouldn't. The leather boots on her feet, usually a familiar sensation that she embraced everyday, felt uncomfortably warm- which was strange, considering the cool air that made the sweat now dripping down her forehead seem like a second, sticky skin. She claimed each step carefully, trying to ignore every creak, and trying not to flinch at every moan made by the ancient wood of the front porch. She was acting like a stranger to this three story dwelling, like she hadn't spent every moment she could there. At this point, she wanted to be a stranger. She didn't want to remember. She didn't want the pain. She was so lost in her thoughts that she was shocked to suddenly find her hand grasping the soul-sucking, cold brass doorknob. The doorknob was so worn and old in appearance that it looked to be even more of a relic than the one hundred year old house itself. The cold of the brass bit into her skin as she twisted it, its shrieks of protest a familiar comfort long forgotten, and she suppressed a gasp of emotional agony. Her grandma had always joked that she was going to get the old thing replaced, but she had, truth be told, loved it- maybe more even than the house. Now, she definitely couldn't. Another wave of grief seized her, and it became a struggle to breathe.

Apparently, fate thought she was being too slow and needed some assistance, because suddenly, the door swung open wide and the hooks in her stomach tightened their hold. Cringing, she expected to hear it crash into the wall from the force of the swing, which she assumed must have been from the wind. She didn't dare imagine it to be something more exciting than that. It was November, after all. But a feeling in her gut was telling her that it wasn't just the wind- it was something far less ordinary than the wind, as cliché as that sounded. She scarcely allowed herself to hope for anything more- because her dreams had always stayed in her head. And how could she even enjoy living out her visions of freedom and fantasy when she had so much grief weighing so heavily on her heart?

Ignoring the feeling that she was walking into the introduction of a new episode of *Supernatural*, she continued forward, her feet still dragging her along, almost unwillingly. A layer of dust had settled across the floor and encased the window frames. An odd sort of resentment filled her chest. Life, already so unfair, seemed to get darker. Her grandmother would never have allowed her house to look like that. She never had, in all the years she lived there; it felt wrong. While it appeared the same outside, it was barren on the inside. Just like Arabella felt. Entering slowly, she glanced quickly around, but was jerked forward by the hooks and the motion of her feet moving of their own accord from the invisible strings that tugged her along like a rag doll. The strings led her to the stairs in the back of the grand entryway; dust caking the room.

The print of her boot-tread followed behind her like a ghost. Every step she took marked her path, cutting through the powder on the ground. With the feel of the chilly air combined with the white hue of the dust, she could almost imagine herself as a small girl playing in the snow. She needed to let that thought go, because it would never be like that again. The stairs, once carpeted with what used to be a pristine white plush, were now leaning toward more tan than white, from both old age and recent neglect. By the time she reached the second floor, she was feeling dejected and alone. Goosebumps covered her skin, and a soft whimper escaped her lips when her aching feet crossed the landing and carried her onto the third floor. Arabella felt her dread rising as the strange feeling of having no control continued to drag her into her grandmother's room.

Tears that had been gathering in her eyes fell down her cheeks in heavy, hot droplets that smudged her already grimy shirt. Still moving against her will, she continued into her grandmother's walk-in closet, right next to the four poster king-sized bed that used to be dressed in luxurious, sateen, dark blue sheets. She really wanted to dash out of the room and across the hall into the bathroom, so she could sit down and have a good cry, but she couldn't. She opened the door to the closet and slipped in. She had been expecting to be greeted with the sight of a barren, vacant closet, just like the rest of the house, but instead found herself in a state of paralysis to discover that it wasn't empty at all. At least not completely, because inside the closet was **the bird**.

Arabella studied the bird, and it studied her. It was just as beautiful and lethal-looking up close as it was from afar. Its large black eyes peered at her with a kind of intelligence that she didn't expect from an animal. The saying, 'bird brain' didn't typically imply intellect. As the bird regarded her, she decided to take a step closer, but just then, it flew past her as if to take its leave- a mesmerizing sight. Oddly, she had honestly never really liked birds before. She had always imagined them aggressively flying at her and getting tangled in her hair, or scratching her face to ribbons, or tearing her eyes out- usually something along those gruesome lines. They seemed like stinky, diseased animals. But this creature...

With gentle steps, Arabella Grace's feet pulled her forward once more, and a resentful sort of acceptance came into her consciousness as she came to the spot where the bird had stood. She felt her knees bend at the joint from a detached point of view. The dull awareness of the hooks that had been tugging her along spread to all of her extremities until her head was the only thing she was in control of. A hand, her hand, reached forward and grasped the carpet on the floor. She noticed that there was a rectangular outline in the floor, and when Arabella's hand tugged in that spot, it came up in a large piece. Arabella carefully placed the square of carpet aside and gasped.

There was a medium-sized box made of a rich rosewood wrapped in veins of inlaid iridescent green and blue mother of pearl that held it together like a bow. Silver text shimmered underneath the lid, interwoven with the mother of pearl as if the words were archaic ruins with vines growing around them. It read:

In the third generation, eight heroes shall be born.
A Clock Keeper like no other shall grace this earth.
Loss will shake one to the core, and rage fill her with no remorse.
After death fills her breath, she'll discover the person who can give her rest.

It reminded Arabella of a prophecy from one of her favorite books or TV shows, but maybe one that wasn't quite finished...

On top, there was a card. It read: ***For Arabella, Happy Birthday. Love, your grandparents.***

Arabella remembered some of her grandmother's final words about her present. *The Bird wanted me to find my birthday present?* Arabella questioned. Well, that was nice and all... *but is this really the reason I'm here?* Arabella had plenty of opportunities to come and get this over the past two weeks, but wasn't ready and didn't want to. But now that it was here and facing her, its gleaming surface begged her to run her fingers up and down it. Her breath became thin, sharp inhalations as she tried to force her own body to stop moving against her bidding. Her fingers reached forward, although she fought against it, because somewhere deep inside her, she knew that once she opened that box, there was no going back. Yet, her hands continued steadily toward their objective, the only evidence of resistance a slight tremor of her fingers. She grasped the box, the polished rosewood surface cool and smooth in her hands, and she lifted it out of its hiding spot, her lack of upper body strength making it comically difficult. *I really need to start lifting,* she mused deliriously.

She sighed in momentary relief when it finally sat upon the carpet by her side. Turning, she tugged the lip of the thin lid and slid it off easily. She gasped. *Gasping is starting to become a habit,* she thought. She had been struck and shoved off-kilter by two things. One: by the contents of the container; and two: because her new tattoo began to burn in such a way that it felt as if it was being etched on all over again. Instantaneously. The pain momentarily distracted her from the quirky prizes before her, but once the fire fled from her flesh and the white stopped clouding her eyes, she focused on her own unfolding mystery.

The first item she spied inside the magnificent package was not your ordinary Sweet 16 gift. She had maybe expected some new clothes, a couple of Pop Vinyl figures, and some books. That's not what she got. She got a shiny, razor-sharp arming sword- sleek and beautiful. It was super wicked, in fact. Its handle was wrapped in aged black leather. The hilt was silver, with more blue, green, and white mother of pearl inlay, and its doubled edged blade was as long as her arm. Goosebumps rose across her skin, and a familiar energy seemingly radiated out from the blade as she plucked it from its resting place. It was incredible. It was something from one of her own fantasies. The hole in her soul grew slightly smaller as the smell of adventure floated on the electrified air. It called to her, and she was not so shocked to realize that she felt surprisingly at peace with it. It was exhilaratingly terrifying, but she had never felt better; she felt like she was finally where she was supposed to be. She had never felt more at home than she did with that sword in her hand.

She tore her gaze away from the temptress of a blade toward the second item in the box as she placed the weapon on the ground. It was a delicate watch made of glittering metal, with three overlapping, gilded, angel-like wings on the right side of the face. The band was made of unblemished black leather. The wings ranged in size like the hands of a clock- arranged smallest to largest, darkest to lightest. The watch thrummed like an ancestral drum as it ticked away; the strange way it pulsed enticed her. It was as if she was watching time itself move forward. She picked it up, careful to avoid the wings, which looked like a weapon in and of themselves. Her theory was proven correct when the upper wing brushed against her palm, drawing a thin red seam that welled with droplets of blood. She didn't have time to dwell on the minor wound, because the undeniable force pushed her further. She watched as she placed it on her wrist with her own hand, in a smooth and confident motion. The watch latched onto her, not even giving her an option other than wearing the beautiful timepiece. She started to recoil from it, but stopped. The metal wasn't cool like she thought it would be. It molded itself onto her wrist like it was part of her limb. It didn't feel bulky or clumsy like most watches or bracelets. It was warm and seamless, like a second skin- like an extension of herself. It felt like the sword had felt- like she had never truly been at home without it.

An invisible hand grabbed her own and guided her. She picked up the sword in a practiced motion. She stood, her back still searing, and leveled the blade. She was unaware that her feet were inches off the ground. The pain in her back felt different now and she reached back to try to smooth the discomfort. What met her fingers wasn't the texture of her cool cotton shirt, but warm, soft feathers.

Wings. Strangely light wings. Appendages that large should have weighed a ton, but ironically felt as light as a feather.

Her mind whirled, and her heart raced. In that moment, life changed- forever. She would never be able to go back. There wasn't any unseen force guiding her now, nor would there ever be again. It was her own soul and thirst for adventure that drove her.

Chapter 3: One That Squeaked Hello.

She dropped to the carpeted floor with a dull thud and rose back to her feet, not so gracefully. Her wings were no longer there, maybe they never had been, and she was grateful that her feet were now moving on her own command. She raced out of the room, hardly giving it a second glance as she tumbled through the empty and hollow space. She flew down the stairs, her thoughts a mismatched pattern of panic and chaos. She numbly realized that she was still holding onto the sword, and the watch was still clasped onto her wrist with such force that the jaws of life would have been proud.

Finally outside, she placed her hands behind her head and turned in circles trying to focus on anything other than the sword still clutched in one hand. She gave herself a small break to catch her breath. She focused momentarily on the sunlight streaming softly through the autumn leaves. And then she completely freaked out. Her breath came out in harsh, sharp pants that left her gasping for air. She pressed her hands harder against her head, hoping for two things- one, that it would better open up her airway, and two, that the pain would bring her to her senses. She was in such shock, that she could hardly feel anything, not even the pain in her palm from the shallow cut or the lightweight sword conspicuously dangling from one of her hands down the back of her neck and across her shoulder blade. Her eyes watered, carving a trail through the dust that must have collected there from when she was inside the cursed house.

When she finally calmed down, and her breathing became less frantic and gasping, she reached up and brushed the tears from her eyes. She started walking home, rubbing her sweaty and tear-stained palms against her jeans, trying to figure out what she was going to tell her parents. *I had a panic attack and a complete mental breakdown after school.* That was at the top of her list. She didn't want to sound weak or whiny- but what was the alternative? She let out a sigh and rubbed her eyes again, her skin felt hot and itchy, as if it wasn't her own. Her back burned with searing waves of pain.

What is going on with me?

Everything was backwards and upside down. She felt like she was in a book- something she used to dream about. But now (no matter how awesome being able to fly was), she just wanted things to go back to normal. Right? What was the normal response here- to freak out or want to go back? She tried to tell herself that the 'normal' response was what she was having. But she wasn't, not really, and that scared her more than anything. Even though she kept telling herself that she didn't want these powers, or the sword in her hand; even as she was wondering what in the world was up with the wristwatch, and was truthfully pretty exasperated....everything else in her screamed... well, that she did want this. She was an emotional wreck.

She silently begged the cosmos for an answer.

She limped the distance to her own house, eyes clouded over with pain, wrestling with her jumbled thoughts and feelings. She entered the house like a ghost, mumbling some lame excuse to her parents and sister who were watching TV in the living room. She tried to conceal the sword behind her back and side, hiding the long blade awkwardly under her shirt.

She suddenly felt extremely grateful for the simple blessing of living in a one story house as she dragged herself down the hallway to the comforting familiarity of her black, white and purple room. The sight of her bed almost made her cry in relief. She stared longingly at it and exhaled in exhaustion as she realized what she needed to do first. She reached under her bed, her back scalding, and stashed the sword there behind some shallow boxes full of old papers and letters. She reached to take the watch off, careful to avoid the razor edge of the wings, but was horrified to find that she could not remove it. It fit nicely when it was just sitting there on her wrist, its tarnished silver gleaming in the dim light of her room. Each time she attempted to take it off, it latched on like there was no tomorrow. She was too tired to care and distantly acknowledged how alarmed she should have felt at that realization.

She collapsed on her comfy bed and promptly fell

asleep on top of the covers, clothes and all. She was soon a tangle of blonde hair and long limbs clothed in a black T-shirt, jeans, and heavy motorcycle boots, all twisted around her soft cotton sheets.

The next Monday was surprisingly uneventful, or so she thought. By the time lunch rolled around, she was completely underwhelmed by the lack of activity. Class had been boring, and nothing of significance had occurred. The teachers were the same as always, and she felt like she couldn't care less. That is, until their eyes suddenly met from across the cafeteria, blocking out the dull roar that filled her High School lunch room. Sparks flew. The eyes themselves were a bright hazel with green threaded through them in such a delicate pattern that Arabella nearly got lost in the dance. She was entranced as they mutually locked gazes.

Never had she seen someone who looked so... murderous.

Seriously, the girl sitting across from her was glaring daggers at her. Arabella Grace had the impression that the girl wanted to strangle her, and would have done so through the means of telekinesis if she were able. Her initial observation of the girl's features revealed that she was shorter than Arabella by about a head (which wasn't that hard). She was Snow White pale and had a wild mane of brunette locks that seemed to match her unwieldy temperament. Arabella was surprised by the fact that she could see the details of the villainess's eyes so well, and was a little taken aback by it. Arabella twisted away from her fellow teen's glare and turned fully in her seat. Now she was facing Diana, her purple-loving, pixie haircut-ed friend, who was watching her again in confusion and worry. "Who's the new girl?" she asked Diana as she played nervously with her hair.

"Oh, I heard her name is December. She registered over the weekend and started today," she answered, locking her big doe-brown eyes with Arabella's ice blue ones.

"That's weird, I didn't hear anything about a new student," Arabella replied, confused. She couldn't help but feel a little out of the loop. Well, she had felt a little out of it in general. Her mind flashed back to Saturday's events, which she hadn't even had time to process yet.

"It's a big school," Diana shrugged, like it was no big deal. For some reason though, Arabella felt it was. "In fact, there are two new students- December, and a new boy named Gabriel."

"Really?" Arabella replied, genuinely shocked by the lack of gossip she had heard today. She itched absently at her burning back. The pain was unpleasantly icy-hot.

"Yeah, Bella, didn't you hear me say that Cadence

was showing the new guy around?" Diana shot a look at Arabella, noticing that her gaze was distant and far away.

"Huh?" She glanced around the table and noted for the first time that Cadence wasn't there.

"You didn't even notice he was gone? Last time that happened, you freaked and sent out a search party," Diana remembered, laughing at the memory of their group running around the school interviewing all of his teachers. With a quick glance at Arabella's almost slack face, she nudged her, "are you feeling okay? You've been out of it today." She took a bite out of her sandwich.

Arabella Grace followed her lead and hummed in delight as peanut butter and homemade jelly goodness filled her mouth and exploded against her tastebuds. "Yeah, just a lot on my mind with my grandma and everything..." she mumbled through a mouth full. Despite her muffled words, Diana still gave her an understanding look.

"Okay, you know if you ever need to tell me anything, I'm here for you," she softly offered, then nodded to Cadence, who was walking up behind them with a slow swagger-tastic gait, his hands crammed in the front pockets of his dark blue jeans. His gray shirt had some sarcastic quip about gaming on it.

"What's up?" he uttered with his signature lopsided smirk. He combed his long, oil stained fingers through his auburn hair to get it out of his blue eyes. He plopped himself down next to Arabella, his lanky frame squishing her into Diana. He then proceeded to sprawl leisurely. He placed his books pertaining to flight and schoolwork on the table. Cade had been flying with his adoptive dad ever since he was a little kid, and his real dream in life was to fly for a private airline company. These past few years, he'd really been buckling down and studying. He went to flight school almost everyday after school; nearing 17, he was almost eligible to get his private pilot's license.

"Move," Arabella ordered him in a threateningly playful way. All he did was look at her expectantly. "Please," she corrected herself.

"Alright," he said smiling again, "besides, I need to find my ward." He stood up, bopped her on the head playfully, and, ignoring her glare, went over to the lunch line for some cardboard they passed off as pizza.

Her mind whirled with possibilities about this mystery student. Would he be tall and handsome, with dark hair and green eyes? She imagined impossible scenarios where their eyes would meet and they'd fall instantly and devastatingly in love. They'd spend the rest of their days listening to music, watching movies, and reading books. *Sigh.*

Her perfect little fantasy was ruined by a manicured hand being waved in front of her face.

"Whoa!" She jumped, ripped back to reality. "What are you doing?" she impatiently questioned Diana.

"Look," Diana said, nudging her in the ribs rather

hard.

"What? What am I looking at?" Arabella testily whispered.

She pointed one perfectly painted nail to Arabella's right. "Over there. Cadence and the new kid, Gabriel." She gestured obviously to the boys, her hands waving wildly toward them.

Okay, her jaw might have dropped a little (it was practically unhinged) when she saw him, but dang, the boy was fine.

He was really tall, probably around 6 foot (perfect for her 5'10" frame), and had all of her favorite features. From what she could tell from across the room, his hair was midnight black, but had a faint dusting of silvery grey highlights on top, giving it the over all feeling of being the color and sheen of coal. His frame wasn't lanky, like you would think for someone his height and age. Instead, he had a strong, lean body- like a swimmer. He was pale, like herself, and had startling, bottle-green eyes that sparkled with mirth. He was, um... hot.

He wore worn looking jeans and a green frayed T-shirt that matched his eyes perfectly. He wore motorcycle boots, *swoon,* and his smile was a cute, mischievous little smirk, although he looked a little unsure. She noticed that when Cadence said something to him and he laughed heartily, he had braces. They were the closest color you could get to Arabella's eyes- ice blue.

They both came over to her, playing dodge the traffic (every High Schooler is a professional at this game), weaving in and out of student after student. They might as well have tried to work their way through a pack of wild animals. Then Cadence, being Cadence, sat next to Arabella and had Gabriel sit next to Claire. *Come on, she already has a boyfriend.* Meanwhile, Arabella was as single as a Pringle and very much wanting to mingle. With the cute boy on the other side of her friend. Why couldn't Cadence read minds?

She was sadly reflecting on the realization that she was **more** single than a Pringle, when Cadence interrupted her quiet contemplation. "Hey guys, this is Gabriel," he announced.

There were a lot of 'hey's and hi's' said amongst the table, and one person that squeaked hello- that may or may not have been her.

"Hi," he gave a cute little half wave and cheeky smile, his braces barely peeking through.

Cadence chortled, "so Gabe, since none of these **rude** people want to introduce themselves, I'll do it for them. The girl next to you is Claire. Next to her is her boyfriend, Zuriel. Then Luke, obviously Zuriel's twin. Then you have Diana." He pointed out each one of them around the round table. "And this is my girl, Arabella," he explained, giving her a quick half hug.

Was it just Arabella, or did Gabriel look a little sad

when Cadence said that? She suddenly had a very strong urge to stand on top of the table and declare just how single she was.

But she didn't, she just sat there... *I'm lame.*

All through lunch she sat staring at her food, when she usually devoured lunch like a ravenous wolf. Really, the only relationship she had was with food. Every once in a while she would sneak a quick glance at Gabriel from the corner of her eye. In fact, she was so focused on not looking like she was looking at him, she was able to completely ignore the burning sensation in her back. It had been almost unnoticeable, as if it were slowly fading. He reached across the table to grab something at the same time she had distractedly reached over to exchange an apple for a bag of Pirate's Booty- and **zap.** Their hands connected. All other thoughts flew out of Arabella's mind. The moment stood still. It was an indescribable feeling- to know, somehow, that time had stopped. It felt like magic. Not hocus pocus, but real, tangible, magnetic, living magic. There was only her and him. Deeply connected. Bonded to the very essence of their beings. **Snap.**

It was just static electricity, she told herself as she retracted her hand quickly. But she knew it wasn't static. She was too busy staring at her hand to notice Gabriel doing the same, as the rest of their table's occupants continued their conversations, totally unaware.

Being slammed into the lockers wasn't a pleasant experience. The metal was cold, harsh and extremely ungiving. Her shoulder cried out in pain when it happened. It was something Arabella had never experienced. Until then, that was. Because, well, she was just slammed into a locker at that very moment. She rebounded off it painfully. Apparently, lockers are not made of cotton candy. Arabella gasped and turned around faster than she knew she could, staring in shock as she watched the new girl storm past her. What was her name- Autumn? August? December... yes, that was it.

As December stalked past in a huff (after she pushed Arabella Grace into a locker), Arabella couldn't help but wonder if she had done something to make her mad. To find out, she raced to catch up with crazy pants, her boots clunking loudly against the laminated floor. She was used to the sound and the stare it attracted.

"Hey, December!" she all but yelled, finally being able to match her quick pace.

"Yes?" December retorted in a coarse, hot tone, staring straight ahead- not even glancing Arabella's way.

Taken aback by her rudeness, Arabella took a moment to respond. "Did I do something to make you mad?"

"You're acting like an idiot," December snapped in

the same hot tone. Now that Arabella could see her features better, she noticed that December's wild mane of glossy hair was the color of rich chocolate, with candied caramel ribbons twisting through it. Her big hazel eyes were accented by a button nose and a pretty, full mouth, with dark lips. Her pale, porcelain skin was flawless. Yet despite all of these features, she was far from delicate or fragile in any way. She was like an untamed, warrior-like goddess. In fact, she was even dressed like one- she wore military style pants and a plain black tee. She was definitely "too cool for school." This school, anyway. Her face wore a fierce expression and an angry twitch played at the corner of her mouth as she continued, "we're part of the most important mission given to anyone, ever! And you're laughing in its face. Instead of training and working harder to fulfill your duty, you're daydreaming and making googly eyes. With everything that's at stake, you should be taking this seriously... I just wanted to remind you that no matter where you are, you're not safe. Neither are your loved ones, and the thing you're protecting above all else is certainly far from safe-especially in your hands. So take this seriously, or I'll make you. It's bad enough that all you want to do is *protect,* that you won't fight those who would hurt the mission if they had the chance." She would have continued further, but stopped when she noticed Arabella's confused and incredibly startled expression. "But you don't even know that, do you? Oh! **Of course** you don't! How perfect!" she huffed, her voice dripping with sarcasm. On that note, she stomped off down the hallway and out of the school's double doors.

Arabella just stood there staring after her in dumbfounded confusion.

The shrill ringing of the bell shattered her frozen state of mind, and she watched for a few seconds as the last of the scrambling students skittered off to their assigned classes before she also bolted off to biology.

Grrr. She was officially late to class... which meant she was officially doomed, now for more than one reason.

He stared in wonder, not for the first time today. His first day in a public school, ever, and it was pure pandemonium... *which is brilliant...* he thought sarcastically. Getting used to the dizzyingly chaotic dance through the maze of a building would take some getting used to. The only reprieve was the stunning girl he was now sitting directly across from. He had wanted to sit down next to her and make a witty remark that would make her instantly fall for his charms... but, that didn't happen. Instead, he sat next to Claire, and Cade sat next to the girl. She was ridiculously pretty. She was matchless when it came to her persona; just his type. And he would have said most girls were his type, up until five minutes ago, but she was captivating in a way that he had never seen before. Something about her captured his heart. She had long, beach blonde hair, a heart shaped face, and also a small heart shaped mouth, with straight white teeth that glimmered when she smiled, which she did often. She had pale, peaches-and-cream skin, with a light golden hue to it. She was tall, athletic, and strong. Her eyes were bright, light crystal blue, ringed with a darker blue the color of the water in the deepest canyon on the ocean floor. The same midnight tone fragmented in delicate, slivered, azure shards throughout her eyes, breaking up the solid, silvery ice color that they would have been. The effect was like dancing starlight during a meteor shower. They had certainly captured his attention, at any rate. Yet, despite how much he wanted to sit next to her, he didn't have the nerve. *Since when do I chicken out about talking to a girl?* he thought, bewildered.

The desire to draw her was overwhelming, and he started fidgeting with his Rubik's cube. He could feel the waxy texture of the navy colored pastels he would ribbon around her, bringing out the color of her eyes. The way he would draw her hair like liquid gold, all lit up from a blazing sun behind her. *The only problem,* he thought studying her, *would be to really capture that smile.* He would draw her on a beach. The waves, sky, sand, and sun would match her coloring perfectly. He had a feeling that her personality matched the ocean too- wild, fearless, deep, and unknown- like she could crash into you and steal your breath and your feet out from under you. Gabriel always had the desire to draw, paint, and photograph the people around him, figuring out where they fit in the world. It was always a fleeting thought: what texture, what medium, the background and the colors. But he wanted to sketch her with a passion that was overwhelming, a crushing, all consuming passion that he hadn't felt in a long time... not since his mom left. She awakened him. And he didn't even know her name. *Figures.* He thought with a scoff.

Cadence (who he would draw in crayons, in a red rock canyon on a cloudless day) had introduced each one of his friends. He hardly payed attention to the others. The sketches he would draw of them quickly flashed through his head: hanging out in malls, by streams, in front of a screen, or smiling in the moonlight. He was just waiting for her turn, so he could put a name to the face. When it finally came, he beamed in appreciation. Arabella, *how unique.*

When the bell rang to go back to class, he made it a point to walk by Arabella. Taking a breath of confidence, he extended a suddenly nervous hand, "Arabella, right?" As he grasped her fingers, he experienced an unexpected jolt of electricity course through his veins, just like the one he had felt when their hands brushed at the lunch table. She smiled sweetly as she welcomed him to the new school and offered to show him around sometime. As she walked away, he felt a throbbing ache in his heart, and a faint, sharp pain in his back- right near his shoulder blades.

Chapter 4: Pretty and Wicked.

She heard a single, sharp bird whistle sound behind her and spun around as she entered the school, the excitement that it was Friday thrumming through her body.

"Sorry, didn't mean to scare you," a smooth voice soothed. Squinting, she let her eyes adjust to coming inside from the bright day as she paused behind the double doors.

At first, all she saw was a figure leaning against the wall. As her eyesight slowly balanced out, she had to contain the gasp that desperately wanted to be freed from her lips. *We have another new student,* she thought, dazed. Standing at around 6 feet tall, his stark white hair was cropped short and his eyes were the color of cognac. It looked as if copper and gold were swirling, liquified, around his pupils. He had flawless pale skin, and when he smiled, his grin was akin to freshly fallen snow. He looked as if he could have been chiseled from stone.

He was wearing an expensive looking, charcoal hoodie and dark washed jeans with shiny-new black Converse. He was lean, with a jawline almost as sharp as the glint in his eyes.

"You didn't... scare me, I mean.." she stammered out, feeling like a fool. *But wow...*

"Sure," he crooned and gave a knowing smile. Stepping away from the wall, he reached out lithely to shake her hand. And for the life of her, she couldn't figure out why she didn't just take it right away. Instead, she just

stared at his hand in awkward silence until somewhere in
the darkest corners of her mind, a little voice peeped up
reminding her that she was supposed to shake it. Quickly
and awkwardly, while transferring her binder from her right
arm to her left, she shook his hand with trembling, sweaty
palms. *Awesome,* she thought sarcastically.

"I'm Arabella," she smiled bashfully, just trying to
break the awkward silence that had settled between the two.

He chuckled with a dark lilt to his voice.

No, a shiver did not just go down my spine, she
thought in denial.

"I'm Harrison," he replied in the same smooth
tone, still holding her hand, which he had long since
stopped shaking. He bent down and set his soft lips to the
top of it. Releasing her, he straightened back up and gave
her an alluring smile.

"Oh. That was my grandpa's name," she said,
shocked, suddenly missing his endearing bear hugs
immensely.

"Is that a good thing?" he asked with a sly smile.

"Very, he was an amazing person. He always knew
how to make people smile."

"I guess that is good, then." he said with the same
fox like grin.

"Yeah, it is," she agreed, but couldn't help
inquiring, "are you new?" she fumbled stupidly. *Of course
he's new.* She would have remembered meeting someone

like him.

Winking, he smiled charmingly. "Yes, I just transferred here this morning. We moved here from Phoenix."

"That's cool-" the bell rang, causing her to rush through the rest of her sentence. "Maybe we can hang out sometime, if you just moved here, you probably don't know that many people... let me know if you're interested." Giving him one last fleeting glance as she hurried off to her next class, she sighed, knowing that it was most likely the last time she was ever going to talk to him again. People like him typically didn't talk to people like her. Arabella and her friends weren't outcasts by any means, they were just sort of, in the middle. They weren't the most popular kids, but not the bottom of the food chain either. She hated that she just had that thought. High School was so silly. It was just a brief time in your life, not a definition of who you were or would become. She liked to think she had a broader view of the world than the narrow scope of her teenage years, and whether or not she was "popular". She liked who she was, and she had big plans about who she would be someday.

"I would like that very much. Come find me later today and we can figure it out."

Shock zipped through her like lightning, and a Cheshire grin illuminated her face.

Arabella Grace couldn't help but squeal with giddiness at the sight before her. She just loved her friends! The gang was at a retro video game arcade in Eagle, Idaho, on the outskirts of Boise. The room had low ceilings and dim lighting that made it hard to see anything besides the video screens. There were about 70-something games in their hangout- ranging from the well known to the obscure. There was a bar along one side where you could get a soda and a snack, a few soundless TVs, and some tables and chairs. Otherwise, it was a sea of game consoles as far as the eye could see. And the best part- they were all a quarter. Arabella and her friends were currently hanging out toward the back of the room at the sit down Pac-Man game, where the screen was a table and they sat around it. She watched with child-like delight as Cadence and Gabriel challenged one another on one of her most nostalgic childhood video games. They were exchanging insults, each attempting at trash talk more ridiculous than the last. Currently, Gabriel was winning. If he continued to win, Arabella would play him next. Little did he know that she had spent countless hours in this place, playing this exact game since her Freshman year. She lived to play it. But holy heck if she was good, then he was only slightly worse or maybe even slightly better.

Suddenly it was her turn.

"Ohhhh, too bad, so sad," she taunted Cade.

"Yeah, yeah. Just so you know, I expect you to avenge me," he challenged, giving her a high-five. She sat down and pulled up her chair, acutely aware of how soothed her back suddenly felt.

"Okay, well, ladies first," Gabriel stated, gesturing to the backlit grid and rubbing his shoulder with an unreadable expression.

"You're going to regret saying that," she teased, firing up the game.

"I'll believe that when I see it." He leaned back cockily in his chair and clasped his hands behind his head. She couldn't help but laugh at his taunt, and she also couldn't help but stare at his arms. But back to the game. She was going to have him eating his words.

"Oh, you are so on," she shot back laughingly, raising one blonde eyebrow. "In fact, let's make this interesting." She pretended to think about it for a moment, still engaged in the game. "How about the loser buys the winner a soda," she insisted, jerking her chin back toward the counter.

"Fine. I'll take your deal. Let's shake on it," he accepted the challenge with a confident smirk.

She shook with her one free hand and couldn't help but notice how much bigger and more calloused his hands were- his hands were rough, but still somehow gentle.

She played the game with ease... until her wrist

suddenly felt uncomfortably warm from exhaustion, and she apparently wasn't paying enough attention, because her Pac-Man ran into a ghost. *Dang it!*

"Ooh, that's rough, blue eyes. I guess you just couldn't handle the heat," Gabriel sniggered playfully and started up his first round. He was staring at the screen, but she was staring at him. Her eyes were instinctively trained on his face, her heart hammering, but her thoughts were distant.

She knew she had just met him, but she found herself wondering if he would ever forget her; it was something that she had always feared- being forgotten. Her irrational fear was that she was just a blip on the map of the infinite Universe, unimportant and easily disregarded. If she accomplished nothing of significance, or never had her great adventure, no one would even remember her name after she was gone. Usually, she could push past the ice cold distress that she associated with this paralyzing fear, but when she looked at him and thought about him forgetting her- it somehow seemed more real, and more painful than she could've thought possible.

The pain was almost as bad as the actual physical pain she'd been having in her back, which had all but disappeared when she sat down. Her thoughts interrupted, she rubbed her wrist, "blue eyes?" *Huh, I kinda like that,* she thought.

"I thought it fit pretty well... when I picture you, I

picture those crazy blue eyes," she heard him stutter humorously. *Does that mean he thinks about me?*

She was blushing so profusely he could probably see her cheeks glowing red in the dark of the room. "Oh yeah," she murmured dreamily, still rubbing her wrist. It wasn't burning now, but she was still surprised by the intense pain. She was also kind of surprised she could still be shocked. Little did she know that these were the least of the surprises she was yet to receive.

"Hey, you okay?" Cade tapped her shoulder, noticing the haunted, far off look in her eyes. He knew her too well. It was a look she had been wearing far too often, which she knew concerned him.

Looking behind her, she answered as truthfully as she could without sounding crazy. "Yeah, my wrist just kind of hurts." She rubbed it again and looked down at the watch that she still wasn't able to get off- she had definitely tried, many times.

"Why?" His question was heavily laced with concern.The others had turned their amused gazes and stopped their side conversations to look worriedly at Cade and Arabella, trying to catch snippets of their hushed dialogue. They were all still watching out for Arabella. They knew how hard losing her grandparents had been on her.

"As if I could possibly know, I'm not a doctor, my

last name is Grace, not Grey," she tried to joke. Yet, even to her, it sounded forced. Despite that, he knew it was time to let it go. His cornflower blue eyes communicated that they would talk about it later. An awkward silence descended over the group and hung heavy in the air, only unnoticed by Gabriel as he raced his Pac-Man across the screen. Every once in a while, small hoots of delight would escape his lips that would make Arabella Grace's frown become a smile.

"Hey, Arabella, what's that?" Claire asked gently, pointing to the watch on her pale wrist. Her question mercifully caused the dreadful silence to break.

"Oh! It was a birthday present from my grandma," she replied honestly, looking down to find she was still rubbing the gleaming face of the watch. Its time ticked on, enchanting her. Once again, she felt as if it were moving time forward, not just counting it. *That doesn't even make sense,* she thought to herself.

Claire snapped her back to reality, "well, it's pretty and wicked," she complimented.

Cade joined the conversation. "When did she give it to you?"

"I found it while I was cleaning out her stuff. It had a note attached that said it was for me," she said, again trying to stay truthful. When did she become a liar? Oh yeah, when she found a super creepy box in her grandma's house, and then she **flew**- because apparently, she has wings. She kept that part out of her explanation. She turned her head slightly to address Claire, her long ponytail tickling her neck. She had to clear her throat a few times to get her attention though, because she and Zuriel were in their own world.

"Yes?" Claire finally answered, smiling.

"I was just gonna say thank you, you know, for saying that the watch was pretty and wicked." Arabella smiled graciously at her and then watched them for a few seconds more before turning her gaze back to Gabriel.

"It's the truth," Claire returned. Arabella could hear the smile in her voice.

She turned once more toward them, just in time for Zuriel to add, "yeah, definitely," as he wrapped his arms around his girlfriend and held her lovingly from behind.

She didn't want to feel pitiful, but couldn't help but wonder- when was she going to have that? She snuck a peak at Gabriel, who was still playing. He was definitely going to win.

Her suspicions were confirmed, not even thirty seconds later, when his triumphant hoots echoed throughout the room.

"Looks like you owe me a soda, madame," he announced in a posh accent, his bangs falling into his stark green eyes. He followed his dramatic speech by sweeping out his arms elegantly.

"That I do," she smiled, and a small giggle bubbled

to the surface. She avoided Diana's knowing gaze, because she knew if she made eye contact with her best girlfriend, she would be more than giddy at the thought of being alone with him and wouldn't be able to keep her face from breaking into a dumb, blushing school-girl grin.

Standing up, they walked the short distance to the counter. Quiet fell between them once away from their friends. Cue the awkward silence. She propped her elbows against the counter's black surface and took a quick glance at the menu while tapping her fingers and toes to the familiar 80's song that was playing.

"Can I get you something?" cooed a smiling brunette waitress who came out from the kitchen door to stand behind the bar. She was skinny and pretty... *great.* She had brown eyes, a small, slightly upturned nose, bow shaped lips, and her face was slender with high cheek bones. Her skin was almost perfect. She basically had all of the features Arabella wished she had. It wasn't that she didn't know she was pretty. She did. But she was always self conscious of her athletic build; she had always been taller and curvier than the petite, stick-figured girls her age, and her skin wasn't terrible, but it wasn't flawless. No one else seemed to notice, but she wished it was satin smooth. Ah, the joys of being a teenager.

She was so caught up in the comparison, she didn't

even notice that Gabriel was staring at her like she held up the sky. She shook off the negative thoughts. She knew better than that. Or at least, most of the time she did.

"I'll have a Diet Coke, oh, and no ice, please..." Arabella decided, smiling widely. Then she turned to Gabriel, "and what would you like, kind sir?" She coated her words with a fake southern accent and smiled coyly, her hands now on her hips.

"I'll have a grape soda, oh, and no ice, please," he mimicked Arabella's request playfully. Out of the corner of her eye, she saw the waitress nod and go to get their drinks. He turned and smiled at the girl, and Arabella felt the smile like a hot poker in the ribs.

Quick to change the subject, Arabella asked him a question, "so, you don't like ice in your drinks either?" She was happy that they had something to talk about, but felt a little silly exploring this subject. She leaned against the counter with her back to it, its edge biting into her spine. Thoughts of her crumbling life played in the back of her mind, even in a simple moment of teenage flirtation.

Once again following her lead, he did the same and turned around, his elbow touching hers against the counter. "Yeah, it just seems like A: a waste of space, and B: it waters down the drink," he cited, a broad, adorably dimpled smile painted across his face. In fact, it was so wide, his braces were showing. Arabella noticed that he liked to keep them hidden, but she thought they were cute.

"Exactly! You know, I've never met anyone that thinks like I do on this important matter. Now for the true test of character." She spun dramatically toward him and challenged him with her eyes. Pretending to intimidate him with a slight pout, she pointed her fingers like a gun and aimed them at his well defined chest. Not that she had noticed. She felt cheesy, fun, and... well... flirty. She was excited in a way that she hadn't felt in a long time. He made her happy.

"Oh, is that so? Well, bring it on." He swept his wicked black bangs away from his face in an exaggerated show of 'Challenge Accepted'.

"So, at night- to help distract myself and sleep- I'll bring in a cup of ice to eat. Honestly, it doesn't have to be at night, I just like to eat ice," she admitted truthfully as a shy blush rode on her cheeks.

"I'm not alone!" he triumphantly howled and threw his hands up like he had just won a quidditch game.

A 'cough, cough' sound drew their attention away from each other's flushed faces. "Huh? Oh right, the drinks." Arabella turned around to find the waitress with a pleasant, yet strained smile, one that implied she had been standing there a long time. Arabella smiled apologetically, feeling a little bad... but at the same time thinking, *whoops,* with a hint of selfish glee. "Thank you very much," Arabella emphasized with a quick, sunny, slightly-forced smile and took the drinks from her. Handing Gabriel his, she took a quick gulp of her own- she loved its bittersweet taste as it slid past her teeth and its cool texture as it bubbled down her tongue and into her throat. It was cold, **even without ice**.

"So do you want to sit at that table and talk more or head back to the group?" he babbled, pointing at a nearby table, then toward the group in the corner, who were currently trying to see how many Skittles Luke could fit in his mouth. She heard them shout that he was currently up to 35... *boys*.

"Um, lets sit down," she quickly insisted and rushed over to the table, avoiding the gaze of her friends, particularly Diana and Cade.

"Good choice," he agreed and quickly strolled over to where she sat. Sitting down on opposite sides of the black table, they set down their drinks and leaned as close to each other as each party would dare. Butterflies settled in her stomach in a fantastically flighty way.

"So, how did the ice thing start for you?" he questioned, trying to sound serious, but failing miserably due to his dimpled smile. His endearing blue braces were shining in the glow of the arcade's LED lights.

"It's just a habit that I developed out of boredom, and now it's become a ritual I almost have to do before I go to sleep. What about you?" she replied, fidgeting with her straw as she answered. She moved to tuck some stray pieces of her hair back, but he beat her to it. His hands were warm and gentle. He looked into her eyes and she looked into his. Blue met green, light met dark. It seemed as if the two had blended together to become a sea of blue and green, and again she noticed the lack of pain in her back.

Slowly moving his hand away, breaking the spell, he replied, "it's something my mom did. She'd buy a cup of ice at a gas station and munch as we drove, and well, my parents are divorced now..." He laughed in the way people laugh when the only other option was crying. "It's just one way for me to stay connected to her. I think of her every time I grab a cup to snack on. It helps me remember that no matter how mad I get at her, she is still my mom," he finished, taking a shaky breath, "and that's why we moved here."

Arabella placed her hand on top of his; he looked down at it with a sad smile on his face. She wanted to erase any semblance of sadness on his face. She wanted to interrupt him and start telling a funny story or something, but she knew just by looking at his face that he needed this- needed to get it all out.

"Apparently, that's what we do in this family, we leave when it gets rough- or at least, that's what my mom did."

"I don't think you're like that," she whispered, giving him a reassuring smile.

"Well, you don't know me," he dejectedly smirked.

"Maybe not yet, but I will." She could just tell, like

she was always meant to.

Bing, bing, bing.

"Oh crap, that's my phone. To be continued?" she asked, giving him a pointed look and a lopsided grin that tugged at the edge of her mouth.

"Yeah, definitely," he added with a soft smile of his own, so different from his usual charming half-smirk. She decided she almost liked it better.

Arabella reached into the back pocket of her blue jeans and pulled out her phone. She held the small device in her palm and used her thumb to turn it on, her back screen was a picture of her and her friends from last Halloween- dressed as demigods, Hogwarts students, shadowhunters, demon hunters, and various Disney characters. The little green text bar said she had a text from her mom-

Mom: Hey, dinner's almost ready. Do you think you could be home soon?

Arabella: Ya, I'll be as quick as I can. See you in a few:)

Mom:...

Mom: Okay, see you soon.

That's weird, Arabella couldn't help but think when she saw her mother's lack of emojis; she always used emojis, all the time. Honestly, she was kind of obsessed. *Oh well*, she shrugged it off, figuring that her mom must have just been in a hurry.

"What's wrong?" Gabriel asked, noticing her

frown. He looked distinctly displeased about it.

"Nothing," she deflected quickly. Jumping up, her eyes glanced away from the bright little screen and locked onto his intent gaze. "My mom just wants me home for dinner, so I have to go. But, to be continued," she reiterated with fake confidence.

"Right," he countered with his own confident smile, a smirk playing at the edges. He rubbed his hands over his arms in a nervous manner, undermining his false cockiness.

"Okay, great," she answered, walking backwards toward the door. Or at least she was walking backwards until she almost tripped over a table, causing Gabriel to laugh silently and Arabella to squeak as a blush rose in her cheeks. She lowered her gaze to the floor as she steadied herself.

"I think I'm going to walk, um, this way," she tried to sound cool, pointing behind her and turning fully around.

"Good idea," he chuckled under his breath, but she could still hear him.

"Okay, well, tell the guys goodbye for me," she waved over her shoulder.

"I will," he replied. Her back was already turned, yet he waved back anyway.

And with that, she was gone.

Arabella pulled up to the front of her one story house in her light blue Bug- it was used, but still in really good condition. She had gotten it from her uncle for a steal. In fact, she had exchanged working on his farm in Emmett as a ranch-hand. Honestly, she had probably worked for them longer than need be, but she had felt really grateful. Tonight, she had driven home lost in her head, analyzing every little thing said between her and Gabriel. She continued to do so as she climbed out of her car, wrapped up in the emotions and thoughts that came along with him. She probably would have been analyzing their conversation for the rest of the night if she hadn't been stopped short by the sight of December, the girl who had scared and scarred her for life in the hallway at school.

December was leaning against the front of her house, arms crossed and a small frown gracing her fine features. She was in her army garb and looked displeased as usual (from what Arabella could tell). Her hair was down. Like before, it was a strange contrast, considering she seemed to always have a stick up her behind. You would think that someone that stiff would have their hair up in a perfect, painful ponytail. Arabella had met people like her before, where all they wanted was to walk the path that life set for them, which is fine if you're into that, but that path was definitely not for her. She wanted to color outside the lines and create her own work of art. Yet, even though

December fit the type, she had never met someone, besides her grandma, who had said such cryptic words to her.

"What are you doing here?" Arabella asked, her eyes taking in her surroundings and trying to figure out if it would be quicker to run up to the front door or back to her car, and which would be a safer escape route. She had read enough books to know that whenever a shady stranger approaches you, you should check which would be the fastest way to get out of Dodge.

"We need to talk," was all she replied, if you could call it that, detaching herself from the wall and stalking toward Arabella Grace at a brisk pace, her arms rigid at her sides as if she were marching.

"What about?" Arabella asked dubiously, but in the back of her mind, her suspicion grew; the images that had been playing there for days came up full force.

"I obviously need to tell you, and you clearly, desperately need to know, but not here," December snapped at her. They were now standing toe to toe. "And if you want to find out, you have to come with me." She remained cool and smoldering at the same time. *How does she do that?* Arabella wondered. "Just a quick walk, I promise," she chuckled with a knowing smile.

"Just a walk?" Arabella beseeched, her voice bleak and quiet. She hung her head slightly and released the death grip she had been holding on her keys. She needed answers... and if this was the only way... she also had a feeling deep inside her soul that this **was** the only way she was going to fill the craving inside her that called for adventure like a lonely wolf cried into the night.

"Just a walk," December quipped, smiling viciously as she cracked her knuckles. *How comforting.*

Chapter 5: Arabella's Arsenal.

"Any questions before we begin?" December inquired, casually standing in Arabella's front lawn like this sort of thing happened every day. She looked strange against all the whimsical lawn art that decorated her walkway.

"Look," Arabella started and took a deep breath that sounded dangerously on the verge of hyperventilating. "As much as I want to find out what's going on, I just remembered that my mom's expecting me." She went to move around the army-clad girl.

December pulled her hair up in a ponytail and Arabella noticed something she hadn't before, the mysterious new girl was becoming even more mysterious. *I didn't think that was possible.* She had a tattoo in white ink, similar to her own. It was the basic silhouette of a cat, about the size of Arabella's palm. It was placed right below her right ear and its tail wrapped around her jawline. It was subtle and pretty, and actually fit December really well. How strange. Arabella wouldn't have expected December to have ink.

Noticing her stare, December let her wild chestnut ringlets fall back down. "Actually, she isn't."

"What are you talking about?" She froze and realized she had been touching her jaw where the other girl's tattoo was, absently wondering how she would look with it. Ember was too preoccupied to even notice the gesture.

She sighed, exasperated, "I'm talking about how your mom thinks you're at Cadence's, or 'Cade's' house, and you thought that you were supposed to come home. Really, your family isn't even here. They went to go get dinner to celebrate your sister's math score. In reality, both of you are wrong, and you were talking to me," she explained, like it would clear everything up, but it just made Arabella more confused. Noticing this, she went further into depth about what she meant. "I have some connections and was able to tap into your phones, and well, just look." She handed Arabella her phone with noticeably rough hands that brushed against hers when she took it. She found the phone unlocked and already open- it displayed Arabella's mother's number and message in green on top of the screen.

"Wha-" Arabella questioned and grabbed the phone, it was almost a little rude, and December glared at her for it.

December: Hey mom, can I go and eat at Cade's for dinner?
Sarah Grace: Ya:) Just remember that it's a school night:)
December: Okay I will.

"You hacked my phone!" she blurted out, dumb-founded.

Instead of answering her, December just rolled her eyes and went on like Arabella had never spoken. "You see, nothing's wrong. In fact, she thinks you are at Cadence's. So let's walk."

"A couple of days ago, you had no problem talking to me in public, heck, you confronted me the first time in the hallway. So why do we need to talk now in private?" she asked, trying to understand December's rationale.

"Because before, I wasn't going to say anything conspicuous. Why do you think I was being ominous, for giggles? We don't know who we can trust, and that means we have to be extra careful," December whispered, dead serious. Arabella would have written her off as crazy, if it weren't for what was going on. If someone told her that they had flown, she would have written them off as crazy also. She couldn't judge December for what she was saying, because she might be the only way to discover the truth. "So just come on a walk with me."

"Okay," Arabella agreed hesitantly. And when December started to walk away, she quickly followed, because she felt like she didn't really have a choice.

"Before I get into it, is there anything specific you want to know?" December began, irritated and stiff, just like her walk, only minus the marching arms.

She began hesitantly, biting her lip so hard it turned white and swinging her arm behind her and clasping it with the other hand at the elbow. Her skin was cold and clammy, and she had a feeling it was from the chilly weather, making her wish she had worn a coat. "Gabriel, I want to know about Gabriel," she answered finally, her voice small at first but slowly growing louder with confidence. There was something too coincidental about him showing up, and if he was trouble, she wanted to know now. Before her heart paid the price.

"Who?" December stopped, clearly shocked and taken aback, like she wasn't expecting that question to be in Arabella's arsenal.

"Oh, you don't know him? I just thought-" she resigned, and let her pale arms drop to her sides, "never mind." She took a quick glance around at the houses as they continued trudging along the sidewalk, every single one exactly the same.

"No, why?" December questioned, now clearly curious, her gaze never wavering from some unknown fixed point in the distance.

"It's just...you two showed up at the same time. I just thought that-" she broke off with a sigh that floated through the crisp night air- seeing her breath had always fascinated her, she would fantasize that she was an ice princess in some far off land. She was so caught up in her past, she had to jump out of the way when a little white car whizzed by, its tire skimming the sidewalk. The little old lady driving gave her an apologetic smile.

December had been nodding along like she was

talking to herself and chuckled at Arabella almost getting hit by a car. She stopped when she computed Arabella's words. "Oh," December acknowledged softly, her voice still frosty, but her features registering understanding. "It's possible..." she whispered under her breath, which, to Arabella, sounded like her usual grumbling.

"It's just that,... don't you think it's weird? You both just randomly showed up at the same time? And with everything that's going on, I just thought..." she finally snapped, done with the cryptic answers. She was now staring down at the fierce little brunette, not even watching the path as they moved along. She had been promised her answers and so far wasn't getting any. A small voice in the back of her head said maybe she was asking about the wrong boy, and cognac colored eyes flashed briefly to her conscious mind.

"Fate works in weird ways," was December's oh-so-witty retort.

"Oh, thank you, Little Miss Military. And here I thought you were going to give me answers," she huffed in annoyance, her patience wearing extremely thin.

December raised one dark eyebrow at the nickname and cleared her throat. "I said I would, but honestly, I don't think I'm the best person to ask about **that** subject. If it's what I think it is."

Arabella threw her hands in the air. "What subject?

You still haven't given me any answers, just more questions." Her voice grew in volume as they turned off the sidewalk and onto a bike trail that veered off into the woods by the Boise River. Shadows danced along the edges of the trail. The setting sun in the distance gave everything an even more ominous feel. If she didn't know better, she would imagine this would be a pretty good place and time to kill someone, but she knew December better than that-

Wait.

"Well, all you have to do is ask," she quipped, so-very- helpfully. Every time she spoke, it sounded like she was stalling, *but stalling for what?* December continued her brisk pace, and Arabella almost had to jog to keep up. How could someone with such short legs move so fast?

"I did ask!" Arabella repeated loud enough that birds flew from nearby trees, and a cyclist passing by gave her a sideways glance.

"Just not about that. But I bet you have questions about the Clock around your wrist and why you can't take it off." December had a smug look about her.

Denial and bewilderment melted off of Arabella's features as recognition took their place. "Why did my grandma leave me this... and why can't I take it off... and what's with the sword?" she questioned, looking over in shock.

"I'll explain it all as soon as I can. Like I said, I

know things you don't. That makes you dangerous. You have no idea the power you hold. So that's why I'm here; to tell you, so you don't get us all killed." The laugh she gave at the end of her little speech was cold and bitter, causing the hairs on the back of Arabella's neck to rise. She reached back and smoothed them down. Even though the girl's words frightened her, a sense of adventure ignited in her soul. It was pretty awesome, all things considered. Flying, magical items, supernatural creatures, tattoos, cute boys, and mysterious strangers. It was like a dream unraveling before her awakened eyes.

"Okay, so what's this- watch thing? Can you at least explain that?" She pointed to the clunk of metal on her right wrist and shook it violently.

Her haughty companion turned slightly and gave her a bored, deadpan look, then continued briskly; she acted as if she was in some great hurry to get somewhere. "The better question is- what **are** you?" A cold gleam appeared in December's hazel eyes, then she turned around once more, her face hard and her gaze searching Arabella's own. Yet to Arabella, it still sounded like stalling.

"What am I, December?" Arabella was starting to sweat, and anxiety ate at her insides; a ball of tension started to form in her stomach, and she swallowed the lump in her throat, which was suddenly dry. She wanted her grandmother to be here to tell her what was going on instead of this haughty and distant girl who was acting stranger by the minute. "Wha- what's going on; why won't you give me an answer?" Her voice was small and meek, yet yearning for a resolution. The way she was walking... and all the aloofness... it was as if she were trying to lead Arabella somewhere.

Suddenly at attention, December murmured, "I don't like The Shadows." Her head shot up- like a dog's when it catches a scent- and her already stiff posture became even more alert. "Shhh!" she whispered harshly, cursed and spat, "that's right. You're un-bound...I shouldn't have met you. Not now. I'm so freshly bound. I was trying to get you there as quickly as possible. I-" She cursed again.

"Wha-?" Arabella started, but was quickly cut off when a hand covered her mouth. December's palm was clammy. Arabella hated when people touched her face. She was a teenager, after all. Sweat and germs break you out.

"I told you, shhh." December commanded, still whispering.

"Why?" the blonde teen attempted to ask, but it came out muffled.

"Because I said so, so shhhh," she answered, taking her hand off of Arabella's mouth and wiping her palm disdainfully against her pants. She reached up from behind her and into her shirt tail. When December brought her hands away, they were far from empty. They held two odd looking pistols.

"Why do you have those!?" Arabella whispered in alarm, remembering to keep quiet.

The gunslinger shot her a look of annoyance and then locked her gaze on the tree line, but all Arabella could see were shadows. The pistols had round, broom-stick handles with dark wood looking to be inlaid with copper and garnet. "Never use that tone when talking about my babies. These beauties aren't just guns, they are both Mauser C96s, and I have them because-" she suddenly cut off and looked over Arabella's shoulder, her eyes widened and her pupils dilated in fear. "Because of that," she spit out.

December pushed her down and fired a round of shots at some unknown assailant before Arabella could even think about what was going on. It all happened so fast, she couldn't even function.

When she looked behind her to see what had caused December to be so vigilant, and to **shoot at something,** she was shocked to see that no one was there... just shadows...

Nope. Never mind, the shadows moved.

They rose out of the ground like liquid, then solidified into humanoid shapes, with long twisted arms and oily taloned fingers. They had no features; they were just a mass of black that seemed to absorb all the light around them. There were several, and they looked like the demons from her dreams a couple weeks back. The scars from which had healed completely, but left her terrified.

They were moving toward Arabella.

She tried to choke down the scream that rose in her throat. Terror clung to her insides, shaking her ribs. But her attention was averted from The Shadows when December shook her shoulder roughly. She drug her panicked, rabbit-like stare toward the brunette.

"Come on, we have to go," she hissed, sounding almost frightened. It was the first time Arabella had heard any real emotion in the other girl's voice. "There will be more of them coming, and I can't carry your dead weight," she snapped, her face tight and set in a stubborn line. She holstered her guns. But when Arabella didn't move or respond, just continued to stare in shock at the creatures still steadily stalking toward them, December gave a sigh and yanked her up. She then proceeded to drag her along roughly- moving faster than Arabella could've dreamed she could go. But adrenaline mixed with fear was a pretty good kickstart.

Still moving like Hell was on their heels, Arabella looked back to see how close they were to having The Shadows grasp them. When Arabella looked, the creatures were far behind them. Yet, December continued to rush them toward the unknown.

Chapter 6: Change the World.

"What. Just. Happened? Where are we going?" Arabella finally stopped abruptly in the middle of the path, gasping for breath and ripping her hand away from December's death grip.

Stopping as well, December turned, not even out of breath, and faced Arabella. She crossed her arms over her chest with one hip cocked. "We need to go, we don't have time for this," she answered in her now familiar, cool and brisk tone.

Arabella shook her head slightly at the words. "No! You need to tell me what's happening," Arabella was able to gasp out through her panting breaths that fogged the air in front of her and made December a blurry mess in her vision- or maybe it was her tears doing that.

"I will reiterate, we don't have the time!" she snapped, "I will explain, but not now! Those things can come out of nowhere. They're born out of the shadows, so every single dark nook and cranny all around is compromised." As if to prove her point, she gestured to the ground along the path and Arabella noticed how shadows danced all around them. "The sun's going to be completely set soon, so we need to hurry. If we don't get to the settlement soon, we'll either be dead or taken. And if you're taken, you'll want to be dead," she fumed abruptly, looking down at her wrist. Arabella noticed for the first time that she had a watch eerily similar to her own.

December's voice became dark and dangerous as she uttered the next words. "Believe me. You. Don't. Want. That. So we need to leave. Now."

Deciding that she probably **didn't** want that, Arabella nodded numbly and mumbled, "alrighty," still in shock and wanting to go home to make sure her family was okay.

"Well, I'm glad we got that out of the way," December spat spitefully, her eyes shining. "Now, lets go!" And with that, she took off again at a dead sprint, like monsters were still grasping at her heels.

With a groan, Arabella took off after her, just not as fast. Barely keeping up with Little Miss Military, she eventually slowed down to more of a jog, keeping December barely in her sights. *Either she's a freak of nature, or I'm really out of shape,* Arabella thought. She started huffing and puffing, following the quick little thing as she led her through twists and turns all over Eagle, following the greenbelt. She finally stopped as they came upon a two story house somewhere in Garden City, from what Arabella could tell. You know, she had never noticed before how lovely the Treasure Valley looked during the Fall season, at night, when you're running in a life or death situation.

The house had four, large front windows, all with their white shutters closed. It was painted a deep eggplant purple and had a white wrap-around porch. December was leaning over the railway of the porch, not even breathing heavily in the slightest, her long hair tumbling wildly over her shoulders. Arabella took a deep breath, and the smell of lavender became apparent.

"Are you even human?" Arabella exclaimed, coming up the house's walkway.

December seemed to contemplate the question, tilting her head from side to side, then shrugged and slinked forward like the cat on her jawline. "I'm just as human as you are," she finally answered. She turned toward the house and walked inside like she owned the place. *Well, she might.* It wasn't like Arabella knew a whole lot about her, besides the fact that she had two guns and knew way too much about Arabella.

On second thought, maybe she shouldn't follow her in. But she knew that if she didn't, she might never find out the truth about herself and her grandmother. So despite the protest that played at the back of her mind (sounding suspiciously like her mom's voice), she walked in. It was better than walking home, anyway. Probably. *No, definitely,* she thought and shivered at the thought of The Shadows she had left behind.

The house was even bigger on the inside. The door opened into a large living room with a strange assortment of furniture all over the place- a desk in the corner made of cherrywood with silver paint wrapped around its legs, a burnt orange sofa, a pink and purple floral loveseat, and a jade green armchair. The end table between the pink and orange sofa was black and had a star-shaped lamp on it. There was a doorway that led to what looked like the kitchen and probably more rooms upstairs. There was a door in the corner of the room that might have led to a closet or maybe a basement. But what struck Arabella, was how vast the room was compared to how it looked on the outside, if that was possible. She couldn't help but whisper gleefully under her breath, "it's bigger on the inside."

"What?" December asked, coming out of the kitchen eating an apple.

"Oh, um it's a TV show thing..." she scratched at her right cheek.

"Hmph," December snorted, clearing her throat, "it's time to talk." Was her face permanently stuck in a glare? And were her arms always crossed and her hair always crazy?

"Yeah, it really is," Arabella agreed. But did she want to know the answers she would find? She hoped so, and she hoped it would fulfill her fantasies. She sighed, her dry lips parted slightly. She licked them- breathing hard in the cold weather had made them chapped. "My first question: um, where are we?" She looked around once more at the strange home.

"Oh, that's easy. We're at, the uh, base," she evaded, and turned her head toward one of the two shuttered windows.

Arabella Grace bit her heart-shaped lips and thought for a second. Her hand subconsciously drifted up to play with her golden hair to calm her nerves. "And the base is what?" she followed up.

Instead of replying, December just continued to stare at the window. Arabella didn't even bother to follow her gaze, that never ended well. But she did notice how fixed the other girl's laser beam focus was- like she wasn't staring at the shutter- but through it- like she could see between each slot. Her hazel eyes seemed to darken the longer she stared, and a trick of the light made them look like they were glowing slightly red.

Arabella heard the creak of the front door behind her and jumped slightly. "Her grandmother's house," came a warm voice from behind her. She turned and almost fell over when she saw an elderly lady coming through it. It was the mystery woman from her grandmother's funeral- the one with the light green eyes.

"Oh!" Arabella could feel her blonde eyebrows shoot up. "I'm Arab-" she started, but was stopped by a raise of the older woman's hand; her lips were still puffed out like a monkey forming the "B" sound in her name.

"Arabella, I know," the mystery woman interrupted warmly. Bright eyes gazed at her fondly.

Creepy- how does she know my name?

"Oh, and you are...?" Arabella questioned, trying to be polite and push past her discomfort.

She laughed heartily. The sound reminded Arabella of warm honey and bells- so different from December's dark, raspy chuckle. "I'm Ailith, Ember's grandma," she supplied with a radiant smile. *Hmm, Ember? Certainly fits the little spitfire, and considering her glare, she might not like it all that much. Hmmmm.* Ailith reminded Arabella terribly of her own grandmother and grief struck her heart. She had a shock of fine silver hair, but her face looked fairly young to be someone's grandmother. She had high cheek bones and a strong wiry build. Her eyes were bright ice green.

"Oh! It's nice to meet you!" Arabella scrambled to reach forward to shake her hand. She was mildly surprised when Ailith reached forward also and grabbed Arabella's hand, only to pull her forward into a fierce hug, her strong arms enfolding her into her short, sturdy frame- Arabella had to bend down to match the woman's embrace. There was something about Ailith that made Arabella want her to like her.

"I've wanted to meet you for far too long," she rhapsodized, right in Arabella's ear, her voice resounding in her eardrums.

Suddenly, a loud cough came from behind Arabella and she tensed at the sound. "You know, as touching as this whole thing is, we really need to focus on the bigger picture, like not only keeping Arabella alive, but fighting for the free will of...**everyone,**" December, or Ember, interrupted.

"You're right." Ailith composed herself and stepped back, straightening her flowing lilac dress (that she somehow made look strong and intimidating) in the process. "Now, let's get to business." Her voice was still warm, but suddenly serious.

"Right." Arabella agreed, "first thing's first," she took a deep breath and played with a lock of her hair, "what's going on!? What were those things?!" she finally exclaimed.

"Did something happen?" Ailith asked, alert.

Ember (formerly December) sighed, "we ran into some Shadows on the way here." As they spoke amongst themselves, Arabella dazedly walked over to the door and took off her black boots, as she was taught was polite when entering someone's home. She blushed when she realized she was wearing mismatched fuzzy socks- one polka dotted and one striped.

She turned back toward the pair. Now that Arabella saw them side by side, she could see the similarities. They had the same soft nose, high cheek bones and warrior build. They were both short and slim, but definitely not slight or petite. These were strong women.

Ailith took a deep breath, ready to answer Arabella's question. "Well sweetheart, you might want to sit down for this," she soothed gently and took Arabella's hands softly in her own. The older woman's hands were calloused beyond belief for someone her age.

Looking down into the older woman's eyes, she stared with deep resolve. "I want to stand," Arabella replied, not unkindly, and took her hands from Ailith's. Her words caused Ember to huff and fold her arms over her black T-shirt.

"You're not helping," Ailith scolded her, looking over at her granddaughter with sharp green eyes.

"Well, she needs to stop acting like a fictional character in a story and accept reality for what it is," she groaned again, recrossing her arms- like a two year old.

Arabella's chest seized in disbelief as all the stress from the last month reached a summit. "Well, excuse me!" She went into a rage, wringing the hem of her black t-shirt. "My whole life has been turned completely upside down!" Her voice bordered on hysteria, "my grandma and grandfather are gone!" she stressed, "and all they left me were questions, worry, fear, anxiety, a stupid watch and a sword. You have no idea what a head trip I've been through... I **flew**!" she cried, letting it all out as Ailith watched on with sympathy, and Ember watched on with intentional boredom. "I've done things these last few days I've only dreamed about," she whispered with a hiss. Slowly, she brought her head up and met Ailith's eyes- ice green against ice blue. "So yes, I think I'll stand," she finished, her voice returning to normal.

"Okay, okay." Ailith tenderly reasoned. "You can stand, but if it's okay with you, my arthritis it acting up, and I'd much rather sit."

"Yeah, that's fine," Arabella gave a watery laugh, which in turn earned yet another cynical laugh from Little Miss Military.

"You know, you're bitter," Arabella snapped at her.

"That's your comeback? So original." Ember glared.

"Oh, well you can take my comeback and-"Arabella started, but was sadly cut off.

"Girls! Now is not the time!" Ailith reprimanded them both.

"Sorry," Arabella apologized.

At the same time, Ember relented, "Yeah, okay."
How nice of her.

"Okay, back to the point," Ailith drew both of their attention back to her. "I'm going to tell you something, and it's going to change your life forever. Once I tell you, there is no going back. Do you understand?" she asked coaxingly, resting her forearms against her legs.

"I just want to know what's going on." Desperation sawed on her vocal chords like a well-used fiddle. Before December could even say or do anything, Arabella held up a finger to shush her.

Ailith played with the edges of her dress. The fact

that she was still wearing her black heels inside bothered Arabella to no end. "Okay, well, where should I start?" She looked up at the ceiling like it held all the answers- or maybe she was counting the cracks in the popcorn texture.

"Maybe at the beginning," December supplied, sitting down by her grandmother, leaning her chin against her forearms.

She shot her a look of fond annoyance. "Yes, Ember, that would be helpful, I suppose," she retorted, then sighed and continued, "when World War II ended in 1945, the history books wrote that the Axis powers surrendered after the events of Nagasaki, and that on September 2, they accepted their defeat. When that happened, the collective leaders of the world- the Allies- all gave a sigh of relief, because nuclear warfare was such a devastating possibility at the time." She was nodding along with her own words.

Arabella nodded slowly, then pursed her lips slightly, wondering what this had to do with anything that was going on.

Ailith nodded back, and Arabella was detachedly amused by the sarcastic nature in which she did it. "History may have ended up that way, but that's not how it began." She shook her head with a sad laugh as a long silver hair fell forward from its folds, the shimmering tendril danced across her silk dress. "The sad truth is, that even reality hides from reality. There's something that the- let's call them the people we report to- call realism reality. It is the facts of antiquities of that time period. The fact that the world ended. Instead of surrendering, the Axis powers retaliated, and the world went atomic."

Arabella's mind was reeling from the new information, and she couldn't help but question dumbly, "realism reality?" *Someone is punking me,* Arabella thought and rubbed her suddenly aching shoulders.

Ailith gave her a reproachful look, "I'm getting to that." She shushed them (Okay, she was talking to Arabella), then swatted at the air in Arabella's direction and let her hands fall back to where she rested them on her knees like she was bracing herself. "Like I said, the world ended. It was destroyed, and almost everything was gone. There were three things that remained. The Warlock-"

"The what?" Arabella exclaimed, thinking about all the books she had been reading and connecting the puzzle pieces. If this was truly anything like the fantastical stories of her yesterday, she knew that she needed to close her lips and listen to Ailith's words; things would go swifter that way. She flushed, remembering the way she had been acting prior to this realization. She didn't even notice that she was biting her lip so hard that it had started to bleed. She tasted the copper tang in her mouth and quickly reached up to brush the blood away, registering pain for the first time. She looked up self-consciously, but the two women seemed to be in a battle-of-wills. Green eyes bore into Ember's hazel ones in a silent, but heated argument happening only between the two.

They both turned toward her, and Arabella tried to duck her head to hide her lip. Ember rolled her eyes and roughly grabbed Arabella's hand. Too shocked to truly do anything, Arabella just stared as Ember closed her eyes and started to... **purr**? Her frame was shaking, and a warm rumbling sound emanated from her chest. What felt like a dozen hot needles poked at Arabella's mouth where it was cut, and she felt a small rush of energy as the blood stopped trickling down her cracked lip. December hastily snatched her hand away, mumbling about Arabella's stupidity and needing to move things along, allowing Arabella to reach up and touch her lip to find the wound completely healed. "How did you?..."

Ailith chuckled and stated, "all in due time."

"Just tell her already!" Ember huffed and flopped backwards where she sat.

"I'm getting to that!" Ailith turned to Arabella, picking back up where she left off after mumbling about disrespectful kids interrupting their elders. "Okay, I'll say it once more, because I know it's a lot- the world went nuclear. Only three things survived: The Warlock, The Residence, and The Mage."

"The Warlock was... well, he was the worst of humanity, no light shone from him. There wasn't a single part of him that wasn't swathed in darkness. He was, is, charming and handsome, which makes him even more dangerous, because he blackens everything he touches, and his reach is widespread. Since the rise of mankind, he has influenced society for the worse, and has been responsible for the most horrific acts and periods of history, for the darker dealings of men. He is the embodiment of the corruption of power, and his devious thoughts have always fed into power hungry minds. Some of the tormented souls he has reaped became so twisted that they turned into The Shadows. That's what you and Ember ran into earlier today. They are his minions- not living, not dead. They crave power, and there's nothing more powerful than the Clocks. If you tried to search The Warlock in any history books, you wouldn't find anything about him, he is devilishly clever. But those who know that truth of our reality, know this to be as much of a fact as the colors of our nation's flag. He has had a monstrous influence on some of history's most heinous leaders, such as Caligula and Hitler. He spoon fed lies and deceit into their very souls, he stoked the fires of their fear, ego and hatred until they became real life villains. They were his puppets. He does it still. Turn on any news channel and you'll hear of the fruits of his treacherous labor." She stopped to let the horrific information sink in- she chuckled darkly at Arabella's wide-eyed expression.

"The Residence I mentioned is a house, a home,

and is the origination or source, like a natural spring or reservoir, of all power in the supernatural world. As I'm sure you've already suspected, life is far from mundane. The house's power continues to flow pure and steady to this day, it will flow until the end of time, if necessary. Its magic was bestowed by the ancient brothers who used to live there: The Warlock and The Mage. Arabella Grace, you must know that the only thing that can make magic impure is the person who wields it. The Book Keepers, who I mentioned earlier as the people we report to, keep and maintain The Residence, along with the spell books and journals contained there. They also recover and preserve magical artifacts and history. We'll talk more about these things later. The Book Keepers ensure that these sacred treasures can all be passed down through the generations of Clock Keepers and Book Keepers alike. Their role is as crucial as ours is for maintaining peace in the world. Protection and knowledge. Yin and Yang. Never forget that we need each other. The last time that happened... it didn't end well for either side."

"Yeah, but we got some pretty cool stuff," Ember interjected.

"Which we lost a Clock Keeper generation later. It's not our place to protect knowledge- just the Clocks," Ailith snapped, seeming angry for the first time. "We both have our respective gifts, and while we share some traditions and traits, The Mage didn't intend for us to share all things.

"As I recall, they still have their presents from our 'tiff' years ago, while some people lost ours."

"That's enough, December," Ailith snapped again.

Arabella watched the two women where she stood as they had a tennis match of wits where they sat.

Ailith turned away suddenly and her pale green eyes bore into Arabella, efficiently ignoring Ember. "The last surviving entity I mentioned," she huffed, "was The Mage." She spoke his name with quiet reverence. "He was the opposite of the Warlock, his brother. No one knew where these beings came from, just that they were older than time itself, and as with most things in the Universe, their collective energy was one of harmony and balance. The Mage was The Warlock's mirror and opposite in every way. He was all that was light and good in the world, supporting those who fought against conformity and the wicked- the artists, poets, inventors, innovators, and freedom fighters. He embodied creativity, growth and progress. He wanted the world to blossom. It was his sacrifice that reversed time and changed history so that we might all live. It is not his body, but his magic and spirit that lives on. They flow through us; they are strong enough to power our devices and our individual powers. We are his legacy. He created a better world by giving up his life, and in doing so, allowed us a second chance. He sacrificed everything and gave it to the Book Keepers and..." with finality she concluded, "...and to us." Her expression was open and waiting.

Arabella sucked in a breath and held up a hand, indicating she needed a minute to think over everything she had learned. It was so much, some of it terrible and horrific, and some of it better than her wildest fantasies. She couldn't decide if she didn't want it to be true or if she needed it to be true. The Warlock, The Residence, and The Mage. From what she understood, there was a time when they were all that was left in the world. Each subject fascinating in its own right. How was she supposed to wrap her mind around that? Her soul felt at odds with itself, half wanting to turn back the clock and go back to when she only dreamed of these things, and the other wanting to throw herself into this fantastical world, embracing the path that destiny seemed to be carving for her. She sucked in a deep breath and asked in a quivering voice, "us?" Fear and excitement played in her crystal blue eyes.

Ailith's gentle smile was filled with pity and regret. "Yes, us," she sounded almost apologetic. Her rough hands smoothed out a non-existent wrinkle in her dress, then dropped back to her sides.

Ember glared at both of them, but her eyes were colder when she looked at Arabella. "Oh please, can you just get on with it and tell her what we are? As much as I enjoy the history lesson- it really isn't necessary. That's what our studies are for. All you need to do is tell her the basics," Ember snapped, unfolding her arms and cramming her hands into her cargo pants while standing and walking to lean against the wall. Like she was some sort of rebel.

Ailith reached up and brushed the one imperfect strand of hair framing her face- now it was perfect. "I'm getting there; I just want to ease her into it," Ailith sighed and tugged at her hair, causing it to be disheveled again.

Ember scoffed, "Well, I think she's been thoroughly 'eased into it'. Now just tell her- the sooner the better for us all." Her head cocked sideways expectantly.

I don't feel like I've been 'eased' into anything! I feel as if I'm diving head first into a car crash. Arabella had observed the exchange with her head on a swivel, and with each passing word they volleyed backward and forward, worry filled her until she was almost drowning in it- her lungs compressed and screamed- she wanted to claw her way back to the surface. Her attention was drawn back to Ailith when she cleared her throat. She looked Arabella over, concern evident in her eyes. Like it weighed on her soul.

"Arabella, it's time you know the truth, forgive me Axelia," she whispered with resolve and straightened her slumped shoulders. Arabella felt a jolt at her grandmother's name being uttered from the older woman's lips.

The need for answers and an adventure won against

any hesitation or grief she felt. Arabella nodded eagerly in confirmation, but inside she was terrified of finally discovering the truth, and was fearful of what the knowledge would bring: dangerous horrors- like demons and shadow creatures made out of corrupted souls. Maybe she already knew too much. But she could still always discover her very own personal monsters under the bed.

Ailith took a deep, steadying breath- to the point of being painful. "Arabella," Ailith confessed with a sweet, heartbreaking smile, "you are a Clock Keeper."

Chapter 7: A Clock Keeper.

Her jaw might have unhinged as the truth she had suspected became a reality. "I'm a what?" Arabella sputtered, flummoxed. Still confused by the meaning of the title, the one thing Ailith didn't expand on and explain in her speech. She was completely dumbfounded. And shocked. She had no idea what that meant, or for that matter, what that meant she was. She felt like Harry Potter when he found out he was a wizard, except she wasn't sure if this was going to be as awesome.

Two laughs sounded throughout the room: one warm and sweet like honey, the other cold and mocking. The dimly lit space seemed to become dimmer.

The corners of Ailith's mouth tugged upwards slightly. "You're a Clock Keeper, dear," she responded encouragingly.

Arabella raised one eyebrow, clearly not amused. "And a Clock Keeper is...?" She bit her lip again- in the same recently healed, but tender spot. Wincing slightly, she stayed focused on Ailith.

She chuckled humorlessly. "A Clock Keeper is pretty much what it sounds like. They keep and protect the Clocks, or as you called it," she mused, "a watch." Her ice green eyes shot down to the metal timepiece, with its three gleaming silver wings.

Arabella looked down at the polished metal that

was permanently attached to her wrist. "Someone gave up their life, not just for the whole world, but for this, specifically?" Remorse sank like a stone in her heart. Life was so precious- it deserved more than anything to be protected and preserved. "Just so they could protect it?" she queried, rambling as a result of her nerves. Now it was her turn to carry on the tradition of having the weight of time rest on her shoulders.

Ailith tossed her head from side to side as she stood, her silky strands spreading across her shoulders like a fan as she swayed. "Well, yes. If a Clock was ever broken or manipulated, if the wrong person or being got a hold of one, all would be lost. And that sacrifice wasn't just made for that Clock you wear, but for this one too," she snatched December's arm quickly and pointed to the one Arabella had briefly noticed before. Now that she had a better look, she could see that Ember's Clock was bulkier. While Arabella's had a thin, black, leather band, December's strap was made of the same metal as the face of her watch. The metal was a bright copper, and the face was inlaid with rubies and garnets. Under its face and hands and numbers, there was an eye- a large, glass cat pupil etched onto overlapping gem stones of garnet, ruby, amethyst, jasper and yellow apatite that were cut to resemble flames. "And for two others."

"There are four of these!?" she exclaimed in shock.

She heard Ember scoff quietly, her smugness radiating from the corner.

"Yes, there are four Clock Keepers born every other generation to protect the four Clocks."

"Huh?" she questioned, earning another scoff from Little Miss Sunshine.

"When The Mage left his estate to the Book Keepers, they found his Last Will and Testament amongst his possessions. In that Will, he left specific instructions on how the Clocks were to be kept safe, and whom should carry out his wishes according to the magic and events he had set in motion using the last of his strength and force. He called forward two sets of Keepers. The Clock Keepers and the Book Keepers. As I've said, they're the yin to our yang. They keep us in balance. As we protect, so they keep. There cannot be one without the other. They have their own set of inherited rules, responsibilities, powers and gifts."

"You said that in the first generation of Clock Keepers and Book Keepers, something happened. What was it?"

Ailith heaved a sigh. "That was my grandmother's generation. She told me that they were just figuring out how the world worked and what it meant to protect the Clocks from not only The Warlock, but life. The two factions had extremely different views on how that should happen. The Clock Keepers wanted to take the fight straight to the Warlock, while the Book Keepers wanted to sit back and observe as things unfolded. Soon it became a huge political debate between the two groups and their supernatural allies, who all had to pick a side. Eventually, it morphed into something even worse; it became a feud between nationalities. When The Mage chose who was to become his successors, he cared about content of character, not where they were born or what their heritage was. So, once that issue became part of the Book Keepers' argument, all bets were off. Especially for your great, great grandmother, who was German. Eventually, the dust settled, and both sides were given gifts from the other as a token of peace and to strengthen bonds and understanding between the two groups."

Blinking in surprise, Arabella whispered, "wow, I mean, I knew I had some German in my ancestry, but I had no idea it was so close. I didn't know any of this."

Ailith gave her a sympathetic smile. "I told Axelia that you needed to know. But you were her sweet little angel, and she didn't want to expose you to the darkness of this world before it was absolutely necessary."

"That would be her, always wanting to protect the ones she loved."

"Would you like to know what you will be learning about if you decide to become a Clock Keeper?" Ailith inquired.

"I have a choice?" Arabella questioned with a

mixture of hope and fear. Like she had thought earlier, on one hand, she just wanted to go back, but how was she supposed to step away from the fantastic and horrific society that she had been shown? How was she supposed to turn her back on, according to Ember and Ailith, the safety of the world?

"Everyone has a choice," Ember stated firmly, "that's why we're doing this."

"What happens if this isn't what I want?"

"The responsibility and powers would go to your closest female family member who matches the qualifications mentally, physically and spiritually. From what I've learned, that would be your younger sister."

Arabella pictured Kat's sweet face, how it lit up and the way it would crumble in terror at the demons, Shadows, and who knows what else. She would never allow that to be a possibility; she would protect her at all costs.

"I want to learn, I want this." She spoke grimly, with a note of finality to her words.

Ailith nodded with a small, sad smile, "If you are anything like your grandmother, I knew you would." Sitting back down, Ailith lovingly squeezed her shoulder as she passed. "Your studies will be extensive, but the main things you need to know about will entail: weapons, including Imprint Weapons- like your sword, The Haunt, animal companions, and your powers. Our weapons have been modified to fit the the modern era, or at the very least have been maintained to stay in perfect condition. But they're still the same weapons we started with all those years ago; they are tailor-made for each of our families-imprinted for only our blood. Our powers are varying between families, between Clocks- you will learn how to wield them, but it will be incredibly difficult. It's a lot of power and it is hard to maintain. Your body can't handle it for too long. Eventually, you'll be able to share the energy of the Clock with your Anam Cara- or your soulmate," she finished with a knowing smile. She folded her hands casually in her lap as if she hadn't just altered Arabella's world forever.

"I have one question-" Arabella started, mentally tucking the rest of the information away to be examined in full later, when she was safe to ponder the questions floating about her tumbling mind. Weapons and magic and soulmates. *Oh my*.

"Just one?" Ailith arched a silver eyebrow.

"Okay, more than one," she admitted. "But just one for now."

Ailith encouraged her, "and your 'one question for now' is?"

"What exactly does my Clock do?" Arabella searched with quiet desperation.

"Oh, dear me, I've been talking for so long, I

almost forgot," she giggled in an almost self deprecating way, and Arabella heard Ember mutter something sarcastic about it not being that important anyway, just the reason they were there in the first place- or something to that effect.

Ignoring her granddaughter, Ailith pressed on with her first lesson. "As I said, there are four Clocks, and each Clock contains one of the core essences of humanity. There has to be balance in order to save humanity, therefore The Mage had to capture the defining essences of humankind. But there's always a price to pay for magic like that. The four Clocks are: the Guardian Clock, the War Clock, The Love Clock, And the Knowledge Clock. The reason The Mage chose Clocks to hold this power, is because he needed a way to keep time moving forward after he had "rewound" it, so to speak, because if he hadn't created a physical entity of the movement of time, it would have continued to reverse. Eventually time would have collapsed in on itself. So the Clocks were created and the powers bestowed upon them to ensure that time would always move onward. If one of these Clocks is ever destroyed, part of humanity would be destroyed along with it, and time would slow. They are the four keys to life as we know it. Whoever possesses at least three of them could control the world. It is crucial that they never fall into the wrong hands. The person who tried to wield them would become so corrupted with power, they would no longer be a conscious entity, but a vortex of destruction. They would only lust for more power. And if they ever fell into the hands of The Warlock...."

Arabella felt her eyes widen. "That's... wow," she whistled, hoping to prevent that from ever happening. She was never going to let Kat be a part of this, not when there was so much room for her to be in danger.

Ailith laughed with such force it shook her whole frame. "Exactly, that's why The Mage left the power to women." They all had to agree to that, amusedly.

"Is that true?" Arabella asked.

"Yes, the responsibility and power is passed down to the female of every other generation. The Clock and its sacred burdens are passed down from grandmother to granddaughter," Ailith confirmed.

"So you were a Clock Keeper?"

"Up until a few months ago. I miss it- but I don't envy you nearly as much as I thought I would." She looked off to the side, her gaze far away.

"A few months ago...?" Arabella looked back at Ember.

"You see, dear, you only become a Clock Keeper on your 16th birthday, and Ember turned 16 just last summer, and I passed it on to her. She's been studying to take the responsibility of the Clock for years, learning what she needs to know in order to harness her powers and their physical manifestations- like your tattoos." She reached up and pulled her curtain of hair aside to show the outline of a cat in white ink just like Ember's, and pointed to Embers copper, cat eye Clock.

"So which Clock Keeper were you?" Arabella excitedly inquired, and then more tentatively added, "which Clock Keeper am I?"

A cocky grin spread across her usually gentle mouth and she stretched her wrinkled arms behind her head, "I was the Clock Keeper of War. You my dearest, are the Guardian Clock Keeper of Protection- just like your grandmother."

Arabella thought back to her grandmother and everything that had transpired between them, and suddenly, not only did it make sense, but it made her miss her even more severely. The fierce aching need to be in her arms almost brought her to her knees.

"Well, what do you think?" Ailith asked, ignoring the tears in Arabella's eyes.

"I think... I need to sit down." Arabella surrendered with a near hysterical snicker.

After a while of sitting there just digesting the news, Arabella was feeling glad that she'd have lessons to dive more in depth later, because most of the details had flown from her head from lack of space. Arabella finally got all of her mental ducks in a row, and knew what questions she wanted to ask. "So, you said that the Imprint weapons were tied to our bloodlines, that's the sword I found?" She uncrossed and recrossed her legs, scratching at one jean-clad knee and playing with her hair.

Ailith nodded slowly in confirmation.

"And that there is also such a thing as an animal counterpart- which is why you have a tattoo of a cat, and why I have bird wings- it's also why I can fly."

She nodded again, but this time it was secretive, like she knew something Arabella didn't. Ailith added, "and why Ember can heal, and has amazing vision and grace- you got one huge attribute from your Clock's animal, while Ember and I got a bunch of small traits. Your animal counterpart is a snow falcon, and that's why your tattoo gives you the ability to fly, and Ember's tattoo gives her feline attributes, like keen eyesight, hearing, and a sense of smell. She also has minor healing abilities, like what she did for your lip, but she can't heal much more than that. Anything that requires stitches or is broken is out of the question. She also has natural speed, strength and grace. It's not just one thing that encompasses her power, but many, unlike you. Yours should only give you the power of flight, but you are a Clock Keeper, and generally we tend to have advanced senses- including speed, strength and grace, but that usually comes with training. That's really all you need to know for now. It's enough to keep you alive. We'll go deeper down the rabbit hole in your lessons." She paused and thought for a moment. "You know, you haven't asked about that."

"About what?" Arabella asked, taken aback.

"Your training. You haven't asked about why you need it."

"Oh, um, I just assumed, it's understood that if you're fated to protect the world, or at least your bloodline is, you should know how to go about it." *I mean, that seems pretty logical,* she thought, and fiddled with a string that was hanging off her sleeve.

"That's reasonable, and part of it, but it's also to prove you have the ability to protect humanity. You must undergo The Trials. They are a set of tasks given to you by the Book Keepers to make sure you are deserving and eligible to be a Clock Keeper. So it's more than just training, it's preparing you for the biggest test of your life.

"And if I fail The Trials, Kat takes my place?" she asked fearfully.

"If you're deemed unworthy of being entrusted with the Clock, then yes, your little sister would take your place and you would have all of your powers stripped."

"No," she choked out, knowing that she could never allow that to happen.

"It's the only way to ensure the Clock's safety."

"But isn't Kat too young?"

"We would wait until she was older to bestow the

Clock upon her, and if she didn't work out, it would be given to one of your cousins, no matter how distant."

"Who would protect the Clock in the meantime?" Arabella asked, pressing on after the disturbing piece of information.

Ailith took a deep breath, but was cut off by Ember.

"It would be returned to the box you found it in and would have to be protected by the nearest available Clock Keeper, ie, me. Which I hope won't be necessary, because the more power I keep, the bigger the target painted on my back is," she spat, glaring at Arabella. She launched herself off the wall, knocking into Arabella where she sat as she passed her and retreated into the kitchen and out of view.

"Oh." Arabella dumbfounded.

"Yeah. Oh." Ailith whispered back sadly.

A knock sounded on the door, causing Arabella Grace to spring up, already tense from the events of not only today, but the last few weeks.

"Are you expecting anyone?" She looked at Ailith, prepared to step between her and whoever was behind the door.

"Yes, now sit down- you're worse than Ember," she teased.

Okay, she might have deserved that.

"Who's worse than me?" Ember questioned, coming back into the room, still looking rather angry and eating another apple.

"How tense and rigid Arabella is," Ailith confessed, still laughing, heading toward the door.

"Impossible," Ember smirked, "have you seen her posture? Even if she tried to stand up straight, her shoulders would still hunch."

Okay, that was uncalled for. Sure, Arabella had heard her mom tell her plenty of times to sit up straight because blah, blah, blah. But when Ember said it, it was like she was chewing on something vile and needed to get the poison out of her mouth.

"Well, listen here, Little Miss Military-"Arabella stood up and began walking toward Ember, her long legs eating the ground.

"Girls!" Ailith reprimand sharply, causing them to pause their glaring match and glance over at Ailith and... the, uh, **woman** next to her. Or at least, she was female. Her characteristics included lots of normal traits. She was about 5'6" and was wearing short black heels, stockings, a pencil skirt, a white blouse, and a button up jacket that hung loosely over her shoulders. She had a petite figure with gentle curves that accentuated her small waist. She looked to be somewhere in her mid-thirties to early forties. That's where her normal traits ended. She had smooth, green skin, and a wild tangle of flaming, bright pink hair that was pulled back into a high ponytail. Her eyes looked human- sort of- they were human in shape, and had a pupil and an iris, but the iris was a color that she had never seen on a human before. Arabella Grace would have thought they were contacts if her skin and hair had been "normal", because her eyes were a curry gold.

"Woah!" Arabella yelled, jumping back. Again, inciting a little chortle from the peanut gallery.

"Oh dear, did you not tell her about me?" the woman inquired of Ailith with a spanish lilt to her words. She flashed her bright, burnt gold eyes at Arabella.

"I thought it would be better to surprise her," Ailith remarked, chuckling.

"Oh, dear Mage," the woman countered morosely, shaking her head. "I'm Mika Reyes," she stated, taking a step forward to shake Arabella's hand, which caused Arabella to stumble backwards.

With hurt reflecting in her golden gaze, Mika grimly commented, "I see," then closed her eyes. Arabella watched in awe as strand by strand, her fuchsia hair transformed into a deep brunette color, a shade redder than Ember's, and as pigment by pigment, her skin faded into a warm cocoa brown. "Is this better?" she challenged, opening her eyes again to reveal the same turmeric orbs. "Or I could do this," she teased and grew taller, "or this," and grew wider. "Maybe this," she continued and changed everything about her over and over, remaking herself until Arabella had viewed thousands of combinations. Everything changed, except her eyes.

Finally she stopped and went back to her small frame and plant-like coloring.

"Tha- that was was amazing," Arabella sputtered.

Mika's curry eyes widened slightly.

"Why, thank you," she responded like that wasn't what she was expecting Arabella to say.

"I have to know something," she said experimentally, not sure how Mika was going to react and trying to test the waters.

"And that is?" she demanded knowingly.

"What are you?"

"I'm your instructor to prepare you for The Trials, and that was your first lesson.

Chapter 8: Scalding Hot Torture.

Arabella opened her mouth to ask a question, but was cut off.

"Yes, Arabella Grace, you passed the 'pop quiz', she chuckled. "You were cautious and aware of your surroundings the whole time. You assessed the situation before you reacted, and you made sure to assert yourself as friendly to a potential hostile before asking a possibly offensive question. And to answer your other query, I'm a Simper Nimph, or a Morph," Mika Reyes explained elegantly.

"Oh, well it's very nice to meet you Mika," Arabella tried to appear calm.

"Likewise, Arabella, I've heard so much about you from your grandparents."

"You knew my grandparents?" Grief struck her once more. She couldn't help but be shocked, but then realized that it made sense for Mika to have known her grandparents if Ailith did. She just hadn't ever imagined her grandmother having a green friend with a hot pink mane. Ailith had been at her grandparent's funeral, maybe Mika had been as well. She had been a little too... distracted to notice most of the crowd that had gathered on that rainy day.

"Yes, we all did," she indicated, spreading her arms, then shrugged as they dropped back to her sides. "Well, except Ember."

"Really?" she chirped excitedly. She was dying to find out as much about her grandparents and their secret lives as she could; she was about to ask more, but was cut off by the sound of her phone going off. She darted a glance over at Ember, who shook her head as if to say, 'not me'.

Mom: Hey, it's time to head home. Tell Cadence hi for me:)

Guilt ate at Arabella as she read the text. She thought for a moment, chewing on her lip, before replying.

Arabella: Okay, headed home now. Love you:)

She looked up from her screen to find three pairs of curious eyes on her, some kinder than others. "It's my mom, she wants me to come home," she explained meekly. She demurely tucked a piece of hair behind her ear and looked up, her ice blue eyes searching for something- she wasn't even sure what. "What do I tell her?" Her voice was soft and desperate.

"Nothing, you can't tell her anything. It would just cause her to worry. It would just get in the way." Ailith explained with gentle firmness. "Hardly anyone from the human world can know- not even family."

"Ailith is right, I'm sorry, Arabella," Mika agreed sympathetically.

"Okay, well as touching as all of this is, I'd rather

not go to juvie for kidnapping- so goodbye," Ember cut in, irritated, and waved her toward the doors, shooing Arabella out.

"Alright, well, bye." Arabella shrugged awkwardly and gave a little wave, her mouth tugging downward. She thought suddenly of the shadows lurking outside now that the sun had set.

"Alright, dearest, it was so nice to meet you finally. Why don't I give you a ride home?" Ailith assured her, pulling her into a hug that reminded Arabella that they had only met just that day.

Mika waved, pity apparent in her eyes for the dumbfounded girl. "Bye, Arabella, and remember: training starts tomorrow- be here at 4:45 p.m. sharp. That should give you enough time to do schoolwork." Mika formally shook her hand. "Oh! And you'll meet my daughter."

"Cool," Arabella responded excitedly; she had a good feeling about that.

"Bye." Ember coolly dismissed her and disappeared through the back door of the room.

Arabella smiled weakly one last time at Mika before following Ailith out the door to head for the familiarity of home- feeling utterly and completely at her wit's ends.

Arabella entered her house through the front and tip-toed through the foyer and past the kitchen. "Hey, was that Cadence that dropped you off? I saw that your car was still here," Sarah questioned conversationally when she saw Arabella. Sarah had her hair up in a ponytail and was just finishing up washing dishes at the sink. Arabella tried to steady her breathing and pretend that she hadn't been trying to sneak in. Her mother walked toward her nonchalantly, probably just for a hug. Her mom was a perpetual "hugger."

"Yeah, we dropped it off on the way to his house and rode together," Arabella answered nervously.

"Cool. So how are Cade and the rest of the Alderics?" Sarah asked.

"Uh... great, I, um, yeah, he's good. They're good," Arabella replied, feeling a little too high-strung.

Sarah gave her a suspicious look. "That's good," she smiled quizzically while giving her a weird look.

Arabella rubbed her eyes, thinking quickly, "well, I'm pretty tired, so I think I'm going to, um, go to, uh, bed. I'm really tired," Arabella backtracked, repeating herself. To prove her point, she yawned and stretched.

Sarah quickly glanced at the digital clock on the stove. "It's only 7:00," she gave Arabella a startled look, very taken aback.

"Yeah, I know. I'm just, you know, so, so tired- it was a long day," she embellished to her mom, then muttered to herself, "too long."

"What did you say?" She still had an underlying tone of suspicion. Arabella was pretty sure she was covertly sniffing her breath while they spoke, double checking that there was no underage illicit behavior going on. Her mom trusted her, but always reiterated that mistakes were a normal part of life, and she wouldn't be a very responsible parent if she didn't do her due diligence to check up on her kids.

Again, Arabella balked, "just that I was tired."

"Okay... well, goodnight then," Sarah Grace conceded.

"Night," she gave her mom a quick kiss on the cheek before swiftly walking at a good clip down the hallway to her room. She made sure the door was closed, then reached under her bed to grab the sword she had hidden under her box springs. She quickly stood, careful not to bang her head against the bed frame, and examined the sword in the light. It shone proudly with its silver and mother of pearl handle, black leather grip and gleaming edges. Wonder filled her features as she turned it over and over in her hand. This was magical, and someone gave up their life to protect it. And the watch, er, Clock. Its wings, as sharp as ever, glowed like soft moonlight. She couldn't help but stare in awe at the two silver objects. She was the Guardian Clock Keeper, the Clock Keeper of Protection.

What did that even mean?

She hid her sword, her Imprint, under her bed and

quickly got ready to sleep. She wasn't lying about being tired. When she went to bed that night, she slept with the lights on.

Arabella's phone pinged with texts from her friends. She was glad it was the weekend, but nervous about tonight. She needed to get her mind off the fact that she started training this evening. Training to become a BA, almost supernatural being who had magic, a sword, and could fly! It was official- lots of Netflix and books were required today if she was going to distract herself enough to keep from going insane. Luckily, she was saved by the group: they wanted to hang out. A thought came unbidden to her mind. This was probably going to be one of the last times she could really hang out with them. Not only would she be busy, but it would be safest for them if she just distanced herself in general. Maybe that meant starting today. But then she pictured their smiling faces: Diana teasing her mercilessly about how she had stayed up finishing a book the night before; Luke playing Black Ops with her and teaching all the best places to 'camp'; Zuriel, who was always willing to talk to her about any new show she had watched, even if he hadn't seen it; Claire who she could just be a girl with, geek out over guys and talk about what color to paint their nails; and then, of course, there was Cadence. Cadence was her best friend. Her brother. She told him everything, or at least, she used to, before she walled herself in with grief, and by then, it was too late. She might be able to part with the rest, but if she lost Cadence, her heart would shatter even further, and she didn't think she could handle anymore grief. So, she would go and say her mental goodbyes. Then she would start distancing herself. *Just not from Cadence,* a selfish voice whispered in her head. Plus, Gabriel could possibly be there, and there was something about him that made her mouth go dry and her heart race.

She arrived at Cadence's house; everyone was smiling and laughing. Like always. They had all been friends since 8th grade, and she had been friends with Cadence even longer. She had met Diana in math class, bored out of her mind. They had automatically struck up a conversation about books, and... instant friends. Together they had made and kept friends. But Cadence had always been there. They had met when they were 5 and a half, when they had both taken gymnastics. Cadence had lent her a jacket after a class when it was pouring rain outside. They had both promptly dropped gymnastics the year after, but had stayed friends.

They hung out in Cadence's family's gaming/ theater room. Her favorite was on: *Princess Bride*. *"**Inconceivable!**"* Wallace Shane's character exclaimed on-screen as Cade came barreling toward her with Diana in tow.

He gave her a quick hug, a lopsided puppy dog smile stretching across his freckled face. "How are you? Everything okay?" He kept asking her that, every time he saw her, as if he was expecting her to break down like the first time she had called him about her grandmother. She wasn't okay. But saying it out loud somehow made it worse. And above all else, she wanted to tell him about her new-found life. But she couldn't.

"I'm fine," she laughed, brushing him off. Diana squeezed between them and gave her a hug of her own.

"So, guess who I invited?" Diana giggled, her short plum curls bouncing as she spoke. Her nails glinted with gold acrylic as she used her hands to demonstrate her point.

"Who?"

"Gabriel."

"Gabriel?"

"Gabriel." She nodded her head over in his direction, he was cornered by the twins and Claire, who were asking him rapid fire questions about himself.

She started laughing; Cadence and Diana followed her gaze and joined in. "I'm going to go save him," she chuckled.

"Oh, his hero!" Cadence teased.

She shot him a glare and gave him a playful shove.

"You're so funny." She headed over. *This is perfect,* she thought, rationalizing in her head. *I can distance myself by hanging out with Gabriel tonight, and we haven't been friends that long, so if after tonight I don't really talk to him, it won't be weird.* She was strangely sad at the thought of not hanging out with Gabriel anymore, almost as much as not being able to hang out with Cadence anymore. Which she had already admitted probably wasn't going to happen.

"Hey, Gabriel? Can I talk to you?" She nodded her head toward the opposite side of the theater, away from the others.

"Sure." He smiled and came jogging up. When he got close, he leaned over and asked, "is there anything you actually need to talk to me about?"

"Nope," she popped.

A wild smirk appeared and it sparked something in her gut. "Thank you."

She laughed softly, sticking her hands in her front pockets as they strolled over to a comfy couch. "Anytime." *Don't make promises you can't keep,* a nasty voice murmured in her head.

"So besides the ice thing, any other quirks I should be aware of?" he inquired as they sat down, attempting to kick off the conversation where they had left off.

"A few..." she blushed.

"Me too." He laughed and his blue braces peeked

through.

Shrugging, she suggested something that sounded like delirious fun. "Want to rapid fire?"

He cocked one eyebrow. "Rapid Fire?"

"I say one, you say one. Back and forth, faster and faster until one of two things happen: we're both laughing so hard we have a stitch in our sides or are deeply in love." *Did I just say that!?*

He seemed to contemplate it, mirth in his bright eyes. "I'll take those odds." *Thank the Mage.* It seemed she had already picked up the Clock Keeper lingo.

"You start," she laughed, suddenly feeling shy.

He gave a nonchalant shrug and retorted, "I sketch almost everyone I meet."

"What?" She stared at him sideways, a smile breaking across her face.

"Whenever I meet someone, I automatically come up with how I want to draw them... um... what colors I would use, the medium, the setting. That type of thing. And I can't focus on anything else until I sketch it. I get all fidgety, and I just need to get it out. That's why I carry this around," he shrugged, pulling a Rubik's cube seemingly out of nowhere. "I've solved this thing at least a thousand times."

"That's amazing," she laughed genuinely, a stitch already developing. "Ever thought about drawing me?"

His voice dropped to a whisper as he murmured,

"all the time." A real smile lit his face as hers blushed.

"When I'm nervous, I braid and unbraid my hair..." she chuckled, catching herself in the act.

"Cute." He chuckled back.

And they continued like that for the afternoon.

Gabriel Fawkes paced back and forth across his room at a steady jaunt, his painting forgotten in the corner. He cried out softly when yet another wave of sharp pain burnt its way across his back- its ache spreading through his ligaments and tendons. The waves of agony had begun when he had started school a few days before. When he complained about it to his dad, he brushed it off and told Gabriel that he must have pulled a muscle or was having growing pains or something. But it kept getting worse as he paced his room tonight. He knew it was more than that. Not being able to take it anymore, he hopped in the shower, hoping it would soothe the sharp aches. He had just gotten out of the shower when another wave hit him so hard it almost brought him to his knees. As he wrapped a towel around his waist, he decided that he wanted to see what was keeping him in such constant pain. He turned slowly in the mirror and looked over his shoulder.

What he saw caused him to yelp so loudly that his

dad came running up the stairs and pounded on the bathroom door. "You okay in there, champ?" His Dad, Jonathan Fawkes, bellowed, knocking on the door even more fervently.

"Yeah, Dad, just stubbed my toe!" Gabriel called back. He heard his dad leave, muttering. He had said he was fine, but he wasn't so sure. In fact, he was sure that he wasn't fine- he stared in horror at his back. Black ink had spread from the tips of his shoulders blades down to his mid-back, and his inked flesh was scalding to the touch. He flinched away from it and looked back at the design.

It looked kind of like wings... He cringed again as another wave of searing hot agony, as if he were being scorched by a brand, spread even further downward. He watched in horror, then awe, as the wings spread and etched themselves deeper into his tender skin. Feeling claustrophobic, he pushed blindly into his room and got dressed in a hurry. *I need to get out of here,* he thought and rushed out of the house. He had to sneak past his father's lounging figure, drowsily resting on his bed, as he grabbed his dirt bike out of the garage and began pushing it down the street. His dad would be out in minutes and would never even know he was gone. Once he was out of earshot of the house, he fired up his Kawasaki 125cc. His dad had let him upgrade to the Baja designs dual sport kit, so it was also street legal. He knew right where he was headed- to the Egyptian Theater in the heart of Downtown Boise.

When he was a kid, his mom had taken him here every time they passed through town. He bought a ticket to *The Goonies*, which was just starting, and quickly walked through ornate halls, entered the theater, and sat by himself in the back, watching the movie unfold behind the ancient stage. As he sat, his back stinging in silence, he breathed through the fading pain, slowly being able to focus more and more on the cinematic masterpiece before him. *The Goonies* was awesome; it was another one of those things that made him feel nostalgic and at home- it was also something he used to watch with his mom, which made it very sentimental to him. He really missed her.

After the movie, he felt the pain that had been plaguing him for the last few days subside. Breathing a sigh of relief, he leaned against the theater and watched the Boise night life move by, a melting pot of different cultures and lifestyles coexisting and thriving in a laid back, yet exciting city scene.

"Good movie, huh?" a voice asked off to his side.

"Yeah, the best," he answered hesitantly, turning to face whoever had spoken. It was a guy around his age with white hair and striking, liquid copper eyes that were similar in color to a paint he had been using earlier. "Do I know you?" he questioned, confused by this random guy starting up a conversation with him. Gabriel pictured drawing him in ink on a cold night, lit by a single street lamp.

"No, you don't. I'm Harrison, I'm new at your

school; we share a couple of classes together. I think you're friends with Arabella, right?"

"Oh, okay, that's cool- how do you know Arabella?" he replied a little defensively, wondering what she had to do with anything.

"Just met her yesterday. Seems like a sweet girl," he explained with a confident, friendly smile.

"Yeah, she is," he retorted, relaxing and offering a smile of his own.

"Looks like I better back off, " Harrison joked, like they were old friends sharing a laugh.

"What do you mean?" he said tersely, suddenly tense.

"Just that you obviously like her," he returned, smiling.Then he leaned in close, touching his shoulder like he was sharing an inside joke. "Just be careful. Arabella seems like the type of girl that could cause a lot of *pain* and heartache." He chuckled darkly. Where Harrison's hand had touched Gabriel, he suddenly felt very cold.

Gabriel shivered, moving away from him."Right..."

Thankfully, Harrison started walking away. "See you around, Gabriel."

"Okay," he muttered, weirded out by the whole encounter.

Gabriel was currently at the YMCA in Boise right off of Eagle Rd. He was with Cadence, who had, from what Gabriel could tell, taken pity on the new kid. He didn't want to feel like a charity case, but Cadence was pretty cool to hang out with.

They sat at the edge of the pool, their bare feet gliding back and forth just under the surface as their board shorts chafed against the stone ledge.

"So, are we gonna stare at the pretty water all day, or are we gonna get in?" Cade teased.

"Yeah, we can get in," Gabriel brushed off the jest. "I mean, you're the one who's an actual member here..."

"Smart aleck," Cade retorted, reaching behind his back and taking off his shirt before standing up and jumping in feet first. He drenched everything around the edge- including Gabriel.

With a shrug, he reached to remove his own shirt, cringing slightly when his fingers brushed the skin of his back, reminding him of the tattoo he was desperately trying to ignore. Quickly trying to once again banish it from his mind, he followed Cadence's lead by jumping in with a wicked splash.

Gabriel swam over to Cadence and they horsed around for a while, testing each other with contests of who could swim laps the furthest and fastest and hold their breath longer than the other. They also made a competition of who could do the gnarliest and most skillful dives, flops, flips and other awesome stuff. Gabriel was momentarily able to forget about his tattooed back.

That is, until he heard Cadence's shocked exclamation behind him. "Wow! Nice ink! That is so crazy- did you know that Arabella has the same tattoo? Except, hers is in white ink."

"She does?" Alarmed by that news, he couldn't help but feel that there was no way that was a coincidence. He was curious for more than one reason about this new bit of information about Arabella.

"Yeah, she got it because her late grandma had a similar one..." Cade reverently offered as an explanation.

"Oh, that's sweet," Gabe reflected in wonder. "I didn't know Arabella's grandma had passed away," he reflected, wondering if that explained the worry and hurt in Arabella's pale blue eyes.

"Yeah, it was only about a month ago. Actually, she lost both of her grandparents at once. Her grandmother died from a brain hemorrhage, and her grandfather had a sudden heart attack from the grief." He took a terribly deep breath. "I've been so worried about her."

"She doesn't deserve that." He sighed deeply, wanting to take any pain she was feeling away.

"Do you want to play a game of basketball?" Cadence asked, changing the subject.

"Yeah," he answered, wanting once more to get his mind off many things.

Later that day, after a thorough game of basketball-which he won- he and Cade went back to Cadence's house. They were in his home theater watching *Indiana Jones*. Just as Indie was about to head into another death defying situation, Gabriel felt his back suddenly tighten with the pain he thought he had left behind him.

The doorbell rang.

Cadence got up to open the door. Gabriel got up to follow him, with pain raging in his back. He launched himself upward, earning himself a head rush. Stumbling around in the dark for a moment, he felt around until he grabbed a chair and waited for it to fade. When his vision returned to normal, he was greeted by the sublime sight of Cadence leading Arabella into the room. She gave him an empathetic smile- almost as if to say, 'I feel your pain'..

"Hey Arabella, what, uh, what's up?" Smooth. The last time he had seen her had been at lunch two days before, when they had shared food and laughed. She had asked him about his latest sketch, who it was, what it was made of, if he would show her. The last of which he had answered with a 'maybe'. It was the best part of his day. He gave her a smile, ignoring the pain that had spiked in his back and careful to hide his brace-clad teeth. Gosh, she had the best laugh.

She smiled back and he noticed how straight and

white her teeth were. "Oh, hi, I didn't even know you were here," her smile turned apologetic, and she tucked a gleaming, golden blonde strand behind one of her small, pink ears. Her bright, glacier-blue eyes pierced into his bottle-green ones, searching for something.

They were broken out of their reverie by a clueless Cadence's blundering interruption. "Are you guys okay?"

"Nothing, I mean, uh, yeah." Arabella turned toward her best friend, giving Cadence a beaming smile; Gabriel felt a twinge behind his rib cage.

Gabriel cleared his throat, gaining their attention, "so what brings you to, um, Cadences's house?" he inquired awkwardly while scratching his left arm. Smooth. Again.

"Oh! Right. I stopped by to tell Cade that I wouldn't be able to go to dinner tomorrow night," she recited, like she had forgotten, and gave a cute little giggle. Her teeth caught the dim lighting in the room when she threw her head back slightly.

"Really?" Cadence started, as if it were completely abnormal for her to cancel.

"Yeah, just some family stuff?" she asked hesitantly, like it was a question. A huge smile was plastered on her face, and her eyes were averting their gazes. "Well, um, I gotta run, so, bye," she added quickly. She gave Cade a quick hug, then looked at Gabriel with another searching gaze. Then she was gone, practically sprinting out of the house.

Cadence stared at the spot were she had stood seconds before. "Did she seem weird to you?" he questioned, turning toward Gabriel.

Gabriel made a noise indicating he agreed, but not for the reasons Cadence probably thought. His thoughts had turned inward, because he had noticed that as soon as Arabella had left, his pain had stopped. He couldn't help but wonder why.

Arabella showed up for her first lesson with Mika and Ailith feeling nervous beyond belief. She felt like she was doing good just for the fact that she remembered enough from walking there and driving home to know how to get to Ailith's house while trying to keep everything straight in her head. When she pulled up, she was surprised to be doing so at the same time as Mika and another girl, who was around Arabella's age and had flaming pink hair. Arabella assumed she was Mika's daughter. Unlike her mother, who had dark hair and skin, she had golden skin and soft, pastel pink eyes, which, along with her hair, made her seem like she might be a little obsessed with the color. She was slightly below average height and had an extremely petite frame, reminiscent of a bird. She apparently preferred her features to be small- she had a button nose and a cute little pair of pink, round lips. She looked like an anime character. She was the poster child for adorability.

"Hi, I'm Arabella," she introduced herself politely.

"Even I could have guessed that, and I bet in 2014 that Denver was going to win," she said with a cute smile and the same Spanish accent as Mika.

"What?" Arabella laughed, guessing that she meant football of some sort.

"Sorry, I was referencing the Super Bowl a few years back."

"Ahhh, yeah, my brain's wired for art and other things, not sports."

"I figured. Good thing I enjoy sports enough for the both of us."

"Well, thanks for that," she laughed. They both followed Mika inside as she beckoned them.

When they entered giggling, Ember rolled her eyes and muttered, "great," which made them laugh even harder.

The next few days, Gabriel watched Arabella like a hawk. Or like a falcon, he should say, because he had been dreaming about nothing else but two things- Arabella Grace and falcons. Weird. He found that even though he seemed to only be in pain when she was around, she was able to entrance him- even when she was light-heartedly making fun of him for liking pineapple pizza, something he learned she held a great disdain for. He also noticed how distracted she seemed to be, only snapping back to reality after you called her name half a dozen times, and even then, her eyes always seemed glazed over and far away. But strangely, not when she was talking to him, or the new kid that sat with them, Harrison- but he chose to ignore the enamored look she got when he was near. Whenever she looked at Gabriel- her eyes would become clear and intent- like she was seeking answers she could only find in his sea-green depths.

He wasn't sure what she sought, but he knew he was looking for it also. They sat at their regular table at lunch. Gabriel sat next to Arabella and watched as she worked on homework, head bent over in deep concentration. Every once in a while, she would cease her frantic scribbling to chew on the end of her pencil- something he had discovered was a nervous habit of hers, or merely something she did when she was deep in thought. She had her hair up in a high ponytail, and the few strands that had fallen out framed her heart-shaped face. She wore light makeup from what he could tell- light eye shadow that brought out her brilliant blue eyes even more, and some sort of gloss on her rose-colored lips. She almost always wore all black- from her boots, to her jeans, to her leather jacket. She was such a riddle: she listened to heavy punk rock and Indie music, but every Sunday night watched a Disney movie. She loved the night and hated mornings, but couldn't stand the dark. The thought of space never ending gave her a major panic attack, yet she never wanted to die. Everything about her was sweet and optimistic, but at the same time, she almost had a shadowed, dreary air to her.

"Hey, Arabella, what happened to doing your homework the night before it's due?" Harrison charmed, breaking Gabriel out of his staring contest with Arabella's right hand- he had noticed that she had a bandage across her knuckles.

"What?" she asked distractedly, still scribbling away. Harrison shot a sly look at Gabriel, but before he could repeat his question, Arabella's head shot up. "Oh!" Her mouth formed a small zero and she licked her lips rapidly. "I was up, um, reading," her eyes were still clouded. Even Gabriel could tell that it was a lie by the way she forced a smile, but when he looked around, he noticed that despite his worries, no one else seemed to notice her tell of deceit. Her best friends... and Harrison... didn't even notice, and that worried him. But what really concerned him was that he could tell, even though he wasn't certain why.

Bent over her paper, Arabella lightly nibbled on her pencil. Before she set the lead to paper again, she gave him a brief, but intense, look of longing- her crystal eyes clear and focused. She slipped him a warm, but also brief, winning smile. It was the most genuinely cheerful he had seen her. He felt himself falling, and he couldn't tell if that was good or bad. She shot him another enticing look. Okay, maybe he could.

He leaned over with a warm smile in return and started to invite her over after school to hang out, but was interrupted by a wave of sharp pain in his back, followed by a cold feeling. Harrison's words suddenly began floating around in his head, "Arabella seems like the type of girl that could cause a lot of **pain** and heartache."

Chapter 9: She Twirled the Sword.

A whole week had passed since Arabella had started her training. It had also been almost that long since she had last spoken to Gabriel outside of lunch. Why did she always make a fool out of herself in front of him? When she was at Cadence's house last Sunday, she had acted like a complete idiot, tripping over her tongue like she'd never spoken before. She did that all the time in front of Cadence, and it didn't bother her at all, so why was it different in front of Gabriel? Maybe because he was funny, sweet, and tended to really listen to her, even if she was off on a tangent about something silly- like the latest episode of *Super Girl,* which was awesome; she was pretty sure she had been Kara in a different life. She sort of felt like a wreck when it came to her love life, a sentence she had never really been able to say before, and it sucked. She kept waiting for Gabriel to do something or say something- anything at this point. But every time it looked like he was going to talk to her beyond their idle banter, he got this look on his face and then pretended to get distracted or have something else to do.

And then there was Harrison, who had somehow started sitting at their table, which all natural laws should have dictated against. When he came around or talked to her, it was like everything else was eclipsed except for him. All she could see was his perfect smile and his bright eyes. All she could hear was his smooth voice and his rolling laugh. It made no sense. It didn't matter what she was doing, as soon as he spoke or caught her attention, she was automatically fixated on him. He was cool and calm- like the eye of a storm. When he did something, it was like he wasn't a part of her life, she momentarily felt like he *was* her life.

It kind of freaked her out.

But she didn't need to be focusing on guys right now, no matter how cute someone's laughing green eyes were.

She needed to focus on her training. The classes themselves were okay... sometimes they were even fun- especially practicing basic attacks with a bokken, or practice sword. But they were also extremely stressful. Her Trial was supposed to have taken place a month after her birthday, so she was behind the curve, but apparently she hadn't been the only Clock Keeper to not have done their testing on time. One of them, whom she had yet to meet, the Clock Keeper of Love, wasn't old enough yet. Her birthday was about a month out. And the Clock Keeper of Knowledge's bloodline had been estranged from the Keeper world. According to Ailith, they had kept and protected the Clock, but, due to some hurt feelings, wanted nothing to do with the rest of them. The whole thing seemed kind of fishy to Arabella. When she had asked about what happened, all she would get were tight-lipped faces and frenzied eyes, so she had dropped it. Due to her late introduction to this mystical world, Ailith and Mika were able to appeal to the all-powerful, all-knowing (that was sarcasm) Book Keepers and push her Trial date a month back from when her training started. She had three weeks left, and she still felt nowhere near ready. Still being in her first week, all she had done in her few days of training was physical stuff, but she was ready to learn about the supernatural world she felt sure would enchant her the same way her books did. That, and she really wanted to be prepared- for Kat's sake. The more she learned about The Trials, the more she was certain that they were more for the purpose of her demise than for proving her worth. She couldn't fail, she couldn't; it didn't matter what happened, she would protect Kat, no matter the cost.

Now back to the show.

"So far, all we've done is practice movements- albeit complex ones, with the practice sword," Mika said, pacing in front of Arabella and Rosada, her sparing partner and quick, pink-haired amiga. Her new bestie gave her an encouraging smile and walked over to the wall of death, as the blush colored cutie called it. It was a giant, wall-sized weapons rack. She grabbed the leather handle of Arabella's Imprint and took it off the wall, offering it to her. She took it readily.

"Cool," she breathed, excited to move further along in her training.

They were in Ailith's home. When she had visited

the house that first fateful evening, there had been a door in the corner of the absurdly large living room that Arabella had initially assumed was either a closet or a door to the basement. It had turned out to be the latter. Once through the door, you descended a single flight of stairs that led to a corridor, which was more like a labyrinth than a hallway. It was large and wide, and filled with musty texts, weapons, classrooms, and so much more than Arabella had even had a chance to explore yet.

They were currently in one of the larger of the ten or so subterranean chambers. Its floor was padded, along with three of the walls- which, Arabella had learned, came in handy when being slammed into them. The other wall (of death) was covered in weapons, ranging from broadswords, to longbows, to throwing stars. About three feet from the wall of death stood four human-shaped silicon dummies. The majority of her physical training took place in this room, with the remainder of her rigorous routine taking place in the gymnastics room, which had everything for her flexibility needs. Arabella really hated that room; it was where she did most of her training with Ember. *Oh joy.*

"Feet shoulder width apart," Mika said for the thousandth time. Arabella complied. "Slide your right foot a quarter of an inch forward. You want to be leading with it. Bounce on the balls of your feet- you need to be ready for anything. You need to keep your center of gravity central.

This requires a lot of core control, so keep it engaged at all times."

"Okay," Arabella comprehended, bouncing on the balls of her feet and loosening her neck.

"When you hold your sword, it's different than holding your practice stick," Mika reprimanded, and adjusted her grip. "You don't want to hold it so tightly that you tire out, and doing so will create messy and unstable movements. You should hold it with your thumb and first two fingers. The remaining fingers should be loosely curled around the handle." Stepping back, she studied Arabella's grip and nodded in approval.

"Okay, now, 'on guard'?" Arabella asked, laughing, referring to the position.

"Yes," Mika laughed. "You can shoulder parry."

"Right," Arabella replied and moved into position, remembering it from former lessons.

"Remember to keep your wrist relaxed and in line with your forearm, you need to adjust the angle of your weapon. You should be feeling it in your shoulder and maybe the tricep. If you do this, you won't tire as quickly."

Feeling extremely BA, she shot a look at Rosada and did as she was told, feeling the slightest burn of aching muscles. It amazed her how quickly she had gotten into shape this past week, but Ailith said that was natural for Clock Keepers, which was awesome.

"Now you need to cut down with the sword- don't,

I repeat, **don't** wave your arm. You need to move the whole blade in one stroke. Use a small motion from the elbow to move your center of gravity toward the sword. Remember to keep your core engaged, to be in control the whole time. To stop the blade, snap your third and forth fingers." She blew her coach's whistle, the one that Rosada swore she loved more than she loved her.

"When do I start practicing on the dummies and with Rosada and Ember?" she couldn't help but ask, extremely curious.

Mika gave an amused smile, "after you've done this at least a hundred times. It's all about muscle memory, Arabella. It needs to be second nature, instinctual, when you're out there in the real world. You don't have time to remember which foot to lead with and how far in front it should be."

Arabella nodded, knowing that made sense, but feeling a little deflated about it.

"Now remember, footwork is key; you want to move your lead foot and have it land just before, or just as, the blow is landed. Put your body weight behind the blow, but not overly, so you don't lose your balance."

Arabella followed through, remembering the movement easily from doing it with the practice sword.

"I hope you remember, from both your practical and theoretical studies, that there are many types of guards. I want you to practice them as I list them off."

"Since you've already gone through 'on guard', let's move onto 'high guard'."

Arabella moved into position, easily placing the sword defensively above her head, shifting her weight, and lightly rocking on the balls of her feet as she stepped through with her right foot.

"Low guard,"

She brought the sword down in one smooth, practiced, even movement, her arm extended and her blade pointing at the floor.

"Long."

She extended her arm and her body, stretching and tightening her gut to keep balance.

"Hanging right."

She brought the sword handle close to her ear and let the length of the sword angle toward the ground.

"Inside right."

She brought it in close, leveled at mid waist.

"Close right."

Shifting again, she brought the handle to her hip and had the blade pointing toward the room's padded ceiling. She felt sweat dripping down her face and blew through her lips upward, trying to dry her forehead.

"Short."

She brought the blade into herself, breathing heavily. Not even the magic running though her veins kept her from becoming fatigued.

"Side."

She brought the sword up toward her ear again, this time pointing it upward, as if she were going to swing it down.

"Good, you can relax," Mika complimented, clearly pleased, a self satisfied smile filling her features.

Arabella practically collapsed onto her sword as she used it as a cane, not even caring if the sword poked a hole in the mats on the floor. Her muscles quivering and hot, sticky sweat rolled down her face and back.

"Nice," Rosada commented genuinely, laughing where she sat against the far wall, sipping from her water bottle.

That looks really nice... She started to move to get water from her own bottle before hearing Mika's whistle blow. *Are you kidding me?*

"Break's over," she sternly chirped.

"What break?" Arabella muttered, still panting; it was only Kat's smiling face that got her back into position.

"I want you to hold your position as I go over information."

Forget Mark Pellegrino, she is the actual Devil.

"There are seven positions for the ideal attacks: the head, left and right shoulder, right and left gut, and the left and right leg. Now, while the thrust would be the most potent even if your sword is dull, you still need to be careful, because overcommitting to the move would cause a large opening defensively. When guarding your head, you want to block your shoulders at the same time. The easiest way to block a downward thrust or slash to the gut or legs would be to hold your sword point down and use your blade to move the attacker's sword away. Standard footwork is to withdraw the foot on the side of the attack, so an attack on your left will be defended on your right, and vise versa. Defensive patterns to work on in your free time include: Eights, Round the Clock and Diagonals-which are all pretty self explanatory. Now, riposters are a way of switching between defensive and offensive sword play. It's an attack immediately following a defensive move. Before we practice these, however, you need to have perfected your normal defensive moves. There are three basic types of riposters: over the attacker's arm, under the attacker's arm, and against the other side of the attacker's body. You have a single-hand sword, which means that with your opposite hand, you can fight or distract the attacker using grappling and other techniques. That's all for now," she finished, not so quickly. Arabella collapsed to the floor, exhausted and extremely happy that her sword fell the other way instead of under her, it would suck to be impaled.

Arabella was at Ironwood Social, a club/restaurant

by the fairgrounds. It was a huge space that still managed to seem cozy, and it also had a kombucha bar; the bitter and sweet, fermented brewed tea was one of her favorite drinks, and they had several selections on tap. Ironwood Social had two stages, one small one on the right side of the room and one large one on the left. White lights hung from the rafters, and in the corner there were giant, comfy chairs and art supplies that you could use. **For free.** She liked to go there when she was feeling stressed, get a kombucha and a sandwich, listen to music, play trivia on Tuesdays, draw and paint (she once drew an awesome picture of Luna Lovegood), read in the comfy chairs or play pool, video games or one of their table games. Sometimes she just went there to relax and get her homework done.

Which is what she was doing now.

When she was at home, she couldn't seem to get a break- her mom and dad wanted her to do chores, and her sister always wanted her do this or that with her. She adored her sister, but she never really let Arabella rest- she loved her so much that she never wanted her to be alone. That was great, most of the time, except when she was trying to do homework. Mika had run her ragged and left her hardly any time to get anything else done.

She breathed a sigh of relief, settling back in an overly- plush chair as the peaceful silence filled her. Aside from a few patrons on the far side by the glassless, indoor window that opened into the neighboring business, a barber shop, she had her own space. The place was awesome.

Sitting and chewing on the end of her pencil in concentration, she wrote down the answers to equations. She was feeling lucky that she only had one page of math homework, but was dreading the reading she had been assigned in history. Her history book sat as a warning on the side table adjacent to the comfy chair. She spent hours doing homework, yawning as the clock hit 7:00.

"You look tired," a warm voice laughed behind her.

Craning her neck, she found Gabriel standing there, his usually light green eyes twinged with darkness. "Oh, hey, what are doing here?" she asked, suddenly wanting a mirror. "I've been here since 5:00, so..."

"Cade said there was a cool art corner here, so I thought I'd check it out," he smiled, and then, continuing their double dialogue, whistled, "that's a while, what have you been doing?"

Right. Cade, who she had told she was going to be here... oh, they were so going to have words- not all of them kind. "I've been getting homework done. I swear, my teachers keep assigning more and more."

"I know what you mean," he winced. "I think they've been trying to take it easy on me because I'm new, but still."

"Right." She nodded, then remembered something

he had told her a few days before. "You were homeschooled- right?"

"Uh, yeah," he laughed nervously and sat adjacent to her in another overly plush chair. "It's been kind of a shock to the system." He muttered to himself, "I seem to be getting a lot of those."

"What?"

"Nothing," he returned dismissively.

Knowing what it was like to not want to talk about something, she didn't press the issue. "So... why were you homeschooled?" she implored, moving her homework aside, knowing she wasn't going to get anything done.

"My family just liked to move a lot," he offered as an explanation, pushing his soft looking hair out of his eyes.

"What about now?" she asked gently, wanting to know all of his stories.

"Um, my dad wanted to settle down, my mom didn't... I got stuck between the two, but ultimately decided I wanted some semblance of conventional schooling.. and here we are," he whispered.

"Oh, I'm sorry- I know you mentioned that they divorced, but I didn't realize... that's rough, no one deserves that- but you really don't." She wanted to take the pain from his eyes and make it as if it had never been there.

"Thanks," he muttered and looked around the room.

Wanting to lighten the mood, she asked about what she hoped was a safer subject. "So, what are some of the places you've lived?"

He gave a sharp snort. " Pretty much all of the Northwest. I've lived everywhere from Anchorage, Alaska, to California, and have traveled and lived most places in between. I've even traveled out of the states a few times, mostly Canada- but I'm not sure how much that counts."

She gave a twinkling laugh. "I'm jealous, I've always wanted to travel like that."

He smiled, "sometimes it's really great. I can see the appeal- but I have to ask, is there a specific reason you want to travel?"

She reminisced softly, "my mom always says that I'm a free spirit. There's something so right about that; it resonates in me and feels familiar. My soul is filled with wanderlust- I crave adventure the same way a starving man hungers for nourishment. When I was a kid, I knew that the part of my soul that was missing, was adventure." It looked like she was finally getting what she had wished for.

The first true smile he had displayed through their whole conversation lit his face. "Thank you."

"For what?" she asked a little breathlessly, realizing how close they were. Somehow, subconsciously during their discussion, they had both leaned drastically forward, their knees were almost touching.

"Cheering me up." He spoke and smiled softly.

She ducked her head to hide her scarlet stained cheeks. As she did so, a piece of hair escaped from where she had tucked it behind her ears. Déjà vu struck her as Gabriel beat her to it, tucking it behind her ear, staring into her blue eyes and cupping her cheek gently.

She gazed back deeply into his eyes, and electricity lit the air between them. She was as hypnotized as he was mesmerized.

Both leaning even closer together, the world slowed from spinning one thousand miles per hour to ten.

Then he pulled away.

Pain spread across his face and he stood up quickly, almost knocking over the plush chair.

"I have to go," he mumbled hastily and fled, leaving Arabella to stare after him in a cloud of confusion and hurt.

She's going to cause you pain, Gabriel thought, remembering Harrison's words as torment spread across his shoulders. For most of their conversation, he was able to ignore the burning agony that spread across his back. But the closer he got to her, the more torture he was in until he couldn't stand it anymore. He had started noticing a pattern. Whenever he was near Arabella, his mysterious tattoo throbbed with pain. A voice that was almost foreign to him was telling him that it was the beautiful and sweet girl's fault. She was the cause of his suffering.

Chapter 10: It Was as if Her Fantasies Had Left Her Bookshelf.

"Again!" Mika called as Arabella finished going through her sword play positions. She sighed, almost wanting to cry and not sure she wasn't already or if that was just sweat dripping down her eyes.

"Okay," she sighed, and her muscles moved on their own accord without any mental exertion.

"Actually, I have a better idea. Rosada, December, come over here," she called to the two girls. Rosada was practicing her specialty- knife throwing on a wooden target, and Ember was practicing her hand-to-hand combat on the silicon dummies in a manner that reminded Arabella of Jackie Chan.

"What's up, mom?" Rosada asked, skipping up, her ponytail bouncing. December followed, marching behind her.

"I want you three to play dodgeball," Mika insisted, amused.

"Why?" Ember asked with calculation in her eyes.

"I want Arabella to work on her reflexes- what better way to do that than by trying to avoid flying, red rubber balls."

Arabella groaned. "This is like gym class from Hell. Don't I suffer enough humiliation by having to do stuff like this at school?"

Rosada laughed silently beside her and shook her

head in agreement. "Even I don't see the point in this game." That was saying a lot, considering she could rattle off stats for every sport ever- even curling.

"It's either this or I have Ember wack you with a wooden staff," Mika asserted. Ember cracked her knuckles while giving her a sadistic grin.

"Dodgeball sounds awesome!" she remarked with as much enthusiasm as she could muster.

Mika smiled slyly, "that's what I thought."

Mika walked out of the training room, assumedly to get dodgeballs.

"Are you sure he was going to kiss you?" Rosada begged, bringing up the conversation they had been having before class. Ember rolled her eyes and stalked away to practice something that involved throwing stars.

"I swear to you, he was. I've never been kissed before, but even I'm not so oblivious that I didn't pick up on the painfully obvious hints he was dropping," she answered, running a frustrated hand through her ponytail and staring at the padded ceiling. "Beorn from *The Hobbit* could have picked up on those signals, and he was a bear creature living in an isolated cabin. Wait... are Hobbits real?"

Rosada laughed and shook her head at the latter question before inquiring about something **much** more important. "What do you think made him pull away?" Her voice had a sympathetic tone to it.

"I have no idea!" she groaned, feeling frustrated. "He looked like he was almost in pain. Also, I wasn't kidding about Hobbits." She closed her eyes, feeling hurt.

"I'm sure there's something similar...but, wait, that's not the point. I'm sure it wasn't because of you," Rosada comforted.

"I hope not," she sighed... "I really like him," she confessed.

"I'm sure it will all work out," Rosada eased and slugged her lightly on the shoulder. "You are too awesome for him to be completely blind to it."

"I sure hope so," she lamented.

"What about the other guy-" Rosada started, but was cut off by Mika coming into the room.

"You guys ready?" she asked, holding a net bag filled with red rubber balls.

"Totally," Ember remarked and joined them once more, her sock clad feet padding softly against the mats with cat-like silence.

Mika blew her whistle, and without further ado, released the orbs of doom. Arabella felt her joints wanting to freeze as both Ember and Rosada dove for the balls.

Rosada was quick, just a pink streak racing across the room, grabbing whatever ball fell across her path. Ember, somehow, did a freaking ninja-roll type thing where she grabbed around ten balls, and by the time she was crouching, had them stationed behind her.

Both of them armed, both of them deadly accurate-
and she was caught between the two.

Scrambling, she grabbed a few dodgeballs and tried
to swiftly move out of the crosshairs. She threw a ball at
Ember, who softly deflected it with one of her own, then
she threw one at Rosada, who almost fell backwards when
she ducked back. A ghost of a smile touched the corners of
Arabella's lips. *Okay this might be a little fun.*

Ember threw a ball at Rosada, and Rosada threw
one at Arabella. It was like time slowed, the way it usually
did when she was in school. The rubber ball flew toward
her and she moved. It was that simple; all she had to do was
move. Bouncing on the balls of her feet, she threw a few
more, collecting them off the ground and even catching
them out of the air. She deflected and moved with a
precision she had never had. It was like she was flying all
over again. The few times any of them were hit, it was from
ganging up on one another. By the end, they all came away
laughing, with only a few red welts (which Ember promptly
healed). She was feeling more and more like the
granddaughter that would have made her grandmother
proud.

They were in the classroom. In the maze that Ailith

called a basement, there were only a few rooms she really used. The classroom was dark, musty, and filled with books; she loved it. The room was, by far, the smallest that she had seen so far in the large labyrinth of a basement, but was, in her opinion, the best. Its walls held built-in bookcases; its floors were warm cherrywood, and instead of the desks that you would find in a regular classroom, this room held four, big, comfy, soft leather chairs. Arabella's favorite was bright green with blue accents. The other three were mint with purple trim, black with red, and teal with burnt orange. In front of each chair was a single, brown, wooden end table. The room's lighting, unlike most classrooms, wasn't artificial and sterile, but made up of a series of lanterns that hung from the low ceiling. Something about the whole place was reminiscent of a dream.

It was her first official lesson. She had been in here once to discuss her lesson plan, but now she was finally going to learn about her newfound world. Starting now, she was going to have three lessons every week until her Trials.

"Realism Reality," Ailith started, leaning against the large oak desk at the front of the room, "is what would have happened, what should have happened, if The Mage hadn't stepped in. As I told you, the Axis powers attained the atomic bomb at the same time we did, and they persevered instead of surrendering, like we've learned they did- like the whole world learned. In actuality, they rallied and retaliated. The tide of war was precarious, and instead of tipping in the Allies' favor, it tipped in theirs. After that, it was a domino effect. World leaders such as Winston Churchill and The President failed to get the edge, and the whole world fell apart. The Rome-Berlin-Tokyo Axis coordinated their efforts better; they were so consumed by war, so proud, and so corrupted by The Warlock, they couldn't stand the idea of losing. They would've rather died than lose the power they had. Once they went full scale, so did everyone else- we were at a stalemate, and that stalemate turned into mutual annihilation. It was a chain reaction of death and destruction. Eventually, there was nothing left to destroy and no one left to destroy it. There were only three things left-"

Shifting uncomfortably in her comfortable seat, Arabella whispered, "The Mage, The Residence and The Warlock." She shuddered, thinking about the world being so empty... all of those lives lost...

"Exactly," Ailith voiced with a defiant anger. It was as if she wanted to go back in time herself so that she could punch The Warlock in the face. "If The Mage hadn't stepped in, if he hadn't deemed mankind worthy enough to save, none of us would be here." She talked about The Mage with such reverence and respect that Arabella felt in awe of the man, barely knowing anything about him, except that he had saved all of their lives.

"The Mage was a force older than time. He was

one side of a coin: the light, the good. His brother... the opposite." A wistful expression suddenly appeared on her face. "You find the more you learn about life, the more you realize that everything demands balance. The light and the dark. The Warlock And Mage were the purest embodiment of this. One brother born of light, the other of darkness."

All Arabella could do was stare. It was as if her fantasies had left her bookshelf and now decorated her life. The only question was: where did she fit in with all these fantastical truths?

Ailith continued speaking, as enraptured in her words as Arabella was. "He created us- the Clock Keepers and Book Keepers- to keep that balance." Scoffing, she refolded her arms as Ember entered the room- but instead of making some snarky remark, Ember just sat in the black and red chair adjacent to Arabella's. "He kept records of everything- from who the latest artist in Europe was, to social erosion in the East. He was dazzled by humanity. But most of all, what he wrote about was how throughout history, he just picked up after his brother's messes," she remarked with a bitter accent to her words.

Arabella raised her hand, feeling almost like a child in her naïveté. "Why were the brothers so different?" She hated not knowing things.

Sighing deeply in contemplation, she explained. "Keeping in mind that everything must be balanced, we understand that so must the supernatural world. The world of magic exists from the energy of knowledge- with the creation of creativity and emotions, there was the creation of magic and life as we know it. Because it originated from those things, it was reliant on those things. But not every individual creature is the same. Like people, some are good, some are bad. But species as a whole are typically attracted to one type of energy or emotion. Some exist and draw their power from negativity- everything bad in the world feeds them. In order to survive, they cause more chaos and destruction. That's what The Warlock is. All that he is, his very essence, is made up of humanity's faults."

"Wow," Arabella responded, her head swimming with the information that the decisions people make everyday supplement either evil or good. She was beginning to think that someone was messing with her, because how could real life be this insane? But then again, she had wings and was suddenly in a weird love triangle- or at least she thought she was- she had no idea what went on in teenage guys' heads. She could just be imagining the whole thing. But if she was right, and those things really could happen to her, then anything was possible. "And The Mage?"

"He was the opposite- he was fulfilled by the good in all of us, but it was more than that. He was amazed by us. There was a letter he wrote regarding his meeting of Abraham Lincoln."

"Whoa, that's like, my favorite President," Arabella

laughed, unable to keep that tidbit to herself. The comment may have earned a scoff from Ember next to her, but it was true. She loved Abraham Lincoln.

Ailith chuckled her honey sweet laugh. "My point, was that the end of his entry read: 'once again, those who choose good astound me'. This became a common way for his journal entries to be concluded. He didn't just need humanity, he believed in us. He was this immortal, all-powerful entity, and yet, we humbled him." She hummed amusedly, clearly fan-girling over The Mage; she idolized him. "He even wrote this quote from Helen Keller on the walls of his library about how the best things in life can only be felt with the heart."

It was all amazing, but something almost didn't make sense to Arabella. "If he was this 'all-powerful being', then how come he died?" she asked, cringing and feeling insensitive, like she was asking about Ailith's recently dead dog.

Ailith's demeanor drooped, and the lines in her face filled with sadness, like rain filling in the cracks of a sidewalk. "Magic comes at a price. Those who perform it expend great energy from themselves. The Mage wrote in his journals that all he remembered was existing, he and his brother simply were. They had always been. They came pre-packaged, already knowing who they were, having infinite knowledge and knowing spells. The Mage was the more powerful of the pair, as light is always brighter than dark, while dark is more cunning. He ended up with with their spell book, but the incantations were so energy depriving, that the few times he used them, he was so drained, it took decades to regain his strength. Even the all-powerful will die without a spark. That's what spells do-they sap up that spark inside you."

Arabella looked over at Ember for confirmation; she was shaking her head like she couldn't believe it herself either, and there was what strangely resembled a hint of a smile on her face.

"He knew that it would take years to regain his strength and didn't want the world to be unprotected. He knew that to sacrifice his spark, his very essence, to create the Clock Keepers and Book Keepers and turn back the Clock on humanity's most devastating mistake would be the only way to ensure that everything would be guarded from his brother's influence."

"This is all so amazing," Arabella frowned, contemplating her lesson, parts of her brain aching from it. But something felt so right about it, like her own spark had known about it all along. It harmonized with her soul.

"Yeah, it is," she agreed, taking a seat in the comfy, buttery, mint and purple chair.

"Thank you," Arabella told her honestly. She packed up her stuff and headed out, but paused in the doorway to say goodbye.

She was brought up short by the sight in front of

her. Ailith held Ember's hand tenderly. "You were quiet," Ailith stated in a whisper; there was so much pride and love directed at her granddaughter; it made Arabella's chest ache.

The closest thing to a gentle smile Arabella had ever seen Ember wear graced her face. "I like that lesson. It reminds me of why I love my cause. It gives purpose to everything I do."

Ailith smiled. "I feel the same way."

The whole exchange left Arabella wondering as she left the house, thanking her lucky stars as she walked home that it wasn't dark yet, what exactly Ember hid behind her guarded mask.

Chapter 11: Her Skin Became Forged in Electricity.

Arabella was very close to writing a *strongly* worded letter to her teachers about the mistreatment and mental abuse they were responsible for by assigning busy work. She had spent six hours doing a packet on the same information that she had grasped when it was explained to her in the first ten minutes of class. Not that she was actually going to send it, but she had a feeling just writing it would be very therapeutic. She fantasized about sending it in a couple of years- after she graduated. Maybe.

Then her phone rang.

Gabriel;) : Any ideas about fun things to do in this town?

Arabella was questioning multiple things about this situation: A) was Ember messing with her, B) why was there suddenly a ;) (winky face) after his name, and C) why was he texting her of all people? He wasn't even here, and she wanted to check to see if she looked okay. That was not how normal people behaved. Plus, he had freaked out the last time they hung out, even going as far as to ignore her at lunch. *Maybe he felt bad?*

The only solution she could come up with was A) Ember doesn't have enough of a sense of humor to do something like this, B) Cadence, C) she had no clue, maybe she wasn't imagining things, at least she hoped she wasn't.

Arabella: yep! Any ideas on what you want to do?

Gabriel;) : I heard there were some cool, quirky places downtown.

Arabella: *awesome. You meant to type awesome. If you're in the mood for that type of venue, then your best bet would either be Freak Alley or The Record Exchange. Two personal favorites of mine.

Gabriel;) : both sound awesome! Want to come?

It didn't take her long to think about how to respond.

Arabella: that could be cool.

She replied, trying to play it cool, but was really grinning like a child hopped up on too much candy. Squealing, she raced into her parents' room where her mother was doing yoga. "You'll never believe what just happened!" she rushed in, almost wanting to jump up and down.

Her mother switched from downward dog to warrior one in one, smooth, graceful lunge. "Hmm, what?" she asked with a warm smile. She loved talking to her mom, she was so supportive of everything Arabella did. Arabella knew that if there was anyone she was comfortable in her own skin around, it was her. Sarah had encouraged Arabella to be her own person, with her own life, though some people might say Arabella had a slight problem with authority and conformity. She needed to be her own person; if she had a problem, she could solve it. She also didn't like telling people things, she tended to be private and closed off, wanting to keep what she felt inside. It felt safer that way, more comfortable. She always told her friends that she would never hesitate to talk to them about her feelings, because she would always be there for them in return, but truthfully, it was always horribly hard to tell people about her own problems. She just preferred to keep her thoughts to herself. But she didn't feel like that with her mom. It wasn't that she **had** to tell her stuff, just that she wanted to. She wanted to tell her when the exciting stuff happened, or when someone was being a jerk at school, or when Cadence was driving her nuts by talking about *A Series of Unfortunate Events* non-stop. She hated that she couldn't tell her about the Clock Keepers. She wanted to tell her about the fact that her dreams had come true, but even she had to agree that it would be in no one's best interest to divulge that information.

"You know how I told you about that boy, Gabriel?" she asked excitedly, flopping back onto her parents' comfy bed.

"The one that's just 'so' cute, with the bright green eyes and a dimply smile? Who you can talk to about everything?... No, never heard of him," she teased, holding the warrior two pose.

"He just asked me to hang out," she gushed,

stretching her arms out into the fluffy comforter like she was preparing to make a snow angel.

"You played it cool, right?" her mom asked, switching gears from relaxed hippie to Mom Mode in two seconds. "Make him chase you, never the other way around."

"I know..." she groaned, having heard this piece of advice thousands of times. "I told him that it 'could' be cool."

"Good," she nodded, content that her daughter was a strong, independent woman who knew her own worth.

Her phone dinged.

Gabriel;) : hey, just pulled up... that chill? I, um, wanted someone local to show me around, and I hope that you're not busy.. if so, then this is really awkward and I'm rambling. Ya. I'm rambling. I'm going to stop now, sorry, I do this sometimes where I try to compensate by over-explaining if I think I'm being rude... and I'm rambling again... someone stop me. Help. Right, so ya, I'm outside, text me if that works for you...

Arabella usually hated it when people blew up her phone. When he did it, it should have been equally annoying, but she couldn't help but think that it was one of the cutest texts anyone had ever sent her.

Gabriel;) : I DID NOT MEAN TO SEND THAT! my thumb slipped... try to ignore the awkwardness and remember that we're going to your favorite places in town, apparently.

Gabriel;) : I hope that your day is going good... :)

Suddenly panicking that he was there, she shot up from the plush bed, now she really wanted to check if she looked okay.

"What caught your hair on fire?" her mom asked, finishing her yoga routine. Arabella felt too nervous to reply and showed her the texts.

All she did was raise her eyebrow and titter, almost in disbelief. "He's definitely chasing you."

Arabella could feel heat coating her face and muttered, practically running to her bathroom to fix her hair. "He's just a friend!" she shouted to her mother.

To which she replied, "I used to say the same thing about your father!"

She quickly got ready and was about to leave. Peeking out the window, she saw him sitting there on a burgundy dirt bike. She ran back to the garage to grab her helmet, stubbing her toe on the freaking corner of the hallway.

Her mom's amused smile vanished as she saw the helmet in Arabella's hands. "Now, I know you weren't going to take your bike without your dad here."

She gave a sheepish smile. "No, I was gonna take Gabriel's."

The look her mom gave her inspired more chills than any supernatural creature ever could.

"Actually, we're going to take my car, yeah, we're taking the car," she rushed, gently putting the helmet down on the bench that held their shoes.

"That's what I thought." Her mom nodded in confirmation and rolled her eyes as she gave Arabella a hug. "Please be safe."

"I promise." She gave her mother a quick peck on the cheek. "I love you!"

Once outside, she pointed to her car and yelled, "I'm driving!"

The drive downtown was mostly silent, save for a few ribs between the two. Arabella explained that her mom didn't like her to ride without her dad. And they discussed Arabella's playlist, which was an eclectic mixture of indie artists such as The Head And The Heart, punk rock bands like Panic! at the Disco, and classic 90's grunge rock, like Eddie Vedder.

"Want to go grab some food?" Arabella asked as they parked the car along the picturesque, tree-lined streets of downtown Boise.

"What?" he started, tearing his gaze from the window. "You know, I haven't actually seen downtown during the day before. It's amazing. Unlike most of the other cities I've been in, it's colorful, clean, historic, hip and cultural. But it's not colorful like Vegas, all artificial and fake- it's just naturally artistic. It's not run down, like so many other historic places, with abandoned buildings and shady districts like Miami or New Orleans have. Everything here has its place. It's not so cutting edge that it takes away from its character, like Seattle or Portland. The culture is all its own. I love it. There's nature everywhere and art painted on everything, including the utility boxes."

Arabella laughed, delighted someone saw Boise the same way she did. "That's why there's nowhere I'd rather call home. I want to see the world, but I know deep inside that I'll always return to Boise."

"I'm starting to feel the same." He gave her a smile; she didn't quite know what it meant.

For some reason, rosy heat spread up to her hair roots. She cleared her throat and asked once more, "do you want to get something to eat?"

Contemplating the question, he ended up shaking his head. "Let's grab something after we go to the places you like."

"So, Freak Alley? Or Record Exchange?" she asked, getting out of the car.

"Um, what's closer?"

She took a look around; they were parked in front of a bank on West Idaho Street. "Record Exchange, probably, we're kind of in between the two, but RX is a bit closer," she concluded, pointing toward where she believed it was. While, thankfully, she mostly had her dad's sense of direction, she still had her mom's tendency to get turned around.

"Sweet," he smiled at her and stepped back. "Ladies first."

"Um, thank you," she muttered, ducking her head. Arabella Grace knew that once more- judging by the heat in her cheeks and neck- she was blushing. In her opinion, being pale should have meant that her ability to blush had decreased, not the opposite.

Leading the way, they walked leisurely down the sidewalk as the sun started to dip below the foothills, painting the sky in pinks and oranges. Seemingly simultaneously, street lights and white lights on cafe patios blinked on. An impish smile stretched across her face, she really did love Boise.

Beside her, Gabriel took a savoring inhale of the night air. "Every city has a different smell- Vegas smells hot and dry and vaguely like cigarettes, yet somehow sweet at the same time. Alaska smells cold and hard, like the steely water in the rivers and the glacial bays made of silty clay that dot its grey and blue landscape. Miami smells of hot, sweet garbage, with a pervasive stench of salty brine and city fumes. And so on and so forth. My point is, Boise is the best out of all of them. It's fresh and clean, like newly cut grass, sage and pine."

Arabella laughed, awe filling her voice for multiple reasons. "I kinda love it here."

"I do too," he said, nudging her as they walked. She attempted to playfully hit him... extremely awkwardly... in the shoulder, effectively killing whatever cute, warm and fuzzy mood they had going on. *I have the social skills of a 30 year old living in their mom's basement,* she mentally groaned, *what, what, what, am I doing?? What is life? I'm so bad, I need to buy one of those self help books.*

When they got to the Record Exchange, she saw the wonder light up Gabriel's brilliant green eyes, and whatever awkwardness she felt melted into a pile of deliciousness in her stomach. *Girls who handle deadly weapons in their spare time should not be able to feel like a gooey chocolate chip cookie.* Yet, she did. She didn't know whether to squeal or to groan- because of the timing- to be this into a boy. Anytime he got close, her skin became forged in electricity, her palms went clammy, her heart raced, her cheeks turned pink, and she lost all ability to think.

"I don't even know where to begin..." he smirked, glancing around as they entered the coffee shop side of the store. The Record Exchange was cozy and warm, and smelled like vinyl, coffee and blessedly aged card-stock. The space was almost split in two, one side housing a somewhat ordered disorder of sprawling rows of CDs and records, all waiting to be shuffled through, and a small stage in the corner reserved for occasional performances by live local or touring bands. The other side featured a small coffee counter, a couple of old fashioned 50s diner booths, and a mish-mosh of gifts: crazy, outlandish knick-knacks, notebooks, novelty socks and T-shirts, and locally crafted wares.

It was a lot to take in, the type of place you could spend forever exploring, discovering its little secrets. The place was so wicked.

"Let's start with the music," she nodded enthusiastically, like a kid who had candy mixed with Red Bull in their system.

"Wise choice." Gabriel cackled, twisting his hands together like a villain. "Okay. That was weird, sorry, let's go look at music," he cringed, smiling so big that his braces were adorably blinding.

The world started to go fuzzy from lack of oxygen because she was laughing so hard. All she heard was, "oh, you think that's funny?" And then he picked her up the couple of inches that it took to make their heads level- actually picked her up- grabbed her around the waist and spun her around. When he stopped, they were face to face. "Will you forgive me for being a dork?" he whispered boyishly, grinning in a small half-smirk.

"Uh, yeah," Arabella whispered back, wetting her

lips, feeling dizzy and light headed- from the spinning, she was sure.

"Sweet," he quipped and dropped her, her newly adopted grace keeping her light on her toes. She was happy just being with Gabriel throughout the evening. They had moments where all of the sudden, the weirdness between them would disappear, like there was something stronger connecting them, something almost tangible. Their gazes would lock, and his bottle-green eyes would be all she could see, and she would realize that he was her magnet- drawing her to him, no matter what. It was as if her skin was on fire and he was a bottomless pool. The world could end and she would still be drawn to him. When they were in the same space, she would automatically gravitate toward him. She couldn't help but look at his face and hope to see his enjoyment whenever they discovered something new or interesting. She randomly caught him stealing a glance as she did the same. She would start braiding and unbraiding her hair, and he would start fidgeting with his Rubick's cube. She had noticed the habit since he had pointed it out to her a week ago. He had mentioned it before he tried to kiss her- the almost kiss she really wanted to bring up, but was hoping he would first. So instead, she just looked around the awesome store.

They looked at the CDs, records, journals, posters and merch; they looked at comic books and old fashioned toys. By the end of it, Arabella walked out with two new records, more than she needed, and Gabriel left with a pair of sloth socks... at least she had found out what his favorite animal was. Hers was a dolphin, or at least it used to be- but now, since she found the Clock, she had really grown attached to the idea of snow falcons.

They quickly moved on to Freak Alley, lucky to catch it in the last illuminating rays of daylight. It gave the tucked away nook a magical feel. Freak Alley was an actual alley between 8th Street and Bannock that was also an art gallery. All types of artists were allowed to paint murals on the walls of the alley. It was a coordinated effort and annual event; she was pretty sure there was a waiting list and approval process. The alley even had a store attached that displayed art from past painters and other types of art that couldn't be painted on the walls. She hung back, relishing the look on his face. She had almost forgotten that he was an artist himself. But there was no way anyone could take him for anything else as he stood there gazing appraisingly up at a giant spray painted Bob Dylan, his mouth quirked up into an amazed smile. She took a step back and really looked at him. His matte coal hair was mussed from running his fingers through it. His sparkling green eyes were lit up in appreciation. Long, artistic fingers stained with ink and paint rested in the belt loops of his black jeans, and his denim button-up rustled softly in the wind.

She left him to his musings and wandered around,

taking in the art. Every single inch of the walls were blanketed in paint; there wasn't a single brick that wasn't brightly covered in color. The scenes ranged from strange to haunting; each abstract piece as fascinating as the next. She stopped at one mural that depicted a battlefield. A thousand things popped into her head. She had seen this piece before, and it usually filled her with a detached sadness. But suddenly, it was personal. She wasn't sure if she felt that way because of The Mage who lost his life protecting the world from a war we started, or if the feelings she was having were for her grandmother, who had lived her life fighting the same battle, or if they were for herself and the war she had been thrust into. Or, maybe, they were for her brother, who was gone fighting another battle they had started. She didn't even know where; he had been very vague with their family about his location.

"You okay?" Gabriel gently inquired, standing directly behind her, his fingertips outstretched enough in front of his body that if she leaned back a quarter of an inch, he would be embracing her.

Clearing her throat, she shook the sadness from her eyes. "Yeah, I was just thinking about my brother."

"Is he in the military?" His voice and questions were a soft caress across her skin.

"Yeah, " she muttered, shutting her eyes and clenching her jaw, willing herself not to cry. "I miss him terribly, and I'm terrified for him, for my family, for myself. He was like, my best friend before he left, we were really close when we were young. There's so much I want to tell him, and there's no way I'll know if I can ever utter a single word to him again. I don't know if I'll ever be able to tell him anything ever again, because I don't know when or if I **will** see him again." She couldn't prevent the single trail of silvery tears from escaping down her cheek and dropping gently off her chin, causing a spot on her chest to glisten where they landed.

"...Oh, Arabella." And then he did hug her.

Two things happened: an enraged scream rolled and echoed- ringing through the alleyway, and Gabriel stiffened, pulling swiftly away from Arabella as if he had been burned.

But Gabriel's increasingly frequent mood swings were the last thing on her mind.

"Where do think that came from?" she asked, turning in circles, her eyes sharp, trying to gauge where it could have emanated from.

"Who do you think you are?!" The scream came again, this time in the form of angry shouts of dialogue at the mouth of the alley. "Don't touch me!"

When the latter reached Arabella's ears, she reacted before her mind, before her body, could. Her soul reacted. Turning, she sprinted to the front of the alley and saw a young couple. The girl was struggling against a guy whose hands were entrapping her wrists.

"Cecile! Listen to me; you have to let me explain!" the man shouted, pulling her closer.

"Explain what? You lied to me! Now leave me alone!" She screamed and twisted and turned in his grasp. Arabella had heard enough. "She said to leave her alone!" She started stalking across the street.

"I can't believe this! I trusted you!" The girl started to cry.

"I wasn't cheating on you, Cecile!" he argued back, taking Arabella by surprise. But even so, she kept walking toward them, wanting to get the unwilling girl away from her situation.

"Really? Because you were buying a ring with another girl!" she spat, struggling harder, and fat tears rolled down her youthful cheeks.

"The ring was for you!"

Arabella registered the words at the same time the girl stopped struggling upon hearing the admission.

A horn blared, and in the dusk, a pair of headlights beamed.

"Arabella!" Someone screamed her name like a prayer. The sound of it was ragged and frightened, as if it had been ripped from their throat.

But who she didn't know. Because all her joints had locked, and her jaw had clenched as she realized that she had turned into a deer in the headlights. She closed her eyes, and all that ran through her head was- *of all the stupid ways for me to die.* A violent shove came from her right side instead of straight on, and someone that wasn't her yelled out in pain. In sudden, amazed awareness, she assessed the situation. The young couple now stood clutching each other with hand covered mouths. A green car sat frozen, engine roaring, a horrified driver manning the wheel a shocking 15 feet from her. And Gabriel, the reason that the car was 15 feet away, was right next to her; clutching his leg to his chest, groaning, his face scrunched in pain. *He pushed me out of the way. No. He can't be hurt. He shouldn't have done that for me. Not for me. He can't be hurt. Why did he push me out of the way? Please be okay. I think I...*

Another groan of pain interrupted her thoughts."Gabriel! Oh my gosh!" She rushed to his side, distressed that he had gotten hurt on her behalf. That he had gotten injured at all.

"Where does it hurt?" She tried to ask the question calmly, but her heart was hammering like a jack rabbit's.

"Is he okay?!" The driver that got out was a handsome, middle-aged man in khakis and a T-shirt.

"I don't know!" she snapped, and then cringed apologetically. "That's what I'm trying to find out."

The young couple came over, they had to be about 8 years older than Arabella, about 24 years old she would guess- both brunettes. The girl was tall and lanky, the guy had a similar build and coloring.

"Let's get him out of the road," the guy supplied, grabbing Gabriel under the arms. Arabella moved to gently remove his right leg from where he was clutching it.

"My leg!" Gabriel yelped. Arabella immediately released it and looked to see what had him in so much pain. His black jeans were torn down the side of his calf, and the skin underneath was just as torn. Blood wept from the gash and turned the black denim a darker shade, the scent of iron touched the air.

The nameless guy looked ill. "Should we call 911 or something?" he asked, grimacing at the sight.

The driver went white. "Whatever you need, I'll pay for it. I promise." Sitting back on her heals, Arabella contemplated the situation. She could honestly just call Ember and have the gash fixed right away. But that would entail Gabriel finding out about her secret life, and would most likely put him in danger. Arabella already felt horribly guilty for the car clipping him.

"Gabriel, do you think you can stand?"

Grimacing, he nodded. "I don't know if you noticed, blue eyes, but I'm kind of bleeding out on the road here. If we can somehow stop that, well, that would be awesome. It's kind of a lame impression to make on a first date."

Blushing once more, she cleared her throat and nodded. "Okay, on three, we're going to try and help you up."

"Can I help?" asked a familiar voice behind the bunch. Standing, she turned around, shocked to see Harrison there as if he had been conjured out of thin air.

"Uh, yeah," Arabella replied, affronted at the pale boy's sudden appearance. She felt strangely at odds with herself at him being there with her and Gabriel.

Standing out of the way, she watched in fascination as Harrison and the young man helped Gabriel stand with ease.

"Why don't we get him to your car?" Harrison suggested, holding Gabriel up on the side of his bad leg.

"Right, okay," Arabella breathed, feeling awareness shrink into a small part of her mind.

Harrison smiled kindly at everyone and told them thank you and that they could all go home, that they could take it from there. It was a really nice thing for him to do, and everyone, especially the driver, looked relieved.

Arabella led the way in a dazed haze, watching Harrison gently lower Gabriel into the backseat in the sweetest manner. She didn't offer one snippet of disagreement when Harrison asked for her keys so he could drive.

They drove to the nearest ER. And for a second, it took Arabella a moment to remember why they had to go at all. Because all she could think about was Harrison's long graceful fingers as they gripped her steering wheel and whether or not he played an instrument.

Chapter 12: This Gift of a Burden.

Gabriel was in Hell. His leg burned, and hot blood felt sticky on his skin as his leg alternated between cramping in and out of crippling pain. His back felt like a thousand flames were crawling up every nerve, and there was Arabella, making googly eyes at a guy he absolutely detested. But he couldn't even voice his opinion, because he was constantly trying to stop himself from screaming.

They pulled up to the hospital, and he remembered the first time he had gotten stitches. It was sadly amusing that needing stitches when he was seven from jumping from bed to bed in a hotel room, and then slipping, effectively cutting his head open on the end table, sucked less than right now. *My life is just awesome. Big'ole thumbs up for me. Hurray!*

But back then, he had his mom- her kind smile with pretty smile lines that accented the corners, her big, brown eyes and crazy, dirty blonde hair. She had leaned down and picked him up, stopping his tears with a single nurturing look. His mom had lived life like it was a constant party, and the words she said to him then had always resonated: "don't you know that in order to live by your own rules, you have to accept living with the pain of your choices? Being able to live with the consequences of your actions is the only way to be able to continue living by those rules." And then she had taken him into the hospital.

At the time, he had thought that had meant that

jumping on the bed was totally cool, but he was bound to fall down. Now, he knew it meant that you reap what you sow. That's what she did. She wanted to continue living by her own rules, living in the never setting sun of her partying- traveling the world and never having an Earthly care.

She looked down upon the mundane, looked down on the mothers who made their kids' lunches and joined the neighborhood watch. The pain? Losing your son, who wanted a stable life, a husband, who wanted to be the best father he could be, that should have been painful.

Maybe it was the agony talking, or maybe it was the realization that sometimes, the risk was worth the reward, but suddenly, he wasn't mad at his mother anymore. He knew that she loved him; he saw a new light shed on her motives that he had never seen before. She had known that she was never going to be that mother, the one that went to the PTA meetings and his school showcases. Maybe she had wanted a clean break. She had always hated false hope and hadn't wanted to give him any. He still loved his mom, although the sting would probably never completely go away. But as he thought about his dad, and Cadence- his first real friend in forever, and Arabella, and everyone else who had welcomed him with open arms, he felt stronger than he had in a long time. Less broken and fragile. Belonging. There were so many people that supported him, cared for him and loved him. He knew that he was going to turn out just fine.

Getting the stitches had sucked. Arabella, Harrison and his dad had waited in the hallway. Sitting there with his freshly numbed leg, all he could think about was what the former pair were doing. And if the leg thing would get him out of turning his math homework in tomorrow. And that his dad had been so pissed! He mostly thought about the first thing and the last. His dad had met them at the hospital with a tight-lipped expression that only returned to its proud grin when he was told the story of Gabriel's heroics. He had begun counting the speckles in the floor in an effort to clear those things from his mind and to ignore the feeling of his flesh being sown back together. Tug, pull, tug, pull, tug, pull, tug, pull. *197, 198, 199, 200, 201, 202, 203, 204. And done!* He hopped gingerly off the table, wobbling on his anesthetized appendage.

The doctor gave him some simple instructions on how to care for it. And then it was back to Hell. When he rejoined the group, Harrison had given him a devilish grin, and Arabella had started ignoring him again; she seemed to only have eyes for his nemesis. His back was beginning to hurt again. The pain made him feel mentally ill, not to mention the tattoo- he had to tell Cadence what was going on. Shifting uncomfortably, he mumbled that he was going to the bathroom. He noticed that the farther away he got, the less his back hurt. The moment he returned, his pain rematerialized. His leg was numb, and he briefly considered asking his doctor to do the same to his back, but knew that would attract some unwanted questions. Was Harrison the cause? Was Gabriel somehow allergic to all jerks or just Harrison? He contemplated this conundrum as they helped him walk to his dad's car. But Harrison couldn't be the cause; he wasn't there every time it started hurting.

"Here you go, man," Harrison sneered, helping him into the front seat; he was having trouble walking on his numbed leg. "Thanks." He gritted his teeth, feeling his pain disperse as he got farther away from Arabella, who had lagged behind talking to his dad. "So, after this, are you going to get your car from downtown?"

"Uh, no. I took an Uber, so... I'm just gonna have Arabella take me back home. But, don't worry, we're going to bring your bike to your house."

"Okay," Gabriel stated.

Harrison leaned in closer, his hand on Gabriel's back suddenly felt scalding, and his head felt as if someone was hammering a nail into it. He whispered into his ear, "I told you she was going to cause you a lot of pain. She must drive you crazy. How can you help but hate her?" Leaning back, he let go of Gabriel.. "I hope you feel better."

And suddenly everything made so much sense. And it made him sick.

"So, where are we headed?" Arabella murmured, watching Harrison as he turned further Southeast, winding his way toward Bogus Basin.

"Just wanted to take a little drive," he replied with a debonair grin.

"Okay," she sighed with a smile full of sleepy happiness. She felt like she just needed to close her eyes for a second, but was a little sad that she was so tired; she wanted to watch Harrison forever.

When she woke up, they were stopped, and it was completely dark out. In some hidden corner of her mind, she knew that she should have been afraid. She knew that she should always be afraid of the dark. And of being in the middle of nowhere with a boy she barely knew. But she didn't care. Harrison was next to her, and everything about him made her dizzy. The heat that emanated from his warm gaze, his intoxicating scent that filled the small space of her car, and his smile- his straight, white, perfect smile. An image of bright braces flashed in her mind, but flashed away as swiftly as the thought had come. As if it had never been there at all.

"Where are we?" she whispered, rubbing the sleep from her eyes.

"At the top of Bogus," he murmured back, his rich voice reaching her ears softly.

"I need to text my mom," she blinked, reaching for her phone, feeling detached from the whole experience. "She'll be worried."

"No, she won't," he comforted, almost sounding like he was boasting.

"She won't?" she questioned, dumbfounded.

"No, she knows that you're perfectly safe." He smiled with a cockiness that left Arabella feeling distantly confused.

"That's good," she blinked again.

Any other thoughts about her mother flew from her mind when his arm slid around her in an unfamiliar embrace.

She could feel the beginning of a long-winded ramble perch on the tip of her tongue. Before the first stuttered syllable could fall from her suddenly dry lips, Harrison was kissing her. And it was like a guy who was tall, dark and handsome, with an unhindered smirk and bright green eyes had never existed.

Arabella had worked herself into a tizzy. She was trying to focus, trying to keep Harrison's cognac eyes from worming their way into her vision as she thought of her new boyfriend.

"Arabella! What are you doing?" Ember growled

as she pushed Arabella against the wall with ease.

"I... I... nothing," she stammered, thinking about what Ember's expression would look like if she told her that she was thinking about a boy. Luckily, Rosada and Mika weren't down here; one look at her pink best friend's face would have given her away.

Ember paced as Arabella picked herself up from the floor. The brunette had her hair pulled harshly back, her delicate features and ornate tattoo contrasting greatly with the scowl on her face. "Just get out of here. Go see my grandma or something. What would your grandmother say if she knew your head was this far in the clouds?" she snapped again and left the room in a huff.

The comment was a low blow, and Arabella felt as if she had been slapped in the face. What would her grandmother say? What would her grandfather say?

Taking Ember's advice, she left the training room and walked through the concrete corridors of Ailith's basement. There had been a time when she had wanted to count all the doors, a battle she had quickly given up. She thought about what Ember had said once more. The words raced through her mind like cars on a track, tracing their way on a loop, over and over at an unimaginable pace. This was the last time she would let some guy affect her during practice, during her journey to becoming the Clock Keeper that would make her grandparents proud. A sly grin slid into place. But after school and at home? She thought that would be perfectly acceptable.

Opening the door to the cozy room, with its low lighting and overstuffed chairs, she was surprisingly not surprised to find Ailith in there. Most days, you could find her in the classroom, pouring over the worn texts. Mika would often joke that she would make a good Book Keeper, to which Ailith would reply by throwing a pen with such deadly precision that it would neatly tear a hole in Mika's blouse on the side. She did this without ever once looking up from her leather bound book.

Today was no exception.

Arabella stood awkwardly in the doorway. The only indication that Ailith knew she was there was the cat-like tilt of her head. Shuffling, Arabella sat opposite of Ember's grandmother, who was sitting in the bright green chair. Arabella found herself drawn to the color. She couldn't remember who it reminded her of. But something warm lit in her chest at the sight. Then pale skin and light hair flashed in her mind. *No. No boys. Not here.*

She cleared her throat.

Ailith looked up quizzically from her book. Comically large, round glasses perched on her delicate nose- the glasses reminded Arabella of the 60s. "Yes?" She gave a small, sweetly amused smile.

"I want to know more about who I am. What a Clock Keeper is."

She stood up with warrior-like grace. "Well, fortunately, that's our next lesson," she revealed, kindness shining in her mint green eyes. She walked in front of the blackboard and started writing as she spoke. "Clock Keepers, the Clocks, and the Book Keepers, were created when The Mage died. He wanted to ensure that humanity would be protected. In order to protect and keep the Clocks, he made the Clock Keepers. He set up a number of things to ensure their safety and that we would have the tools required."

All of that made sense to Arabella, and she was prepared to learn more- it was funny, she almost felt as if she should be taking notes.

"The tools he gave us are: our animal counterparts, which correlate with our tattoos; our Imprint weapons, which are tied to the metal and stone specific to each Clock, and therefore, its Keeper; and our Anam Caras."

Arabella Grace kept her promise to herself by keeping her mouth shut and settled back further in her seat.

"As you may recall, there are four types of Clock Keepers, each guarding a specific Clock. Each Clock safeguards a characteristic of humanity- The Mage was trying to ensure that humanity could never go so far off the deep end again. The Love Clock is the root of all emotion. You will find that everything you feel is born of love, even- no especially- hate. The War Clock is the primal need to fight for survival, for the betterment of humanity, to expand, to change, and to keep your beliefs. All of the things worth fighting for. The Knowledge Clock is the ever present need to strive to learn, grow, and know about the world around us and beyond. The Guardian Clock is the need, the basic need, to protect what you have, your family, your home. Each Clock is unique, and looks completely different from the others. The Clocks are made of types of stone and metal that are linked to our animal counterparts. Metals and precious stones have inherent powers that balance out and enhance our own powers. They are created in the Earth, and bind us to it, but have otherworldly properties as well. It is no accident that your Clock is a wristwatch made of silver with a leather strap, or that it's decorated with wings and nacre, or mother of pearl, inlay around the face. Mine- I mean Ember's- is also a wristwatch, and is made of copper. It has a glass cat eye cut into the garnet and ruby. The band is made of interlocking copper, instead of leather like yours."

Arabella studied her Clock in the warm lighting. Its face shone brightly and glinted off the walls. The wings were sharp and sleek, so well designed that they could almost be real. The pink, puckered scar on her palm reminded her of how sharp they were. It was beautiful and deadly. A weapon all its own. They were their own protection.

Ailith kept talking, a wisp of a smile on her face. It

was as if the remnants of a bittersweet memory were playing across her expression. "The Knowledge Clock is a pocket watch made of dark chrome, with a snake slithering up the front. The inside holds a simple face. Practical. But in the chain, there's a yellow stone, malachite, woven through, mixing with the metal. The Love Clock is also a pocket watch. It's made of white gold, and a dragonfly graces its casing; there's amethyst along the edge of the face. It's a mesmerizing piece. Delicate and strong. Completely alluring."

Ailith stopped, as if to check that Arabella was still with her. She was not only with her, but was completely enthralled. This was her family's legacy. This was the power that thrummed inside her, pacing like a caged animal preparing to be released. And this was her, learning to set it free.

Satisfied with her bewitched expression, Ailith pressed on. "The Clock's power isn't fused to you yet. That's why, physically, you can't take it off. The power isn't completely yours yet. Once you complete The Trials, you'll be completely bonded to it."

"And then I'll be able to take it off?" Arabella asked in a semi-desperate plea. She'd had an itch right where the Clock was fastened ever since she had put it on. It was, frankly, driving her nuts. She almost wanted to try to get a screwdriver under the thing.

"No," Ailith chuckled. "After you bond with your

Anam Cara, then you'll be able to take it off."

"I can only take it off once I find my soulmate?" Arabella narrowed her eyes after she rolled them. "Sure, that should just be so easy. How peachy," she scoffed, but a thought was rising in her mind. Before it fully developed, it was squashed, and she had forgotten what it was that she was thinking about at all. Suddenly, Harrison's sparkling smile flashed, and she frowned to herself. She needed to focus on Ailith. But..if she had found her soulmate, she would realize it, right? Harrison being her soulmate was completely impossible. Sure, he made her feel breathless and dizzy. Whenever he was around, her world seemed to shrink until all that mattered was him. But it couldn't be him. As much as he enthralled her, there was something in her soul that said no. But maybe...ah, now was seriously not the time to think about her newfound love life.

"In essence- yes." Ailith gave a small smile and hurried to explain, moving from where she leaned back to her chair. "You need the Anam Cara to split the power, because once the Clock fuses to you... it can be rather intense, to say the least. Plus, once the magic is shared like that, in that kind of commitment, it almost guarantees that it's safe. Once that happens, it can be taken off."

"Okay." Arabella nodded, worrying her nails. A pained expression crossed Ailith's face.

"But back to the Clocks. If a Clock's hands are ever stopped, time will slow. I'm not kidding, Arabella: this must never be allowed to happen, because once all four Clocks' hands are stopped... time actually stops. It's not just humanity that's at risk if the Clocks fail. It's everything. The very fabric that weaves this universe together will collapse. That's why you need to take this seriously."

The sudden mood change threw Arabella. But it was understandable that with something this important, you couldn't, she couldn't, joke around or take it lightly. Dread built in her stomach. Arabella used to think that time moving on without her was her worst fear. Now she realized that it was the thought of it stopping entirely. "I will never allow that to happen," she promised fiercely.

Ailith searched her eyes, looking for a hint of wavering, and making sure that this wasn't all just for Arabella's sister that she wanted to be tasked with this gift of a burden. But there wasn't a hint of doubt. Arabella's usually soft blue eyes were hard with steely determination. "Another piece of advice: if someone wears the Clock and they're not a Keeper-"

"They'll die in a burning ball of fire?" Arabella guessed, feeling a little morbid..but hey, it was the first thing to pop to mind, and sometimes she really didn't have a filter.

Ailith stared at her with wide eyes for a second. Then she shook her head, strands of silver hair catching the light as she chuckled. "Um... no." She rolled her eyes and absently rubbed at her wrist. "If they take the Clock and they're not a Keeper, the magic won't fuse to them. So the powers will lay dormant."

"Okay, then why can I use the powers if the Clock hasn't fused to me?"

A simple twinkle lit her eyes. "Arabella, it's in your blood. The residue left is enough to kick start your powers. But even now, you're not the strongest you're going to be, not the fastest, nor the sharpest; and you're not going to be able to fly as high and as far as you want to."

I was made for this, she thought.

"Anyway, if someone would stop interrupting..." cue pointed stare. "We could finally get to the point. The power of the Clock is more of an abstract concept. It doesn't give power to the wearer. It's a pure entity; it unlocks and bonds with the powers the bearer already has. It enables that aspect of humanity to be controlled. That kind of control will eventually kill a wrongful wearer, but if that person is strong enough, they could cause some real damage before that happens. Not to mention The Warlock, who would be strong enough to handle one.

In order to protect these parts of humanity, we were given a number of weapons- our Imprints, which we will actually have a lesson on later. But basically, they're the weapons connected to the Clock Keepers bloodlines. The metals and stones in your weapons can also conduct magic. They were forged to be deadly and strong.

The animal counterparts are another weapon, and a

way for the Anam Cara to expend energy. You can only tap into a small part of the animal, while your soulmate can actually become it. The tattoos are how we access the powers from these animal counterparts. All power has some kind of price. They're the physical representation."

"How does that work?" Arabella asked, confused. "I mean, I got mine done by, like, a regular tattoo artist."

There was a mischievous glint in Ailith's eye. "And how did you learn about that tattoo artist?"

"It was in my grandma's Will..." Arabella said slowly. The whole thing had been an ordeal, understandably. Shock and grief had made the world loose and bleak, details vague and lines blurred. The ink on paper blotted with tears.

Now that smile had a twinge of bitter to its sweet. "The tattoo will either appear, slowly, when you turn 16, or you can get it done by a Book Keeper. I assume, knowing Axelia, that she was trying to protect you from the shock of finding the tattoo."

"Was there a reason I had to have it in white ink? Why are yours and Ember's as well?"

"The white represents one side of a coin. Balance, remember? The Anam Caras have Black ink for their tattoos. It symbolizes that you are each other's other halves. As you know, the Guardian Clock Keeper's tat is of a snow falcon's wings- your animal- it unlocks your ability to fly. The War Clock Keeper has the outline of a cat, as you've seen on Ember and myself." She tucked her hair behind her ear and stuck out her chin proudly. "Instead of one big thing, like flying, I...Ember, has several things that are feline in nature. Sight, hearing, reflexes, smell, and the ability to heal minor wounds, bruises, and cuts."

Arabella nodded, impressed, but couldn't stop herself. "I have two questions: one- how can she heal herself and others? I'm pretty sure cats can't do that. And two- what would her Anam Cara turn into?"

Ailith supplied, "cats can actually heal themselves through purring. Before the Clock bound itself to her, she could only heal herself. But ever since, the power has become amplified by the Clock, she can now heal herself and others too. And her Anam Cara turns into a snow leopard."

"That's pretty sweet," she mused and leaned back deeper in her chair, practically lounging.

"Very," she agreed and got back to business. The Love Clock Keeper's tattoo is a Dragonfly, in the same white ink, on the left hand- more specifically, on the ring finger. It has a strong influence over peoples' emotions, not permanently, but it is powerful." Her face tightened. "The Knowledge Clock Keeper is a white snake wound around the right ankle- it enables the power of camouflage, unless someone knows they're there. And they are ridiculously fast. I think they can move about ten feet per eye blink." She paused for a moment before adding, "that really covers most of what you need to know about the Clocks." She gave a sweet smile.

"Arabella, that's who you are. You're a part of the third generation of Clock Keepers. Arabella blinked in shock at the familiar words.

"Oh, like the prophecy I found?"

Now it was Ailith's turn to blink. "What prophecy?"

Shaking her head, Arabella started braiding her hair. "The prophecy I found on the box holding my Imprint and Clock?" Her head hurt, like she was trying to piece together a particularly difficult puzzle.

"What?" Ailith stared at her with wide green eyes. Arabella described how she found the box and recited the passage. For some reason, the words came easily.

"That clever old man," she chuckled, "The Mage must have put a spell on it so the text would materialize in your generation." She enunciated clearly and deliberately, working it out as she spoke out loud. Ember, who had snuck in during the last part of the lesson and had been silent against the wall for once, stood up stick straight as Ailith abruptly turned and addressed her. Calculation filled the brunette's hazel gaze. "Ember, go and get the box that held your guns and Clock."

When Ember returned with her maple wood box,

they all witnessed that the garnet and ruby inlay that adorned the top was interwoven with a continued verse of the prophecy in delicate copper cursive:

Love will prevail once temptation stirs.

Through it all, silver wings, fiery eyes, and purple light

will fight through The Shadows and the night.

Only to discover a bigger surprise.

"It's been years since I've looked at this box," Ailith whispered, "I have to tell the Book Keepers."

Chapter 13: Nearly Demons.

Her lessons started to pass in a blur of information. She learned everything she could. She felt like she was getting better at all of it. Her fighting skills, her knowledge- it all made her feel empowered. The fact that she was learning it all for Kat made her feel even more so. She had completed almost all of her lessons. And they had all really stuck in her head. Especially the one about The Warlock, which had kept her in horrified silence. As did learning about The Shadows... and, as much as it hurt, she loved learning about her grandmother...

"The Warlock is the dark to the light," Ailith started, her voice grave. "He is the brother of The Mage. He truly did love his brother in his dark and twisted way. Perhaps he just loved the idea of him. Perhaps he took comfort in the knowledge that there would always be someone out there to challenge him. Before The Mage's sacrifice, he had merely made humans his play things. But now..." She took a quick inhale of breath and Arabella felt that it was all coming too fast. Too fast. "He hates them, hates us. He has always been evil, and relishes further influencing the darkness in our own world. All throughout history, you can find echoes of his presence. Hiding in the shadows, he had- has- the power to implant thoughts and ideas, slowly driving people mad. To make matters worse, he is a devil in disguise of sorts. Sometimes, the most beautiful things in life can cut us the deepest. As

Shakespeare said, all that glitters is not gold. He is a deceiver, and can hide in plain sight as our deepest desire and want." A pained expression crossed her face before she continued her whispered chant, like she was afraid someone might overhear. "He was the corrupter of human emotions. He filled the people that worshipped him, worshipped his charm and beauty, with greed. He would prey on the ones who were the easiest targets, those who already craved power."

"So, he wants to destroy us?" Arabella asked, feeling fear rear its head, but she couldn't be afraid- not now, not ever.

"No. He needs us now. We feed into his power. We make him stronger. If he destroyed us, he'd have no more puppets.

The ones who are corrupted become The Shadows. They crave, hunger, for power. They are the essence of destruction and decay. Their souls have become so blackened, they bleed their darkness from the inside out."

"That's what Ember and I saw?" Arabella thought of the soul-less nearly-demons, with twisted limbs and featureless faces.

"Yes." She nodded grimly. "They are also," she inhaled deeply, "what killed my son, Ember's father. And her mother." She cleared her throat, red rimming her eyes. "They're what killed your grandmother as well. I'm sorry."

Arabella felt like the breath had been stolen from

her lungs. She stood up, wanting to destroy something, anything. She could feel an icy hot chill spread from the tips of her shoulder blades to her clenched fists. Turning swiftly, she brought one of them up and put her hand through the wall. Stone flew; she hardly acknowledged the biting pain of her split knuckles and possibly broken fingers. She turned, breathing like an enraged beast. Which she might have been. She expected Ailith to look horrified, maybe even disgusted. But instead, her face was laced with understanding. She gently walked over and took Arabella's hand. Warmth flooded her as Ailith's faded tattoo glowed a dull red. Arabella watched as her skin knit back together and she felt everything pop back into place.

"See, even having the residue of the power is enough."She chuckled weakly. "The Shadows are drawn to power. Most of the time we can hide it, but there are a few times when the Clock's power isn't masked by our protection. When it's just too powerful."

"When?"

"When a Keeper comes into power at 16. They almost always show up, or around that time. It's also common for them to show up when there's more than two Clocks together and one of them is unbound to its Keeper." She seemed to search for the right explanation. "It's like it amplifies the other's power because it's trying to latch on to its stability."

She thought of her and Ember's run-in with

them. "But, I don't.." She failed for words. "There weren't any Shadows when I turned 16, and I'm still unbound, why haven't they come here?"

"They can't come here, because I had wards placed on the house, your house, and your school by the Book Keepers. When you're out and about by yourself or with friends, Ember isn't with you, and you are far enough past your coming of age, you should be safe. Are you sure there hasn't been anything? No sign of The Shadows?"

She thought back to it, to the terrifying dream.

"Well, there were a couple of dreams, and one seemed so real... but it was just a dream."

Ailith gave a bitterly knowing smile. "The Warlock's power is to play with perception. If it was a dream, it was probably he who planted it there, but you didn't have the Clock then, did you?"

"No. I didn't."

"The Clock power protects us from The Warlock as much as we protect it from him. It creates something similar to the ward, it shields us from him. That's why you are supposed to be bound to the Clock when you turn 16- you weren't able to. If he had found you before you were bound, he should have, would have, killed you."

She thought of the horrifying figure and its dark, cackling laugh. "Why didn't he kill me?"

Ailith reflected for a moment, clearly analyzing

what she knew about strategy- she had never looked more like Ember than in that moment. "I don't know."

The uncertainty scared Arabella more than anything.

"The Trials..." Ailith started humming to herself as she sorted through loose papers strewn across her desk, "... are how you prove your worth as a Clock Keeper."

Arabella nodded, understanding that already, ready to find out what type of beast she would truly be up against. Her mind unwillingly started to dissolve once again into the happy fog it had been in since she had started dating Harrison. Who wanted to think about or do anything else when they had found the love of their life? He intoxicated her, made it where the only thing she wanted to to do was spend time with him. Her lessons were the exception; something inside of her kept pushing her toward them. Maybe it was the image of Kat's face, or maybe it was Ember's words, or maybe it was the memory of her grandma's smile. Whatever it was, it kept her on the path of a Clock Keeper, and allowed her to shut Harrison out of her mind, at least for a little while- not that she'd want to for long. Yet, for some reason, it seemed like the only time she wasn't completely consumed by thoughts of him was when she was at Ailith's house. Her head felt almost clear, at least, clear enough to work. "What exactly are The Trials? How am I to prove myself?"

Ailith considered her question, tilting her head from side to side, her long hair shining and shimmering like liquid mercury. Her pale green eyes studied Arabella. It was as if she was wondering how much of the truth pill Arabella could digest. "The Trials are a study of character. The Book Keepers have designed a test that perfectly challenges you and assesses if you have all of the qualities necessary to be a Clock Keeper." She presented a sweet smile that made Arabella warm with the feeling of approval. "Personally, I feel that you posses all the qualities of a Keeper, your grandma would be proud."

Her eyes stung as she accepted the compliment with a tight throat, "thank you."

Ailith cleared her own throat and spoke roughly. "The attributes are Intelligence- including understanding of the supernatural world, optimism, helpfulness, bravery, kindness, loyalty, confidence, love, and forgiveness. You'll do wonderfully."

Arabella hoped so, for it wasn't just her own noose that would tighten with her failure. She tried to picture The Trials, the feelings, who she was as a person. She liked to think she could achieve all of the above, but worry gnawed at her soul. "And if I fail?"

A regretful sigh filled the lantern-lit room.

"First, you'll be stripped of your powers." She

paused, taking in Arabella's flinch. Taking away her spark would be like taking Ga-...Harrison away, and he was her life. Ailith continued with a steadiness that reminded Arabella that she had been the former Clock Keeper of War. "The power would be given to the next available female in your bloodline; it wouldn't have to be a close relative, just a female of the same heritage. Until then, the eldest third generation Clock Keeper," she paused once more, "Ember, would safeguard the Clock, since the best candidate in your bloodline is Kat, and she isn't of age yet."

Arabella's jaw clenched, her muscles tightening and teeth groaning. Kat was gentle, sweet. She was a bright light. When Arabella was in the supernatural world, it made her come alive, made her light shine even brighter. But somehow she knew that the burden would just dim her sister's shine. Arabella Grace knew she wanted to be a Clock Keeper, but she also knew that even more than that, she was doing this because she wanted to protect her sister. "I will pass The Trials." She spoke firmly. Recognition flashed in Ailith's eyes as she saw a strength similar to her own.

"I know." There wasn't a hint of doubt. "The Trials are about finding out that your virtues match the Clock. Once you finish The Trial, your magic will fuse to the Clock."

"But I won't be able to take it off until I'm bound

to my Anam Cara?" Arabella asked, wondering why she felt hollow at words that should excite her.

"Yep." Ailith gave a hesitant smile, and Arabella could tell they were both eager to change the subject.

"Where does The Trial take place?" She pictured traveling to some far off, secret land.

"It will be done right here in Boise, but not just anywhere, I'll summon the Anacora, and it will take place there."

"The Anacora?" Arabella played with the unfamiliar word as it rolled off her tongue.

"It's a gateway or checkpoint between this world and the supernatural one." She smiled like she was sharing an inside joke.

"The worlds are separate?" Arabella pictured a world below her own, a secret society.

"Yes, some creatures prefer to live in the human world, but most live in an almost separate dimension. Their world is just like ours, but it's like there's a curtain separating the two. There's a veil, and they're not behind it, but in it, and that veil is right on top of our world."

Arabella's brow furrowed and a breath escaped in a long-winded laugh. Ailith stared at her, startled, and Arabella was relieved that Ember had been too mad to join this lesson. Then, spitting the words out in the same hoarse tone, she roared, "that's fantastic!"

"Really?" Ailith's look of confusion deepened, and

she ran a hand over her face.

"It just makes so much sense, and I'm so extremely happy to find out that there's more out there. I can't wait to learn more. It's like everything just clicked. Now tell me more about this gate."

"The Anacora is represented in the form of a house. You go through the front door in this world, and if you exit out the back of the house, you'll be in the veil. But what's truly special about it, is that any room can be used for whatever it is you need."

"Like the room of requirements?" Arabella asked excitedly.

"What..." she started, perplexed, and then as her expression cleared, it turned flat, and her voice was dry. "From *Harry Potter*?" She seemed to consider it and an amused expression hinted on her face. "I suppose."

"Awesome," Arabella breathed, eyes alight.

"If you think that's awesome, then you'll be even more excited to find out that while the Book Keeper council, myself, Mika, Rosada and Ember will be watching in the Anacora, the actual Trial will take place in a pocket dimension that the Book Keepers control. Everything will be based on your own mental suggestions- your desires and fears. "

"Yep, that's pretty cool," she concluded, blown away.

She dodged the spear by pivoting her body to the side and promptly swallowed the lump of coal in her throat. The next spear was much closer to hitting its mark and tore a hole straight through the hem of her shirt. She had just bought this black T-shirt, because the same thing happened to the last one.

"Come on Arabella, you can do better than that!" Ember taunted; she was in one of her rare good moods. Unfortunately, when Ember was in a good mood, it usually meant that Arabella was going to be worked extra hard. Ember hollered and cackled from the sidelines as Rosada threw another spear, this one aimed at Arabella's head. Letting her instincts take over as she was taught, Arabella ducked quickly. In one smooth motion, she grabbed the spear embedded in the padded wall next to her and threw it at Ember. Dodging easily, Ember clucked her tongue at Arabella mockingly.

"Arabella! We've talked about this; you need to stay focused," Mika called authoritatively. She also stood on the sidelines, blowing on her snazzy yellow whistle to stop the match.

"She needs to leave!" Arabella pointed, exasperated, to said person who needed to leave, "she is not helping!" Neither are these dizzying thoughts about Harrison, she admitted to herself, but she wasn't going to tell Mika that. She wasn't going to say that the boy's eyes haunted her throughout her lessons, not as bad as when she was outside of Ailith's house, but enough to leave her slightly distracted and her thoughts murky.

Mika took a deep breath as they went down this road again, "in the real world-" she started, but was cut off.

"There are distractions, I know. But I doubt any of the distractions are as annoying as her," Arabella huffed.

"Okay," Mika dejectedly slumped her shoulders in defeat, "let's take five and have a small water break," she gestured widely to the room before spinning on her toes and gliding out the door, but not before giving Rosada a pointed look. Ember promptly followed her, something Arabella was grateful for. Stepping off the wrestling pad, Arabella went over to the taped sidelines to grab her water bottle from her bag. Beside her purple bag sat a pink one.

"You know, you shouldn't let her get to you," Rosada said, searching through her own bag for a water.

"I know, and I really do try to just brush her off, but something about her just gets under my skin, ya know?" She took a quick swig from her green water bottle.

"Well, just look at it this way, you two are complete opposite ends of the spectrum of humanity. She's the Clock Keeper of War- the offense, and you're the Clock Keeper of Protection- the defense."

"So, what your saying is that this is all just one big sporting event?" she snickered.

"Yep, the Clock Keeper of Knowledge is the coach, and the Clock Keeper of Love is the die-hard, screaming fan that hides in the team bus after the game," Rosada concluded, straight faced, causing both her and Arabella to break out in hysterical fits of laughter.

"That's so Rosada of you, Rosada," Arabella joked, coming down from a never ending bout of belly laughing.

"Why, thank you," she purred and brushed her bright pink hair out of her face. Rosada Nasima, or Rosie as Arabella sometimes affectionately called her, was the only thing that kept Arabella sane- well mostly sane. She was an energetic sports nut who was obsessed with anything and everything pink. That was probably because she **was** pink. Well, at least her eyes were. Rosie was a Simper Nimph, like her mother. So, she, like all Simper Nimph, as Arabella had come to learn, could alter anything about her appearance on a whim, except for their eyes. The species' eyes could never change, for no two Simper Nimphs had the same colored eyes. It was the only thing in their appearance that was permanent. Rosada's eyes just happened to be a rosy hue. She really did adore the color. Mix in her big attitude, and the fact that she could tell you every statistic about almost every sport team or athlete ever, and she could wrap just about anybody around her tiny, but strong, finger. Even Arabella's best friend wasn't immune, it seemed. When the red headed boy had stopped by her house the night before to find out why Arabella had missed all their plans that week, she had guiltily lied and said it was because she was tutoring Rosada, when in reality it was the other way around. He had appeared to be instantly and openly smitten.

Speaking of reality, Arabella was being called back to it by the sound of Mika blowing her whistle.

"Ready for gymnastics practice with Little Miss Military?" Rosada whispered to Arabella as they both quickly sat on the blue mat and began stretching.

She gave a little snort in response to Rosie's question and continued to pull on her feet, her hair irritatingly falling in her face from where it had come loose from her pony tail.

"What happened last time? She gave you a black eye, didn't she?" Rosada teased.

"It's not funny!" she whispered back sharply before sighing in defeat. "Yes, she did," she confirmed somberly, blowing hair out of her face again.

"That's brilliant!" Rosie barked out, laughing uncontrollably. "Well, at least she can heal it after she breaks it."

Arabella shrugged and muttered, "that still doesn't change how much it hurts when it happens." She finally gave up on keeping her hair down and pulled it up into a low ponytail.

"Okay, that's enough stretching, girls! It's time for

practice. Rosada, you can go practice knife throwing," Mika declared and pointed to the row of dummies on the opposite wall from Arabella and her daughter. She then gave Rosada a look that Arabella couldn't decipher. It was happening more and more- the closer Arabella and Rosada became, the harsher Mika was.

"My specialty!" Rosada beamed and practically skipped over to her favorite training area.

They were in Ailith's maze of a basement once more. Its numerous rooms now familiar, the secrets it held were a well-kept friend. The training room bubbled around her. *I've changed,* she thought in full surprise. But what surprised her more was that the room hadn't. But maybe that was because she had done most of her changing in it. The three padded walls were no longer a foe. She knew how to use them as an ally and how to avoid receiving their fabric tattoos. Now she could name, and use, almost all of the shining instruments of destruction that hung invitingly against the wall of death, and the silicon dummies that stood like toy soldiers could attest to that- with the new tears and rips in their gummy armor to prove it. Similarly, the gymnastics room was now a mountain she was able to climb. She could now leave it with a semblance of dignity, instead of just leaving with screaming ligaments. But all of it still paled in comparison to the comfort she felt in the classroom. Its lantern lighting and hugging walls gave the impression of a safety she had long since forgotten. It was where she could could focus the most, where she could block Harrison from the foreground of her mind. He was sooo amazing- and that was distracting.

She refocused on the present as she greedily gulped the cold water from her bottle for a minute too long. She had been doing an exhausting weight lifting routine that left her lack of upper body muscles sore.

Mika stood, with whistle in hand, looking dangerously close to blowing it. "Arabella, first you have acrobatics training with Ember for thirty minutes."

Arabella groaned, her bones and muscles aching with a hollow agony.

Mika only acknowledged the shuddering sound of pain with a raise of her perfectly formed eyebrow. "After that, you have a choice. You can either, A: go to the classroom with Ailith, or B: do some mixed martial arts practice, also with Ember," Mika finished. When the second option came around, December gave Arabella an especially bone-chilling smile and cracked her knuckles- as if on cue.

"I think I'm going to have my lesson with Ailith," she decided, wide eyed, in fervent self denial of her nerves.

"Coward!" Rosada called, throwing another knife

dead center into the dummy's head. Ember simply shrugged, but Arabella knew she would pay for it later. Ember wanted to make Arabella the most capable she could be, no matter the cost.

Chapter 14: Some Super Secret Ninja Stuff.

Turned out she was right. Ember had made up for it during their acrobatics session. Arabella swayed, nauseated and feeling the desire to empty the contents of her stomach into the toilet at her feet. Because someone *cough* had thought it would be a good idea for Arabella to attempt three backflips while Mika went to check on Rosie. Without her there to save her, Arabella had been at Ember's mercy, with no way to stop the world from swirling out of control. Arabella willed herself not to be sick. She breathed deeply through her nose and ignored the acidic taste and burn at the back of her throat. If she upchucked, she would just be exhausted afterward and unable to go on her date with Harrison later. She swore on The Mage that she would kill Ember if that happened. Arabella blinked, startled to realize she had almost completely meant the sentiment.

"Okay, that's enough, cupcake!" Ember called through the bathroom door.

Arabella sluggishly stalked to the baby blue countertop, steadied herself, and threw some water on her face. She stared into the antique mirror, the white paint on the frame was faded and flaking; water dripped off the roundish chin of her 16 year old baby face. Her normally bright blue eyes looked muted and exhausted, and heavy bags betrayed her late nights of sword practice that she would often engage in instead of homework. Her rosy red lips dipped down at the corners in a slight frown, and her skin seemed even more ashen than usual, giving her heated cheeks an undesirable flushed and ruddy appearance. What would Harrison think if he saw her like this?

An annoyed tap rapped harshly against the door again. She opened the lime green door. The bathroom in the basement was done in the same random and strange assortment of colors as the rest of the house.

"You know, I have a question for you," Arabella started, glaring at Ember, clearly irritated.

Ember raised one eyebrow. "And that would be?" she quipped, staring blankly at her, her smug expression a permanent fixture on her striking features.

Arabella walked out of the bathroom and into the hallway. "Were you held as a child? If not, that would explain a lot." She grimaced at the unbidden words that flew harshly from her mouth. Yet she couldn't regret them as much as she would've if the onslaught had been aimed at someone else.

"Yes, I was held. But I don't see the point in niceties, or anything as trivial as sugar-coated words, or cultivating relationships. All love gets you is hate, and hate destroys you from the inside out." She spat, turned on her heal, and stalked down the hallway.

Arabella stared after her with less exasperation than usual and maybe a twinge of pity. She truly believed that to love was to destroy?

"You know, you shouldn't be so quick to judge

her," remarked a voice from behind Arabella.

"Holy Hades, don't do that!" Arabella exclaimed, holding one hand to her pounding heart and the other reaching for where her sword usually hung at her hip; she spun to look at the older woman.

"I'm sorry to startle you, my dear," Ailith laughed softly, "but that doesn't make what I said any less true."

Arabella crossed her arms firmly over her chest and was happily surprised to find them more defined than they were a mere week before. "Why? That's all she does to me. She criticizes me and makes fun of me. She's bitter and unpleasant- why?" Arabella ranted, questioning Ailith with wide, tired eyes.

Ailith gave a watery laugh, "my granddaughter wasn't always like this. She wasn't. She was sweet and loving. She was so full of life; you remind me a lot of her."

Arabella snorted at that.

"You may not believe me, but it's true. But she changed," Ailith trailed off sadly and rubbed tiredly at her cheek.

"Her parents passed away, right? Shadows?" Arabella couldn't help but question, rubbing a finger sleepily under her right eye before recrossing her arms defensively.

"Yes, Shadows." She closed her eyes tightly, shielding herself from the sadness. Ailith took a sharp and painful intake of breath and Arabella winced at the sound.

"When Ember received her Clock, she knew what it was. She had always known what it was. Your grandmother chose to wait to expose you to this world, while I chose to train Ember from birth. She grew up knowing that the most important thing in this world was her mission: fighting to maintain the delicately balanced order The Mage had created. There was one day between her receiving and her Trials. One day before she was bound to the Clock. It was enough. She wore the Clock on her 16th birthday, but she had plans to celebrate with a friend and wanted to wait to get bonded; she didn't think The Shadows would be so fast, would find her that quickly." Ailith paused, a broken sob seemed to choke her, "when she came home, her parents...my son... they were gone. Ember swore from that day on that she would never put anything above the Clock- not friends, not feelings, not love. She wants you to do the same, she needs you to protect your Clock," Ailith finished with silver tears streaming down her face. She gave Arabella a quick nod and then exited the halls and headed up the stairs. She paused at the top step, still crying. "That's why my granddaughter is the way she is... Why don't you go home Arabella, just for today." She flashed her a reassuring smile that left a bad taste in Arabella's mouth.

Arabella was at her house with Rosie. They were

rushing out of the door to leave, because training started in 10. *Frak*! They were going to be in so much trouble.

"Rosie, hurry your skinny butt up! We need to leave, or we're going to be late!" she called from the kitchen, knowing that Rosie was in Arabella's room, presumably changing clothes. At least, she hoped she was changing and not playing with Arabella's two dogs. Rosie had an obsession with the two 'fluff balls'. They were alone, because Arabella's parents and sister were at her sister's school's annual winter fundraiser. So she could be as loud as she wanted.

Or at least, they were supposed to be home alone. Suddenly, someone asked, "going to be late to where?" Arabella did two things- the first one was awesome, the second one- not so much. The first thing she did was nail whoever had spoken with a wickedly fast spin kick. The second thing she did was scream.

"Holy crap! Where did you learn to do that?" moaned Cade, laying on the kitchen floor, clutching his face in pain.

"Cadence!" Arabella exclaimed and rushed over to her friend. "I am so, so sorry!" She was horrified when she realized that she had bloodied his nose.

And that's when Rosada came in. "What did you do?" she questioned in alarm. She was now wearing black yoga pants and a black T-shirt like Arabella's, instead of her pink sundress. Her bright pink hair was up in a messy bun.

I accidentally spun..spin..kicked my friend's face," Arabella confessed, grabbing some paper towels from near the sink and handing them to said friend who was now sitting up and tilting his head back. The blood coming from his nose was the same color as his hair.

"Spin kicked," she supplied, quirking a pink eyebrow at Arabella. "Well, at least we know those lessons are paying off," she retorted while chancing a glance, not-so-shamelessly, at Cadence. "How did he even get in?" She leaned against the counter and looked almost bored (or at least, she tried to).

Arabella arched her own blonde eyebrow, considering it. "That's a good question." Arabella turned to Cadence, who was now mostly blood free.

"I used my key. That your mom had you give me. When we were 5," he concluded, looking at Arabella in a way that clearly conveyed- 'is that a crime now?'

"Right. I... duh," Arabella flushed with shame, feeling frazzled.

Rosada merely gave her a bemused look while shooting another quick glance at Cade- one that Arabella by no means missed.

Cade gave an understandably frustrated sigh, "well you gave it to me. I just don't use it often. I'm only using it now because I'm trying to figure out what's up with you."

"What do you mean, what's up with me?" Arabella asked, cringing.

"Well, I'm not sitting on the floor for fun," he pointed out. "But I've worked it out now," he triumphed, still wiping blood from his nose. "You have?" Both Arabella and Rosada deadpanned in shock.

"Yeah, you're taking lessons from the pink ninja here. Glad to see you again. Sick contacts by the way." He pointed in her direction and stood up to lean against the counter next to her. Rosada blushed big time, her cheeks almost the same color as her eyes and hair, then mumbled, "thank you." Her eyes glanced away from Cade and focused on a black spot on the granite countertop like it was the most interesting thing on Earth.

Arabella mumbled, "oh yeah, you know me, ninja-ing it up." She gave a nervous laugh, her blush deepening. Thank goodness he was too busy 'talking' *cough* flirting with Rosie to notice her poor excuse of a lie.

The pair were busy laughing together about something, and don't think that Arabella didn't catch Rosada give him her number. "Well, like I said, if Arabella ever hurts you again, don't be afraid to call me. I'll protect you," she heard Rosie laugh out loud. Just like that, she knew Cade had fallen for her rose colored friend, enchanted by her lilting Spanish accent.

This is way too weird, was all that raced through her mind as she awkwardly scratched at the back of her neck. "Okay, well, it's nice to see that you two are hitting it off, but Rosada, we really need to go." She cleared her throat, and the couple jumped back from nose touching distance like they had just noticed how close they had been.

"Right, Arabella's right. We need to go," Rosie echoed, stepping away from him and looking sad just to say it.

"Go where?" he asked dreamily- his blue eyes glazed over sweetly. He cleared his throat. "I mean, where are you guys going?" he inquired further in a more serious tone.

"We have some super secret ninja stuff to take care of," Arabella answered quickly, not putting it past Rosada at this point to tell the truth.

"I'm assuming that's the same excuse you'll use when I ask why you missed Diana's going away party?" Cadence spoke with barely contained fury, losing any schoolboy charm that he had previously portrayed.

"Diana, what?" Arabella questioned, her heart sinking.

"Her going away party." He spoke slowly. "Her Dad got a new job in Europe, and they had to move- she told us, like, two weeks ago." He gave a deep sigh and dragged oil stained fingers down his freckled face. "I know with what happened to your grandparents, you've been out of it. I'm out of it. I miss them too."

Arabella flushed at that. Cadence's adoptive grandparents had never taken to him like his adoptive parents had. Her grandparents had been all too happy to fill that void, dragging him to the movies and baseball games along with Arabella.

"But, I can't help but feel like something's weird. Let me in. What's going on in that gypsy brain of yours?" He sounded so defeated. This was her best friend, her brother, and she was giving him the cold shoulder. She opened her mouth, prepared to tell him.

Then he said, "it's not Harrison, is it? Because I thought you liked Gabriel, but you haven't so much as mentioned him for a while, and he's acting weird. If Harrison's being controlling, or... just tell me what's happening."

Arabella's mouth snapped shut. Her eyes turned flat, the sympathy in her irises vanished. "Look Cadence, we have to go. See you later." She couldn't believe he would say that, and who was this Gabriel guy he was talking about? She briefly remembered a guy with laughing green eyes, but the memory was gone with the next intake of breath. She grabbed a strangely silent Rosie's hand and hauled tail out of the house. She shook her head, all anger disappearing, wondering what had just happened between the two of them.

Once they were half way up the road in Arabella's car- her little baby blue Bug- Rosada spoke. "It's probably good you did that, for the both of us." Her voice was quiet, and she was as contemplative as Arabella had ever seen her.

"Did what?" Arabella muttered, her voice as tight

as her grip on the steering wheel.

"Pushed him away." Rosie's voice held a quality that Arabella had never heard from the small rose.

"I... I didn't." She hadn't meant to. "What do you mean best for both of us?"

"Morphs are bigots." Rosada spat, the words flying like venom from her tongue.

"What?" She was so surprised she almost jerked the steering wheel into the other lane.

"Simper Nimphs are purists. We're barely allowed to interact with other creatures, let alone humans. And dating...falling in love? Out of the question."

"I didn't know that. What about us? Us being friends?"

She spoke in a deep, phony voice. "I'm helping to 'train the world's protectors'. Since that's the way it's seen, as some greater duty, it's fine. But if they knew I was so close to you, if the King knew... I would never see the outside of our kingdom again."

"I had no idea," Arabella stammered, realizing that explained some of the warning looks she had seen Mika giving Rosie.

"Yeah, we don't really like talking about it. It's like some unspoken taboo," Rosada muttered, chipping at her pink nail polish.

"You like him, don't you?" Arabella asked, but

could already guess the answer by the far away look in her magenta eyes.

"Wha...? No. Never. Pfft; what would even make you think I... okay. You caught me. He's just really cute," she babbled excitedly and ran a manicured hand through her hair.

Arabella chuckled under her breath darkly and clucked her tongue against her teeth. "Honestly, I should have guessed he would be your type- tall, funny, freckled, and blue eyed. And let's not forget red-headed. That's about as close as you can get to pink."

"Yeah," she agreed dreamily, her hands fidgeting with her seatbelt shoulder strap. "He is really cute and funny, and don't even get me started on that hair. He caught my eye the other day when we ran into him, and yes, I thought he was cute. But now...well, yeah..I definitely like him," she admitted, frowning slightly. "That doesn't bother you, right? Because if it does... well, I guess it doesn't matter. It can't happen anyway." Arabella could see her studying her through the corner of her eye as she tried to focus on traffic.

"Rosie," she proceeded with confidence, "I don't want you to get hurt, I don't want Cadence to get hurt. But I think you need to do what you feel is right. I will always be there for the two of you." She would always support the people she loved.

"I think I will."

Chapter 15: A Handsomely Dressed Snake.

Arabella panted heavily and drew in a great gulp of air that exhaled in forced gasps as she held her sword aloft for three consecutive minutes- her homework from Mika. She only got five minutes rest in between each rep. After, she practiced her offensive parlays, so that at her next practice, Ember and Rosada wouldn't take her head off . *Oh joy.*

The timer shrilled off on her phone, signaling another set was over. She gratefully let the sword drop to the floor, its heavy blade resounded with a dull thunk against the carpet in her room. The weapon looked strangely out of place against her black, white and purple Parisian decorated walls, yet was perfectly at place in her presence.

She glanced at the clock on her phone once more and groaned, realizing her break was up and that she had in fact gone one minute over. She reached over and turned the timer on with jelly-like arms; just once more. At least she wast more used to it than when she had first started doing it every night. Every. Night. She let out another sigh.

She walked out of the house, her thoughts erasing into pure sunlight at the beautiful sight that was in front of her. Harrison was there, leaning against her car, his snow white hair glinting in the winter sunlight and his dark skin seeming to radiate heat the closer she got, keeping the cold away. Automatically, her mind was intoxicated by his presence.

"Am I giving you a ride to school?" she asked brightly, beaming like a sun ray, not even bothering to think of how he got to her house in the first place, just happy he was there.

"Not exactly." He gave her his infamous debonair smile. It made her heartbeat flutter like a caged butterfly.

"What exactly, then?" she asked, with a pliant smile. He whistled out a haunting tune that made her drift closer to him, her feet floating and lightly scraping across the asphalt. He trailed a finger down her cheek. "Let's not go."

The fog was briefly lifted as at last she saw the light. "Not go?" Her voice was thick with disbelief. "We can't, it's school."

He gave a chuckle that was warm and dark. "Yes, we can, unless-" he stated offhandedly, "you want to see Gabriel."

No recognition flashed at the name. "Who?" Her head became buttery warm and her whole body tingled. If this was what he wanted, then, of course, she would do it. "Okay, let's not go." Then her world went dark as Harrison's lips twisted into a sinister sneer.

Arabella woke up feeling cold, detached, and

befuddled. "Mom?" she croaked, her throat scratching and screaming for water.

An obsidian cackle sounded.

Fear slithered down her spine; it conflicted with an overwhelming feeling of safety. "Harrison?" she asked, unseating herself in a flurry from the rickety chair she was perched on. "Where are we?"

Dark laughter was all that she was given in response.

"What's going on?" she called again, feeling fuzzy. It was also dark, too dark. There was a reason she was scared of the dark. Wasn't there? She stood shivering, hugging herself.

"Do you care about me?" Harrison's liquid voice wrapped around her.

"Of course," she nodded into the inky blackness.

"Do you obey me?"

Now her voice came out in automatic monotone. "Of course," she breathed, hypnotized.

"Am I your whole world?"

"Of course."

"Do you strive to be like me?"

"Of course."

"Am I all you want?"

"Of course." Her mind went blank, her body limp. Cold swept through her eyes. Darkness started bleeding from her fingertips. Shadows wrapped around her face.

Cold pierced her heart and she gasped. She had one thought and one thought only. She wanted power, and The Warlock could give it to her.

His voice called once more, dream-like, as if reflecting on something nostalgic. "At first, when I figured out that this new generation was coming around, I realized that it was my chance. I would finally be able to locate the Clocks. I mean, the amount of power my brother gave you guys..." He snickered cynically. "It was amazing, and you being unbound, giving off all that power and unable to hide it- it was more than I could resist. I started with that girl, Ember, or I had my Shadows try to. They failed. Now she is bound, and I had to move on." He hummed to himself and Arabella felt something brush her cheek. "But you," he whispered, "you were so," he seemed to search for the word, "inexperienced. Powerful from the Clock, but not really a Clock Keeper. So I waited. But that boy," he spit out the name, "Gabriel, made it so hard. Again, my brother really outdid himself. I had to know that the power of 'love' wasn't going to get in the way of my plans. Best way to do that, you may ask? Actually, you won't... but I'll tell you anyway." Again, his voice became a whisper in her ear. "Make him hate you. I made it to where he was in so much pain every time he went near you..." he barked out a laugh. "It was delicious, and incredibly devious- even by my standards. Just watching that boy fight himself- day in, day out- trying to reconcile between the power of the Clock and my powers was amazing. But now, you don't even remember his name, and he only associates you with pain. Just look at you- so enamored with me. And now I control you, I control your power. You're my Shadow."

Arabella absorbed his speech, detached. She didn't care how it happened, she was just content to be near him. He whispered one last thing. "Now, just say you love me."

Arabella opened her mouth. But nothing came out.

His voice bordered on unrestrained desperation. "Arabella. Just. Say. It."

"I..." *No,* she thought, shaking her head, trying to clear the cobwebs.

"Just say it!" he howled, losing his patience. Losing his sanity.

"I... no," she muttered, her head was suddenly clear. Her chest boiled with anger, and disgust roiled through her gut in turmoil. "This isn't right. None of this is right. You're The Warlock..." she said slowly. "I..." her mind reeled as it made sense of all of this. "You're the embodiment of evil and corruption. And even if you weren't," she gave a bitterly barking laugh, "I would never love you, you're cruel and controlling and consuming. If someone was worthy of my love, they would have to earn it. Our love wouldn't be a paper consumed by flames, burning hot and sudden, leaving nothing but ashes behind. It would be like the ocean tide- powerful and constant. I wouldn't just care about him, I would protect him. He would protect me. I wouldn't obey him, I would respect him. He would respect me. We wouldn't be enamored with each other- we would be ourselves with each other. He wouldn't be my world, he would help me make a better one. He would be by my side, but he would never be controlling or needy. I am my own person, I am powerful. I will do as I please, and I know that when I love someone, they'll let me be free. Not only will I soar unhindered, but they'll fly beside me." Bottle-green eyes and blue braces quirked into a smile raced through her mind.

He gave a slow clap. Yet something was off, his movement was staggered. It reminded Arabella of a robot whose cord had been unplugged and was about to power down. "Well, I tried."

Arabella shot up, her eyes blinking at the sudden onslaught of light as her world came into focus. Her back was against the frozen ground, dead grass bit into her palms. Her heart was a jack rabbit, and a frog sat in her throat as she awoke. She was exactly where she had been when she first talked to Harrison- The Warlock- that morning. Bile rose in her throat with an acid rush. He was still standing in front of her, handsome as ever, a handsomely dressed snake. She scrambled to her feet, grass stained her palms. She planted one foot and then the other. *Steady*. With her hands in tight fists and her teeth clenched, she ground herself, raising her arms to block her face- she was prepared to fight. Her core tightened and a growl resounded in her throat, her black T-shirt clung, sticky cold to her flesh. This was her home, and he wasn't coming anywhere near it. He chuckled his once charming chortle, but now, it made her stomach roll with that morning's breakfast of toast and strawberries. "See you around, Arabella." He winked and vanished, flickering away with a concerned look on his face. The Warlock was the master of deception, making you see things that weren't there, bending your reality and perception of things. He played mind tricks. He had been doing just that, Arabella realized. *The whole thing had been in my head*, she thought. It explained the dark space that she had occupied while enthralled by his control. It hadn't actually occurred. But it felt like the most real thing that had ever happened to her. Arabella stumbled into her house, shaking, life drained from her features, anxiety causing her heart to race in trepidation. Her chest welled with despair, and panic seized her soul. *My family!* she thought, terrified. He knew where she lived. He knew about her family. That horrified her more than anything. She texted them and was relieved when they all replied, her sister even going as far as to sass her about texting her while she was in school, her mom sending an ample amount of emojis and her dad sending her a Star Wars meme. She prayed they would stay safe at work and school. She called Ember, her voice wobbling as she leaned against her countertop, recalling the whole incident to the best of her recollection and sharing her concerns. She wished she could be three places at once, and for the first time since his deployment, was happy for Thom's absence.

"What should I do?" she gasped, breathless. Ember's voice was as fiercely cool and calculated as it usually was.

"Just calm down. I'm coming right over and we can make a plan from there." Ember called to Ailith, and then Arabella heard the telltale click of her hanging up.

She leaned her head against the dark granite counters, the cold stone cooled her flushed flesh. She was trying to focus on her breathing and block out the dark possibilities ribboning through her brain. The roar of two engines made the still morning air shatter, splintering the comfortable bubble of suburbia.

Groan, squeak, and crash. The door fell open from the force of a concerned Ailith storming through her foyer and rushing into the kitchen. Light green eyes flashed fiercely over Arabella, searching for any hint of injury. Arabella wanted to dive into Ailith's arms, cry herself into exhaustion and sleep for years. But she couldn't, she wouldn't. She would stand strong, wipe the tears from her eyes and discover the best route to protect her family.

"Are you okay?" Ailith asked as Ember came walking in behind her, her granddaughter was stalking through Arabella's house, inspecting every corner for any hint of a Shadow. Ember's hands rested in a position

Arabella was familiar with- comfortably against her holsters.

Arabella swallowed the lump in her throat, her tastebuds felt like they were coated in a dry powder. "I'm fine." She spoke quickly, stuffing down her own disappointment and deflation. She focused on her concern for her family. "I... I'm concerned for my friends, my family- Cadence, Kat, my mom, my dad."

Ember made what was the closest thing to a sympathetic sound that Arabella had ever heard the young woman utter, and her surprise thickened when the cold combatant reached up and squeezed Arabella's hand as she passed, then continued her survey of the room.

"What can I do to protect them?" Arabella questioned, feeling helpless and needing to do something, anything. Arabella trusted Ember to go after The Warlock, she didn't need revenge, she needed reassurance.

Ailith was quiet for a really long time. "Arabella, you've already done it!" she finally responded, snapping her fingers and coming to some form of deliberate conclusion. "The Book Keepers have been studying lore for years, trying to piece together what exactly killed The Mage, what could kill The Warlock. I know what it means, the puzzle pieces finally fit. The Mage and The Warlock were complete opposites, they fed off of completely different energy. To simplify: they survived off of two different things, good and bad. The Mage died because there was only destruction left in the world. He didn't have a lot of power left and he needed all of the light and good in him to restore the balance. That's what killed him. The Warlock is the opposite, he feeds of off corruption, and he tried to degrade you, to use the most powerful force of good in the world against you. Love. But he couldn't, you were already hard to lead astray- what takes hours for most people, took months with you. And in the end, he couldn't do it. You love so purely that anything else would be impossible. That love has weakened him. That love is the same thing your family feels for you, and that connection between you will protect them. He can't use it against you. It drains him. It kills him. It scares him. Arabella, you are the most dangerous thing he's ever encountered, and the more of a Clock Keeper you become, the more protected you and the ones you love will be. Once you're Bound- he won't be able to touch you.

Chapter 16: There is a Price You Pay.

Arabella threw herself into her training. When she wasn't training, she was with her family. Ember followed her between the two houses, between classes (because yeah, she went back to Arabella's High School), and everywhere else that wasn't reinforced by wards placed by Book Keepers. Despite Ailith's completed puzzle, Ember still wanted to be extra diligent. Which Arabella didn't exactly mind, except that she drove her nuts and made Cadence very confused at the short brunette's constant presence. It was either Ember's weird way of expressing her friendship, or she was using Arabella as bait. Luckily though, in the case of Cadence, he was too wrapped up in Rosada, who was protecting him almost as well as Arabella, to really notice any strange behavior. They really cared about each other, and that was the most horribly amazing thing in Arabella's life. Besides Gabriel- who she wasn't thinking about. The Warlock's words about him danced in stilettos around her skull. It was dizzying and confusing, and she wanted to forget about it. Her family came first. That meant no boys. That meant being a Clock Keeper, that meant keeping The Warlock from her family, and that meant keeping Kat away from a fate unsuited for young girls with bright green eyes and ballet slippers.

Blood dripped from her chin, and sweat bled into her eyes. Her breath was a pant as she pushed herself. She imagined that Ember's hazel eyes were replaced by swirling cognac eyes as she swung her sword with a snarl. Ember ducked and spun, hopping lightly on her feet away from Arabella's reach. She lunged. Silver glinted off the training room walls as Arabella's Imprint crashed violently against Ember's short sword.

Then Arabella was flat on her back, Ember's leg having successfully swept her feet from under her. A dark chortle escaped from the small girl as she stared down at Arabella- the only time she looked down upon the blonde was when she had bested her in training- but a begrudging respect shown in her eyes. Ember reached down and helped Arabella up; in the process she repaired Arabella's wound with a warm rush and a flash of red.

A surprised thank you started to fall from Arabella's lips, but she was stopped short by December's cold glare. Still, it was... progress.

Mika clapped her hands once, then twice, then thrice. She smiled proudly. "That was great! Arabella, your in-combat thinking was quick and calculated. You're focused in a way I haven't seen before."

That's because Arabella was more focused on this than anything else in her life. She finally understood Ember and her need to put the Clocks above everything else. It was both reassuring and terrifying.

Rosada gave a whoop of delight and animatedly

proclaimed her excitement at Arabella's 'triumph'. "That's what I'm talking about! You had her, you had it! You were in the zone!"

Arabella quirked an eyebrow. "Right," she started, her voice bathed in sarcasm. "Until I wasn't."

Rosie flashed a dimpled smile and shouldered a shrug. "You'll get her next time."

Ember demonstrated her patented, disbelieving snort. "Unlikely."

Mika blew her yellow whistle and said to go once more. "Again!"

"The Book Keepers," Ailith stated, drawing in swooping cursive as she spoke, the white chalk bleeding onto the blackboard with a whine.

She started making bullet points.

"The Book Keepers live in the Residence, which is The Mage's home. From it stems the magic that weaves the supernatural world and our world together."

"Is that the same as the Anacora?"

"No, the Anacora isn't for anyone to live in, it's just a gateway; the Residence is just a house that's in our world and the next. But, back to the Books Keepers- they have many important jobs and are our equals. They guard and study The Mage's journals, keep records, and go on missions recovering artifacts and finding other Book Keepers."

"Finding other Book Keepers?"

"Being a Book Keeper, like being a Clock Keeper, is all about DNA. The Mage established the magic through science- we just have to have one microscopic strand of ourselves touched by magic. Except that the Book Keepers gene can mutate into any gender and lineage, as long as they're worthy of it. Like the Anam Cara gene."

"So, do they have Anam Caras?"

"In a way... Book Keepers have something called a periglour- the difference, is that instead of being their own form of magical counterpart, the periglours are other Book Keepers. Hence the Book Keeper gene needing to mutate into new families and generations."

"Oh, okay." It was amazing how similar, yet different, the two factions were.

"The Book Keepers are made up of a council of seven elders, they're the ones who will be overseeing your Trials. They oversee basically all of the human and magical world. Now, Book Keepers come into their powers at the age of 18. The gene is passed down from grandparent to their first grandchild. The Book Keepers have what is called a mark. It's what identifies them as a Book Keeper, and their periglours have the same mark. It's the physical manifestation of their powers and appears when they come of age."

"What does the mark look like?" Arabella inquired. Ailith exhibited her honey sweet laugh. Her arm moved with liquid grace and she scrawled in script the words she voiced. "A Book Keeper's mark is completely unique, only two Book Keepers will have the same mark. Their matching feature is what marks them as periglours. I've seen it be as simple as a strand of hair that is a shade different than the rest, or as complex as a whole arm covered in wyvern scales."

"Awesome," Arabella breathed. Because how could she not be enraptured? She was a fangirl at heart, and this appealed to the nerdiest part of her soul. If she ever got to meet anyone that had cat shaped pupils and wore too much glitter, she'd lose her mind. The excitement of her new world allowed her to forget her regrets and troubles. At least for now.

"Yep." Ailith's lilting laugh betrayed her perpetual amusement at Arabella's excitement toward all things non-human. "Now, as I was saying, the Book Keepers received the other half of The Mage's powers, the ones that we didn't acquire. Their abilities are different than ours, closer to what The Mage had. Their main gifts are those pertaining to knowledge and power. Because of that, they're able to alter other people's knowledge; they can create, erase, and hypnotize. Their purpose is to reveal the truth when it's needed and shield it when it isn't. We protect the human world, not only from other species, but from themselves. Book Keepers tend to be in places of power: the police, military, politics, show business. Another directive of theirs is to clean up messes from the supernatural world that were made in our world. Their training involves being versed in all forms of education- math, music, combat, science, history in the human and magical worlds, spell books from The Mage, his journals, language arts and humanities, as well as the languages and customs of almost every culture. They are able to manipulate dimensional magic and change small parts of the fabric of the world, but only for a small amount of time. But they're powerful all the same."

Their most commonly used spells are: warding, hypnotism, altering memories and the public's knowledge of events, absorbing knowledge from others, slowing time to analyze every detail, and having perfect recall- which is basically photographic memory- that they can turn on and off.

They can only perform more complex spells if they read it straight from the source; they do that with the Anam Cara ritual. They are the watchers of society and our closest allies.

They collect and preserve things from history. They are the watchdogs of the world to make sure no one person or people get too powerful. That's why the human world is kept from the veil, because the supernatural would be too easily manipulated by the mundane. They're the border patrol for the Anacora, and make sure nothing evil gets out of one world and into the other. Book Keepers, once done with their basic training, are able to specialize in one field. Whether it's being a delegate in a particular mythical creature society, being a scholar at the Residence, gaining position in politics in the human world, recovering magical artifacts and spell books, doing clean up, or being a planner- which is a strategist for war and organized fighting- they're the barrier and bridge between the magical world and the human, while the Clock Keepers are the sole protectors of the Clocks and mankind.

Since what we think and assume we know is how we see the world in its physical or metaphysical representation- is our reality- the Book Keepers can change that knowledge. They alter the reality of what we can think. That's why when you start wearing your gear, it will feel like it weighs no more than your workout clothes."

"That's amazing, so they can basically do anything?" Arabella asked, astounded by their scope and range of power.

Ailith laughed once more. "No, all power- especially magic- comes from within. There is a price to be paid for all magic; anything that requires a lot of power will drain you pretty completely of energy. Some laws of science still apply. It's a 1:1 ratio. Too much energy expelled could kill the Book Keeper wielding it."

Wisps of Arabella's hair had escaped from her bun and were now stuck to the back of her sweat covered neck, the cool breeze covered and cooled her panting flesh, and with the wind came the smell of dry heat that slowly gave away to a dry chill. Her tongue tasted like dead sage, and the high desert atmosphere overwhelmed her sense of smell as she breathed in deeply through her nose. A huff escaped her lips as she struggled to catch her breath. The foothills were mostly deserted at this point in the year. Most Idahoans, with the exception of the die hards, believed it was too cold to hike up in the high desert above Camel's Back during this season. Good thing Arabella was running.

Ember and Rosie huffed next to her, all of them tired from the uphill battle of sprinting the steep inclines of sand that qualified for hills around here. Sand was everywhere- in her socks, between her toes; the little grains rubbed gratingly across her flesh with every stride. But that was the point. This part of her training was all about keeping her footing. That meant flying downhill, hopping from one little divot and rock in the trail to another. She was just praying she wouldn't face plant and tumble, snowballing out of control. Running uphill was just as much of a challenge, the ground was slick from years of wear from other travelers, the fine gravel, and a thin layer of frost (even with the warm winter sun beating down).

"Okay, that's long enough of a break," Ember declared as Rosada took another gulp from her water bottle, and Arabella applied more sunblock.

She didn't fall downhill once.

Afterward, Rosada rode with Arabella in her car, and Ember rode her bike, visible in the review mirror as she trailed behind them.

Rosie fiddled with her nails, chipping at recently repainted holes. "I need to ask a favor."

Arabella gave her a sideways glance. "Of course, anything."

"So you know how I took your advice and became friends with Cadence?" she asked nervously as she jiggled her legging-clad leg.

Arabella rolled her eyes but nodded anyway. "All I said was that I wanted you to be happy. But if you want to go with that it was my idea... go ahead." She reached over and turned down the radio, hating that she was blocking out Eddie Vedder as he belted out a spine shivering lyric, but recognizing that this conversation probably needed her full attention.

"Well, he's amazing... and well... you see..." she gave an adorably nervous laugh. Arabella waited patiently for her to spit it out. "He... asked me out. Last night, and.." Rosada took a calming breath. "Would you cover for me? I mean, it's just one date, and it's not like a date, date. Well... I guess it is. And I'm leaving to go home after your training... I just... I need to do this, just once. Please?" She turned her bright pink puppy dog eyes on Arabella.

Arabella glanced away from the road quickly and saw something in Rosada's eyes that made her heart clench. Love. Knowing Cadence, he probably felt the same, with his big heart and open smile. Hoping she was doing the right thing, she sighed softly and whispered, "of course."

"Thank you!" Rosada squealed. Arabella had to laugh.

Arabella let herself become consumed in her classes, both school and training. During family movies, she would work on homework, the same thing she would do at lunch. When she had any free time, she was over at Ailith's or with Ember, forming some sort of shared goal or bond between the two. And if she wasn't completely engrossed in her lessons, she was worrying. She was worried about her Trials. Scared what it could mean if she failed. Scared of The Warlock, who hadn't been seen since Arabella's small triumph. Scared for her family, for her friends. Especially for the two who were wrapped up in each other, when they weren't focusing on their own lives. Cadence was close to graduating flight school and Rosada was busy with training Arabella, and the two somehow still made it work. Arabella walked into a room as Rosie was texting him with a big grin on her face. Whenever she and Cade had their weekly 'sibling' night where they watched cheesy movies and made goofy commentary, Rosada seemed to be mentioned in 90% of the comments. It was so cute, and she shipped them hardcore. But... the danger... Mika was getting increasingly suspicious. If she found out, then Arabella would never see Rosie again, and Cade would never see her again either. They wouldn't even be able to FaceTime, which Arabella was counting on for her own sanity, when Rosada had to go back to Spain. Plus Cade... whenever Arabella asked what would happen to him should they get found out, Rosada got really tightlipped. But Arabella trusted Rosie, even if that meant trusting her with Cadence.

"Rock wall climbing?" Arabella inquired, dumbfounded. She, Ember and Rosada were standing outside Asana, the rock climbing gym in Garden City.

"Yeah," Ember grumbled and stalked inside.

Rosada sighed and explained, "indoor rock climbing is a great full-body workout for both strength and cardio. You end up building the muscles in your delt's, bi's, and tri's. The climbing itself engages your core from using both your arms and legs. You'll develop strong arms, shoulders, thighs, back, neck, and forearm muscles. You'll create better endurance and perseverance."

"Right." Arabella blinked. "Rock wall climbing."

"Also," Rosada said offhandedly has they walked in, "there's a really cool concert I want to see next door."

And that's how they ended up dragging Ember to her first rock concert, and despite leaning on the wall the whole night, December left with a smile on her face.

"Years ago, there was a war. Between the Book Keepers and the Clock Keepers," Ailith explained. "It was our version of the Civil War."

They were back in the classroom. Its dim lighting, overstuffed cushy chairs, and the smell of aged parchment and chalk dust brought Arabella small comfort. The bright green chair she sat on reminded her of things she was painfully ignoring. The Warlock's words had brought confusion about a boy who was now ignoring her. A boy she subsequently remembered vividly. A boy she ached over.

"There was a lot of chaos after The Mage created our new reality." Ailith's words were soft, and she had the smile of a sweet child. "My grandma used to spin such wonderful stories about it. Dark, twisted, magical stories. It was a new world, a new truth. There was peace, and in a world filled with strife, peace wasn't a comfort. Two factions of people now had powers that were previously unattainable by humans. They both had different ideas of what the world order should be. Now, neither view was wrong. Just different. The Book Keepers wanted to lock the Anacora, make sure that the supernatural world never interfered with ours again, and send any creatures that did live here back there. Then they would send a couple of Book Keepers there to make sure the creatures didn't die, of course."

"Die?" Arabella asked, alarmed.

Ailith nodded dourly. "Yes. The supernatural world is a little more black and white than the human world. They are split into two categories. The righteous and the grim. The righteous are fueled by humanity's positive energy-creativity, love, compassion, etc. The grim are powered by negative energies- hate, distrust, jealousy, etc."

"Like The Mage and The..." Arabella's voice wobbled at the sudden onslaught of memories. Darkness covered fingers. Eyes filled with smoke. Inky desire wrapped around her heart. "The Warlock."

"Exactly," Ailith confirmed, running a hand through her static free locks, silver twisting around her fingers as she twirled a strand. As she brushed her hair behind her ear, she brushed past Arabella's pain. "So they were going to send liaisons of Book Keepers over there to keep the creatures alive, at least the good ones. But the

Clock Keepers wanted something different. They felt that segregation was the root of what had originally brought humanity to its knees. Then someone told your great grandmother, who was German and a Clock Keeper of course, that that was rich coming from a German."

Arabella's eyebrow quirked to her hairline and a scowl of disgust twisted her blushed lips. "What?!"

Ailith met her gaze with her icy green eyes. She had a stare like a thousand soldiers, "it was not a proud time in our history. We went to war, because not all creatures like interacting in the human world- like Morphs- they had as many allies as we did."

"Who won?" Arabella asked, curious about how they operated so peacefully now.

"It ended in a truce. They weren't doing their job, and they realized that, that was the most important thing. Included in that truce were some gifts- tokens of good faith- from each side to the other. We were given a spell book with combat charms. They were allowed to study our Imprint weapons and create some of their own." Ailith again had that far away look she often got when speaking of her past.

"I'm going to learn magic!" Arabella exclaimed, eyes aglow with wonder and her spine rod straight as she shifted, suddenly un-sunk from her seat. She couldn't help but feel excited. She was a nerd after all. The thought of magic and spells being softly uttered from her awed lips made her shiver with delight. Her skin crawled as if the elated feeling in her core was too much for her to contain. It was. Because... Magic.

"No." Ailith's hard expression softened at Arabella's alarmed eyebrows. "The spells were in The Haunt. The Haunt was... lost a couple of years after I became bound to my Clock."

"The Haunt?" Arabella asked, tumbling the new vocabulary word across her taste buds. "I think I remember Ember mentioning something, but... well, what exactly is it?"

Ailith's voice sounded tight to Arabella's captivated ears. "The Haunt was a single room, it was used as a meeting room and safe haven for the Clock Keepers. It was in what the Book Keepers call a pocket dimension- which are spaces between our world and behind the veil. "

"So is it summoned by a spell, like the Anacora, or... how do you lose something that isn't really there?" Arabella was human, with a couple of upgrades, curiosity was one of the rights she was defending. She was going to use that right, it was her right not to remain silent.

"No. It's not a spell. It's a key. The Mage created a key that, when inserted into any door lock, becomes a doorway into The Haunt. The key is what was lost."

Arabella would have questioned the subject more, but one look at Ailith's drawn face, and she decided against it. No matter how sweet Ailith could be, she was still

Ember's grandmother, and a fire brewed in her soul.
Arabella didn't want to face that fire, and she didn't want to
make Ailith upset by dredging up a better forgotten past.

"Anam Caras, or soulmates."

"Soulmates?" Arabella asked at the start of her next
lesson. She realized she had been dreading a subject she
had previously anticipated.

"Soulmates," Ailith sighed, looking equally
perturbed. "Anam Cara is a Gaelic term, considered an
essential part of spiritual development. Book Keepers, as
we've discussed, call their other half a periglour- which is a
Welsh term. It has the same meaning as Anam Cara, but it's
more about the bonding of the essences of the mind and
spirit, while a Clock Keeper is connected physically and
spiritually to the their Anam Cara. The history behind the
Celtic lore is the philosophy that two souls with a unique
connection can be stronger together than apart. To quote
John Ó Donohue, they are- *a person to whom you could
reveal the hidden intimacies of your life. This friendship
was an Anam Cara, your friendship cut across all
convention and categories. You were joined in an ancient
and eternal way with the friend of your soul.* It is based on
spirituality and the bonding of two souls. Each person was
connected to someone else before time began. They always

recognize each other when they meet again. And when they do find each other, they reestablish that deep connection as their two auras or "Anams" flow together. They see the other person's highest potential." Arabella grimaced. "Your spirit is reflected in them." Ó Donohue also said, *you are joined in an ancient and eternal union with humanity that cuts across all barriers of time, convention, philosophy, and definition. When you are blessed with an Anam Cara, the Irish believe you have arrived at that most sacred place: Home.* Ailith cleared her throat. Then started in a hard, withdrawn tone. "Clock Keepers need their Anam Cara to take off the Clock. Because once a Clock Keeper is bound, the magic at our corc is stable."

"Right, the Trials don't stabilize our magic." Arabella agreed.

"Correct. The Trials bond the Clock's magic to our own. But we're not truly stable until we have bound with our Anam Cara." Ailith was far away. In a time when she was just a girl with the sunrise in her eyes and a future shrouded in choices. Now those choices were made, and she was starting to see a sunset. The difference, was that the sunrise had been too blinding to see, but the sunset was painted with the colors of a beautiful palette. "The Anam Cara gene has mutated into seemingly random people who match the chosen Clock Keepers. But in order for the bond between the two to truly work, you have to choose each other. Love each other. It's a bond in blood. The ritual actually entails cutting into the other's palm and clasping hands. The magic in both parties' DNA is then able to fuse. It's beautiful; you can see your partner's aura so clearly and perfectly." She cleared her throat. "You stand within the Gaelic symbol, Triquetra, which represents unity of spirit. And together you speak this vow: *My soul chose yours long before my mortal nature graced this Earth. With unwavering heart and mind, I give you my soul, and ask in return for yours, with trust supplementing our eternal coupling. I know myself as I know you, a mirror is the likeness of our auras. Let not only the magic at our core fuse, but also the essence of our being bleed together in the same manner as the cuts on our flesh as we become one. We are joined in more than lust, but also friendship, and a melding of hearts willing to withstand the forge. I make this vow evermore- I will love you, fight for you, learn for you. I will never leave your side or your spirit. As you bleed, I bleed. I happily take your burdens as my own. For we shall never part, in life, in death- we will do both together. Your blood binds my soul, and your soul binds my blood. I am your guardian."*

By the end, Arabella had liquid mercury dripping down her face. It was beautiful, and something clicked when Ailith said those words, as she spoke a Clock Keeper's vow to their Anam Cara, and the Anam Cara's vow to their Clock Keeper.

Ailith cleansed her expression. "There are stages to

the Anam Cara bond. The first is being attracted to each other's geographical location, because you have to be able to meet, after all. Once within a familiar distance of each other, the Anam Cara starts to experience his powers for the first time, and begins to dream of his Clock Keeper. Next, he senses the power of the Clock and Imprint weapon, and will lead the Clock Keeper to the source if she hasn't already acquired them. Then, his tattoo will fill in after meeting his Clock Keeper-"

"Tattoo?"

"An Anam Cara has a matching tattoo, which appears after meeting his Clock Keeper, in black ink, unlike a Clock Keeper's white. We balance each other. Once the tattoo fills in, he can control his powers. But he can only access these powers once the Clock Keeper and the Anam Cara are both 16."

"What are their powers?"

"Unlike a Clock Keeper, who only access attributes of the animal counterpart, Anam Caras can turn into the Clock's animal counterpart."

The falcon.

Arabella wanted to lurch forward, propel out of her seat, run out of the room so that she could stare into the sky and ponder the unknown. She had met her soulmate. Her heart soared, and her mind rebelled. Her thick armor was battling her romantic soul. She almost told Ailith of the revelation, that she had been led to her Clock by a silver falcon. But the words didn't come out, and before the thought could be formed into speech, Ailith was continuing on with the lesson.

"The second part of the process is when feelings start to develop. Your twin souls recognize each other; your Clock starts to become more powerful as it senses that you're going to bond soon and unleash the Clock's full power in a healthy way."

"How long do I have before I need to bond to my Anam Cara, how long can I take the Clock's energy?"

Ailith's light eyes darkened. "If you've met your Anam Cara, you typically have two years before you need to be bound. If you haven't, most Clock Keepers have until their 21st birthday."

Even though she knew the answer in her bones, her head needed to ask the question. "What happens if I don't...?"

Ailith fidgeted, and it baffled Arabella. She knew there was something she wasn't telling her. Something to do with Ember's grandfather who had passed years before. It was a mystery that shrouded Ailith whenever the subject got brought up. Grief would cause her eyes to grow foggy, and her posture indicated that any continued conversation wouldn't be welcome. But in the months that Arabella had known the older woman, she had never known her to not be sure of her movements. But now, she was bumbling about as if she were a toddler who had stolen candy and the evidence was on their face.

Ailith squinted at Arabella. She looked at her with her grandmotherly reassurance and spoke in her honey voice. "If a Clock Keeper goes without their Anam Cara for too long, the power of the Clock kills them. When my husband... when he.... when he passed away, I got really sick, and only recovered after giving the Clock to Ember. The only reason I stayed alive at all was that... let's just say that it was a special circumstance."

Arabella wanted desperately to ask what that meant, but was too shocked by the image revealed by a finally completed puzzle. "My grandpa," she choked.

Ailith gave a sad smile. "He loved your grandmother very much."

Arabella knew he had. And now she knew why her grandmother's death took him too. And so quickly. She had to forge on. She had to forget his kind eyes and warm hugs, just for a little bit. Because she was afraid that if she didn't, the void in her heart would swallow her whole. "What's the third step?"

Ailith gave her a look so understanding, it almost broke Arabella. "The third, and final step of the bond is when you're both sure of each other- platonically and romantically. You must truly trust and love each other. When you go through the ritual, it entangles your minds and souls. You will gain each other's knowledge, and you will finally share the power of the Clock."

Arabella Grace had more sleep in her eyes than there were stars in the sky. And she was struggling. An alarm went off in Arabella's head, the sound was shrill, colder than the northern shores, and she dragged herself from the midnight waters of sleep. Her murky mind blinked awake.

And a dark Shadow loomed over her face. She rushed into a sitting position, her legs trying to kick free of the cocoon she had created in the night. The Shadow cackled and smiled into the shaded room. White teeth grinned broad and Arabella's heart lurched. A stampeding horse out of a closed box, the organ gave a horrid shudder and stormed in her chest, crashing against her ribbed walls like thunder and lightning.

Her hand, guided like a magnet, swept under her box frame and came away with her twinkling instrument of graceful destruction, while her other hand flicked on her Hufflepuff nightlight- her only form of salvation.

Ember's features were half revealed in the dim, and she lazily leveled her gaze at Arabella's sword, her hazel eyes lit with warm flames and her grin growing as

Arabella's pant of desperation became a snort of anger, surprise, and relief.

Arabella sputtered and hissed, "what in the-" deep breath. "Ember, why would you do that?" Her eyes shot to the Clock laying comfortably on her wrist. "It's stupid early! I might actually kill you this time!" she hollered in a whisper, aware that the rest of her family were sleeping only rooms away. She shot out of bed and pointed the weapon attached to her arm threateningly at the smug brunette.

The only explanation Ember gave was her infamously bemused grin of a grimace. Instead of telling Arabella anything useful, she mumbled hoarsely, "I want to try something." *Huh, that's not terrifying.*

Turned out, Ember's idea of 'trying something new' was Arabella learning her lesson in a more adrenaline fueled environment. In the cold. At dawn. Did she mention it was cold? That's what led to her standing on the frozen ground, the frost creeping into her boots. No matter how tightly she wrapped the flimsy piece of material she called a 'coat' around her waist, her teeth chattered in her tight scowl, sounding like porcelain drums. Her stomach ached, the only thing having entered her mouth that 'morning' was coffee and toothpaste. The coffee warmed her stomach, but the caffeine jittering in her veins made her even more painfully aware of the lack of food she had consumed. There hadn't even been time for a protein shake. Or at least that's what Ember muttered when they had gone through Arabella's window at 6:00 am.

"What are we doing here, Ember?" She fidgeted from foot to foot, every time growing a little shorter as she sunk further and further into the snow.

The ice queen stalked across the field, making quite a striking image, her hair billowing in dark waves as the sun rose steadily in the lightening sky. Faint rays of morning light caught in Arabella's eyes, and she was squinting into frozen air. "Grandma is going to give you your lesson later today. You'll sit in that cozy little room, in one of those comfy chairs, and learn about real life stuff in a hypothetical situation. I want you to learn and adapt as you go. Discover and deal with things as they're relevant."

"Why can't we do that in the basement?"

"It's the morning-" she started.

Arabella shot her a look that was somewhere along the lines of 'no duh'.

"- and it's cold. The morning will have you feeling unprepared, but the cold will keep your senses alert." While that made sense in a very Ember like way, it still left Arabella pissed. Some people were morning people. They could wake up at dawn and peer at the soft morning light with affection. They could possibly feel refreshed at the prospect of a new day. Arabella was not one of those people. She was a night owl, the later into evening it was, the more refreshed she got. She was more productive and more inquisitive and creative when the stars shone and the moon glowed. But Ember was probably the type of person who woke up at 0500 hours, or something equally as tiring. Arabella was quite clearly fed up with this exercise, and that was before Ember pulled out the blindfold.

"No."

"Arabella,"she warned, growling and snapping.

"No." Arabella answered again, her amusement shown in the sour twist of her lips and the lift of her eyebrows. Ember glowered, the small amount of patience she had slipping away as her eyebrow twitched faster.

"Fine," Arabella breathed and shivered. It was cold. Ember placed the blindfold around Arabella's eyes, the cloth covered her chilled ear tips, a thankful reprieve from the brisk breeze. The knot Ember tied caught in her fine hair. Arabella felt she was far too comfortable with Ember leading her into strange situations that most people would find potentially hazardous.

Arabella heard the the steel of her blade hiss from its sheath as Ember's boots crunched over the ground in front of her. Arabella strained to hear the audible world around her, her only defense against the dark that covered her vision, and she focused on the moment instead of allowing herself to get caught up in her past dark days. The wind picked up, and she shuddered. Somewhere, the tired wear of tires against the road sounded, and the fragrance of winter's chill and a coffee stained morning trailed through the gust. It was ominous and hopeful and daring all at once. The feeling of being at a cliff's edge, right before you take flight. The moment you experience in your life when your wanderlust soul battles fear, and that inner war excites you.

There was a thud. An impact as something hit the snow. And then a screeching sound as silver strained against the friction of frozen ground. It was from the right, but how far she wasn't sure. Then she couldn't hear Ember's footsteps anymore. The fine hairs on her arm stood on end, and goosebumps became more pronounced on her skin. All was still.

Ember's familiar, haughty voice echoed. "Imprint weapons."

"Excuse me?" Arabella deadpanned. She was out here at 6:30 a.m. to learn about the arming sword that had taken residence under her bed almost since her birthday. She recognized the scorn she was feeling and knew that it was mostly petty, but she really hated mornings.

Ember's voice sounded to the left, and Arabella's head whiplashed from where it had been facing the right to the sound of rasped words. "Each Imprint weapon is connected, bound magically, to a specific bloodline. When not in use, they're in their box, like the one you found yours in, which is warded and protects the Clocks and the Imprints. I'm sure grandma has told you, that after our Civil War, Book Keepers were allowed to study our Imprints and create their own, and now their Imprints are a part of their initiation. Your weapon is a part of you, an extension of self; it calls to you, and you will always be able to find it." Arabella swore she heard a smile in Ember's tone as she paused briefly before getting to the point. "Now fight."

Arabella's fingertips suddenly felt frozen, colder than the rest of her body, as if the digits were now buried in the light drifts around her. Ember's footsteps grew loud in the snow, slowly crunching toward her, the sound of metal being unsheathed became apparent. *Concentrate.* Then she could feel it, the silver digging into the frost, the blade glinting in the early morning rays, sharper than diamonds, raw and ready and completely in sync with her own heart. It pulsed as if it were filled with veins of her own blood. 10 feet away, slightly in front of her to the right, was her reflection- her Imprint.

She sprung forward.

She felt Ember's weapon propel past her. Too close. Then she had the silver in her hands, the leather wrapped handle warm and familiar. She heard Ember move and she swung. The tip of her weapon rested lightly against something soft and all was still.

Using her left hand, she took off the blindfold to see Ember, surrendered, a dark smile twisting her features, and Arabella's sword was at her throat.

Ailith handed Arabella a cheat sheet, the permanent scowl she had acquired after learning that Ember had already given Arabella her lesson for the day was finally lessening.

"As I've mentioned before, the supernatural world can generally be divided into two main categories: the righteous and the wicked. The righteous feed off of positive human emotions, and the wicked feed of off negative emotions, just like The Mage and The Warlock, respectively. Those two categories are further split into two more categories of what they have power over- there are phycias, who control the environment, and metalits, who control the mind."

Arabella looked over the list and felt strangely affronted that alicorns were evil. She couldn't help but wonder about each one of these creatures- what they were like, their hopes and dreams. She had to protect them all. Well, maybe not the bad ones.

"Arabella, you need to keep this list. Memorize it, because your life depends on it."

The Supernatural World

The Righteous

-Meno
*creature that controls
light
-Nix
*water spirit
-Culebras
*a humanoid creature
with snakes for hair
and venomous nails
-Yetis
*a giant fur covered
creature that lives in
the mountains
-Nakki
*a pond spirit that
protects people from
Kappas
-Imp
*small mischievous
rodent
-Fairy
*a small creature that
guards the woods and is
very empathetic, they have
tails and no pupils
-Elf
*Craftsman
of the forest,
the size of
trees
-Centaur
*half-man, half-horse
-Golem
*human made of stone
-Nephele
*cloud nymph
-Simper Nimph
*changes appearance
-Witch
*half-elf, half-human

The Wicked

-Koshei
*soul is separated
from body and
kept in an object
-Bugbear
*a demon that feeds
on nightmares
-Pixies
*fairy evil look-alike,
has pupils
-Wyvern
*what dragons are based on
-Chimeras
*a hybrid of deadly
creatures
-Redcap
*murderous dwarf
-Bogle
*spirit that causes
confusion

-Wraith
*evil spirit

-Jotunn
*a troll
-Alicorn
*winged unicorn

-Kappas
*evil water spirit
that drowns its
victims

Chapter 17: Her Blade Met with Her Fiery Foe's.

"Concentrate!" Mika called and then turned to Ember, motioning for her to stand up. *Great.* "Ember is going to show you again." She sighed. They were once again trying to have Arabella attempt to fly.

She had tried at least once a week since finding out she was a Clock Keeper, but something was holding her back; she just couldn't. She would feel the power course through her, would feel the wings start to unfurl from her flesh, and then... nothing. No wings. At first, she thought it was grief holding her back, the thought that her grandma used to feel the same way. Then, in retrospect, she thought The Warlock's hold had been inhibiting her. Now, she knew it was fear, because she knew that the more of a Clock Keeper she became, the darker the world would appear. Yet, she kept trying to fly, because as long as Kat could live the carefree life of a little girl, as long as she wasn't afraid of her own shadow, there would be something to fight for.

Arabella watched Ember, covering her ears as Ember quickly pulled her hair up. Her feline outline flared red, and her eyes glowed like burning coals, she unholstered and discharged her weapon twice. The evidence of her shots fired were embedded in the center mass of the dummies.

They were good shots, the kind that hit vital organs and guaranteed a visit from death or at least a lot of crappy hospital food. But that wasn't what had caught everyone's attention. A small black object floated to the ground, smaller than a pin head; it was still smoking. Ember holstered her two pistols, the copper inlay glinting as she stalked over to the object and gingerly picked it up. She laid it gently across her palm and brought it over for everyone to inspect. A feral grin twisted the brunette's face. It was terrifying how Cheshire it was. Dark and grim... and pretty, which December was. She was as cold as she was fiery.

They leaned in close as Ember showed them what was in her palm.

It was a fly.

The small dead insect laid still against her palm, it wasn't even twitching, completely frozen, untouched, except for the fact that it didn't have any wings. Arabella suspected that it was Ember's attempt at grim humor. For far longer than a second, they stayed in stunned silence.

In the end, it was Rosie whose soft exclamation of, "dang," broke the still air. "That's impressive... creepy... but, still impressive."

Ember gave a satisfied grunt and nod. If Jayne Cobb and John Casey had a love child... Arabella mentally trailed off and shuddered at the thought.

"Now, Arabella." Mika spoke with finality ringing in her words. Moving to the center, Arabella sucked a deep breath in, cleared her head, and blew a gust of wind out, feeling prepared. She envisioned her wings: their soft down, light weight and silver feathers under the lights. She pictured how they would feel resting against her shoulder blades and back. She remembered what it felt like to be weightless, to have nothing but air beneath her feet. She slowly felt magic begin to leave its breathtaking mark underneath her skin, and just like that, she had it. She could feel the wings where they connected to her shoulder blades, rubbing against the cotton of her tank top. The wings spread, their silhouette hitting the cold air. The outlined mist turned solid as feathers started to trickle, one by one materializing into reality, the hot, searing sensation of exhilarating comfort.

Then nothing.

Her eyes stopped glowing blue, her heart stopped thrumming, and fear rose, rushing to fill the cracks in her exterior with bone chilling water. It seized her, gripped the warmth from her inner soul and bled her from the inside out. She was afraid of heights, she was afraid of The Warlock, she was afraid of not being good enough, she was afraid of being weak, she was scared.

She sank to the floor like a sunken stone. Water filled her eyes, and a scream tightened her strangled throat, resting there for later use. Raising a fist, she swiftly brought it down upon the blue mats. She looked at a worried Rosada and a concerned Mika, with wide, faded eyes. "Why can't I do this?" She was lost.

It was Ember who spoke, the anger in her words

barely masked by the steely distance she strived to maintain from the situation.

"Who are you, Arabella?"

Arabella... was brave. She remembered a quote by Nelson Mandela, *I learned that courage was not the absence of fear, but the triumph over it. The brave man is not he who does not feel afraid, but he who conquers that fear.* Was she afraid? That was an outstanding yes. But, there were things far more important than fear. Her family. Her friends. The women standing in this room. She could do this, because her belief in self was stronger than the fears in her head.

A phantom outline of her tattoo was taking shape, solidifying and etching itself into her tender flesh as warm skin met cold air. It connected with her very core from the base of her neck, between her shoulder blades, underneath her tank top. When she felt the wings settle into place, she knew that she would be able to maintain them for the rest of her practice. She opened her blue eyes, they glowed brighter than usual, illuminating a small radius around her.

She turned around in time to be barreled into by her Rosie amiga. "I'm so proud of you!" she gripped her tightly; for someone so small, she was surprisingly strong. "You did it."

Arabella gave a bark of a laugh, feeling very pleased with herself. "I did do it! Didn't I?" she laughed giddily and gave Rosada a crushing squeeze of her own, carefully aware of her own wings, she gave them a little flutter and lifted herself and Rosada just barely off the floor.

"Woah!" Rosie shrieked as they hung there, Arabella's wings keeping them aloft.

Arabella heard amused laughter from behind them. "Alright girls, it's time to return to practice," said a warm, but stern, voice. Arabella lowered them gently to the floor, and they both turned to see Mika waiting.

"Sorry, Mom." Rosada meekly responded to her mom's quirked eyebrow; she turned back to Arabella, "good job," she whispered, then gave her two thumbs up before walking back over to her spot on the floor.

Arabella looked around the room- Mika emanated pride that only an instructor could, and her golden eyes betrayed her amusement. She stood there, her arms loose at her sides in a formal, businesslike manner. Ailith stood next to Rosada with a gentle smile upon her face, grandmotherly love shining in her ice green eyes. Then Arabella turned to Ember, who stood in the corner. Her arms were not crossed for once, but held two weapons- one was one of the steel training staffs, and the other was Arabella's Imprint that she had left hanging on her scabbard.

Ember held both both loosely in her hand. Arabella was surprised to discover fond amusement lining Ember's usually cold features. Just like that, the expression disappeared, and Ember was throwing the arming sword in her direction.

Arabella caught it with a graceful ease that surprised even her, and her eyes widened in response.

Ember sauntered toward her with a wicked grin, the twin to the one that Arabella was now sporting. She twirled the staff like a baton. "Let's spar; I want to see what those wings of yours can do." She grinned again, and Arabella couldn't help but think that this was going to be fun as she glided upward in the air.

She brandished the sword once before her blade met her fiery foe's.

They clashed and danced for what felt like forever, delivering blows in a never ending cycle. She soared over Ember's head and twisted so she was holding the sword to Ember's back as she landed. Without a backwards glance, Ember had Arabella lying flat on the mats. The only sign of the leg swipe the metallic staff that Ember now held behind her. She launched at Ember as she turned. Arabella's sword met her staff and they grinned into each other's faces. Feral.Wild.Wicked.

Ember pushed the sword away and jabbed her in the chest; Arabella could feel a plum sized bruise taking hold of her sternum. Arabella swooped into Ember, knocking her flat, and stood victorious, holding the sword to her throat.

Basking in the afterglow of the hard fought match,

Arabella helped Ember up. They moved to the wall, leaning against it, their breath a series of heavy pants. Both of their powers retreated, their eyes dimmed, and Arabella felt the iridescent ink settle.

She told Ember she had a question, something she was a little curious about now that she had really seen, felt, her wings.

"Shoot," Ember muttered back, pushing some curly damp hair from her forehead. Her voice wasn't as cold as usual.

"So we're 'weres'?" she asked, thinking about her wings from moments before.

"No." Ember responded gruffly, obviously still a little sore about losing; she stalked away, muttering about stupid YA novels.

Rude.

His breath came out in sharp gasps and his soles slipped against the cold, wet cement as Shadows nipped at his feet. They closed in on him, and he could feel their death-like fingers raking at the back of his heels, so close to pulling him into their clutches and to his demise. Terror caught in his throat, and he wheezed as they grew closer. Both were ink, their lack of color was deeper than midnight; long, bony tendrils snaked closer around his ankle, pulling him to the ground. He fell with a crash, and his head bounced off the cement, pushing his braces through his lips. Pain spread from the two points. Blood dripped down his face. His upper lip was in such mind numbing agony, that he was almost incapable of even noticing when they dragged him to a cage. Amongst all the pain, he saw Arabella.

Gabriel shot up in his bed, his sheets askew across his torso. He usually slept fairly peacefully, but tonight, that was far from the case. Nightmares snaked across his vision, and another wave of pain from his back hit him with such force, the breath was cleansed from his lungs. He laid back down, breathing heavily- a cold sweat was dripping down his back. Gabriel tried to fall asleep, tried to ignore the pain in his chest- the panic, the fear.

The heartbreak.

Every time he closed his eyes though, demons played games behind his lids.

She dodged spears and daggers with an ease that she wouldn't have thought possible when she started all of this, but now it felt.. almost easy. Plus, she didn't get out of breath. Ailith said it was because The Mage's magic was starting to take hold as she matured and accepted her responsibilities.

She turned sharply as a well aimed kick almost landed against her face. She felt something at her back and quickly spun to see that Rosada was trying to catch her by surprise. Yelping, she tucked and rolled away from the two currently trying to kill her, and watched in amusement as lithe little Rosie's elbows landed against December's shoulder, right where Arabella's rib had been. *Ouch.* Then she watched as the scene unfolded into something even more comical. Ember slipped from the shock of contact and fell flat. On the way down, her feet tangled with Rosada, so Rosie also ended up on her back.

"December..." Rosada groaned.

Arabella couldn't help but cackle, then launched right back into the fight.

"Arabella, I'm so proud of you!" Rosie squealed, giving her a squeeze that a python would be proud of.

"You know, I think my daughter put it most eloquently; I'm very proud of you as well," Mika echoed, trying to sound formal, but the tears brimming her golden eyes gave her away. "You've only been a part of our world for such a little amount of time, and already you've done amazing, impossible things."

"My dear darling, come here." Ailith called and hugged over the top of Rosada, who still had not let go. "You are ready, and you'll do wonderfully; your will is strong, and your heart," she gave a soft smile, "is so good and pure. You don't have to worry about Kat, because you are a Clock Keeper." She slipped a tear from the corner of her eye. "Now remember, your Trial will take place in the Anacora, between the veil. Get a good night's rest so that you're fresh. Ember will collect you in the morning," she finished and exited through the kitchen after giving her one last watery and sniffling hug. Ember left after giving Arabella an, shall we say, approving nod.

"We also need to go," Mika announced as she nodded to Rosada, who lingered as her mom slipped out the door.

"I'm going to see Cadence tonight, want to come?" Rosada spoke in a hushed tone, and pink lined her face.

Arabella laughed sweetly at her friend. "Not tonight, I need the rest."

"Okay," Rosada laughed along and gave her one last hug. "I'll see you tomorrow.

Chapter 18: She Could Lose Everything.

"Do you want a ride home?" Cade asked as they chatted by Gabriel's locker. His dirt bike didn't work well on the ice, and unfortunately, that morning had been abnormally frosty.

"Yeah," he muttered. He wanted to say no, in case they ran into Arabella, but what was he supposed to say? *I'm pretty sure your best friend wants me dead, is poisoning me, and yet for some reason I can't get her out of my head.* He shook his head; it was crazy... crazy, but true. "Thanks, man," he said instead.

"No problem, dude, but I was wondering if it was okay if we got something to eat first, I'm supposed to meet my girlfriend for dinner." Cadence had a look on his face that made Gabriel itch to photograph it; it was raw and open, he was in love.

"No problem," he sarcastically sighed, taking a deep internal breath. *I can be normal for an hour.*

They drove along the highway, some silly pop song on the radio. "Oof, you seriously listen to this stuff?" Gabriel directed a questioning look toward Cade.

"You sound like Arabella," he laughed and turned the radio up.

Gabriel froze at the comparison and his nightmares of the abyss flew to mind.

Cadence eyed his friend's posture from the corner

of his eye while he tugged at his hair with his permanently oil stained fingers. "What's going on with you two?" Suspicion laced his voice like poison on a blade.

All Gabriel could do was shake his head and let long strands of his dark hair cover his eyes to hide him away from reality. So he didn't notice when they pulled into the parking lot, and he didn't notice when the car lurched to a stop against the black top. He had his hand on his chin, and his fingers splayed against his sharp cheek bones. His bottle-green eyes drifted out the window.

Bang!

The car door across from him slammed shut, and he looked up wildly from the window he had been dazedly staring out.

They were at a fast casual restaurant that seemed vaguely Mexican. Shrugging, he winced as his leather jacket tugged at his cotton T-shirt, raking against his tender skin as he followed Cade inside.

"Hi, how are you, today?" the girl at the counter beamed flirtatiously, her blue eyes sparkling as they bounced between the two boys. She wore the employee uniform and had bright, cherry-red dyed hair tucked under her cap. Gabriel imagined drawing her in a Cola commercial.

"Great!" a spunky girl with electric pink hair

replied, skipping up between he and Cade. She jumped
easily from her short height to Cadence's lofty one and
kissed him on the cheek.

The counter girl's smile tightened, and a frown
played on her features. "How may I help you?" she
questioned, her voice strained. They all quickly rattled off
their orders, and she walked away at a brisk pace, as if the
room were on fire.

"So, how's ninja training going?" Cadence teased
the pink girl, who Gabriel assumed was Rosada. Gabriel
recalled the strange situation that Cadence had told him
about involving Arabella and Rosie. He wanted to like
Rosada, but how could he like someone who was 'besties'
with his tormentor?

They found a table by the window. "Like Michael
Phelps in the Olympics," she quipped. Gabriel's knowledge
was vague, but even he recognized that was good, and it
made something in his spine stiffen. Rosada snuggled a
little closer to Cadence. Honestly, the chairs could only get
so close. Cadence suddenly remembered his manners and
hastily introduced the two. Gabriel noticed that she had
bright, pink colored contacts that were a few shades lighter
than her vibrant hair.

"Here's your food!" The server from before was
back. She casually placed down Cadence and Rosada's
food, but slowed when she put Gabriel's in front of him,
subtly brushing against him in the process.

Rosada cleared her throat loudly. "You know, I would have had Arabella come, but she was... getting some work done on her tattoo."

Gabriel froze, and the waitress left.

Cadence looked at her, only slightly confused. "So, she's not hanging out with Harrison?"

"No." She spoke harshly, firmly, and then tried again. "They broke up."

Gabriel's whole body seized. Desperate to change the subject, he blurted, "I have a tattoo!"

"What?" Rosada pestered.

"Yeah," Cadence answered for him, suddenly energized. "In fact, the crazy part is that it's just like Arabella's, except it's done in black ink."

Rosada's face filled with shocked realization.

The next morning, Arabella stood by her front window. Every few moments, she would part the turquoise curtains to check if Ember had pulled up. She was dressed in black yoga pants, tennis shoes and a T-shirt like any other day, but had been previously informed by Mika that she would be changing into some sort of gear when she got to the Anacora. She nervously braided her hair. Repeatedly.

She was just going to look through the curtains one

more time. Taking a deep breath, she went outside to meet her instead of waiting for her to come and ring the doorbell. Nervous butterflies fluttered in her stomach, her heart was in her stomach, and her stomach was in her throat.

This was it.

She either became a Clock Keeper, or left the weight of the world on Kat's shoulders. She was really starting to regret eating breakfast, even a light one that consisted of an egg and toast. She could lose everything in an hour and no one would know; a secret to the world but a catastrophe to her.

"Ready to go?" Ember called out, flipping up her helmet visor, her eyes in a familiar glare. But Arabella knew the brunette well enough to see the sympathy in her hazel eyes.

"As I'll ever be," she muttered and nodded at Ember, determined to make her grandmother proud.

"You sure you can ride this thing without falling off halfway down the road?" Ember scoffed and patted the bike. She handed her a cherry red helmet, which Arabella secured before answering.

"Yeah, I've ridden before," she rebuffed, swinging her leg smoothly over the bike and feeling the leather give comfortingly where she sat. She explained distractedly, "my dad has always ridden, so I grew up on motorcycles and ATVs. In fact, if I didn't think it would scare my parents to death-"

"Just hang on." Ember cut her off as the crotch rocket sped away from the curb without warning. Then she sighed, "I should check out your bike sometime."

Arabella smirked. "Okay."

They drove to a field in between Eagle and Star, in one of the Treasure Valley's more rural areas. That meant dirt roads, which were not fun to go over in December's sleek little road bike. She could feel every little bump. Eventually, they arrived at a small wheat field- its crop already harvested and frostbitten this late in the year. Nothing but similar fields surrounded them; in the distance, some trees rose and eventually gave way to foothills.

As expected, Arabella Grace counted three, no two, figures in the middle of the field. Two. They were both clearly female and both around the short height of her two instructors. Sometimes she felt a giantess amongst the pixies she surrounded herself with. Where was Rosada? Rosie was her rock, she couldn't do this without her. She made Arabella feel like she wasn't alone.

Arabella and Ember both headed over to meet the other two women. While Ember walked at a brisk pace over to her grandmother and Mika, Arabella trudged along slow and dazed, searching everywhere for a head of pink hair. Panic was starting to claw at her insides, and something rose in her throat as she spun in circles, scanning the space for her friend.

"Arabella!" Someone snapped at her, but she didn't know who. She continued to look around, frantic with panic. "Arabella!" *Oh no, Cade...*

She felt a claw-like hand dig into her shoulder with sharp fingers. She turned to come face to face with Mika, her usually soft golden eyes were cold and hardened. Like molten lava being dipped into water, she could almost hear all signs of warmth sizzle out. "We need to go." Her voice was low and detached, a little more than the whispering of a scorned ghost- an echo, devoid of emotion.

Arabella looked around once more. "But, Rosie? " she questioned. "She's supposed to be here." Her head turned once more on a swivel, hoping to deny the truth that her mind was supplying. She refused to think that her best friends, the star crossed lovers, had been caught. Because that meant that if she had been there last night, she could have saved them.

"We need to go," Mika repeated, her eyes revealing nothing- not one ounce of recognition at her daughter's name. Instead, they stayed cold- still warm, burnt orange in color, but distant. Her voice was just as detached, but her hand did tighten on Arabella's shoulder, however, just enough to show that she had heard her. The gesture didn't reveal if she was trying to be comforting or disapproving.

"But..." her words of protest were drowned out by

Ailith.

"Arabella, dear, it's time to go." Ailith walked over to the pair and gently moved Arabella away from Mika, while Ember hung back waiting for them.

Arabella looked at Ailith, her dread on the tip of her tongue. The older woman merely shook her head, as if to say, 'now is not the time'. Despite her reassurance, or lack thereof, the dread in her stomach grew and constricted her heart. It felt like a breathing monster. It ate away at her self confidence, it caused her whole body to shake and her mind to race. The monster would slowly destroy her from the inside out.

Ailith took a deep breath and cleared her throat. Melancholy hit Arabella between the ribs as she realized, in her spirit, that Ailith was using her Clock's magic for the last time.

"I summon the Anacora, I wish to enter this safe haven with clear and pure intentions. I ask it to reveal itself and to help us. I wish to see into the veil." Even though her words were clear, and she spoke modern English, Arabella honestly couldn't have told you what words had been spoken. She was too busy looking at Ailith. Despite her height, Ailith looked larger than life, and Arabella felt the stark contrast between their maturity- there was so much she didn't see clearly. Admitting that was the most clear sighted she had ever been. Ailith held her hands, laying palm up, straight in front of her. The bright blue sky was dimming and the winter wind chilled around them, but not a single silver hair moved on Ailith's crown. Her tea-green eyes turned red as they emanated the Clock Keeper's glow.

Suddenly, a mansion shimmered in and out of view in waves, until it finally solidified- like her wings. The house (if you could call it that), was approximately six stories tall. From what Arabella could see, there were two front-facing-floor-to-ceiling-bay-windows on every floor. Its large wooden door was split down the middle, and on each side were two brass knockers the size of Arabella's head. While the door was all dark woods and metals, the rest of the house was marble slabs and white crystal columns. The closest thing she could equate it to in her mind was the White House. But that was like comparing a first-edition, author signed hard back to a ratty old journal you found at your weird neighbor's garage sale- one that was missing pages, and was water logged. This structure was the gateway between worlds.

She gasped in shock, Rosie and Cade momentarily forgotten, although the bundle of aching nerves were still there, twisting in her gut and numbing her limbs. The image and reality of this magnificent sight pushed through the buzzing feeling spreading though her veins; she began to glow, softly, and from the corner of her eye, she could see Ember do the same. Then there was Ailith, who bittersweetly gazed upon the two juvenile would-be heroes.

The only person who didn't seem to be

experiencing some type of energy burst from being in the Anacora's presence was Mika, who just stood there as still as stone, and as cold as ice. Arabella was almost surprised when she moved; she had half expected her to stay in the same stoic position forever: years from now, tourists would be lining up, paying to see the statue of the 'pissed off human-ish person'. When she did move, the movement was robotic and alien compared to what Arabella had come to think of Mika's persona. She was completely wrapped up in her thoughts, her posture stiff, with white lined lips and frozen eyes. She marched up the steps. With each step, Arabella could've sworn she heard the hinges creak, until her instructor reached the door, not even hesitating to knock with the brass hula hoops that passed for knockers.

The doors swung open, and the group was able to see what looked like a grand foyer: complete with piano, chandelier, and spotless white marble.

"Creepy," she couldn't help but whisper. She saw Ember nod and heard Ailith chuckle. The robot stayed the same. This wasn't Mika; she just stood on the steps, not going forward or backward. Arabella could tell that it wasn't just the entryway that made her hesitate- she was on the fence about something.

Just then, a man appeared with two guards, they were twins. The man was tall and spindly, with elongated limbs and spider leg-like fingers. The wrinkled appendages were long and thin, and his pale skin clung to his bones like shrink wrap. Yet, despite all of his odd features, you could tell that once upon a time he had been handsome; he now wore age like a finely tailored suit- with his dark, peppered hair, light, twinkling blue eyes, pointed chin, and high-set cheek bones. Against which was something that looked like golden paint splatter, assumedly, his Book Keeper trait. He bowed at the waist, folding his 6'7" foot body in half; a dapper black suit was draped over his lanky frame.

The twins were identical and dressed in what looked like a mix between black pajamas and armor. They both had dirty blonde hair: one had loose surfer dreads and the other short, razor cropped hair. Their Book Keeper traits varied slightly from one another. 'Surfer Dude' had a crow resting beneath his ear, while 'Army' had a blue jay. 'Surfer' was also trying to subtly play candy crush on his smart watch, while 'Army' looked scornfully at his brother. Besides that, they both had big brown eyes, upturned noses, golden skin, and square jaws.

As the man bowed, the juxtapose pair behind him followed suit.

"Hello," he smiled warmly. "I'm Dac Kien- I am master of the Book Keepers, and it is my honor and pleasure to watch over your Clock bonding.

'Surfer Dude' tried to wave, but 'Army' elbowed him and whispered in a voice that everyone heard, "we're not supposed to be distracting."

Dac cleared his throat and smiled. Still standing in

the doorway, he gestured with one willowy arm for them to come in.

They all huddled into the towering mansion, eager to learn its secrets. The three women accompanying Arabella looked comfortable in what she could assume was a semi-familiar setting, while she just felt nerves conflicting with awe.

They all smiled at him and the twins as they passed. Ailith even gave Dac a hug as if they were old friends.

"You, my dear, must be Arabella." Dac turned toward her, his blue eyes twinkling with hope, yet something akin to dread played in the shadows behind the light. "It's a pleasure." He spoke warmly and shook her hand with hands softer than she would have thought possible for someone his age. He could probably feel the cold sweat that she had been trying to erase against her jeans since they arrived.

For some reason, she felt like curtsying, but instead, she merely gave him a warm, if shaky, smile of her own. "For me as well," she replied, her eyes darting to her companions, who gave her reassuring looks that she wasn't messing this all up. Or at least Ailith, was. But Ember didn't look quite as coarse and cold.

"Shall we move on?" he asked with a tight smile. He ushered them down a grand hallway that seemed to suddenly appear. She glanced around and shrugged, then

followed behind Dac. She knew she wasn't alone; she
could feel the others behind her, and the one twin was still
trying to play candy crush when they left them in the foyer.
Despite not being alone, the ball of dread remained rooted
in her gut- a reminder of the failings, the doubt and despair
she couldn't seem to shake. If I had only been there, she
thought, thinking of Rosada.

They walked down the hall for a while, and
Arabella tried to take her mind off of- well everything- by
admiring the glass and marble all up and down the
passageway; even the doors were made of the magnificent
stone. When she asked Dac where they led, he offhandedly
remarked something about other dimensions, slight
variations of our world. *Huh.*

She admired the corridor further and wondered
where the crystal doors led. The lighting was perfect- soft,
glowing light, warm and twinkling with threaded gold. It
radiated from fixtures that uniformly sat above each door.
She abruptly walked into something hard. Actually, that
something hit her right in the forehead. She reached up to
evaluate the damage of the sudden discomfort, happy to
discover no blood, when she realized that she had run into
Dac.

"Terribly sorry," he apologized kindly; she
discovered that he had stopped in front of a door far
different from the rest. It was bright liquid gold. Its surface
seemed to shift and change.

Fear zapped through her like lightning. "Is this it?" *Whoa, I'm nervous.* Her chest felt uncomfortably tight. There was this thing about anticipation that gave her anxiety, drove her insane- it was like a physical sickness; no matter what she told herself or what she did, the dread just wouldn't go away. She could feel a lump at the back of her throat, and she felt like she was constantly choking on it. No matter how much she swallowed, the ball just would not dissipate.

"Unfortunately, yes, my dear." He sighed as if sensing her fear and gave a sad and slow chuckle- his lanky frame shaking only slightly. "You know, it's weird: I've been a Book Keeper since I was 18 years old, and now... well, let's just say I'm older than that." He again gave a low, dry laugh. "I was shown how to do this only once by my own grandpa when it was Ailith's turn. That was my first time, you'll be my second in this generation, following Ember, of course. In January, I'll have my third." He didn't mention a fourth. "All of the sudden, after all these years, we have to do these ceremonies, and our worlds collide anew." Dac pushed open the door, and they were all blinded by a radiant light.

Chapter 19: Her New and Unstable World.

She choked. The light she saw was so bright and pure, like bleached sunlight, and it steamed out of the door frame like Heaven's gates calling home. It was overwhelming; she was physically unable to say the words on the tip of her tongue. The light was so intense- she couldn't recall a time she'd seen anything so vivid. It was certainly more beautiful and natural than the florescent hospital bulbs. The thought brought tears to her eyes as it uncovered her constant companion of grief. Or maybe it was just the light. It enveloped them completely.

Finally, the light died down. "Holy Hades, what was that?!" Arabella rubbed her eyes. When she attempted to focus, black dots filled her vision. All the edges were blurry, and she felt light headed.

She thought about reaching out and leaning against the wall's cool marble surface next to her, but visions of her sliding down its face filled her head. So instead, she stood there, swaying, until she was relieved to feel Ailith grip her upper arm lovingly. She knew it was Ailith immediately from the feel of her coarse, but caring hands. She lowered her hands and raised her eyes. She tried to hold herself confidently, with her chin up, but the effect was ruined by the way it trembled. That didn't matter, because as soon as her eyes opened, her jaw dropped. Yet, in a way, well... she had almost expected the sight in front of her when she opened her eyes. A courtroom sprawled before her, and

Arabella suddenly missed the winding corridors of Ailith's house with a horrible urgency. The room was almost exactly the same as you would imagine any TV-Land courtroom to be. And like them, it was made completely out of wood of the same deep color. It even had practical light fixtures hanging around the room.

"That was an inter-dimensional portal," Dac supplied, shattering the silence.

"Awesome." Arabella spoke plainly and stepped out of Ailith's grip.

She followed Dac into the courtroom, where they were greeted by six assumed colleagues- three men and three women- whom Arabella had just noticed were in the room.

They were all the same- all dressed in grey tweed from head to toe, with slicked-back peppered hair, and they all had their hands folded in front of them. When they did smile, every face looked pinched and pained from the effort. Yet, despite the similarities, they were arranged in unique pairs. She recalled Ailith's lesson regarding how each Book Keeper had unique defining characteristics.

Dac greeted each one of them with a stiff nod, and the rest of his composure became still as well, like he was just realizing why he was there- this day would affect the fate of their world. Then he turned toward her, "Arabella, this is the rest of the Book Keeper Council." He then pointed left to right, from women to men, in the small courtroom. "This is Mrs. Avery Alethea, Mrs. Saffi Darissa, Mrs. Sofia Eldridge, Mr. Nester Alethea, Mr. Quinn Darissa, and Mr. Arif Eldridge. Each couple was completely distinct from the others. The Aletheas both had two little, smooth, white, marble-like dots above their lips- like snake bites. Neither of the two looked like the kind of people who would get the latest piercing fad. The Darissas had blue teeth. Arabella stifled a nervous giggle at the mental image of the stoic duo eating Fun Dip. The Eldridges both had what looked like metal right hands, and it looked to Arabella that they weren't prosthetics, but metallic flesh. They were all so strange, and yet all of them looked completely comfortable and at peace. Well, as peaceful as a stiff suit could look. She decided to mentally dub them 'The Big Wigs'.

"Are you ready?" Mrs. Darissa inquired. She was a willow of a woman, and her blue stained teeth pressed tightly against her thin lips. Her arms were still placed formally, clasped stiffly in front of her placid facade. Panic filled Arabella faster that she could say 'shuddersome'.

"No, she's not ready," came a snap from behind Arabella. She turned slightly, but she really didn't need to; she knew who had spoken from the snippy and pissed off tone of voice. It belonged to the only person (besides maybe Ember) who could possibly sound that mad in this awe worthy moment. Maybe awe was the wrong word, it was more like being in living electricity: shock waves seemed to pulse through the air, and a sizzled, copper taste played a harsh dance- in heels- on her tongue.

"No?" Mr. Darissa raised one perfectly trimmed eyebrow- it was sleek and peppered like his hair. He straightened his monkey suit, and gave one of the most forced, and bluest, smiles that Arabella had ever seen- which was shocking, because she had seen his wife's Botox-esque grin.

"No," she replied again, just as harsh, and Arabella had to shake her head in most ruthful surprise. She turned around again in time to see Ailith place a gentle hand on Mika's shoulder, and pull her slightly back with the shake of her head- clearly saying 'back down'. Ailith jumped to speak before Mika could continue, "what Mrs. Nasima is trying to say, is that Arabella needs to be prepared and get her armor on before we can proceed," she cordially smoothed the tension with her honey sweet voice.

They all nodded, and she felt relief flood through her.

"That is completely acceptable," Dac replied, his voice as crisp as fall air.

Somewhere behind her, she heard Ember huff, and for once, the sound wasn't annoying, but comforting. It reminded her of the small and perfect peace she had managed to acquire this last week and a half in the easy routine of her new life. But Arabella knew that those times were over, and a sort of depressing acceptance fell over her at the thought. The feeling was akin to when your favorite character in a book died. She felt like she was drowning from the inside out. All she had really wanted was to protect her friends and family. She felt alone. But then she realized that wasn't true, because she knew that when Ember huffed, it was her way of showing that she had her back.

"Thank you," Ailith spoke politely and shot a look at Ember that made Arabella want to stand up for the brunette she-devil, who had grown on Arabella. She had come to mean something to her in her new and unstable world, a world that was now crumbling underfoot. Arabella was falling, and even as she plummeted, she knew that Ember was there, spiraling downward with her- and that no one else was falling but the two of them. It was frightening, but inevitable, for the two to spin out of carefully crafted control, control as fragile as glass that had been made with shaking fingers.

Mrs. Eldridge gave what was the closest thing to a sympathetic laugh that Arabella thought she could make. Then she raised her hands, and with the snap of her fingers- literally- a door appeared on the farthest wall from them in the courtroom, right behind the judge's bench.

The door was like the courtroom's door, in the sense that it was completely different from anything else Arabella had ever seen. Instead of being composed of liquid and twisting gold, however, this door was made of pure, warm light- like sunlight falling through fall leaves. The glow illuminated the room, and everyone was squinting, especially Arabella, with her light blue eyes.

"Whoa," Arabella marveled.

At the same time, Ember made a sound akin to a vampire hissing- no doubt this much pure light probably wasn't good for someone with that fair of skin. Now that Arabella thought about it, it probably wasn't very good for hers- she baked like a potato and then turned into a tomato in the sun.

"Well, go on." Arabella turned to see that it was Mrs. Eldridge who was urging her forward. Arabella gave her a small smile, which she thought she saw returned. She inched forward, somehow knowing that the others would follow. She tread gingerly across the courtroom, feeling like she was battling roaring wind to get there. The only thing that seemed to exist in the space was that brilliant light. The closer she got, the warmer the light became. She waded through until she was standing in front of it. Arabella was bathing in the glow, basking in its warmth. She had the enveloping feeling of being curled up with a good book in front of a crackling flame on Christmas Eve, finishing up a steaming cup of cocoa while a cute, good-feels movie played on the TV. She could almost feel how heavy her eyelids would be as sleep finally found her amongst the comforting pages of her novel. It gave her the feeling of being safe and protected, and in spite of her earlier apprehension, she knew she would be safe. She never wanted this feeling to end. A gentle hand touched her shoulder, bringing her back from her daydream. She looked behind her to see Ailith's smiling and sympathetic face. Ailith gave her a gentle and almost imperceptible nod; the nod promised that everything would be fine, for now at least. But, in that moment, she believed in that promise, so she opened the door. Under her breath, she hummed her and Cadence's song- also now Rosie's favorite. She wanted to bring them with her, even if they couldn't be there. But all it did was carve sadness into the edges of her warmth. So instead of dwelling, she reached her right hand into the light. In spite of its intensity, it didn't burn at all, but enhanced the feeling of safety.

Suddenly, Gabriel was brought to mind. That feeling bolstered her courage so she was able to grasp hold of the door knocker and swing the door open as she stepped into the stone room behind it. The room was reminiscent of a chamber from a fairytale castle- with grey stone walls and an ice blue and emerald green stained glass window in the shape of an arch letting in the colored sunlight. What light didn't come from sunlight came from the torches on the walls- their rusted steel sconces and oil scents wafting throughout the room. When she turned, she saw Ember coming in last after the first two; she was closing a wooden door. No more was the warm feeling. All that was left was a pair of twisting eels in her stomach, butterflies in her chest, and water in her lungs. She imagined for a moment that she was dreaming. The erratic flapping of the butterflies' wings matched the way her heart pounded drastically against her chest.

There were three pieces of furniture in the room- a dress form, a paper changing screen, and a small table with a glass pitcher filled to the brim with cool water. Five crystal cut glasses sat next to it. Rosie was supposed be here. Arabella snuck a glance at Mika, whose expression teetered on thinly veiled anger.

On the dummy was a suit of armor- it was made of tough hide. Where it wasn't covered in leather, it was comprised of metallic mesh. There was a black chain mail "hoodie" that went over the top. There was also a leather sword strap and sheath for her Imprint; the beautifully wicked sword would look amazing against all the black leather. The boots seemed high enough to go just below her knees; they were crested at the top and had black steel toes, but the soles had absolutely no heel at all- presumedly to minimize sound. Knowing her luck, she would probably bang her toe against something and alert anything that was after her to her exact location. Stealthy boots only went so far.

"Are you ready?" Ailith asked, gesturing to the armor.

"Yes, I am," she replied with a light nod, not

completely sure. Needing to do something with her nervous energy, she started to re-braid her hair.

Then Arabella took off her light winter coat, placing it on the floor next to the table and started to move behind the screen.

"You can leave that on," Ailith referred to Arabella's black tank top and jeans. "But you're going to have to take off the motorcycle boots."

Scowling, Arabella obliged. At least the other boots were black too. "Thank you," she smiled at her, realizing how hard this probably was for her teacher. Behind her, she heard Mika and Ember lean against the stone wall, which probably wasn't terribly comfortable. Nervousness twisted her intestines, and a lump seemed to have taken up a permanent residence in her throat as she watched Ailith reach for the first article of attire- the pants. "Now as you can see, the pants have plates set in them made of thick wyvern leather on the front of your thigh, and another plate on the back, and also on the front shin. The mesh is made of steel threads."

Arabella took the pants and did the awkward hop around dance to put them on. They were perfect, if slightly cold. She became excited when she saw Ailith grab the next piece of clothing, and suddenly she had a lump in her throat for a different reason- she was practically vibrating with love for her armor. Then Ailith handed her the boots. "The boots are made of softer leather on the outside, and thicker leather on the inside, with black, steel tipped toes and altering layers of leathers in varying densities and textures on the soles. This allows for soft, but strong, stealth movements. In other words, you can still kick butt, but you don't squeak when you walk."

Arabella squeezed them on, and as much as she adored her motorcycle boots, these were made for her.

Then came the shirt. "The shirt is long sleeved and made of the same materials as the pants. It laces up in the back for perfect fit and leaves no room for vulnerabilities." Once Arabella shimmied it on from the front, Ailith came and cinched it up tightly, and Arabella finally understood the need for fainting couches in the 1800s. Then Ailith touched two loops of steel cord at the cusp of each of Arabella's sleeves. "These are for slipping your thumbs through- they are made of the same thickly woven steel thread, and when you pull on them, two slits appear on your back, allowing your wings to unfurl."

Sweet.

Ailith stepped away from her and gave her the chain mail. "This is for extra protection from piercing, and is also inflammable; the metal is enchanted. Plus, the slits are already built in, so when you are ready to fly, again, just hook your thumbs through and tug." Arabella slipped it on over her head, and when she was done... she felt extremely B.A. Yet, something was missing. "There is also a little, discreet, wyvern leather pouch on the side of your lower

thigh for your phone." Then she handed over the black
leather sheath and slid her arming sword, with its intricate
swirls of mother of pearl inlay in the handle, into place. She
slipped her phone into the side pouch, but imagined she
wouldn't be using it much. It's not like you can get on
Pinterest, read, or play Helix Jump while fighting for your
life. She strapped on her sheath, belting it over the chain
mail, loving the way the weight swung against her in a
familiar pattern- moving with her like the waves washing
over the same rocks everyday in a lull of ebb and flow of
give and gentle crash as she moved fluidly in her new gear.

"So, I have a question," she murmured, lovingly
playing with the handle of her sword and feeling her braid
slip over her shoulder as she gazed down upon the Imprint.

"Yes?" It was Mika who answered, not Ailith, as
she stepped out from behind Arabella. Ember followed the
Morph's lead. Her golden eyes flashed dangerously, as if
daring her to ask what was really on her mind.

She swallowed quickly, her panic returning after
her momentary reprieve caused by the buzz induced from
donning her deadly clothing. "Where did all this come
from?"

"Oh," Mika said stiffly.

But before she could say more, Ember
chirped, "Well, I can answer that. This is your room. It
reflects your personality; your essence. This door, room,
portal, represent your dream world, your ideal 'happy

place'. It figures that it would be a mythical, fantasy-era setting. Don't look so dumbfounded. And your things, they were transported here." She answered in a bored tone, and looked like she wished she had a knife to clean the dirt out from under her nails.

There was no reason for her to sound so irritated, Ember was lucky it wasn't the Hufflepuff common room.

"Oh, and before I forget, here's this." Ember threw a small dagger, concealed in an ankle sheath. It looked like one of Rosada's. "Just in case."

"Thanks," Arabella gave her a nod as she knelt down to strap it on, waiting for the snappy quip to follow. She never got one and mentally shrugged it off.

"There is only one thing I can say before you go in," Ailith cautioned as they left the room and returned to the courtroom where the Book Keepers nodded greetings as they re-entered.

"Yes?" the newly armor-clad girl played with the end of her braid and raised her eyebrows curiously.

"The Trials test you on the traits and skills of a Clock Keeper- intelligence, optimism, nobility, kindness, loyalty, self-confidence, love, and forgiveness- so just be yourself, and you'll do great." She gave her a long hug; her words were eerily similar to what her grandmother had said to her only a few short months ago, and grief crept over Arabella. While she felt like she had gotten over her grandmother's death, she would never get over her life. She had to push past the grief and be strong.

It was what her grandma would have wanted.

Her skills and character traits- she was worried that she wouldn't be up to par with all of these standards. She decided that the best thing to do when you were scared was to make a joke, "wait, so all Clock Keepers have these traits? Well then, how in the world did Ember ever pass?" She quirked her right eyebrow.

Ember sneered.

And Ailith giggled. "It varies, some people have some of these traits stronger than others, or are stronger in one and weak in another.

"Thanks," Ember scoffed and walked up to Arabella. "Well, let's hope that this works out for you and me." She had a look upon her face that dared Arabella not to make her proud.

"Yeah, let's hope," she muttered and glanced down at her hand and wrist- she would do this for Kat, she would do this for the Clocks. Suddenly, Ember was gone and sitting in the courtroom's peanut gallery- followed by Ailith.

She turned to Mika, "any last words, coach?" she joked, trying to glimpse the teacher and friend she had grown close to.

"Yeah. Don't die, that would be too much

paperwork for me," she replied harshly, but the words made Arabella snicker, because they were similar to a line she had read recently in a book series she loved- it was definitely similar to something her favorite alchemist would say. Arabella was certain she was joking, but then realized she wasn't. Her curry eyes, usually as warm as honey, were cold and dead, with a twinge of fury lurking behind them. *She knows I know about Rosada and Cade,* Arabella realized with a start.

I know I should have protected them, she tried to communicate to the worried mother with her remorseful eyes. Mika's eyes softened, barely, but it was there. Then she left to sit with the others.

Arabella gave them one last uncertain smile before turning toward Dac.

"Are you ready?" he prompted in his throaty voice as he leaned toward her in a gentlemanly fashion. She half expected him to offer her his arm.

She nodded, unsure at first, then again with no doubt in her mind, thinking of Kat, Rosada, Gabriel, Cadence, her grandma... and herself. "I'm ready," her declaration rang out strong and clear, she almost didn't recognize her own, usually hesitant, pitch. He and the rest of his colleagues nodded together, then circled around her. They snapped simultaneously, and it echoed throughout the room. *Huh, apparently it's slam poetry night*, she joked to herself. There was a sudden flash of light, and then she was gone.

Chapter 20: A Twist of Colors.

She was in a room- a classroom, very much like one from her school. The room contained four white walls, a single white board, and coarse, dark grey carpet that covered the floor space. It smothered creativity while maintaining a frigid air that left Arabella shivering in her leather protection. On the white board was written, **'The Righteous? Or the Wicked?'**

The two terms reflected the black and white landscape, littered with pops of grey, that represented the supernatural world. She wasn't sure what the test would be, but with her hand resting on her Imprint's hilt, she would try to be prepared for anything.

A glow lit the room, and Arabella squinted into the spark. When the glow dissolved, a creature was left in its place. It was a girl, and she was spinning a rock in her hand, grinning. She tossed it higher and higher. Grinning wider and wider. Why would she have a rock? Arabella thought of the supernaturals she had learned about. The girl didn't make any move, just continued to toss her rock. Then, a memory came to mind: *Koshei, a creature whose soul is kept separate from their body. Like Voldemort. And they're wicked.* "Wicked." She spoke clearly. The light flashed once more.

The following beast was down on all fours, with a long, sleek, armored body, colored like a sunset. It had large eyes, floppy ears, and a long, pointed muzzle. It was like an armadillo and a fox had a love child, only the fox was half Labrador, and it had just rolled around in orange sherbet. She wanted one. It glowed slightly, the color of soft afternoon light. *A Meno, a being that controls light.* "Righteous."

They converged in the room in rapid succession, one taking the last's place the moment she had spoken. A girl made of vapor took the Meno's place, with white eyes and a silk dress shifting around her, lightning ran like veins under her cumulus skin. *Nephele, cloud nymph.* "Righteous."

An animal rose, as dark as night, the size of a mammoth and feline in shape, with large, snarling teeth the size of a butter dish. *Bugbear, a demon that feeds on nightmares- fitting.* "Wicked."

It was a fairy the next time, small and made up of an intricate color scheme, with chiffon wings and a long tail. Except she noticed that it had pupils. "Wicked," she said, picking out its true nature. *Not fairy, pixie.*

A giant, scaled dragon appeared, with flickering reptile eyes and a long forked tongue. *A wyvern.* Its scales matched her plated armor. "Wicked."

Two feet of absolute blue followed, with narrowed eyes and an oval shaped mouth. It had bright green irises and rubber smooth skin. *Nix, a water spirit.* "Righteous."

Next came a long snake tail, instead of legs,

attached to a male torso and face, but his hair was comprised of short little snakes, and his nails were long. His eyes were little slits. *Culebras, where Medusa originated from.* "Righteous." *You can't always judge a book by its cover.*

It was giant and covered in white fur: *Yetis.* "Righteous." Each time her voice rang stronger and clearer.

She saw a whole ugly mess of hybrid creatures: *lions and tigers and bears, oh my! A Chimeras.* "Wicked."

Then there was a small dwarf with bright red hair and a long, crooked nose. *Redcap.* "Wicked."

The next one was tall, and its arms dragged against the ground; its skin was the color of mushrooms, and patches of dead grass covered its body. *Bogle, spirit that causes confusion.* "Wicked."

Something the size of a mouse with a mouth full of shark teeth emerged, the glint in its eye was terrifying. *Imp, mischievous rodent.* "Righteous." She eyed it warily.

The next one actually was a fairy, with its long tail and creepy, pupil-less eyes. "Righteous."

Oaky, ashen skin and deep foreboding eyes grew into a figure the size of a tree. *Elven.* "Righteous."

The half-man-half-horse was easy; *centaur.* "Righteous."

Then there was a boy made completely of grey stone and clay- *golem.* "Righteous."

Bright green, smooth skin and flaming pink hair,

with eyes glowing electric blue almost made her tear up. *Simper Nimph, Rosie.* "Righteous," she practically growled.

A flickering ghost, with yellow eyes and rotten teeth.*Wraith, evil spirit.* "Wicked."

A giant troll with large buck teeth and hammers for hands. *Jotunn.* "Wicked."

A shimmering white unicorn with angel wings materialized. *Alicorn.* "Wicked," she pouted.

A small, frog-looking creature with midnight blue water shrouding its body and pitch black eyes that hungered took the alicorn's place. *Kappa, water spirit that drowns its victims.* "Wicked."

She watched as a small turtle that appeared that looked to be made of sparkling plum colored silk with soft grey irises came into focus. It gave a soft smile, revealing thousands of needle-sharp teeth. *Nakki, pond spirit that protects people from kappas.* "Righteous."

There was another girl. She looked human and had a sunflower in her hair...no, it was sprouting from her hair, and Arabella could see small wildflowers sprouting like rings from her fingers, she had earthy coloring with dirty blond hair, tan skin, and dark green eyes. *Witch, half-elf and half-human.* "Righteous."

Arabella was prepared for the next creature to appear, but instead, there was a simple desk, and on that desk, a #2 pencil and a piece of paper. On that paper, a single question:

'What is intelligence?'

It was a simple question, but it left Arabella staring, her mind spinning in circles like a dog chasing its tail. She could have said that intelligence meant being smart, knowing all the answers. But being intelligent was more than that, it meant making the right choices, no matter the circumstances...but that wasn't necessarily true for everyone either. **There isn't a correct answer to this question**, she wrote on the white piece of paper, her pencil lead leaving a swirling trail of letters and sentences. **Intelligence isn't something that can be defined. Some people may call it wisdom, but being smart doesn't mean you're wise. It could be getting a high score on your paper, or being the best in your field. But those are someone else's definitions. It's completely subjective, dependent on the viewer's perspective. But, if I had to choose a definition, I would say that being intelligent is possessing a willingness to understand things, to keep an open mind and heart, to look at the world and question it, question yourself. If you're intelligent, you're willing to discuss topics and create things that are out of society's box. To keep learning and growing. But, that's just my definition in a world full of infinite solutions.**

She finished writing, nervous that she should have just written that intelligence was being smart.

The world swirled and blurred around her in a twist

of colors. The word 'Intelligence' flashed white hot in her head.

When the world stopped being a kaleidoscope of colors and motion, she was in ruins, literally. Everything was shadows and dust, the buildings were little more than foundations. The sky was a black, stormy overcast, and all she could smell and breathe was the sulfur and smoke that singed her lungs and made her eyes water. She just stood there. She had a feeling that this was the world without The Mage. Her hand went over to her sword. As she unsheathed it, it sighed a comforting hiss as it slid free. She held it pointed at the ground in low guard, ready for anything that could possibly come her way. *Think Arabella.* What was going on? She could feel her body start to sag, and the air seemed to become heavier, more smoke filled the wind. A painful cough erupted from her throat and out of her mouth.

She looked around, but all she could see from there to every horizon was destruction. She saw some pieces of gleaming white, but she didn't even want to know the horrible things they could have been.

She walked, unsure, and glanced from left to right once more, her golden braid swinging steadily against her back. Her attention was caught by what looked like a newspaper stand- it was blackened, and the plastic window was replaced by a solid covering of grime. She sheathed her sword and carefully stepped around the crumbled walls as she crept over to it, hopeful that there would be a paper inside. She grasped the handles and could feel the grit embed itself onto her palms and digits, a dirt tattoo. She pulled with all of her might- it wouldn't budge. She braced her other hand against the box and pulled again- nothing. All she had done was wipe some of the dirt away, revealing that it was once glossy red underneath.

Deep breath. She tugged with all of her supernatural strength once more.

Oomph.

She fell backwards and her hands bit into the black shards of gravel that blanketed the ground. The force of her fall had freed the door from its rust. She stood, dusted her hands against her pants quickly, and eagerly grabbed the paper inside. What she saw confirmed her worst intuitions. The paper boldly stated:

The End. A real life apocalypse.

And she had been dropped smack dab in the middle of it. She glanced down at the paper again- she was in Chicago.

Chicago? Why Chicago? Alrighty then.

She closed her eyes to take a deep breath, but they snapped open as soon as she shut them. Her family. And her friends... Gabriel, Rosie, Cadence. Panic seized her chest. She had to get to Boise. Somehow she knew that when she found them, everything would be better. She had to chuckle though- it was like her own personal Hunger Games or Divergent. Hey, she was even in Chicago. Her revelation was her only hope.

So she started to walk in what she somehow knew was the perfect direction.

...

22 days of non-stop walking, nothing more and nothing less of that Hell. She hardly took breaks, and she found that she honestly didn't need them. A couple of months ago she would have been stopping every 10 minutes to catch her breath- now she could go hours without reprieve, into the night and throughout the day. When she did stop, it was usually for a brief nap, or to eat or find water, or so that she could doctor her feet with some bandages and fresh socks that she got from an abandoned convenience store.

She started to feel like it was some sort of karma for all the times she had gotten out of going for hikes with her mom. Oh, how Sarah Grace would be laughing at her now. But Arabella continued, because she knew that despite the situation, it could always get better. She would be able to find her family- she just knew it. Her hair was a wreck; it resembled a bird's nest, and pieces of it had started to dread together. With no baths, it was greasy, and instead of its usual beach blonde, it was stringy brown. Her personal hygiene, or lack thereof, was starting to weigh on her.

Seriously, she was rank! A teenager plus no bath equals a funky smell. But she carried on, walking somewhere on a lonesome highway. She tried to keep track of where she was by road signs, but had been on autopilot for the past couple days and felt like she was on the edge of delirium. Still she trudged on. She would not give up. Then, as if it had always been just over the next hill, the Boise valley miraculously came into view- she was almost home! Her tired limbs seemed to spring to life again as she raced through the familiar city. It reminded her of the time she had chased after Ember, what seemed like years ago- before she knew her destiny.

With her heart feeling renewed and her head held high, she made it to her home at last. The only sound in the decimated city was the light padding of her boots against the concrete. Her limbs strangely didn't ache anymore. She came to a stop in front of her house at a skid, knowing that she had made it this far by never once losing hope.

The gingerbread colored house, with its whimsical yard art and turquoise curtains in the front windows, was a beacon of faith. It was her own personal lighthouse, and she stared at it in wonder as she walked up the walkway, drinking in the landscaping, familiar and comforting. She came upon her dark wood door and placed her hands against the steel doorknob, its cool texture smooth under her calloused finger pads. She pushed it open gently, hearing the sound of bright laughter inside as she opened it.

Then the world spun and the word 'Optimism'
showed under her eyelids.

When she rematerialized, all of her imperfections
from the last task were gone. Her sword was shimmering
and unscarred, and her feet no longer whined. They felt
warm instead of waterlogged. Her hair was once again
slicked back into a braid, and most importantly, she didn't
have that cloud of stink around her anymore (she was pretty
sure she had seen a bug buzz by too close to her and drop
dead- just like that). Instead, she smelled fresh, like her
usual vanilla body spray scent.

She was in an alley, and it wasn't a cool alley like
Freak Alley. It was just a boring alley in between what
looked like two apartment buildings. Both sides were made
of grey cinder block, and both had windows lining the
walls on the higher levels that were dotted by random
planter boxes for those dreamers who were still idealistic.
The alley had two openings, with a street running parallel
on each end. She could see the blur of traffic, and every
once in a while, a lone cyclist from where she stood over a
small storm drain in the middle of the dark passageway.

None of these things should have caused her any
worry, but despite that flimsy reassurance, her palms were
sweaty and her heart raced. She had a flight or fight urge in

her gut that was threading its way through her pulse. Her right hand automatically went to her waist to reach for her sword.

"Can you help me, dearie?" a soft voice asked from behind. She jumped so high she could have hit a bat, then she spun in place and released her sword to meet her assailant's throat... who happened to be about 90 and had the frame of a glass bird. She had what were possibly the largest coke bottle glasses on that Arabella had ever seen and a small wooden cane. She was, sadly, hunched over her cane, with three bags of groceries in each frail little arm. And to top off the look, she was wearing a cotton, floral print muumuu.

You're kidding me.

This lady couldn't inspire fear in a chipmunk. Arabella was sweating. She realized she had her sword out and quickly put it away. She wished she could put her dread away just as easily.

"What a lovely baseball bat that is," the obviously senile woman remarked sweetly. "So, can you?" she repeated.

"Can I what?" Arabella asked in panic. Her eyes darted around the alley, sure that something was lurking in a darkened crevice, biding its time until she dropped her guard, even though she had defeated the darkness.

"Help me?" the woman reiterated sweetly, struggling slightly under the weight of her bags.

"With what?" Arabella implored warily, her eyes darting around. Her palms were sticky, she had to run them against the leather of her pants every few seconds.

"With my bags, of course. I can't get to my apartment by myself. It seems that I overindulged," she chortled, turning her bespectacled owl eyes on Arabella- they were a milky blue. "Please?"

Arabella knew two things in this world- one: that her last name being Grace was some sort of cosmic irony, and two: that if she went with this old lady, something bad was going to happen. She could feel it in her gut- no matter how optimistic she tried to be, the hope from before had dissolved. Something grievous was coming her way. Standing there in that alley, with a crippled old lady and a mountain of guilt swallowing her pride, she drew a shaky breath and chanced one look into the elderly lady's magnified, pleading eyes. She took another gulp of air and blew it out in a gust between her teeth. "Where do you live?"

"Thank you so much; it's hard to find help from young people these days!" She gave Arabella a hug, and in the process, dumped all of her bags into Arabella's not-so-waiting-arms. It was only her recently honed reflexes that prevented her from dropping them.

"My pleasure." She grunted from the weight of the

bags- the old lady was stronger than she looked. It was as if Arabella's heightened strength had all but disappeared. She still couldn't help but feel that terrible danger was near.

"This way!" she called, waving her over with her hands; her voice was distant- probably because she was already at the end of the alley.

How did she...? Arabella decided it was better not to question it- it must be some Trial ju-ju. Arabella raced to catch up with the mysterious older woman. It was what her grandfather would have called a 'blonde' moment. When Arabella glanced behind her, the alley where she had just been standing was no longer bright, but was instead shrouded in darkness. She shuddered and hurriedly ran faster toward the old woman, who just stood there, smiling obliviously.

"This way," she gestured again as she hurried down the busy street, not really watching where she was going and smiling sweetly as people barreled past her, yelling unkind words at her when she was in their way. "You know, it's bothersome how much of a hurry folks are in nowadays, always on their phones, too busy to look around."

Arabella nodded and followed behind, uncertain. Every once in a while, she'd steal a glance behind her. Her anxiety level was as high as it had been after her grandmother had passed, as high as it had been during the aftermath that followed her episode with The Warlock, and as high as it had been when she had started to enter The Trials- the fate of her sister weighing on her shoulders and the fate of the world spinning around her heart.

Finally, the old woman halted at one of the many buildings that lined the streets. Arabella tensed, waiting for the worst as the old lady put her key into the slot. But, all that followed was the click of the door unlocking. When it swung open, Arabella was tempted to ditch the bags and run.

"It's so nice that the door is automatic; it makes it so much easier." The little old lady rambled on cheerfully. She all but skipped inside.

"I'm sure," the younger woman muttered as she silently cursed at herself for jumping to conclusions. But she still couldn't unclench, so she followed behind with growing trepidation, tensing further at every shadow, knowing that they were more than regular shadows. They were evil Shadows. Okay, that sounded pathetic and stupid, even to her. But she honestly couldn't snake the anticipation of something dreadful coming her way. But it couldn't be The Shadows, could it? Hadn't she defeated that demon?

"Well, come on," granny said, scurrying into one of the three elevators against the opposite wall, only giving Arabella enough time to steal a quick glance around the room and note how it was identical to every other apartment lobby in America.

She stepped into the elevator and sniggered to herself as she remembered what she thought of every time she got into a lift. She rearranged the bags and again thought, *man these are heavy.*

"What's so funny?" the aged lady asked her in curious amusement. Arabella looked down at her with a timid smile, "being in an elevator reminds me of my sister,"

"Why's that?" she asked, chuckling.

"My sister is deathly afraid of them." Arabella chortled, remembering Kathryn's fearful face and wide green eyes whenever she saw one. Arabella would do anything to let that remain Kat's biggest fear.

"Little kids are funny that way," she laughed, "how many siblings do you have?"

Arabella guessed that having a conversation was better than listening to crappy elevator music whilst imagining her own demise. "Two- my little sister, Kat, and my older brother, Thom." She thought about her older brother in the army, probably facing a nameless danger, and yet she couldn't help but think that maybe she was currently in the more perilous situation of the two. Walking the woman home was doing a number on her heartbeat. She was afraid that after this, it would be permanently hammering.

"That's nice dear," she patted Arabella's grocery

holding hand like she was a good dog. Arabella scowled at the same time the elevator rang out with an inevitable and annoying, **DING**!

She hobbled her way out and turned left down a stereotypical hallway, complete with a gilded mirror across from the elevator and peeling yellow wallpaper. The carpet was standard hallway carpet, patterned in black, tan, and navy diamond shapes. Arabella was instantly reminded of Gabriel. This building seemed like some of the hotels he had described to her from the time period when he was moving around a lot, before his parents' divorce. She was suddenly hit with an unimaginable amount of grief stricken acceptance- she would never see his brace-filled grin again. The bright blue color of them always made her smile, even when she was under The Warlock's charm and hadn't been able to remember his face, she had remembered his smile. It didn't matter how bad training or homework was, he pulled her mind away from it all and made her feel human once more, made her feel safe.

Just not this time; she grasped onto the memory of his smirk like it was a life preserver, and she was in the middle of an ocean. Focus.

The lady stopped, and Arabella felt unwanted tears fill her crystal blue eyes, a mixture of salt and dread. She thought about her siblings and how her eyes were always a little greener when she cried, a little more like theirs. Their memory, along with her parents', was stored safely in her heart. Hopefully these last images would comfort her before she died.

On top of the fear, her arms ached from carrying the groceries all the way from the alley, and they seemed to grow heavier as the woman struggled with her golden keys. They were the same color as the doorknob and also the little plaque on the cheap wooden door that marked the room number as 366. That was too close to 666 for Arabella's liking.

"Ahhh, here it is!" she triumphantly held up a small gold colored key to Arabella- not only was the coating chipping, revealing the dull, silver metal underneath, but Arabella was pretty sure it was the key she had started with. In retrospect, it was a good thing, it gave her time to think about her loved ones. She remembered hearing somewhere that death doesn't happen to you, it happens to those around you. While she had probably gotten the quote from one of the teenage fantasy fiction shows she stayed up too late to watch, it didn't change the meaning of the words. They had stuck with her for years and had haunted her after the death of her grandma. Now that notion would ring true for her loved ones.

The little old lady placed the key in the door, and as she did, Arabella tensed. She turned the key at an agonizingly slow pace, as if she took pleasure in Arabella's pain.

The door swung open... and her world swirled

again. The word 'Kindness' flashed.

     She stood in a board room, or a place where a council would be held. Arabella thought over her lessons: The Haunt. The Clock Keepers' safe haven and meeting place. The gift that had been lost. The room was shaped like an octagon and made entirely of honey colored wood, except for the ceiling; the roof was made of yellow and tan stained glass, and when the sunlight streamed through, it gave the whole place a calming and comforting ambience. The farthest left wall had an expansive bookshelf, and on the farthest right wall was an oak door, that despite the whimsical quality of the space, was pretty heavy-duty. The majority of the room was taken up by the round table in the center, similar to one you would find in a school cafeteria-except completely different. In lieu of cheap plastic, it was made of a rich, glossy wood, with turned legs and swirling knots and lines that seemed to tell a complex story.

     Eight chairs were stationed around the table, seven of them were occupied. The first couple of people seated were ones she knew. The first person she noticed was Ember. She glared fiercely, her wild, curly mane more unruly than usual. Arabella knew that, for once, her intimidating stare wasn't directed as her, but at the person across the table from her. And the second person she knew was... Gabriel.

Arabella suddenly felt the tight knot in her chest loosen as if she were finally free. She felt relief spread through her limbs, permeating her with a feeling of comfort and protection that only he could bring. It was strange, considering they hadn't spoken since their almost date. Not since Harri- The Warlock. Her heart felt light, and if it weren't for the somber mood in the storybook room, she would have sang. That was, until she noticed that Gabriel was also glaring at the same person that Ember was. Arabella sat down in the open chair next to Gabriel and he reached under the table to hold her hand. He squeezed it lovingly and shot her a soft glance with his warm green eyes- it just felt right. No matter how long she stared into their depths, she was amazed, and she found herself thinking about those very eyes whenever she let her mind wander. He turned his gaze from her and glared at the person again.

Arabella looked over and took a moment to study the object of their intense hatred, or at least extreme displeasure. But when she looked over, shock rocked through her like a bullet and made her quake in her boots. The person across from her was faceless.

Her only defining characteristic was that she was definitely female, but none of her features were distinct. When she focused on one, it would shift and blur so fast that she couldn't tell what exactly it was. For example, her hair went from short to long, from brown to blue, and everything in between, within the span of a second or two. Everything was constantly changing. When Arabella glanced around the table at the other four people, she found them to be the same as the featureless woman. The only differentiating attribute between them was their gender. There was one other girl, besides Arabella and Ember, and three guys, besides Gabriel.

"I won't allow it!" Gabriel suddenly snarled at the blurry girl and slammed his fist into the table with an echoing thud. Arabella jumped a mile high. Her heart raced almost as fervently as it had all throughout the last Trial. This was a different kind of fear.

"Gabriela is right- it can't happen," Ember agreed in her usual, frost coated tone. But there was a hint of an underlying passion to her words- fire and anger. Arabella ignored her use of the nickname, Gabriela, and looked around the sea of faceless wonders. They were all looking at the first unknown girl- holding their breath, waiting for the next decision. Their demeanors were displayed clearly, somehow, on their indistinct features, and it was obvious that they were siding with her on whatever this argument was about. Ember looked sharply at the guy to her right, but he merely stared ahead, purposely ignoring her. "This is not the only way," Ember pleaded, showing emotions that Arabella had rarely seen her display- her voice even seemed on the verge of cracking and breaking. But in a flash, that trace of emotion disappeared, and she was back to a stone cold warrior.

"It's the only way," the nameless female 'said', although Arabella had no idea how she did it; she didn't have a mouth or a nose to speak of. Yet sound radiated from her in a distinctly feminine voice. Arabella knew that if someone asked her what the lady's voice sounded like, she would never be able to recall it; she would never be able to recognize it again.

Arabella decided to speak up, "what's the only way?" she asked in a strong voice. Again, she surprised herself.

The faceless woman looked at her and in her indistinct voice answered, "the only way to save the world- is to erase you."

Um, creepy...

Wait, what?

"Excuse me?" Arabella managed to sputter out. "What do you mean, 'erase me'?" She tried her?hardest to imitate Ember's hostile tone.

"It's the only way," the featureless chick stated, remorse dripping from her tongue.

"Why?" Arabella probed.

"Because, the only way for all of us- everyone on

Earth- to survive, is for you to sacrifice yourself. You would be erased- forever. Gone and forgotten, like you never existed at all."

Ice cold fear shot through Arabella. Forgotten. Erased from the cosmos. The words repeated on a painful loop through her mind- she would be blotted out. She would cease being. Nothing would tie her to this world. She would never have been. This notion terrified her to no end; it was her worst fear. She wouldn't have anything to show for her life. No one would care or remember her. With that thought, tears pricked at the corners of her eyes. She was frozen in her bones. "Why?" She felt weak.

She sensed the faceless girl was about to speak. Gabriel jumped up quickly, his chair clattering with a clash against the lumber floor. "It doesn't matter, because it's not happening."

"Are you just saying that because if she dies, you die? Because that won't matter in this case- it won't affect you. If she doesn't exist, then you'll never have been bonded."

Arabella began to process what the woman said, but his next response left her reeling.

Scoffing, his subtext held a barely contained gruff roar. "No, I'm saying it because I love her."

There was no air in her lungs, just butterflies, and she reached up to squeeze his hand in understanding.

"Gabriel, you know I don't want this anymore than

you do, but it has to be Arabella. She's the only one he wants. He has a vendetta against her. If she doesn't kill him for good, then we're all doomed. This is the only way to destroy him."

"There has to be another way," Ember countered.

"If there was, we would take that road. But there isn't another way! I'm on your side. I'm one of you too, remember? I don't want her to be hurt, but I want everyone to live, and I thought you did too Ember."

Ember glowered. "Never question my dedication." Then she sat back. "Keeping Arabella alive is definitely in favor of the greater good."

Arabella was strangely touched.

The room was silent for a long time, and they all sat, just staring at Arabella. She thought about every debated word thrown around the table and the evil she was willing to face in order to save everyone here. She closed her eyes. Her head felt heavy and her heart felt the same. A stone sat in her stomach, its surface worn smooth by churning and worrying in her gut. She really just wanted to surrender to the inevitable, maybe put her head on the table and sob a little. Instead, she took a deep breath, steeling herself for a moment, and pretended that she was a character from a really good book, one that wouldn't blink in the face of fear. She just didn't want to be forgotten, she wanted to endure, she wanted to **be**. But.. she also remembered the dystopian world from the previous Trial and knew that no matter what, she wouldn't allow that kind of destruction to occur. She re-opened her eyes, the blue in them shining crystal clear. "I'll do it," she faltered nervously, her voice quavering, but she had said it; no going back now.

The other faceless girl placed a bottle on the table. Its contents glowed bright periwinkle and looked more like swirling slime than liquid. "This is your bomb."

...

Arabella was behind the veil in the supernatural world, in a dark cave that echoed with a thousand sounds-running water, a rodent scurrying, and something growling from deep within. It was reminiscent of the room she had dressed in, with the same rough, grey stone walls with old fashioned torches held in sconces set in brackets. Outside, the sun was setting, and the torches were flickering inconsistently against the cave's wall, casting a soft orange glow. She tried to take one for herself, but didn't quite know how to get it off the wall, so she left it and continued alone- her snug boots making a sound akin to a mouse padding its way across the floor as she walked. That is to say, she was as quiet as a mouse.

The glowing bottle was secure in a leather bag that Ember had given her, and her sword was clutched tightly in her hand in a death grip. Her knuckles were white and getting whiter as she delved deeper into the cave. She walked for what felt like miles, the only sound she made was her light tread. Every once in a while, she could hear the splat of fat water droplets hit the cave floor.

"What?" she whispered as she wondered out loud; she was at a dead end.

There was a rough stone wall, the same as the rest of the cave walls, except this one was 20 feet high and 25 feet wide. Arabella suddenly realized that she could no longer hear the ghosts of echoes from the cave's other occupants. She turned in searching circles for signs of color or movement, but the vibrancy had been sucked from the room the same way it had been sucked from her lungs. No longer a mountain cave teeming with life, it had become a black space of dead air. She realized then that the way she had come was covered by pure black- a swirling, consuming, dark abyss. She felt terror grip her heart and she cringed, her sword hand tightening considerably and the other reaching into the cool leather bag to grab the potion. She was using a potion.

If only my friends could see me now.

But when she looked down, her hand was grey like the walls- she was fading. She shot her head up and studied the swirling mass. She backed up for two reasons: it was getting closer, and... it had firefly eyes. And those eyes were grinning at her with sadistic glee. She backed into the dead-end until the stone dug grooves into her back. Still she wanted to move further away- until she became one with the stone, until she was forever away from that thing. She cried out in pain, but even then she knew that she wasn't really feeling it, not really- because she was almost gone. Her skin was ashen, her eyes pale, the veins running through her body shrinking, the blood in her veins turning to dust. Her loved ones probably felt worried, yet had no idea why. She thought of her family. The image of them would would carry her through. She stared at the creature, not in horror, but like she was invincible. Suddenly she felt a rush of bravery, she reached into the bag. She felt her grasp almost slip on the bottle, but she smoothly pulled it out. What if she was too late?

I can do this.

She threw it, like a baseball, right into the darkness. Everything exploded. All that existed at that moment was fire and pain. Then the lights swirled again and she saw 'Nobility' flash white behind her lids.

She was in the dark- not metaphorically- literally. Everything was a steady gloom. There was silence too, a form of quiet that was more deafening than crashing thunder. She stared ahead, almost in panic, but mostly in vertigo. Déjà vu clashed with common sense and the outcome was paranoia.

Where was she?

The abyss seemed a likely answer. Nothing but

pitch black as far as the eye couldn't see.

Then there came a whisper. So quiet, that at first it sounded like the wind blowing demurely through the trees. She struggled to catch if it was just empty noise or actual words. She stood there, her hands at her belt, her mind sharp. The whispers grew louder- the sound was haunting- but still unclear. Then it became a murmur of words mumbled under someone's breath. Finally, the whisper became a breathy screech that chilled her to the bone. Her hand tightened on her hilt. *Tell me,* the words rang in the void.

Tell you what? she thought. The voice answered as if she had said the words out loud

Where she is, it hissed.

"Where who is?" Arabella shouted, not trusting her own mind.

Rosada.

Ice cold fear shot through her like electricity, and she froze, not even wanting to breathe. She knew how she responded could result in not only Rosada's capture, but Cadence's imprisonment- this wasn't just part of The Trials. This was her mind playing tricks, and the Book Keepers trying to be diplomatic. "Never," she swore, her voice strong and clear.

Tell me. Tell me, and it can all be yours, the voice whispered enticingly.

"What can be mine?" her voice sounded warbly to

her own ears- like she was underwater.

A perfect life, the voice rasped once more, sounding closer. Arabella swore she felt warm, sticky breath against her cheek. Then suddenly, the darkness was illuminated. She was in a room- a living room. It was warm looking, with amber walls and two chocolate-velvet love seats. There was a TV mounted on the wall playing a Disney movie, and a few stuffed animals littered the floor. Arabella looked around and noticed that there were pictures on the walls. Stepping closer to look at them, she noticed with a shock that they were of her. There she was holding hands with Gabriel, looking content and in love. Then there was a picture of Gabriel in a black suit, again holding her hands in his. She wore a white gown straight out of a fairytale. They were both beaming like it was the happiest day of their lives. Next, there she was with a smiling little boy, no older than three. He had bright blonde curls and bottle-green eyes. He was the most beautiful thing she had ever seen. She stumbled back in shock, having no memory of these photos. But there they were, as clear as day. She glanced around the room and at the stuffed animals strewn about the floor.

Holy Hades! What kind of 9-5, picket fence life was this?

She felt a pressure in her head- like something was sifting through her thoughts.

A door creaked open somewhere beyond the room

and with it came the sound of Gabriel's voice, deeper and more mature than the one she knew now, "blue eyes, we're home!" he called out clear and booming.

Out of the hallway emerged Gabriel- but he was all grown up- the little boy from the photos rested on his shoulders, giggling madly. "Alexander loved the dentist," he remarked with a rich laugh as he planted a kiss on her cheek. Her skin tingled where his lips had touched. She reached up and touched the spot where his love still lingered, her eyes finally met his. Blue against green.

"He's such a weird kid," she cracked up, "but then again, he's ours, how could he not be?" she joked easily and pecked him back on the cheek. Inside, she was shocked by her words and actions.

He gave another hearty laugh and a dazzling smile. Alexander, still resting on his shoulders, tittered even more insanely. "So, when do they get here?"

She glanced at the watch on her wrist, "five minutes ago, which means you're both late," she replied and he returned her amused grin- he didn't have braces.

"That seems about right," he exclaimed in mock exasperation.

"Yep!" little Alexander joined in giggling, his cheeks impossibly rosy at being a part of the family jest.

"Come here, little man!" Arabella lovingly grabbed him from Gabriel's shoulders. He swung down, and she cradled him adoringly before bestowing raspberries on those rosy cheeks. Then the doorbell rang, its sweet hymn echoing warmly throughout the cozy house. She let Alex down and he waddled off to play with his toys and watch the TV that had been playing in the background. Her heart ached and her arms longed to scoop him up in a maternal embrace once more. Gabriel walked over and sat on the floor, his long legs folding elegantly underneath him as he played with Alex. She walked through the house- knowing exactly where she was going- to open the door. She swung it open enthusiastically, a brilliant smile splitting her face. For once in her life, she felt comfortable in her skin. On the other side was a couple with a small girl the same age as Alex, she looked like the perfect mixture of her parents.

She welcomed them inside out of winter's biting chill with a hello and a hug. Again she felt that pressure in her head. They made it back to the living room and all took a seat. Gabriel stood to greet them as the little girl wiggled out of her mom's arms to go take Gabe's place playing with Alex. Gabriel came and snuggled up to Arabella on the couch with a nuzzle to the nape of her neck that made her entire body respond in sheer rapture.

Across from them, Cade whispered something to Rosada, and she laughed sweetly. She melted into him, her brunette hair pulled into a high ponytail and her brown eyes shining with glee. A pang went through Arabella when she looked into Rosie's eyes. *Weird*. Squeals of delight from the children caught all of their attention as they sat on the floor, enthralled by what was on the TV; the four parents looked on in content amusement at the camaraderie of the two tiny friends.

"So, Arabella," Cadence beamed, "how's the book coming?"

"Great!" she offered ecstatically, "after the first one did so well, the second seems to be writing itself."

"I'm so proud of her," Gabriel gushed- in a manly way. "She's finally getting the credit she deserves, really making her mark on this world."

Arabella could feel heat rise in her cheeks at the compliment. Like he was one to talk, what with his award winning photography and art.

"That is so amazing!" Rosada chimed in. Again, Arabella felt a pang.

Arabella's eyes wandered to where Cadence and Rosada held hands; that pressure returned- like a probe searching in the dark crevices of her mind. She gasped and reached for her sword-it wasn't there.

"What's wrong?" Gabriel examined her, concern showing in his breathtaking, bottle-green eyes.

"This is wrong!" she gasped and sat up so quickly the world spun.

"Sit down!" Gabriel growled. But instead of the deep, warm voice, it was a rough whisper.

Arabella remembered her dagger- the one strapped

to her ankle- the one that looked like Rosada's. She reached down and unsheathed it in one fluid motion. She poised herself in a defensive stance; the dagger positioned in front of her. Even then, she felt that pressure, and she knew that if she wanted to protect Rosada, there was only one thing to be done. She decisively turned that dagger toward herself and plunged its smooth silver into her stomach. The world swirled once more. The word 'Loyalty' was all she saw.

She was in a hospital- it was a painful reminder of her grandmother. But instead of pristine white, this room was a bright cherry red. She knew it was a hospital, nonetheless, because what lay before her was the saddest sight she had ever seen. Kathryn. Her sister was still, asleep- an assumption she made based on the gentle rise and fall of her chest. Her cheeks were sunken and shallow, her skin a sickly yellow. Every shaky breath sounded labored and painful. A doctor stood by her bed, and Arabella growled as he drew blood from the sweet girl- she looked incredibly small in the bed. She was sickly enough without a huge needle being stuck in her and taking blood-she wanted to shout at the doctor to step away from her.

Immediately.

The doctor left, and Arabella was left alone in the

room with Kat and her own weeping mother and father. Her mom never once glanced up at Arabella in the few moments that the doctor was gone, but she swore she heard the faint stirring of a whisper in the otherwise still room.

This is your fault.

Great, more whispers.

But even knowing that this was a test, like she had known deep down with all of the other Trials, her emotions still overrode her logic and control- like they had in all of the others. Guilt crashed into her hard, and she felt tears snake down her cheeks as she stared at her tiny sibling- the one who had always loved her, the one who had let Arabella be her rock.

When the doctor returned, he wore a grim expression. Her mother stood up, and her dad stayed seated, holding his baby girl's hand. They were both still weeping- which made Arabella feel worse...

"How bad is it?" Sarah moaned woefully.

"It's like we thought," the doctor affirmed gravely. The news caused her mom to sob harder, and the sound made Arabella's heart clench. "She must have ingested the flower, but I have absolutely no idea how, it's only indigenous to India. The only reason I recognized the symptoms was because I spent time studying abroad there."

"And the only cure?" Sarah Grace prompted hesitantly. Arabella could tell she already knew the answer.

"The flower itself," he confirmed and turned

toward Arabella, acknowledging her presence for the first time since she appeared in the room, "and you have to retrieve it, Arabella Grace."

...

A picture of the flower stowed in her phone pouch, Arabella began her journey into the deepest part of the jungle. It had been days. She wasn't sure how many at this point. Not only were there things there that wanted to lick the meat from her bones until they gleamed (as if that wasn't bad enough), but the voice was betting against her, testing and taunting her every step of the way. Actually, lots of voices were speaking to her. None of them were cheering her on. They defiled her, criticized her. They seemed to know her weaknesses and insecurities- they knew exactly what to say to get under her skin, and then they dug deeper. All the voices hissed, but Ember's voice was the loudest. It penetrated her mind with every twist and turn; every single word echoed. Every single word spoke of how she was going to fail, how she wasn't good enough, that she wasn't a good person, and nothing could fix her... despair seemed to be her constant companion.

She cut a vine out of her way with her Imprint.

She's going to die.

The whisper floated around her once more. She tripped over some garbled roots and saw something slither over the ground. The air was humid, her leather was stifling, the bugs moved in black clouds that darted across her path and blocked the sun.

You never complete anything- why should this be any different?

· A growl echoed from her right, and her feet ached with every step.

Failure! What would your grandma say, what if she knew your head was this far in the clouds? You don't focus on anything, you don't take anything seriously! Do you really think you're fit to take care of yourself- let alone the world? Ember sneered with a sharp jab.

The humidity made her hair huge and unmanageable, even in her quickly unraveling braid. Once again in The Trials, she stunk, and large chunks of hair clung to the sweat on her neck and face. Perspiration covered her from unruly head to aching toe. *Holy crap- it's hot.*

If they wanted your sister to live, they should have sent someone who doesn't trip on their own feet, someone who can at least keep their best friend safe.

She just kept plunging through the jungle, somehow knowing that she wasn't deep enough- the sounds that resounded throughout the thicket made the hairs on the back of her neck and arms stand up.

They should have sent someone that people can rely on. Someone who could at least have saved their own grandma. You couldn't save her, and you can't save Kat.

Who are you kidding? You, Arabella Grace, are unintelligent, useless, cowardly, uninteresting, uncaring, and a waste of human space. You wouldn't know righteousness if it slapped you in the face. You are worthless. You've already let The Warlock fool you once, who's to say you won't do it again? I don't think you're even capable of love, but if you are, just know that you won't be able to save her. You won't be able to save yourself, and everyone you love will die because you are a spineless worm.

Arabella finally broke.

She sat on a nearby log, heavy sobs racking her body. She wanted her mom. She placed her head in her hands, the sweat making everything sticky. She had run out of water a day ago. She really wasn't sure how long she had been out here. It was just one long cycle of walking and being ridiculed. There was no stopping, arguing with or ignoring the voices. When it was dark, she slept. Even in her sleep, she was told how worthless she was. But honestly, at this point, she was so far in that she didn't know what type of darkness it was. But it didn't matter anymore; she was going to sit there and cry. That, combined with lack of water and how much she was sweating, would surely lead to dehydration. Soon it would finally just be over- the words sounded sweet to her ears. She started to shudder at how casually she could think about her own demise, but decided that she didn't really care anymore. But even as she was thinking these thoughts, she knew deep down inside that these words were not her own. In spite of that, she couldn't make herself feel like caring, not really, she just couldn't anymore. That was asking too much. It was all true. She couldn't save her own grandmother. Or even Rosie and Cade. How could she have thought she could save Kat? She couldn't save her from this, and she couldn't save her from the Clock. It would just be easier to give up. She wasn't a Clock Keeper, not really.

Who had she been kidding...?

She took a deep breath. She hoped her tears could drowned out Ember and the other voices' nasty words. But it wasn't her tears that blocked them.

There was an unexpected stirring in her soul, her own golden light crying out at the suppression it felt.

Her grandma's face surfaced, her eyes were always shining with pride. She thought about her grandpa, with his warm hugs that always made everything better. Rosada's encouraging smile joined her collection of endearment. She thought about Cadence always being there, with his words, his smiles, and his silly movie commentary- he was always willing to just let Arabella be.

And, of course, her mother saying that she was made to do amazing things. And her father, silently giving her an encouraging smile that would crinkle the edges of his eyes; his crow's feet smirk and teasing sarcasm were a welcome form of love.

She thought about her brother, how he always made sure she was protected, would bring her up when she was down. Her sister was ever-sweet, filled with giggles, and always wanting to crawl into bed with her after a hard day.

Her friends, each one with their own personalities, each unique, and each loyal in their love and support for Arabella. Ailith's kind words came to mind also, always patient, never cruel. And Mika and her pride in her Arabella's successes, so joyous to see her student excel. They believed in her. Even December, Ember... she always pushed her forward, and she never once gave up on her. She showed Arabella what it meant to love something so completely that she would never give up on it.

And of course, Gabriel- his laughing eyes, his collection of portraits, his nervous habits, bonding with him over something as silly as how they both liked to chew ice...and then him telling her that he loved her smile.

She sprang from the log. This was for Kat, who would never give up on her. So she wouldn't give up on her, either. Arabella was stronger than that. Sprinting through the jungle, the whispered voices still played through her head, but she thought only of her family. Their presence and love drowned out the noise, because that's all it was- noise.

Let them talk.

As long as she had them in her heart, she was

invincible, she had proven that with The Warlock, and here she was proving it again. She would always protect them. Her limbs rejuvenated, she ran without stopping. The sweat was trivial. The funk- well hey, it was good at scaring animals away. And her Clock Keeper grace returned as she leapt and bound over the obstacles on the forest floor.

Finally, she got to the heart of the jungle, where the light no longer shone. Her eyes searched through the dim.

She was filled with awe.

Pure sunlight came through what had seemed an impenetrable canopy. In that one little spot was a flower- identical to the picture in her phone pouch. She scrambled to it, sweat dripping into her eyes and her thighs burning as they stretched and released against her armored pant-legs. She grasped the stem on the floor as she skidded to a stop on her knees. Hope filled her; her heart was alight, and those horrid voices were finally gone.

Then, once again, the world swirled, and this time, she hoped it would be the last time. Two words appeared- 'Love' and 'Self-Confidence'.

A gun shot rang out.

Arabella was at the mouth of another alley. *A little cliché,* she thought, but hey- she didn't design the tests.

A body dropped in front of her in a flash of silver and lilac. At the end of the alley was a hooded figure, literally holding the smoking gun. Arabella reached for her sword and ran to the victim.

A scream ripped from her throat- the sort of desperate wail that shook people to the bone with its devastating chill. Heavy sobs overtook her body, and she gasped desperately, "no, no, no, no!" like a record skipping. She skidded to the ground, the armor protecting her from scraping the flesh off her knees, but she didn't care, she would have taken a thousand cuts, scrapes, and lacerations in place of the pain she felt now. She cradled the fallen body to her chest and rocked back and forth, sobbing with overwhelming force. She stared down at the familiar green eyes as the light faded from them, and the once vibrant grey hair became painfully dull.

"Ailith!" she pleaded in helpless grief as she crushed her mentor tighter against her trembling body. Bawling uncontrollably into her limp shoulder, she continued to rock her back and forth. "Ailith, please, please! Stay with me! Somebody, help us! Help!" Her voice broke as she agonized in audible sorrow. She cried until the ragged sound escaping her was little more than a pitiful croak, but she continued the wretched noise, the heart wrenching lament, in the hope that it would somehow bring her back. She just wanted to hear that twinkling laughter once more- that soothing honey voice. *Oh, no. Ember.*

Without a thought, she pulled on the strings around her thumbs, pulling apart the flaps in her armor and letting the wisps of her wings free. She hadn't felt strong enough to use them before this point, but now, rage fueled her capabilities. She felt the feathers become matter as she took to the sky.

She had already lost her grandma- she couldn't lose Ailith too. She made it to the hospital lightning fast. She entered, not caring about her strange appearance, no excuse laid in wait on her tongue. The hospital staff stared, but once she put a gun-shot victim on the reception desk, they didn't seem to care anymore- not even about her wings and sword. Some nurses and doctors came and carted her off in a blur of scrubs and tennis shoes. Arabella stared after them. "You better save her!" she yelled desperately, then she whispered for herself, "I promise, I promise I'll be back."

Then she flew out the hospital doors.

It didn't take long to get to the crime scene and find the culprit, thanks to her tracking classes with Ember- also, the dude was kind of chubby and hadn't gotten that far. She swooped down upon him, devouring the distance between them in a dive- he started to sprint harder, and sweat streamed down his slightly jiggling face.

His efforts wouldn't save him.

She landed on him, causing him to flail flat on his stomach. He was in a heap of panicked flesh as he tried to regain the air that had been knocked out of him. It was a good thing that he had extra cushion. The gun went clattering out of his hands, thankfully it was on safety, and skidded a few feet away. She kicked him in the back with her steel-toe boot. He whimpered in pain. *Pathetic*.

She rolled him over. Almost automatically, he raised his hands to cover his cowering face- like that would help him. She embraced the burning rage that had ensnared her soul.

"You!" she spat, like the very word was venom on her tongue. Her mouth felt heavy with the words yet to come. She unsheathed her sword and raised it up to point it just under his double chin.

"Please, don't," he whimpered once again and raised his beefy arms to cover his face even more. Arabella noticed that he had a slightly upturned and wide nose that was smashed to his face like a pig and beady eyes to go with it.

Arabella still held her sword aloft. She gave him a vicious look. "Why shouldn't I? Why shouldn't I just let this sword drop a few inches and slice through your throat like it was made of butter?" Her voice was cruel and avenging. Somewhere inside, she was appalled by herself. But rage and grief, new and old, squashed the guilt quickly. "You may have killed her," she hissed, fire burning in her eyes, and she felt the glow of a Clock Keeper emanate from her. She was invincible, especially against this little pig of a man. She was drunk on anger and revenge.

"I'm sorry!" he sobbed.

"Sorry?" she barked with a cackle. She looked around in disbelief. *Yeah, I bet you are.* "You shot her! She's probably dead. You can't apologize for that. It's not okay, it will never be okay," she thundered, feeling like the Goddess Nemesis- the Goddess of Revenge. And she would have vengeance.

"I didn't mean to!" he pled.

"You didn't mean to? How do you accidentally kill someone?" she growled out. "You had a gun in your hand and shot her, there's no mistaking that." She moved to swing her sword in swift justice, knowing she was making a choice that she could never come back from.

"No!" he yelped with a shudder, and she rolled her eyes- glad once more for the deserted street. "I swear, I swear- it wasn't supposed to be her- it was a money drop, someone is ransoming my daughter- my little girl- I was going to give whoever took her their ransom," he quivered.

"And the gun?" she hesitated.

"Just in case it went south!" he howled, arms still raised. "But when I got there and saw somebody standing there, I panicked and shot. Only when her body dropped and I saw who it was, a little old lady, did I realize that I had messed up. So I panicked and ran. Please, I can't express my regret enough," he blubbered with genuine remorse. When Arabella looked at his squinty eyes, she saw that they held truth. Honesty shone through them.

But Ailith was still dead, or near it.

With a wretched, mournful sob, she brought her sword down.

It bounced off the concrete by his head- nicking the quaking man's ear in the process, she sunk to one knee with a battle cry. The only thing keeping her up was her sword. She turned her head and stared at the man. "Go," she croaked weakly. He didn't need to be told twice- he scrambled off. Hopefully, he could still save his daughter in time.

Then the world, instead of swirling, exploded like a supernova, and one last word was stamped into her skull. 'Forgiveness'.

Chapter 21: A Tear Slipped Down Her Cheek.

She was back.

She stood, battered and bruised, pride shaken, more than a little tear stained, but still, she stood. Her back was straight and proud (she could practically hear her mom compliment her perfect posture). Her Imprint was back in its place. Arabella was finally safe. Or as safe as a Clock Keeper could be. Kat was safe.

She stared out at the audience surrounding her. Slowly, they began to clap. The stiff Book Keepers, with their perfect, pinned-back hair and strange features. Mika, her instructor, clapped with the first warmth she had shown all day. Ember clapped, respect evident in her eyes. Ailith clapped with grandmotherly love. She almost looked on, expecting to see Rosie clapping and hollering like her favorite team had just won the state championship, but the recollection that she wasn't there came crashing back like a gut punch. She was suddenly bombarded with hugs- at first by Ailith, then by a reluctant Ember, and finally by Mika. Thankfully, the Book Keepers hung back, though she might have been okay with Dac hugging her.

Arabella looked at Mika again, her curry eyes were no longer as tight, but worry was evident in their depths, and Arabella knew it was for her teacher's daughter.

Arabella broke- she hoped for the last time that day. She let it all out, sobbing for all the times she had been beaten and battered, her brain turned to mush, all the times every single one of her walls had been torn down and she had to compromise some part of herself. She just cried and cried in sweet release.

Eventually, she pulled back as if ready to be let go, and they all complied. She looked their faces over and knew that she loved each and every one of them- even Ember, strangely enough. Okay, maybe love was too strong a word, but she knew that without these brave women, she never would have survived.

"Did I pass?" she blurted out through a watery laugh. A Book Keeper- Arabella honestly didn't remember her name- it was the one who had a metal hand- remarked, "yes, with flying colors," and let a bit of warmth illuminate her features. She looked a lot prettier with it.

Ailith nodded, and Arabella felt relief at seeing her alive and well. "We were able to watch. They had a one-sided portal open- it's like a window in an interrogation room- where we can see and hear you and the scenarios you are facing, but you can't see or hear us." She paused to give her one of her signature warm smiles. "And you, my dear, you did perfectly."

Arabella flushed. *They saw everything!* She had a lot of embarrassing moments in there, and some moments that she'd rather no one knew about. Even so, she nodded in understanding, feeling a weight lift, but strangely enough, as soon as it left, another kind of weight took its place.

"I think it's time to go." Dac prompted kindly, pointing toward the swirling door with a willowy arm. The exit twisted and shifted in varying shades of sparkling gold.

"Yes, it is," Arabella concurred.

Then he snapped his fingers, and Arabella was back in her winter coat and civilian clothing- but thankfully, her cool new boots remained. Her armor was folded neatly in her arms, with her sword, dagger and phone placed on top. She turned to go put them back in the room she had found them in.

"Oh, I wouldn't do that, dear- I have a feeling you'll be needing those rather soon," Dac called and gestured once more toward the golden vortex.

"Okay..." she acquiesced, before complying and leaving the courtroom, the others following behind her. Ember caught up to her as they walked along the hallway, easily matching Arabella's long stride with her short legs. "What do you think he meant by that?" Arabella whispered to her.

"I have no idea- but it worries me," she stated, her apprehension apparent only in the way her voice trailed off at the end.

They walked on in silence, nodding solemnly to the twins- 'Surfer dude' had somehow 'lost' his watch; his brother looked rather smug next to him. They exited through the giant oak doors, still strange and out of place against the crystal and marble. They stood for a moment in the barren field, watching as the sun started to dip behind the horizon, marking the middle of the winter day. It disappeared along with the Anacora, both gone for now. Before she could could climb on the bike with the she-devil, she was called aside by Mika, who placed a piece of paper in her hand before stalking off and getting into the car with Ailith.

Huh?

Arabella palmed the note and stuffed it in her coat pocket, awkwardly balancing her armor. She swung her leg and mounted the bike with Ember, and they zipped off into the cool evening.

> Red Baron Airpark-1id9, Old Highway 30. Oasis, ID 83647- 8:00 pm. Don't be late.

It was 6:45 p.m.

She had Googled the place on maps; it was 51 miles away. It was also a flight school, strangely enough- The Red Baron Airpark. She wondered briefly if Mika wanted to add on to her training, but finally admitted to herself that she knew the real answer- this was about Rosada and Cadence.

Maybe when she witnessed Arabella's Trials, Mika

saw that she could trust her to always be loyal to her friend. She hoped that she hadn't truly been furious with Arabella, just a little upset that she had been an accomplice to the trouble Rosie might be in. While the Book Keepers and Clock Keepers both believed in equality and continued to strive for peace and balance, the Morph world was run by a King with very biased views and tyrannical rules and consequences.

It all just left her feeling so drained.

When she got home, she hugged her family tightly, despite their surprise at the unexplained affection; the crushing hug she gave Kat left the smaller blonde looking begrudgingly happy. She had to laugh at the fact that her mom's only response was to sweetly ask, "how was your day, are those new shoes?"

She checked her phone for the first time in what felt like years, only to find a bunch of missed calls and texts- some were from her friend group at school, who either naturally or by design had now drifted away from her- but, strangely, the majority of them were from Gabriel. She and he hadn't talked since The Warlock. Something happened on both ends. She knew why she stopped; if The Trials were any indication, she didn't want him to get hurt (even if she did suspect he was designed for her world). But why he had disappeared from her life, she had yet to discover. She didn't bother answering the texts. She was heartbroken. Gabriel was the greatest mystery in her life yet, but he was one she wasn't prepared to delve into. Was it wrong of her to want to keep her heart locked up a little longer?

She started to re-braid her hair.

She thought of Mika's note, and she thought of Rosie and Cade.

She glanced at her clock, as red block numbers read 7:00 p.m. She supposed it was now or never. Throwing a hoodie on over her armor, she thought about riding her motorcycle, but didn't want to have to explain to her parents her sudden need to travel faster. She started heading outside, yelling a quick, "I'm going to Rosada's!" over her shoulder, before racing out the door, not even waiting for a response. She was definitely going to be in trouble when she got home. So even at the risk of being grounded forever, she went to go save her friends.

"You have arrived at your destination," her British male Siri confirmed. She wondered deliriously if he would learn someday that Chinden Boulevard was pronounced 'shin-den', not 'chine-den. Clicking it off, she stuffed her phone back into the phone pouch of her armor. She stared left and right through the windshield of Baby Blue. Darkness fell through the sky, and the Idaho sunset faded on the edge of the horizon in an array of soft pinks and oranges as the retreating orb finally sank into the ground. Through the dirt and bug spattered glass, she saw miles and miles of chain link fence on either side. A little metal box was posted in the driveway, and she rolled up next to it. She stared unconfidently at the keypad on it. She had a similar one at her family's old apartment building in Meridian when she was young, before they moved to their house. To get in, you had to enter a passcode and wait for the lights to flash either red or green.

What now?

She slumped back into her pleather seat and cranked up the heat. It was cold.

She sat there, stumped, scanning the area for security cameras, when her phone buzzed. She fished it out to find she had a text from Mika.

> **Mika: Pull around the corner and ditch the car-if you are wondering how to get in, remember, you can fly.**
>
> **Arabella: Right!**

She pulled around the corner, her car humming gently as she parked it on the shoulder of the road. She ducked when a lone semi-truck passed by; she had to roll her eyes at herself and her paranoid response. Really, there was no one around. The dread in her gut thickened.

Stepping into the cool air, she stretched her arms, preparing to unleash her wings. She took her hoodie off and threw it into her car. She pulled on the loops around her thumbs and the flaps slid away. Closing her eyes, she focused on the the power racing through her veins, a network of live wires lived under her flesh. She had been able to feel it as soon as The Trials had ended; it was like she was made of crashing white water- powerful, alive, relentless.

The ghost of her wings spread across her back, and the feeling of sunlight wrapped around her. The wings solidified as a gasp broke free of her tight lips. She opened her eyes, knowing they were alight with electric blue. She took off from her position, gliding up through the choppy air until it smoothed out like glass, flying higher than she could have dreamed of before. Her stomach twisted at the height, but her soul felt quenched of its thirst for adventure.

The airstrip came back into view. She gulped and dove, the wind harsh against her face, her braid snapping like a whip against her neck. She felt tears collect in her eyes, causing the mascara on her lashes to leave windblown smears across her cheekbones.

I need goggles.

As she approached the ground, the wind caught her wings. Her feet touched down with a soft thud and she stood ready for an attack. She was yanked by the arm, hard, into one of the warehouses she had landed by.

Inside the hanger, she came face to face with Mika-the Morph's muted copper eyes held a fierceness, a fire Arabella had never seen before, but there was also fear lingering under the surface.

Arabella swallowed a gasp and reeled back, only to be pulled forward again by Mika's surprising strength. There were lean muscles under all those pant suits.

"What's going on?" Arabella whispered to the older woman, who was now only two inches away.

"Follow me," was all she got in response as Mika spun on her flats, walking deeper into the hanger at a brisk pace. Arabella desperately wanted to ask what was going to happen. But she trusted Mika to have a need for secrecy.

This is going to be fun, Arabella thought with strong sarcasm and hurried to keep up. Even with her long strides, the petite woman gave her a run for her money.

They reached the end of the long hanger without any hitches, the only sound the soft padding of Arabella's boots and the slight click of Mika's flats. Trepidation creeping in, Arabella started to re-braid her hair, but stopped, wanting her hands to be free. Then suddenly, a song started looping in her mind, she strongly ignored the instinct to hum. Stupid Fall Out Boy and their catchy tunes.

She was brought to an instant halt by Mika when the mentor brought up her bronzed hand abruptly. Skidding slightly, she looked around for what would have caused such a startling stop. She listened through the silence, she was a Clock Keeper, she was built to survive and protect-not to be caught off guard. The sound of whispers were carried to her ears. Low sounds that cast unpredictable echoes across the walls of the hanger, she strained to hear what was being said and grabbed her sword's hilt. She looked around for a place to hide while Mika looked prepared to fight. Arabella grabbed her hand and yanked her under one of the Cessna planes that were scattered throughout the hanger.

Mika glared at Arabella. Arabella merely pointed to her ears. They needed to listen, and then Mika could tell Arabella what was going on.

Arabella tuned in the best she could, catching only fragments of words.

"Tragedy," she gathered from one guy's murmurs.

"Mistake," she heard from another's.

"Treason," she heard the first one say. "Disgrace."

"Thought," something, something, "trouble," she snagged the words from the whispers between the two. Arabella also thought it funny that the first man started all of his sentences with the letter 't'. It wasn't until the man said his final words that she felt ice cold fear zip down her spine.

"Imprisonment- both of them," his whisper was more like a shout in her ears.

She turned sharply toward Mika, her chin scraping slightly against the concrete ground they hugged, and saw tears streaming down Mika's cheeks. Catching Arabella's gaze, she hurriedly wiped away her sadness and they both turned back to the men. They were only able to glimpse the tips of their feet. They had black FBI-looking dress shoes on. She watched the 'agents' walk away. The hanger door opened and florescent light streamed outside, overexposing the night air. A scream rang out.

It was Rosada. The shrill and terrified sound rang in her ears like a gong. She rushed forward, scraping her armor against the floor in a scramble to get to her friend; this time, Mika held her back.

"Let me go get her," Arabella breathed in despair. The need to protect her friend burned and overtook her body.

"No," Mika whispered back, her eyes clearing like she had remembered something. "I want to go to her too, but I have a plan."

"Mika, what's happening?" Arabella asked, even though she dreaded the answer she already suspected. It had been a long day. Mental, physical, and emotional exhaustion wore down on her like chains shackling her to the ground. Still, she was dying to move in, because Cade and Rosada were her best friends. So she stared at Mika, wondering if her instructor could teach her one last lesson.

Burnt gold eyes, filled with hurt and sadness, bore into her own exhausted ones. "They found out about Cadence and Rosada."

"You knew?" Arabella gasped in shock.

Mika gave a pitiful laugh, "of course I knew, I'm her mother. But seeing her so happy was worth any risk I was taking. The way they looked at each other was worth any risk." She searched Arabella's face, an unanswerable question in her eyes. "How was I supposed to stop that?" She took a deep, shaky breath. "I assume you know about the bigotry in our world. In order to enforce his laws, the King will send a surprise visit from his officers to our kind in the human world from time to time to make sure we're not getting too friendly. The officer found Rosada with Cade," tears welled in her eyes once more. "He immediately hauled the two of them away."

Her worst fear realized.

She could lose Rosie.

She could lose Cade.

She was worried for Rosie, but she was terrified for Cade. He was an innocent in all of this. This was the guy who had been with her when she had learned how to ride a bike. The guy who was there when she got her first pet. He was her big brother when her real one couldn't be, warding off guys and offering a supportive shoulder to cry on. He was the one who had punched her first boyfriend in the nose when they were in 8th grade because the jerk had asked Mindy Carny to Winter Carnival instead of Arabella. Afterward, he bought her chocolate ice cream and skipped school with her to watch action movies all day. He had been there at every theater performance, cheering alongside her family. He asked her about every art piece she ever made. He cared. Through the ups and the downs, he had been there. He knew everything- all the good, all the bad- her hopes and dreams of being a travel journalist, her fear of dying and being just another faceless person, forgotten by the masses.

He knew everything. Everything except that she was a Clock Keeper, a fact that was most likely going to get him hurt, maybe even get him killed. She had let go of all of her other friends. She had hung onto Cadence's friendship and introduced him to this world without telling him what it was, without his knowledge or consent. It was as if she had blindfolded him and given him pet a wolf, all the while telling him it was a dog, she thinking the wolf was tame, until it bit his hand off. She had to save him. She had introduced him to this world, she would be the one to rescue him from it. She wouldn't fail him.

"What are we going to do?" She turned, asking Mika. "We're going to..."

Boom!

"Wait for the explosion," she finished.

"What was that?" Arabella jolted, her ears ringing. Mika turned toward her- her coppery eyes flashing with dangerous mischief. A smug grin curved her face, like the Cheshire Cat, and she raised one eyebrow coolly. "A diversion."

Arabella stared in stunned silence, her jaw ached

with the need to drop to the floor. She blinked a few times and nodded, mostly to herself. Before, she had respected Mika as you would a teacher- a mentor. But, now, she respected her as someone who was a good ally.

Mika grabbed her hand in a vise-grip and pulled her out from under the plane, away from where the explosion had sounded. *Whoa, she really thought this through*, she realized as their footsteps raced toward Rosada's scream.

They ran from the hanger and wove through several buildings before coming upon an idling, small private plane (very villain-esque). Two men stood by, one holding a handcuffed Cadence and the other holding not only a handcuffed, but gagged, Rosada. Arabella beamed, knowing she had probably been sassy to her captives to earn the muzzle.

The minute they saw Arabella and Mika, Cadence froze in his struggle against his captors, his indigo eyes were wide with shock as he took in Arabella's appearance in disbelief. Rosada thrashed wildly and started shouting against the gag like a mad woman. She decidedly stomped on the goon's toe, and he yelped in surprise and released her. Tears of relief flooded her pink eyes as she ran toward them. She reached Arabella and stared at her pleadingly- if there was one thing Rosada hated, it was being silenced. Reaching forward, Arabella pulled off the gag.

"Thanks!" she gasped and nodded her head toward

the cuffs. "Now," she grinned, "can you do something about these so we can really get this party started?"

A laugh bubbled from her relieved heart in the heat of the moment.

Arabella reached for her sword. In one slice, the cuffs came away clean. Arabella bent down and grabbed her dagger. "I figured you just might need this."

Rosada snickered, "I just might."

They ran toward the running plane. Cadence was standing off to the side, dazed. Mika was battling the two guys by herself, spinning two chakrams- which was something Arabella couldn't do, but it just so happened to be Rosada's mother's specialty. Arabella felt torn between standing in front of Rosada or blocking Cade; she wanted to protect them both from the two FBI looking guys.

Her body reacted before her mind could when one of the men broke off from Mika and charged toward Cadence. Arabella sprinted ahead of Rosada and stopped a blow aimed at her BFF.

Déjà vu.

Standing protectively in front of Cade, she twisted the man's arm. His fist still firmly in her grasp, he turned toward her, his elbow catching her chin and throwing her head back. She felt a crack in her neck. *That can't be good*, she thought, but continued to fight. She was a Clock Keeper- she'd heal.

A pink blur came in view. Arabella round-housed

her attacker, effectively pushing him down. This gave her a split second to yell at Rosada, "protect Cade!"

Her friend's face showed mixed emotions between wanting to help Arabella and her desire to run to Cadence's aid. But her words ultimately pushed Rosie to run to him, her dagger at the ready.

A kick was delivered to her gut. She doubled over, the wind cleaned from her lungs. Her attacker used the distraction to corner her friends.

I don't think so.

The words echoed in her head as she spun, ignoring the pain in her lungs and abdomen. He was fast, but she was faster. With lighting speed, she grabbed his shoulders and whipped him around so he was facing her. They danced under the lamp posts.

He shouldn't have messed with them, she thought bitterly. She gripped his shoulders, turned, and pulled him into her. Bending her knees, she lifted him onto her back and rolled him so that he went slamming onto the ground. She pinned his arms to his sides with her knees as she crouched and hooked him as hard as she could. The blow connected with his nose; blood gushed as his head rebounded off the concrete.

She stood, woozy, adrenaline still pumping through her body. Her injuries didn't hurt, yet, and tomorrow she would go see Ember about them. Another well timed explosion sounded, also courtesy of Mika (she assumed), keeping back up at bay.

She faced her friends.

Cade was, understandably, in shock, while Rosada looked cool and calm, and even a little cocky. Though, a small amount of concern showed in her pink eyes. Mika stood there, her opponent moaning on the ground.

"Rosada, say your goodbyes- we have to go," Mika stated hesitantly, her voice filled with an ocean's worth of regret.

Rosie blanched, "what?" she yelped.

"Shh," Mika warned, "do you want the whole place to hear you?" She took a deep breath, sadness filling every line on her cocoa skin; she seemed to momentarily age ten years. "We need to leave. If we're going to be free, we **have** to leave. So, say your goodbyes. Once we leave, take Cade home immediately, Arabella." Her golden eyes showed desperation and sorrow at having to make this decision to keep her daughter safe.

Arabella felt like she should respect that decision, except she couldn't, because this was Rosada. Her Rosie. Her bright pink, sports loving, always-first-to-call-shotgun (even if it was only the two of them) best friend. She felt as though someone had cut a hole in her heart.

When she looked over at Cade's face, she could tell that he felt what Arabella did, except deeper- pain was carved into his heart, and time would never be able to heal it. A determined look came across his freckled face. "No." The word rang as clear as a bell across the airstrip, even over the rumble of the plane's engine. *Way to make a great first impression, dude.*

"I can fly her out of here. We leave together, or I'm not leaving at all." He looked at Rosada. "I love her."

Both of their faces shone brightly with love.

Arabella's eyes enlarged, "Cade, you can't," she begged. She couldn't let her friend go deeper into this world. "You don't know what you're getting yourself into."

"No, you're wrong. I do," he argued back. "She told me what she was a long time ago."

Startled, Arabella looked back and forth between the two. Rosie's face turned down in guilt. "I had to, because I love him too."

"Did you tell him about me?" she blurted out, suddenly worried that he knew about her secret, her lie, her betrayal.

"No," Rosie rejected fervently, "I would never."

Cade looked extremely taken aback. "What? I mean there were the lessons, but... what?" he fumbled over the words with confusion written all over his face.

"We don't have time for this!" Mika hissed in exasperation. She pointed to Arabella- "she is a Clock Keeper and she can explain what that is later. Right now, we need to go, because as sweet as this is- Cade, you have a family. And I hate to admit, but it will be a tight squeeze if you do come, I imagine that before, one of the guards was going to stay, and Cade was going to be put in baggage."

Arabella felt sick at the idea of what had very nearly taken place.

Mika continued,"they're more likely to go after Rosada, she is the one who committed treason, it's safer if you stay."

Rosie flinched, but regret abstained from her features.

"I can pilot the plane," he spat out, quick to give any reason that kept him with her.

Mika looked at him, surprised, "what?" She looked at Arabella for confirmation. She confirmed it with a subtle nod of her head. "Oh."

"And," Rosada jumped in, "if you come with me, they'll double their efforts."

They all sat in silence for a moment. There was another explosion, but these distractions couldn't keep them at bay for long. Finally, Arabella piped up, alarmed by the sound of rapidly approaching footsteps. "Just go!" Worry knotted her stomach at the thought- she wanted to go with them. She couldn't control what might happen if they left alone; she couldn't protect them.

Catching her gaze, Rosada saw the concern in her eyes and shook her head; a sad light dimmed her eyes.

"Wait," Mika fretted. "What about your family,

Cadence?"

Pain fit itself onto his features. "They'll miss me, but they won't look for long- or at least, the police will write them off, I'll be 18 in a year, and...," his voice was tight, and the freckles on his face were thin disks. A waver seemed to weave its way into his tone. "I was a foster kid before they adopted me." His blue eyes dropped to the ground. "Our kind is 'liable' to run away."

Pain stabbed Arabella in the heart with a fast jab, a tear slipped down her cheek. She knew how much Cade's family meant to him. He was one of the lucky ones- or at least that's what he had always said, taken in young and officially becoming theirs a few years ago.

When Cade was barely a year old, he had been dropped off at an orphanage. Why anyone would abandon their kid was beyond her. During his time there, an older girl named Kara had taken care of him, had become his protector. She was only 10, and yet she had looked after him up until his fostering at age 5. He had met Arabella shortly after. He and Kara had stayed in touch for a time, but when Cade turned 9, she had disappeared. Considering she had never been able to stick to one home, the state decided to write her off as a troubled kid after a minimal search of a couple months. It had never sat right with Cade. Arabella knew that's why he learned how to fly, so he could find her. He had wanted the freedom to go anywhere. To always look for her. But in spite of that story, his family was his family. They loved him, and he loved them. She saw the heartbreak in his eyes. And she also knew that no matter how much he loved his family, he had never completely felt like he belonged. With Rosada, he finally felt that sense of home. Arabella could see how determined he was to keep Rosie safe; he wanted to be with her, no matter the cost. She realized in that moment how much he loved Rosada and the lengths he would go to for her. They locked eyes. No matter what, no matter who came and went in her life, this was her best friend, and no amount of time or space would that change.

Flinging herself at him, she gave a quick sob into his shoulder and hugged the living daylights out of him. Her hands bunched in the fabric of his shirt and gripped so tightly that they cramped, and she feared they may never unclench. Placing her head in the crook of his neck, she cried harder. She could feel him shake against her as he hugged her back just as hard.

She stepped back, aware that the longer they stood there, the longer she endangered their lives. She wiped her nose and looked toward the sky, silently weeping. It wasn't fair that the stars shone so brightly when her whole world seemed to dim. "Be careful, you big idiot," she sniffed and lightly punched his shoulder, trying not to break down.

"Hey, you know me- 'Careful' is my middle I name," he attempted to joke, but his smile broke, giving him away, "I love you, nerd girl."

She almost broke down at the nickname he had given her. "I love you too, fly guy," she returned with her own broken smile. She turned toward Rosada. Her pink hair and eyes seemed to glow. "Gosh," she mumbled and pulled her into a fierce hug; the pink ninja only came up to her collar bone. "Don't you dare ever change," Arabella mumbled intensely and rested her head on top of Rosada's. "Please take care of him."

Rosada's bright pink eyes softened. "I promise. I'm so lucky to have met you."

Arabella shook her head and felt the same bittersweet warmth race through her veins. "No, I'm the lucky one. Take care of yourself, too."

She smiled. Her gaze drifted away from Arabella's face and over her shoulder. Giving Arabella one last quick hug, Rosada broke away and walked over to her mom.

The hug that the mother and daughter shared was unique in the way that only a maternal embrace can be, it is the only one that can express that much love. Arabella's heart clenched, suddenly wanting her own mom to hold her and take her far away from any of this. The words spoken between them that weren't drowned out by the roar of the engine were lost on the wind. Only soft murmurs met Arabella's ears, and she felt that whatever transpired between the two of them in that moment would be sacredly kept there. No more explosions sounded. There was nothing to hide the thundering of footsteps, the distant shouting, and the ringing sirens. They had to split up.

"I love you!" Arabella shouted to the pair as they boarded the plane.

"Bye!" Cadence called back.

"Oh!" Rosada's eyes were suddenly wide. "I have to tell you something!"

The footsteps grew louder.

Arabella unfurled her wings. "What?"

"Gabriel is your-" a vehicle barreled toward them, its headlights blinding.

"It doesn't matter, just go!" Arabella yelled, cutting her off. Her curiosity could wait.

Gabriel's my what?

Then they were gone. The plane lurched forward with sudden urgency, and soon the wheels stopped touching the ground. The sounds of a fresh fight grew closer. Arabella, with new tears still rolling down her cheeks, grabbed Mika, and suddenly the cool night air was caressing her salt soaked face and rolling off to splash on the fluttering feathers that extended from her back as the two winged their way through the evening sky.

She alighted to the soft ground near her baby blue Bug with Ember-like grace. Mika had lost some of the light in her eyes, but she stood tall as she climbed into the car, mumbling something about not wanting to take another Uber.

Well, that certainly explains her ability to mysteriously appear.

A sharp exhale worked its way up from her chest and parted her lips as Arabella Grace got into the driver's seat. The victorious, yet defeated, pair drove off into the star painted horizon.

After she dropped Mika off at Ailith's, Arabella drove home in silent contemplation.

What a long freaking day.

And it had all felt like Hell.

When her gingerbread house came into view, with the friendly yard art sprinkled about the suburban green lawn, she nearly cried. Okay, she did cry. In fact, she lost it. Huge, ugly, tears covered her face and left a salty taste in her mouth as she surrendered to the bittersweet release of her utter and complete breakdown.

The tears quickly dried up, however, when shock rang through her as she realized this day just refused to end.

Gabriel stood there, a black hoodie shadowing his face, the fabric blending into his hair. She could just see the outline of his semi-full lips pressed into a hard line. It wasn't a comforting sight.

Despite that, Arabella couldn't help but be self-conscious of how she looked. Suddenly, she imagined all the places the armor seemed lumpy and how flat the padding and chain mail hoodie made her look. Her face was a sweaty mess, with stray blonde strands flying every which way like a bird's nest. Her complexion was certain to be all blotchy and flushed from sweating and crying; she probably resembled a raccoon with her mascara stained eyes. She quickly ran a hand from the top to the bottom of her braid repeatedly. Then she rubbed at her eyes. She was surprised at how many callouses she had on her own hands. Her once soft hands that she used to lotion and manicure were now cracked and dry. When she pulled her hands away, they were covered in dark smudges as if she had been sketching all day and had graphite blackened fingers. She decided to clasp them behind her back; she was strangely concerned about him seeing their worn down state. She thought about her clothes- a million lies filled her mind. One rose easily to the tip of her tongue, and her soul recoiled at the ease at which she was able to deceive the truth.

I've been cosplaying.

When she stepped closer to him, she became less aware of her own haggard appearance and more aware of his. His bright green pupils were matted with pain, lines were sketched across his face in tight contours, and dark circles ringed his eyes. His shoulders were slumped, and he hunched in on himself like a gnarled beast.

Her mouth thinned in concern.

The sun was now completely set, and the stars were their twinkling companions, along with a full moon and Arabella's porch light that lit the path. The walkway was cast in dangerous shadows that set Arabella on edge. "Are you okay?" The words popped out of her mouth.

Hollow laughter filled the empty space.

A violent flinch wracked her body. His once warm laugh was now a sinister call. Her vertebrate clinked together as her spine shivered. She was cold, she was lonely, and she was facing the hope she had lost.

"Honestly..." he shook his head fervently. " I don't know how I didn't see it, you must have thought I was the biggest idiot in the world." He hissed and growled the words out.

"Excuse me?" she blinked.

"What are you, Arabella Grace?"

She stared at him, blinking the panic in her eyes rapidly away.

"A witch, a demon, a goddess, or are you Hell itself? Why me, why not Cade or... Harrison?" he spat, accusing her of something she wasn't even aware of.

She flinched again at the mention of The Warlock while confusion battled with shame in her head. When she looked deep into his eyes, it was like she was watching something come unhinged in them. She had never wanted those eyes to change.

Gabriel, it had always come back to Gabriel. The Warlock had been hell-bent on keeping him away from her. In The Trials, he had been by her side every step of the way, he played through her mind and made her heart sing.

He saw her, and she... she loved him. "Gabriel," she started calmly, intoning softly, "how can I help you?"

"Stop!" he screeched. Arabella stumbled backward. "Stop the act. I know, I know what you've done. I can see clearly now."

"Gabriel, I don't know what you're talking about," she tried to reason.

"You're hurting me!" he cried and tugged his hoodie off, despite the winter's chill that had her shivering in her gear. Underneath the hoodie, he was bare skinned. He turned his exposed back to her. Beautiful, black wings spread the expanse of his smooth and muscled torso, wrapping and bending across his shoulder blades and dipping with grace toward his waist. It was intricate and lifelike, and not unlike her own tattoo. Arabella wanted to reach out to feel whether or not soft feathers would meet her finger pads.

It was true. He was, in fact, her Anam Cara.

That explained The Warlock's behavior and was probably what Rosada had been trying to tell her too. Arabella had suspected, but she hadn't dared dream.

He turned back around, struggling to pull his hoodie back on. Arabella had gotten a glimpse of his toned and lean torso, and she briefly daydreamed before the seriousness of the situation returned to her and had her searching for his pained gaze once more.

"It started with the blackouts."

The bird. Just as she thought.

"Then, I had this killer pain in my back, and this tattoo slowly appeared, bit by painful bit."

That must have begun when she met him, the day she shook his hand at school.

"And then it just kept hurting, burning, digging into my flesh."

What?

"It never stopped, but it wasn't constant. It only happened at certain times. Finally I realized the pattern- it only happened when I was around... **you**. I only burned when I was with you. When I found out from Cade that you have the exact same one, I knew you had to be the cause."

That didn't make sense, the bond didn't work that way. After the tattoo's completion, he should have been fine, and the Clock should have been pushing them together. Something was very wrong.

"What have you done to me? Why are you hurting me?" Tears gathered in his eyes and rushed down his face in light catching droplets.

"Nothing! I swear, I'm not!" she pleaded.

"Don't lie to me!" he cried, and Arabella reached out, wishing to help him in some way. "I came here to ask you, to beg you, to stop. But you're a monster, and now I see that you'll never stop. I'm going to run so far out of your reach, you'll never be able to hurt me again." He snarled and shoved her down.

Arabella gasped and tumbled, hitting the ground with a thud. Ice and snow bit into her palms and instantly chilled her flesh. She heard the roar of a bike's engine and the peeling of tires. She was going to be sick, bile rose in her throat, and acid filled her mouth. "What?" she whispered.

Chapter 22: Cold, Biting Silver.

He tossed in his bed. Every position felt like pins and needles. Flames seemed to lick up his back. When he shut his eyes, flashes from his most recent blackout came back to him. None of the images made sense, it was like his childhood fantasies had come back to haunt him. He was 20 feet in the air, drifting over highways and houses, untouchable, the ground a moment away in his crystal clear sight. He twisted in his sheets. After seeing Arabella that evening, his tattoo had been worse than ever. It screamed against his skin with a ragged sting. His sheets, once satin smooth and cool against his burning flesh, had become as rough and scorched as the desert floor.

He had come home that night with the intention of packing his backpack and running far away. Far from Arabella and her alluring, agonizing presence. But his dad had been home, and he had smiled at him with crow's feet crinkling around his eyes, and... he couldn't leave him, not like she had left. So he had mumbled a goodnight and crawled into bed. He was going to make his dad homeschool him again. He was going to stay in his house, locked in his room, and never leave. He would never see Arabella again, because he would not depart his dad's side.

The rage slowly died down within him as sleep wrapped her hands around his eyes and pulled him into a fitful slumber.

Behind his lids, he was drowning. Water filled his

mouth and dripped like ice into his lungs. Salt stained his nose and froth covered his vision. He struggled and kicked, but was immobilized in his chilled prison. The frozen ocean around him started to heat up. It was comforting at first, but it soon turned into a full boil, rushing and combing over his form in scalding waves that made his skin go raw, tender. His flesh slipped and slid over his bones like it was in danger of falling from his body. The temperature continued to increase until the taste of salt was washed away and something molten took its place. He tried to scream, but that just let more magma fill the cavities between his teeth. His gums felt singed. Then a hand, cool and relieving, gripped his shoulder and pulled him from the burning pit. He saw silver wings and golden hair, and he resented the sight.

It all went black.

He stood in his own mind, covered in a blanket of darkness; the air was damp and pressed in with a suffocating weight.

Then, crystal clear, rang Harrison's smooth voice, "I warned you, Gabriel." He sounded awfully smug.

"What?" he scoffed.

"I told you she was going to cause you a lot of pain." He didn't give Harrison the satisfaction of answering. "Can I tell you a secret?" Harrison whispered, all dark and hypnotic. Gabriel found himself lending his ear. "She hurt me too. She and her kind destroyed everything I hold dear."

"Like what?" he asked as sympathy started to bleed into his speech.

"They killed my brother," he spat.

"Arabella killed someone?" no matter the pain she had caused him, he couldn't picture her doing something so fundamentally wrong.

"Not Arabella specifically, but her family. They hurt and kill and murder. They think The Shadows are bad, but humans are so messy, and the dark is so clean. She wants to kill me, and she'll be the end of you. Help me, and we can stop all of that. Who would your dad have if you died?"

Something pressed into his mind, and once again it was like his vision had become filled with crystal clear smoke. "What do you need me to do?"

Gabriel shot awake, terror, or realization, making his back ruler straight as he blinked into his dusk covered room. His blankets were wrapped tightly around his body- a sign of the unpleasant rest he had just awoken from. He thought of Arabella, he thought of stopping her.

"Excellent..." Harrison's voice echoed through his head.

A house rose in his mind; he had been there before. He knew where he was supposed to go.

Pulling his forgotten hoodie over his head, he

relished the feeling of his back suddenly being doused in relief. It was easy enough, slipping out of the house. His ink stained hands made quick work of crawling down the garden trellis. Scaling his way down the lattice, he climbed onto his bike and pushed it a safe distance away before barreling through the streets.

He arrived at a towering dark house with floral print curtains in all six windows, and a rich, buttercup yellow door. It was extremely striking against the charcoal grey paint that covered the rest of the dwelling. It was the same structure from his first recollection of blacking out. The yellow door swung open and the situation became even more unsettling. As soon as his boot-clad foot touched the bottom step of the porch, he realized he might have made a mistake listening to the voice in his head. It was like staring at a corpse. The house was large- but it felt like what had made it a home was now hollowed out.

Still, he pressed on, entering at a hesitant pace. His lost soul and heart the only things keeping him going, because everything else was telling him to turn back. He should have listened.

He entered an almost vacant foyer, it had hallways branching off in either direction and a large staircase in the middle of the back center wall. At the bottom of the flight of stairs stood Harrison. Two demons stood watchful by his side.

"You were so meddling. But now... now I see your

value." He smiled sweetly, and it made Gabriel feel bitter.

Silver. That's what he first awoke to. Cold, biting silver- like Arabella's tattoo. Light reflected and bounced around him in dim waves, and water dripped in the distance to a lethargic rhythm. Soon after, the cold hit him. It seeped into his bones from the concrete floor he sat on. Piercing pangs rang sharp and disorienting through his wrist. He glanced down with a frantic jerk of his head. He was handcuffed. With more silver. He glanced around. His world became pinpoint small.

He was in a cage.

A cage. Trapped. Completely bound in silver.

The fire on his shoulders and spine came back more intensely than before. He screamed before the blackness reclaimed him.

The next time he woke up, it could have been an hour, or it could have been a day. He was shrouded in shadows. Fear clung to his heart. He hadn't been aware that the human body could feel such depths of complete and utter terror. Another shot of lancing pain rang through him, but his raw throat was too ragged when he tried to yell. To be blunt: it sucked.

There was a bowl of slop near him. Or that was

what he mentally dubbed what appeared to be the food they were supplying him with. He used the term 'food' lightly. After what his pain fazed mind guessed was roughly thirty minutes of staring and sweating into the dim, a shadowy hand pushed the food toward Gabriel with a slow deliberate scratch against the concert floor, as if drawing out the nightmarish process. All he could do was scurry further back in his cage. He ignored the protests of agony that his body gave to the best of his ability. Finally, the hand retreated. Sleep thundered over him again.

He was roused by a bright flood of light.

And a rich laugh.

"Oh," he groaned and shied away from the light, hissing like an overexposed vampire. Despite the increased wattage, it was still darker than his room, even on his most 'sulking teenager' days, when he transformed his bedroom into a 'cave'. Thinking of his dad's kind and teasing nature was like being socked in the sternum. So much for not leaving.

I love you dad.

He blinked a few times to adjust his vision, but everything just felt raw and overstimulated.

Then Harrison laughed again. It was still that disturbingly warm pitch that was wrapped in villainous intentions. "Are you enjoying your," he paused for wicked effect, "imprisonment?"

"Well, let's just say that I'm not leaving a good

review on trip advisor," he groaned out amongst the head splitting pain. "But, if you tried a little harder, added the right lighting, you could make it downright swell in here. Have you considered becoming an Airbnb?" He had the satisfaction of glimpsing his captor's leer darken into a snarl.

"I'll keep that in mind," he countered, maintaining neutrality. "It doesn't really matter, you won't be here for long." He held something high in the air where he lounged, far from Gabriel, against the opposite wall. Gabriel strained to make out the shape of his backpack. "You really do have some lovely things in here." A flash struck the room.

Gabriel cried out in surprise, recognizing his camera's shuttered click that followed the blinding light. He tried to rub his eyes with his tethered hands but only succeeded in pulling the skin around the handcuffs to reduce it to even further rawness.

"I just needed to give someone motivation," he snarked.

"Who?" he asked, fearing for his dad and Cade.

"Arabella..." he answered with dark satisfaction.

Gabriel's stomach swooped to the inner circles of the Earth. "Arabella?"

Again, he sniggered with sinister insanity. "At first you made me so enraged. The perfect little Anam Cara, showing up right in time to distract her from me. I couldn't have even begun to use her while you were stealing her time. But in the end, she rejected me. But then I saw the opportunity I had. At first, I made you hate her so you would stay away. Then, I realized that if I pushed you just a little further, I could inspire an emotional reaction from her that would cause you to no longer be under her protection. If you broke her heart, you would break her spell. She still loves you, but she doesn't trust you- not after last night. And true love is built on trust. I've destroyed enough of it to know that. So you became the perfect bait. She'll always come to save you- at the very least, for the Clock's sake. And if she comes here, I can kill her."

His voice trembled as he felt the bile rise. "What are you saying?"

"Arabella wasn't the one hurting you. I was." He seemed to find peace in the words.

Gabriel was sick as he saw every rotten memory of the blue eyed girl shift back into glittering light.

Arabella, what have I done? He jerked against the cuffs again. "You can't do this!"

Harrison smiled wide, revealing pearly white teeth before his appearance melted away into a ghastly form. "I already have."

Chapter 23: His Wicked Smirk and His Gentle Grin.

Arabella stared after Gabriel; she considered flying after him. But she too was confused by the events he had described and ached to talk to Ailith before she poured her heart out to the guy who had just thrown her to the floor. She took a deep breath. The air shined with shimmery, frozen mist.

"Arabella!" Her mom's voice shrilled like a tsunami over their yard.

Oh no.

She took one look at Sarah Grace's furious face, and... didn't see any anger. She just saw the one person who had always loved her unconditionally. Arabella met her mom's greenish-blue gaze and cracked a heartbroken smile against a soldier's stare. The motherly figure's expression softened, and Arabella felt the tears start to stream down her face in wet, hot rivulets.

Sarah grabbed Arabella and pulled her right against her. Feeling the warmth from her mom and the comfort she provided was what Arabella had been seeking all day. She broke down. Her body shook in sorrow, her frayed nerves finally turned to jelly. She cried- with loss, with grief, with girlish heartbreak, and with the world on her shoulders. She was completely emotionally exposed and raw. Both her mind and her body were exhausted to the point of processing nothing more than the smell of tea tree oil in her mom's hair. She didn't even realize that they had stepped into the warm folds of their home. She was only a kid.

So she cried, and the sobs echoed against the vaulted ceiling. Her already bruised ribs felt like they might fracture from how hard she cried. Her tears were so thick, she couldn't see, which she was grateful for when her sister and dad came in. She didn't want their pity and worry. But she did want a hug from Kat. She wrapped Kathryn into a warm hug and inhaled the smell of her strawberry shampoo. *All for you.*

Her parents joined them, and they sunk to the floor, holding on for dear life.

She woke up late in the afternoon. She had fallen asleep the night before in her 'cosplay' outfit. She sighed, contemplating the lies she had told. She had convinced her parents that she had gone out because Cadence's mom had called to tell Arabella that he was missing. All had been forgiven with the understanding that she would communicate next time. They trusted her.

My life is a scattered jigsaw, with no picture for reference, she realized bitterly, feeling at odds with it all. She was a Clock Keeper, and she was glad she was. And also, she had saved her friends. But she had also lost her friends. She was exhausted. And to top it all off, her Anam Cara bond appeared to be broken.

Wind me up, and I'll play half the song.

She mechanically crawled out of bed, stretching, cracking like a glow stick. Her armor already on, she thought that it was better than anything she had in her closet. Who knew how the day would go? She should probably go straight to Gabriel. Not only did she... need him, but her Clock needed him too. Even after only truly realizing the entirety of her feelings for him last night, it was strumming with a strange urgency that left her cheeks stained with a blush.

First things first- personal hygiene. She didn't have the energy to shower, as much as she needed to, so she bathed instead in vanilla perfume and rose deodorant. Her oval mirror reflected, in the seconds between each splash of water on her face, the damage that the prior day had inflicted: a bruise on her chin in sickening yellow and plum purple; her red rimmed eyes and smeared mascara; her white hair from the amount of dry shampoo she had just sprayed through it to soak up the sweat and grime of yesterday.

She slathered on foundation and mascara and called it good.

She stared at the mirror and she saw herself. Strong, willowy, beautiful. The Clock glowed with ancient light, its wings just as sleek as ever. The The mother of pearl inlaid in its silver face glimmered no matter which way it lay. Something rejuvenated in her eyes, a spark. Her pouty funk wasn't worth the toll it would take on her heart. She had to find him.

She rushed out of the house, mumbling an excuse about Cadence with red cheeks, which her mom thankfully bought. A protein bar was the fuel she devoured on her way to Ailith's house.

She walked into the familiar porch-wrapped house without even knocking.

She dodged the knife that embedded itself in the wall next to her head.

She gave Ember an unamused look. She meant business. But Ember wasn't even watching her- she appeared to be watching *Dirty Dancing* on her grandma's old box TV.

Good choice.

Ember glanced at her with cold eyes, but they warmed slightly when she really looked at Arabella. "What's wrong?" she asked with a twinge of a emotion.

"Nothing, Ember, I just need to talk to Ailith," Arabella deflected and picked at her glittering chain mail.

"Well, tough. She's with Mika, some business about Rosada, it has the uppers in a tizzy."

Arabella scoffed, that sounded like an

understatement."I'll be going then." She turned and opened the door. Sunlight streamed in, like the world was pretending it was the perfect Sunday.

"Wait..." Ember stopped her, lazily drawing out the word. Her eyes flickered around the room. "Why did you come here?"

"Because I need to talk to Ailith," she repeated. "Why do you care?"

She hesitated and stared down with graceful wonder at her Clock. "Before The Trials, I was hard on you. Because I needed you to be better, for the Clocks' sake. But you've proven yourself. No matter how little I understand your... actions. I do respect you." She rubbed the Clock's face. "We're connected."

Arabella took that with a grain of salt. But still, something inside of her warmed at Ember's admission. In a lot of ways, they were all each other had. Maybe she should learn to depend on that. "I found my Anam Cara," she blurted out.

"You what?" Ember stared at her, perplexed, and stood from where she sat on her grandma's burnt orange sofa.

"And something's wrong," she admitted, worrying her lip. She started to braid her hair. She explained the whole scenario- Gabriel's paranoia and ravings from the night before. The pain he had felt.

Ember's hazel eyes narrowed, and she combed a

hand through her unruly cocoa locks. "That doesn't just happen," December pondered.

Thanks for stating the obvious.

"In fact, it sounds a lot like..." she cursed. "Do you love him?"

Arabella blanched. "What?"

She narrowed her eyes. "Did you ever, even come close to loving him?"

She thought back to the few weeks she had spent getting to know him- before The Warlock. She thought about the wonder in his eyes when he saw artwork, how adorable he was in his sloth socks, and his eagerness to comfort others. "I think... I think I was starting to, but then, that was before The Warlock's spell."

She urgently beckoned Arabella to follow her as she went into Ailith's basement. They entered an armory, one Arabella had never seen before. Ember explained her theory as she dressed in armor similar to Arabella's- except hers had holsters for her 'babies'. "The Warlock controls perception. If he altered Gabriel's perception of you, it could undue the Clocks. We need our Anam Caras." She sounded bitter. "The Warlock thought that if Gabriel wasn't in the way, then he could manipulate you, but that didn't work. Yet, at the same time, the only thing protecting Gabriel, and those around you, was your love for them. And from the sounds of it, Gabriel broke your heart last night- or at least dampened your schoolgirl view of him. He isn't protected now, he became vulnerable- which makes him the perfect bait."

"How do you figure?" Arabella gulped, referring to multiple things.

"Are you asking how I know what The Warlock will do? That's easy. I know War." She tilted her head with feline curiosity. "Or are you asking why Gabriel would be perfect bait? That's also easy, because you care. Right now, you're confused. But at the center of your being is a warm, sticky mess. No matter how hurt you feel- you will never leave someone you care about in danger. Especially someone you love."

Arabella began to protest.

"Don't forget, I saw your Trials. Your brain may be saying no, but your soul is singing. There is something about that boy that makes you glow. It could be as simple as his smile."

Arabella thought about his wicked smirk and also of his gentle grin. Guilt struck her, she couldn't desert him in the middle of her own mess. He didn't deserve that. What had he done besides be there for her, notice her, humor her, be her only match in this whole world?

How had I not known?

Ember finished throwing on her own chain mail hoodie, and stuck her hair in a high, frizzy ponytail. She wore her tattoo with pride. "We need to find him before The Warlock does."

She thought about his words from the night before.

"Let's hope we do." She couldn't live with herself if they didn't.

They pulled up to Gabriel's house in record time, Ember had somehow ended up driving Arabella's Bug, and they had woven through traffic, over highways, and through residential areas at an alarming speed. Ember utilized her Clock Keeper powers the whole time for cat like reflexes. It had been terrifying.

Arabella got out of the car with an apprehensive air. She looked questioningly at Ember.

"You've got this," she mouthed and gave a sarcastic thumbs up.

Nice.

She had only been here one other time to drop Cade. *Cadence*, she thought woefully.

Her memory of the home didn't do it justice. It was a picturesque, dark grey townhouse, only a hop from the Boise River.

She knocked slowly on their white door, the paint smooth and chilled against her scraped knuckles.

"Hello?" Gabriel's dad opened the door. He was a more mature version of Gabriel, except with blue eyes. Still, he wasn't unlike the Gabriel from her Trials. "Can I help you?" he asked, squinting with recognition, hopefully remembering her from when Gabriel had hurt his leg.

"Hi!" She responded brightly. She wanted

Gabriel's dad to like her, and not just because she needed his cooperation right now. "Gabriel and I are working on a project together for school. Is he here?" she figured that was more believable than the truth, even if her voice did break.

He sounded dazed. "No, I'm sorry, Gabriel stayed over at his friend Cadence's house last night, and he's staying there again tonight."

Her world spun, and her skin prickled. They were too late. No. There had to be something more she could do. She forced a smile. "Can I check to see if the project is in his room?"

"Sure," he smiled back and directed her to Gabriel's room.

She raced up to the second floor of his house and threw the door open. His room was painted navy blue, plastic glow-in-the-dark stars decorated his ceiling. Black and white photos of various cityscapes had been hung with care, and one whole wall was taken up by a mural of the ocean at night. There was a twin bed in the center of the room and other odd bits of furniture. Arabella looked around for his backpack, remembering how Gabriel had lovingly described his one constant possession. It wasn't there. She focused on Gabriel's bed.

She was going to be sick.

A picture lay on his forest green comforter,

delicately balancing atop the blanket. It was of Gabriel, his eyes were bagged and red, making him look ill. His hair hung around him, limp and greasy, and his wrists were mangled and bloody from the handcuffs he was wearing cutting into them. He was cramped and folded like a chair in a little cage.

Worst of all, she knew where the picture had been taken.

Chapter 24: She was Bound In Silver.

Arabella and Ember thundered through the house, giving Arabella no time to recollect and dwell on the memories collecting like dust particles between her ears. They moved through the living room and into the kitchen, stopping before the basement door. Ember shot off the doorknob without even checking the lock.

"It's a trap!" Gabriel yelled as they raided the dark and dank room. The voice was a rush of relief to her ears and it made her heart thud with a little less panic.

Arabella huffed, "no duh."

She vaulted the basement's short flight of steps and cut his cage door off its hinges without breaking stride. He gave her a stupefied look.

"You came for me? Why?" He sounded surprised, like a man looking hope fresh in the face.

"Because I wanted to," she answered with complete resolve as she carefully used her Imprint and her Clock Keeper might to cut away his handcuffs. He gave a sweet smile as she examined his wrists, the first signs of infection were setting in, and blood pooled haphazardly around his boots, staining the leather crimson. She hoped he hadn't lost too much of it.

Her fear was realized when she pulled him from his prison. The second he started to stand, he began to sway.

"Whoa," he gulped and clung to her.

She cringed. "Ember, I need your help."

Together, they supported him and started up the stairs at a brisk pace.

Gabriel's eyes started to droop.

"Gabriel, Gabriel, stay with me," she pleaded. She tried to get him to start talking. "What's your favorite childhood memory?"

Ember gave her a judgmental look.

"Um," he tried to focus. "When I was a kid, my mom would sometimes send me to bed pretty early. But my dad would come into my room sometimes, like.. an hour later, with graham crackers and milk, and watch a movie with me." He blinked.

Arabella was about to respond when The Shadows crept into motion. The rift between her and Gabriel had left them all vulnerable to attack from those nasty creatures for the first time in a long while. With her left hand holding her unsheathed sword, she fought the darkness, her silver companion giving them their final peace. Ember, on the other side of her, had taken out a gun. She was firing shots off into the room. The basement sounded with echoed gun fire and silvery steel. Gabriel drifted off between them.

They needed to hurry. She decapitated and parried anything in her way with confidence, slicing away their reaching hands. She could see the light of the kitchen. She cleared the way, carving one from shoulder to hip as it folded to the floor in a dripping pile. Ember's gun exploded once more. Gabriel was in a worrisome state of silence.

They heaved into the the kitchen.

Yes. Almost there.

They made it all the way to the entryway before it all went to Hell. Gabriel murmured Harrison's name.

But Harrison wasn't who appeared in front of them. Smoke billowed around them in a whirlwind that whipped Arabella's braid with sharp snaps. The dust from the abandoned house unsettled in a tornado that twisted and turned before resettling in front of the door. A cackle echoed, and the fair hairs on Arabella's neck stood on end. The fracture in their bond had also left them vulnerable to **him.**

A hooded figure stood in front of them, pale and covered in a patchwork of purple veins. Black eyes replaced pupils, and a shark-like smile swallowed his charm. The snake had shed its skin.

"Arabella," he rasped.

Ugh. She had kissed that.

Sometimes your first kiss really isn't Prince Charming. She shuddered.

She felt enraged. Dumping all of Gabriel's weight onto Ember, she rushed him. A sword appeared in his own gnarled hands. Sparks flew as the blades clashed and slid against each other.

"I'm not afraid of you!" she snarled, trying to get closer to his face, trying to see her own terrifying reflection in his soulless eyes. She wanted to see his face when she killed him. She was strong enough. She had her glittering Clock and her shining sword, she was bound in silver. She heard Ember struggle not to throw Gabriel to the floor.

"Yes, you are," he replied smoothly. She pulled back just in time for him to barely nick her cheek.

She pressed forward, pushing him toward the door. "No, I am not. You don't have any power over me."

His eyes narrowed dangerously as he blocked a swipe aimed for his torso. "Maybe not, but I do over him." His eyes flickered toward Gabriel."

"Not anymore." Their faces were close, their steel pressed one to another, the only barrier between them. Arabella slipped her sword away from his, and in one smooth motion, cut down against his shoulder as she poured her soul into the words, "because I love him."

Blood bloomed where her sword hit, and The Warlock's eyes widened. He was hers, hers to destroy.

She brought her sword down in an arc, a battle cry was ripped from her stained lips as he flickered once like a ghostly smile and then disappeared, the last thing she saw of him was fear rushing into his eyes.

Her Imprint embedded into the wooden floor.

Her devastation was short lived. "Arabella." Ember caught her attention. She looked back at Gabriel, he was deathly pale. "He needs to go to the hospital. Now."

She looked around, panicked that there might be

more Shadows. But it was only the three of them in the empty house. As they scurried outside, Arabella hoped it would be the last time she saw her grandmother's home.

Ember was gently placing Gabriel in the Bug's backseat when Arabella, keeping a watchful eye over them both, heard a soft voice come from the trees. A British accented male voice surprised them all as it broke the silence. "I was sent to find you." A figure stepped out of the forest's protective shadows.

The Clocks Will Keep Ticking.

Acknowledgements

I appreciate so many people, it makes it difficult to express the gratitude I feel for those who supported me. First and foremost, I would like to thank the person who put the most effort into helping me with this book, who spent countless mornings and even more nights reading version after version of this novel (even the awkward first draft). So, thank you mom. You are my biggest fan and most loving supporter, and without you, I would never have even started writing. You are the only reason I do it 'right'. Secondly, I would like to thank my step-dad and my little brother- you guys are the best. And also my grandparents, who are always the first to boast my work. Big hugs to my Uncle Reno for teaching me what real literature is when he gave me his personal and well loved copy of his favorite Hemingway novel. Katie Eastman deserves a special thanks for the night she spent brainstorming character and Clock names. And, of course, thank you to my dad, my whole entire family, and all my friends for always lending their ears and eyes when I need an opinion.

Another person who deserves huge credit for the completion and betterment of this novel is Bev Heyer- she is seriously one of the best editors someone could ask for! And also Evelyn Hadden, for her helpful insights and inspiring words of encouragement, her opinion meant everything. Many thanks to Hunter G, Johanna French, and Brigitte London for the honor they did me to be my beta readers.

I would like to give a huge shout out to all of the illustrations that these amazing and talented artists did for my work: Gabby Cano, Salvador Castaneda & Bella Benlian. I send my gratitude to the Fieselmans for being the supportive family friends that they are; you guys are so sweet. Thank you to Pandora, Netflix, chocolate, and the undo button. I would also like to acknowledge all of the great artists that came before me that really and truly inspired me from the moment I could walk. Without their guiding hands and inspiring works, I never would have dreamed of creating my own world and sharing it with all of you.

About The Author

It was an insatiable love of reading that inspired thirteen year old Marie Grace to begin writing Bound in Silver, the first novel in the The Clock Keeper Chronicles. "I wanted to create a world of characters and adventures that an avid YA fan like myself would love to read," Grace divulged. With her first book published at age sixteen and the next installment of the six book series in the works, she spends the rest of her time pursuing the creative and beautiful things in life such as photography and the culinary arts, as well as hanging out with her family and two adorably annoying Pomeranians in her hometown of Boise, Idaho.

Arabella

Find more graphics and
information about The Clocks
and their Keepers at https://
m.facebook.com/m.gracebooks

BOUND IN SILVER

Marie Grace

"Every great dream begins with
a dreamer. Always remember,
you have within you the
strength, the patience, and the
passion to reach for the stars to
change the world."

-Harriet Tubman

Made in the USA
Columbia, SC
29 April 2019